THE SYRIAN SUNSET

Howard Kaplan

D1519766

CONTENTS

CHAPTER 1

DARAA, SYRIA

THE ARAB SPRING

2011

O n March 21, 2011, trying to hold onto hope that was vanishing like blue skies as a storm gusted in, Lilia Wassaf hurried towards the main square in Daraa, Syria. The Jasmine Revolution in Tunisia had blown the winds of the Arab Spring a seemingly impossible distance to Damascus. Snared by their satellite dishes, Al-Jazeera television from Qatar gave voice to the voiceless. People spoke of the sweet fragrance of living without whispering, of an end to the secret police knocking on their doors at any hour, of some of their loved ones and neighbors whisked away over decades emerging from the dark cells.

A warm breeze lifted the ends of Lilia's multi-colored headscarf, and she brushed them defiantly from her face. With each step, electric fear jolted through her, and Lilia hoped she would not bolt home. When she heard what had happened to those Daraa boys ten days ago, she had fallen to the floor in her parents' house, cried helplessly, and could not move. Finally, two days later, she had slipped outside far behind her two brothers and, unseen, followed them halfway to the massing male crowd before turning back.

At thirty-two and slight, Lilia favored the western dress of the middle class, black pants and a red floral blouse she had hunted for in the faraway stores of the capital to the north. As long as she could remember, even as a girl, she had dreamed of something more than marrying and pushing out children but never could put both hands on what she wanted. She acquiesced to becoming a teacher. Her exasperated parents and furious mother ushered potential suitors into their *ablaq* mosaic-floored courtyard with its small trickling fountain. Like a horse's tail swatting at flies, she sent them scurrying. Lilia preferred to sit in the hills alone, reading and dreaming.

She had been certain those fresh winds would sweep away the grit and grime of Syria. Everybody who wasn't too beaten down thirsted for change. Most of those who argued for the safety of the status quo were older and remembered too well the eccentricities of the president's father, Hafez al-Assad. They still spoke of the 1982 massacre of twenty thousand in rebellious Hama, 200 kilometers north of Damascus, only after looking to see who might be listening.

Like Arab stallions running free in the desert, the ordinary people had trampled the leaders of Tunisia and Egypt and dragged them into small, barred rooms. Syria's Bashar al-Assad, trained as an ophthalmologist before replacing his long-serving father as president, promised reform that, like most assurances Lilia had heard, never made it from fabric into a dress. Bashar had married Asma, a British socialite of Syrian pedigree, pale, on occasion blonde, but more typically her short wavy hair framed her face in a restrained brown. Degreed in computer science and French literature, textbook provenance for the new kinder Syria the Assads heralded, Asma gazed out often from the covers of international magazines who clamored for a walk and talk through their 340,000 square foot marbled hallways. That was n palace on the mountaintop compound in the western Damascus suburbs. Everything a dictator under duress might need immediately was a stroll away on the plateau: a hospital and the Republican Guard headquarters.

Asma excitedly told these correspondents in her endearing British lilt of her progressive programs for women's rights and education, which she had come to Syria to achieve. She soon bore three, still very young, children. Out of the spotlight, she stood regally by Bashar's side as people disappeared. For someone as shy and gangly as Bashar, you had to rule a country, grand or tin pot, and Syria was a good deal of both, to snare a looker like Asma. Lilia admired or hated her depending on her activities on any given day.

On Friday, March 4, five boys aged eleven to sixteen snuck out of their parents' homes late at night and gathered at their school. Earlier, they had happened across cans of red spray paint. They scaled the short perimeter stone wall, the older kids boosting and lifting the smaller over, undeterred by the dark in their familiarity with the grounds, approached the stone building. In flowing red Arabic script, they scrawled everywhere on the outside limestones and similarly adorned the low stone wall. Their handiwork read: *'jayeek el door, ya daktor'* (you are next, doctor) *'asjaab yurid tsqat al-nizam'* (the people want to bring down the regime.) At that hour, the boys believed they were unseen. Informers fearing their neighbors' settling of scores, never slept soundly.

Saturday morning, the five, along with more than a dozen classmates, *who weren't even there*, Lilia thought, so angry she suddenly wished she had her brother's knife to use on anyone who questioned her, were yanked from their beds. Driven away, they disappeared into an adjacent province. Soldiers brushed over the slogans with thick, uneven black strokes. The girls in the nearby school where she taught couldn't manage even learning games and cried all week.

Lilia quickened her step, excited that women were welcome at the demonstrations in the main square for the first time. Her face suddenly felt hot as she thought about those shot dead there three days ago.

Terrifyingly, not a murmur reached Daraa about the missing boys; certainly, the torturers were plying their skills on the boys' soft bodies. Most of these children, *children*, she repeated to herself as she strode determinedly, were from her Abazeid clan. She had secreted her brother's small hunting knife in her long pocket but at the last minute returned it, afraid she'd start shaking and draw the secret police to the blade. The elders, of course only men in this backward country, approached local officials who lamented that they were powerless to free the boys. Whole days later, the elders were allowed into the room to see Atef Najib, Bashar al-Assad's cousin, head of the local *mukhabarat*, the secret police, and the only man in Daraa who could, with a sweep of his hand, release them.

Fathers and elders shuffled before Najib and begged forgiveness: they were good boys, guilty only of youthful indiscretion, and would never again display such disloyalty. The men were told to forget their children. They should bring their women and the *mukhabarat* would impregnate their wives, this way replacing the boys.

Like every person in Daraa, Lilia lost her mind at the affront. Resentment and rage burned like an inferno through every home; even regime supporters demanded amends and the children's return. More meetings between the burgeoning number of elders and the *mukhabarat* chief in nearby Suwayda, where their boys were being bloodied, failed to bring them home.

Lilia reached the main square. At the extremity of southern Syria, Daraa hugged the border with Sunni Jordan. Daraa was proudly Sunni. Bashar was Alawite, an offshoot of Shia Islam and a minority in Sunni Syria, so he required repression to rule. Lilia felt so many emotions simultaneously that she feared her skin might split and they'd burst out. She loved her city and the Syrian people the way she promised herself she would love the right man one day. She simply required more first. She looked at the old stone minaret of the Omari Mosque; the minaret facades alternated between sections of light-colored limestone and black volcanic rock. To her right, three arches rose in the old, dark stone mosque wall. The dome shined white. A few motor scooters puttered in the two-lane street wide enough for dozens, maybe hundreds, of jammed-together protestors. Billowing white clouds blotted out most of the blue sky. The beauty nearly spilled tears from her eyes.

Two days ago, Friday afternoon, thousands wedged between the single-story shops on one side and the volcanic wall opposite. Voices competed like at a sports match with a rival region. Some aging men warned: if the demonstrators don't stop, they will free the *ghuls* from the cemeteries to roam their streets. Lilia had laughed at that. Two days ago, she stayed at home, frustrated and restless, and helped her mother prepare the afternoon meal of kebab Hindi, rolled lamb with onion and pomegranate molasses. She had hungered to join her brothers, but it was not then allowed.

Her brothers had texted her with their every step. *Word echoed from nearby mosques. Hundreds march and shout 'Hurriyeh, hurriyeh' (freedom, freedom.)* Instantly: *Proud elders in tribal attire.* Nothing, nobody could turn back this tidal wave. Bashar, too would be toppled.

The *mukhabarat* broadcast from the minaret loudspeaker, tinny pleas she heard through the boys' phone calls. They asked the protestors to write down their demands and return home peacefully. The regime would listen. Nobody need be killed. Familiar with the ploy, the crowd roared its refusal. *Standoff, more people joining by the minute,* her younger brother texted. *No more can fit but more come. And more!* Lila had been more excited than she ever remembered.

The sea of people, lest they flatten each other, headed towards the provincial government headquarters in al-Mahata. People argued. Some shouted: reform the regime. Others threw bottles at the large photo of Bashar at the intersection. Uniformed police reinforcements burst from buses and split into groups, each commanded by plainclothes *mukhabarat* officers. Young men and many teenage boys chanted and pumped their fists. Emotion, long stomped on, silenced, sang to the heavens. Their boys must be freed! *"Ba'al el youm ma fi khouf"* (no fear after today) rose like an anthem. As the trapped crowd thinned in the forward march, some pounded on their motor scooter horns and shouted, *"Allah Akbar"* (God is great).

Lilia too had felt brave clutching her phone outside by their fountain despite her fear for her brothers, for everybody. Then the beating in the air drowned the sounds of their trickling water. She looked up. Helicopters were noisy overhead, and from the courtyard she saw them descend towards nearby fields below the hills overlooking the city. Her bravado deserted her alone by her fountain, and she dropped to the ground and leaned back against it. More texts: *In black. Mukhabarat. Sharpshooters running into shops.* And soon: *On roofs. Aiming. I love you, Lilia.*

Then hot angry tears spilled helplessly from her coal-black eyes. She grabbed the edge of the fountain for support and screamed. *Sending video to Al-Jazeera.* She was so afraid for him; she dropped to the floor and covered her ears with both hands. Her other brother phoned. Her damp fingers answered.

"Lilia, *listen,*" he implored her, panicked.

She heard the loudspeakers pointed in all directions from the minaret just below its pointed peak. Electronic voices sounding disembodied, inhuman, and maybe frightened like her called through them for the crowd to go home, repeating that their demands could be met if they did. The crowd, emboldened by their numbers, not believing doom could strike when the just were so many, erupted in screams of "Liars, liars. Down with Bashar. End the regime." Lila's call abruptly cut off, and her heart dropped down through her body.

Almost immediately, her brother sent the video. She watched. It was like being there but safe, she thought, ashamed. Black-clad police pushed the crowd back, it then surging forward like a boomerang. Truncheons pummeled protestors. They kicked men and boys and threw them into black vans that burst away and weaved through the fleeing crowd. Those who moved too slowly were slammed to the ground, to the sound of metal against bone.

Incredibly hours passed. Lilia couldn't bear waiting any longer. She had to act, not think. She silently eased out the front door, ran halfway there, then stopped, her heartbeat wild. Alone in the street, she saw up ahead that neither side gave ground. Tires burned, the smell acrid. A fusillade of rocks pelted the security forces. The sharpshooters fired into the air. People in the street ducked. She suddenly realized she was vulnerable and ran to the side of the nearby shop, whole lambs hanging from hooks in the window, mouths drooped. She crouched low and watched.

Then as if in a dream, sharpshooters fired into the crowd. The sounds weren't real, she tried to convince herself, only the backfire of cars. Men screamed. Most seemed hit in bleeding arms. The mob scattered. At the crack of bullets, more fell, shot in the legs. Though she felt she could not count on Allah, she thanked him for the sharpshooter's sure aim. The crowd ran back towards the Omari Mosque, shouting, "Someone was hit in the head. *He's dead.*" She saw another drop, blood exploding from his chest, and he collapsed like a doll. The *mukhabarat* grabbed the bodies, a man at the head and another at the feet, ran with them, pushed the lifeless into cars and sped away. The crowd scattered. Uniformed black *ghuls* wielding black batons gave chase.

Her younger brother called to tell her he was not hurt and impart the news. She dared not tell him she was near and saw. She started back towards her house in a daze, keeping low and against the shops. She could not cry as she stumbled forward.

The next day cowed elders met with Bashar's cousin, Najib, and promised to fulfill his every order. Najib released the dead bodies on condition that they be interred immediately, quietly and without a mass funeral or another mass protest. He then raised a finger as a warning and a threat. Without discussion, the elders agreed. The population felt otherwise; the martyr's sacrifice had to be honored. Lilia had joined a sea of people, tens of thousands, covering the ground to the cemetery like ants.

After the funeral young men and boys, emotion spilling like a fountain overflowing in a downpour, raged into the streets. Bearing tents and food, they encamped in the stone Omari Mosque courtyard. Authorities ordered them to leave. Not a soul budged. Security officers wielded their truncheons and strode between and on them, the black wood wet with red. The courtyard emptied, and then within an hour, everyone surged back. For fear of reprisals or worse, nearby clinics refused to treat the wounded. A makeshift hospital under a tent flew up in the mosque courtyard, sides dancing in the wind. All day Lilia made the rounds to pharmacists and clinics, begging for supplies, bandages, and medicines. The activity, the stealth, the weight of her parcels, and the edging through alleyways to avoid undesired eyes considerably calmed her. As long as they were not seen, the merchants donated readily. Some men trembled as they filled plastic bags. Others wept; most hurried and stayed silent.

The following day, Lilia walked across the stained black stone and entered the treatment tent in the mosque courtyard. All morning, shots burst into flesh, the death toll over thirty. It was inconceivable and, at the same time, exactly why they seized the streets. About half a dozen girls darted from blanket to blanket where men lay on the ground. Despite her horror, Lilia was hopeful as these girls had crossed an ancient line into a new present. There would be no going back. As a schoolteacher, she had taken the required course in medical first aid, and her heart leaped that the men welcomed her here. She washed wounds, applied creams, and wrapped gauze until her scarf was wet from sweat and her clothes dyed with blood. She felt free and knew a Daraa husband would never have allowed her here.

An hour before sunset, word bounded from house to house that the boys had been released. Bruised, broken, all with electric shock bites in their skin, none could walk on their own. Several were near lifeless. Joy and rage crashed together inside her like thunder. She willed herself to believe that a regime that would do this to its children must certainly collapse under the weight of such evil. Yet as she brushed aside some unruly hair that had fallen over her face, she knew Hafez al-Assad had rampaged for three decades. Bashar had absorbed it all at his father's knee.

As she noticed the sun meeting the horizon, a yellow ball visible through the end of the tent, the sky pink and purple like the beautiful wound of a hurting country, her elder brother touched her shoulder and motioned his head. She understood. Girls could not remain among the all-night protestors at the mosque.

In the half-light, she walked alone in the empty street towards her home. Wild dogs howled from the fields. It was cold, and she shivered in her damp clothes. Her father had accepted her presence at the healing tent, and she thought she saw approval in his silent, red-veined watery eyes. Her mother fumed. Lilia easily ignored her mother's upset at what the extended family would think.

She turned the corner and saw a dreaded *mukhabarat* black van parked ahead of her. She was not sure why it was hidden, as they could take anyone anywhere. Some instinct made her stop and walk backward. Suddenly she sensed someone behind her, but before she could spin, she felt a hand clasp her mouth.

"We're friends, don't struggle," the voice said, but it was not the Daraa accent, nor the softer Damascus dialect, nor from anywhere else she immediately recognized. She felt herself lifted into the air, did not resist, and to her surprise, being held felt comforting. She was just crazy tired, she told herself.

Her feet did not touch the ground until she was inside the van. The man released her, and almost in the same motion, the driver eased the vehicle ahead.

"No cake?" she asked, not surprised at herself, given nobody was beating, restraining, or blindfolding her. "I like *barazek*."

"I prefer *kleicha*," the small, thin man beside her in *mukhabarat* black said, describing the pastry rolled between layers of date spread. "You've certainly had a long day. It seems we've not come completely prepared. My apologies."

Kleicha, she knew, was beloved to the east in neighboring Iraq.

For some strange reason, she was not scared. She assumed she had trembled in such stark terror in recent days that this didn't seem extraordinary. Tires crunched over the dirt of the side street.

"We are not from the *mukhabarat*," the Iraqi said.

They had to be, she thought. This was how they lied, snuck into your brain.

"We have been watching you the last few days, attending the funerals, gathering supplies, and especially in the medical tent."

Fear arched through her. For sneaking in medicines, they might hang her the way they did, indoors, unseen. She said nothing, thinking about the gentle way he had raised her in the air.

"Why watch *me?*"

"If this is the beginning of civil war, and we think it is, it will not go easily for those who desire change as you have witnessed. It will take a lot to remove the regime. Syria has powerful friends in Iran and Russia that the leaders in Egypt and Tunisia lacked."

"Why am I here?"

"You have your identity card with you?"

"Of course."

"Good. You are already someone risking everything for

her people. You could be arrested tomorrow. And disappear."
She could not see through the blackened windows. They were
outside the city now and, from the added bumping, moving
through the fields below the low mountains.

"I know," she said. "I'm afraid. Most of the time, that
doesn't stop me."

"You can do much good. You already are. But you are
limited, and I don't mean because you are a woman, and there
is only so much the society will allow, even as it's stretching.
The regime could run tanks through the mosque courtyard at
any time."

"We *know*," she said angrily. "Our eyes are open."

"I propose to offer you the prospect of doing far more.
Would you be interested?"

"You think I long to bandage wounds?" She was
becoming impatient though suddenly she was no longer tired.

"The last few days show you what's ahead. It's going to
be even worse than Hama. Unlike his father, Bashar is weak.
So he will try to prove otherwise. I can offer you the chance to
help save thousands of lives, maybe tens of thousands of your
people across Syria."

She closed her eyes. Now she *was* dreaming. She had to
be. When she opened them, she would wake up in her bed, no
matter that she could feel the van jumping on uneven dirt.

Her eyelids parted. "Why me?"

"The truth is, it is not because of your commitment or
unparalleled bravery, despite both in insufficient supply in the
larger world. It is the way more things work. Mere chance,
on this occasion, because of how you look. I cannot tell you
more now. I have not exaggerated what you will contribute.
That said, if you wish, I can drop you somewhere where you
can walk home. Otherwise, you'll leave Syria with us now. We
listen to the communications. A massive crackdown is coming
at the mosque. They are deciding when."

"Then I'm needed here."

"That is your choice. But ask yourself how much *you*

can accomplish? They will empty your courtyard, tear your medical tent to shreds. Many will die. It advances nothing if you are among them."

She imagined the roar of regime tanks, saw herself under the treads, and feared more for her loved ones who'd see it. "What about my family? My brothers. When will I talk to them again?"

"They will believe the *mukhabarat* have taken you for your various activities. We cannot inform your family you were not that you are safe. They will believe you among the disappeared."

She was cold, beginning to shake again. "I have often thought, maybe more hoped, that there was something I was *supposed* to do. Maybe this is it?"

"I want to suggest you think differently," the man said with the thoughtfulness of the scholar he was when time cooperated. "If you believe this is the universe's plan, when you are bored and very lonely, you will experience a crisis. You may grow resentful, and become unsure of everything you believe in. In the real world, you are here because of a coincidence. Because of that, you have a chance to do something remarkable. The only thing the universe has planned is to expand through the heavens, and that is for a reason we don't know. If it doesn't care about electrodes placed on those boy's genitals, it's not much concerned about what you or I do."

She laughed. "You're talking me out of this?"

"I sincerely hope the contrary. So I am being direct with you."

"You have clothes for me to change into?"

The driver tossed a bag of clothing from a local shop back from the front seat he had spent time selecting as if for one of his two daughters. He had another one beside it that was not for Lilia.

"We don't nearly always succeed," the Iraqi said. "But we try."

"Okay, tell him to stop this thing so I can get out and

change. I'm freezing."

The driver pulled off the secondary road into the olive fields. As they bounced in the dirt, Lilia held onto the front seatback. The van stopped, and without asking, she got out. Olive leaves shimmered silver in the three-quarters moon. Deeper in the grove, she saw a heavy truck with wood slat sides and white Syrian plates. In the cool wind that rustled the leaves from that direction, she smelled apricots, Damascus' most prized export.

"The Nasib Crossing?" she asked.

The Iraqi let loose a grin and revealed to Lilia surprisingly white teeth. "Have you been to Jordan?" he asked.

"What? You don't know whether I have or haven't?" She smiled between chattering teeth. "I have not, but it seems I'm about to."

The border crossing was 16 kilometers from Daraa on the M5 Damascus-Amman Highway, the primary trade thoroughfare from Syria to the Gulf States. With the bag of clothes, Lilia ran in a swath of moonlight between dark trees. Behind a thick trunk, she wrestled off her wet clothing. She laughed when she found a bra that seemed her size. She had never been out of Syria and was excited. Soon she retrieved her old clothes, assuming they would want them and the imaginings of her family would be worse if they were discovered.

In the front seat, her small body fit comfortably between them. The Syrian border guard leered at her and her uncovered head when they stopped at the checkpoint. The driver silently passed him folded green Syrian lira, the outdoor Roman theater at Palmyra visible. The thousand-pound notes flew into his back pocket. He waved them through with his rifle muzzle, and the truck bounded into the Jordanian desert.

CHAPTER 2

DAMASCUS

2011

Breathing hard, Yussuf Fuad stood at his office window on the highest of the ten floors of his new, impregnable Military Intelligence Directorate. He absorbed the commanding view of the southern outskirts of Damascus and beyond the orchards that embraced the stone city on three sides, the branches clouds of blossoms now that it was spring. The Barada River gathered in underground caverns in the Lebanon Mountains, roared beneath the desert, and broke the surface into the karst spring of Ain-al-Fijah, twenty-five kilometers to the south. From there, it plummeted through steep gorges and arrived here, separated into seven serpentine branches that birthed the oasis of Damascus. Behind Fuad to the north, suburbs and restaurants with panoramic views through glass walls reached up the lower third of the brown, desolate Mount Qasioun.

Headed towards the cliff of 65 years old, Fuad believed his salt-and-pepper but thick hair made him appear younger. His youthful air mattered only to thwart those darting from the underbrush like rattlesnakes to supplant him as head of the Military Intelligence Directorate of the *mukhabarat*.

He climbed the stairs early and always arrived before those dozing reptiles who had not slithered into the lower floors. This morning sharp calf spasms had thrust him awake at 4 a.m., which often happened now as the civil war exigencies reduced his hiking on Mount Qasioun. It was one of the sudden ways age laughed at those who believed themselves immune. Diminutive and only ten pounds heftier than when he nervously and uncertain of himself joined the army at eighteen, Fuad leaned his head against the cool glass to help him relax. Before he retired, he was in the midst of one last attempt, secreted from his colleagues, to save Syria from itself.

Of the four branches of the *mukhabarat*—the others, the Air Force Intelligence Directorate, the General Security Directorate, and the Political Security Directorate—Air Force Intelligence flew above them all. Hafez al-Assad had climbed into a cockpit at the Homs Military Academy in 1952, later trained in MiG-17s in Russia and rose to command the Air Force. The Assad's still ruled from the air.

Under Fuad's farsighted expansion, Military Intelligence provided succor to radical groups that lined up behind the president and undermined those abroad that did not. Warm, joking, and rarely flustered, with the uprising blowing across the country like the hot desert *hamsin* sands, he found himself on a tightrope between his position and his love of the people. He gazed down. He had sketched this building's original design and decided on three subterranean interrogation floors, sufficient but not excessive, outfitted with traditional Syrian tools of persuasion.

A few clouds hung low in the bright blue sky. Rather than address the reports of overnight unrest stacked on his desk—with a slight twist on the dial of fate, he would have found himself among the rebels—he let his thoughts loose to roam the past. As a young military intelligence officer, he had not been ambitious, never imagined or desired vaulting to such stature. Then an unexpected offer in London, the entire purpose he discovered only then of the course he had attended, and his immediate acceptance soon pitched him into the upper echelons of the *mukhabarat* without compromising much. Not for a moment would he consider betraying Syria.

Long married, Fuad welcomed none of the young women who offered themselves like naked meat dangling in the *souq*. As a young, single intelligence officer, despite his lack of stature, his quiet direct talk and unusual blue eyes drew the prettiest to him like mosquitos to bright light. He had no tolerance for deception in courting. He promised no favors to these young paramours, married or not, that he failed to deliver immediately. After he wedded Fatima, he stopped, not quite on a dime but more like pulling the emergency cord in the London underground. He gradually screeched to a halt. Then a cloudless sky opened and released the lightning bolt of Margaret Eido, the French foreign aide worker, who lasted the blink of an eye. An agreed upon two weeks. After these many years, he often still saw her copper-flecked green eyes when he closed his. He had not allowed another near since. When alone in the car, he sometimes talked of his troubles to the empty space where she had sat.

Below the morning crawl to the central city clogged the three northbound lanes of the Qazzaz Highway, southbound leading to Damascus International Airport nearly empty. At 7:30 a.m. across the highway, the dense suburb of al-Qazzaz stirred; exhaust rose from tailpipes, and women in long dresses wonderfully balanced empty baskets on their heads as they moved gracefully to the marketplace. Behind his building, the satellite dish-crowned cinderblock shacks of the Palestinian Jarameh Refugee Camp sprawled.

Fuad brought his gaze to the imposing concrete barrier that circled the building, protecting it like a father's hug of his son in a storm, welcome but maybe not sufficient given the rising rage of both man and nature. An additional low concrete wall lined the highway's edge to discourage vehicles from straying like wild dogs.

Fuad had not considered the threat of a raging rebellion

when planning the new Directorate outside the inner cordon. Checkpoints were impossible here, given the crush of cars. Just then, as if Allah had been listening and laughing at his puny musings, Fuad first heard and then felt the colossal blast. Flames from the highway towered almost across from him, black smoke in their wake. Then the shock wave threw him back like he was a leaf. His head banged on the too-solid mahogany desk, and pain pummeled him. For a fleeting moment, he thought of those he had ordered tortured.

Fuad heard only the buzzing in his ears, then gradually outside sounds returned, the loudest some kind of cracking. He had glimpsed a truck, he thought, exploding on the highway, turning cars ablaze, and slapping away the high barrier like it was paper. Then the ringing in his ears was overwhelmed by the crash as the entire side of the building gave way. He touched the back of his head, felt no wetness. Though he should try and make it to the back stairs, he staggered to the window.

His floor and the one below hung in the air like balconies; the entire facade below them was gone. On the highway, dozens of cars burned, flames licking carcasses bare as a long dead camel in the desert. Thick gray smoke billowed. As the dark cloud spread, people emerged from cars farther away in both directions and ran to help. It must have been 1,000 kilograms of fertilizer, Fuad realized. He staggered back towards his desk, the chair on its side across the room. Leaning against the polished wood, he pulled the cell phone from his pants and, with difficulty, managed to dial Kassem's satellite number. It would pick up in the underground hallways of Institute 3000 on Mount Qasioun.

"We heard it even here," his son said, terror high in his voice. "I couldn't get through to you. If you're talking, then you are not badly injured."

Fuad managed a smile at his son's scientific precision. "It is the right conclusion."

"I'm coming."

Another explosion raged outside. Fuad squeezed his eyes. It was intended to mow down those who, of course, would hurry to help. Despair sunk and flooded through him for all the innocents maimed and murdered across this roiling land.

Singsong sirens of the Red Crescent ambulances filled the quiet. This time he headed not for the window but to safety. He would not risk the elevators, even if operable, as electricity could ignite at any moment.

Outside his office door, women screamed, some bloodied; overhead fluorescents flickered. His breaths refusing to leave him easily, Fuad headed down the corridor, alternately dark and lit, his steps unsure, his head spinning. A soldier Fuad did not recognize, of no rank and in camouflage fatigues with a Makarov pistol at his waist, approached from ahead of him.

"General, may I help?" He dared not touch Fuad without invitation.

"Of course. Thank you."

The soldier slung an arm around his waist and pulled Fuad's flank to his.

"The stairs," Fuad said, feeling the body warmth and only then realized he was cold.

"The rear elevator is working."

"*Stairs*," Fuad said hostilely.

"Of course, sir."

Lightheaded, Fuad unnecessarily shared what he was thinking. "Watch the Saudis claim Air Force Intelligence blew up the building on the president's orders to discredit the opposition."

"I don't understand. Maybe take it easy, general. I'll get you out safe."

Fuad grabbed onto the interior railing past the heavy steel stairwell door as the soldier awkwardly held him. Pain pulsed inside his head. It was difficult to descend this way, but he could hardly catch his breath. They moved slowly. At each floor landing, Fuad stopped to rest. He consoled himself that the delay would allow Kassem time to arrive. At the fifth floor, Fuad pushed the soldier's arm away and walked himself, sliding one hand down the round wood railing in case he needed to grab it. He must appear strong outside, not to save face but to beat back the circle of hyenas. He had watched them surround a zebra standing to give birth in Tanzania's Ngorongoro Crater. If the foal released on all fours did not immediately walk, they would tear it apart. This one, blood on one hind leg, had staggered safely on its feet. He often returned to that image when challenged.

As Fuad stepped from the building, the smell engulfed him: a cocktail of flesh, smoke, and petrol. Undaunted by the second car bomb, men had emerged like ants swarming to help. In a standing mass, others rhythmically raised fists in unison with chants in support of Bashar when they should have been running to pull the trapped from the rubble. They were like helpless children, Fuad thought, reverting to the comfort of uniformity. Medics in their loose red shirts, red and white crescents on the backs, grasping stretchers, trotted rhythmically into the building. Orange and, closer to the ground, yellow flames licked the car frames. With little remaining to burn, metal skeletons, car fragments, and ash covered the highway like dark snow. Everything was black: the road and the dead.

Suddenly a man staggered in front of him, unable to walk, braced on both sides by civilians. He was gray ash, his hair down to his shoes, save for the blood staining his shirt and jeans. He held a surprisingly white cloth to the stump where his hand had recently resided. His eyes were bright, distant, mercifully more in shock than pain. Fuad exhausted no emotion in rage or mourning. The scene focused his determination.

A plainclothes security officer, whom Fuad knew but suddenly could not recall his name, gripping an AK-104 with a telescopic sight ran towards him. "General, it's not safe. I must get you to the Defense Ministry."

"Have snipers fired?"

"No."

"Leave me."

Fuad turned and looked back. The left side of the building had been sheared off cleanly as if by a surgeon's scalpel, exposing the northern switchback stairs. Men stepped up and down them, some with stretchers. Then Fuad laughed. Those in the interrogation cells below ground had been protected.

A slowed siren wailed like a trapped cat. The red Mercedes fire engine attempting to approach was blocked by a smashed yellow car, somehow intact and not burning. A dozen men surrounded it, lifted the vehicle with noisy exertion, and carried it to the side. Nobody in this country did not stop when a vehicle stalled in the desert, the way their ancestors always welcomed strangers into their tents.

Kassem ran towards him. Fuad released his breath and only then realized he had been holding it. Tall with curly black hair, Kassem was gangly yet calm. At twenty-nine, he towered over Fuad by two heads. That his curly thick hair was unlike Fuad's straight locks had never particularly struck Kassem though Fuad felt the reason for the difference more days than not. Fuad's short frame was broad, his legs muscled. He and Kassem had hiked through the mountains since the boy was five, when Fuad hauled him on his back up the steepest ascents. His son worried obsessively about small matters but acted quickly and calmly in an emergency, on the latter count like Fuad.

Kassem bent, hugged and kissed his father on both cheeks.

"I must see where it exploded," Fuad said, adding quietly, "Don't hold my arm."

Vigilant and protective, Kassem grew afraid when Fuad sometimes slid back a little on loose mountain trails, but his father refused to relinquish these ascents for flatter ground. As they approached a small crowd, seeing him, people moved away. Fuad glimpsed the first of the two craters. Black hunks of the highway had toppled in. No sign of the vaporized truck.

Fuad lifted his eyes in both directions and took in maybe thirty blackened and burning vehicles and the dead. He saw many small, blackened bones.

Red Crescent men carried two corpses on a single stretcher, one's head smashed, revealing the brains, the other bleeding only from his mouth.

"How many dead?" Kassem asked the medic.

"Too early. Inside, about forty so far, but we'll find more."

"How many people are in the building?" Kassem asked his father.

"Eight hundred. Many had not yet arrived. They wanted the commuters and to blame us."

"Hundreds are trapped," the Red Crescent man said. "We hear them."

Kassem's heart raced as he imagined arms reaching up through the broken stone. The yellow car rested now against the shattered roadside barrier. Firemen clad in heavy black with yellow identifying stripes sprayed from powerful hoses like striking snakes. As water struck the car frames, steam sizzled.

"Children were heading to school," Kassem said. Tears filled his small coal eyes and breached the dam of his eyelids. He then peered at his father's office window, just barely there. His face fell. Stone suddenly tumbled from below the two remaining floors, skipping against the facade on the descent.

"This is what the Free Syrian Army wants," Kassem raged. "To murder school children. They're terrorists."

Fuad returned to his familiar tightrope walk with his son, concerned now and almost for the first time that one or both of them would fall off. With tremendous guilt at disregarding Kassem's autonomy, he had steered him to a career atop the regime's chemical weapons complex.

"Not the Free Syria Army. It's al-Nusra." In vehicles rippling black flags with white script, these Syrian Salafist jihadis rampaged and bulldozed regional history as they went. From the ashes, with their transnational brothers, they would raise the Islamic State. Al-Nusra, the newly birthed Syrian cousins of al-Qaeda, postponed worldwide jihad to trample the Syrian state. The idea for the *global* Muslim caliphate first sprouted in the parched mountains of Afghanistan, where Islamic fighters waiting to bestow on the Soviets the welcome uninvited guests might expect, had a lot of time on their hands.

"Dad, you had intelligence on the attack?"

"No. I would have closed the highway. It has al-Nusra's signature. It is like a lover. A woman always recognizes a man's signature in bed. Even if he returns after many years. The FSA would gladly destroy the building. But not when cars were packed with children. This is al-Nusra, like a man who tries to win a woman by first destroying her."

Not knowing what he felt, Kassem said, "I suppose women have signatures too." He was bookish and shy, with unrestrained curiosity.

"Yes, as distinct as any man. However, they can be different with different lovers. Men are tediously the same. Even me." He let loose a smile that refreshed him. "You will experience more in time."

"Given how little I have, it would seem inevitable."

Fuad felt such profound love, it could not have filled him fuller. He put an arm around Kassem's waist to support himself. To hell with anybody who salivated that this was weakness.

"Come, I need to give orders. I want the names of the dead. I will call each family myself."

Kassem felt his father tremble slightly against him and was nervous that he would exhaust himself. "You can assign that."

"And I could have sent you to boarding school in England rather than read to you."

"Okay," Kassem said. "But I'm taking you home after you make arrangements. You can start the calls tomorrow."

"Yes, General," Fuad said playfully. A fresh wind of

blackened flesh reached Fuad's nostrils, and his face collapsed. "Kassem, I'm glad you're here."

Fuad knew he had to tell his son soon about the path he had paved for him. Fuad's head hurt too much now for him to worry again about how his son would react to the details of how and why he had been misled for so long.

* * *

Shai Shaham was unaccustomed to the fear he felt. When wearing a South Lebanon Army colonel's uniform in a jeep at a Hezbollah checkpoint above a craggy Beqaa Valley ravine beside an actual Christian South Lebanese general, his heartbeat hardly hastened.

Worry, on the other hand, to the Mossad Deputy Director of Operations was a lifelong partner. Like an actual one, occasionally vexing but more often comforting in its familiarity. For Shai, worry was as common as walking, and the two often found company together, though his legs always hurt when his mind carried them farther than they liked.

Shai had changed little over his considerable decades other than in increasing girth, though he began as a chubby child and, even when bolting to six feet, never escaped it. In addition to trudging preoccupied, often unaware either where he was headed or had been, he was known to fret through a lot of food. He did not expect much would ever change, such as the intractable conflict with their Palestinian brothers. Nevertheless, he found joyful surprise that his small Toyota now unlocked and started without his fumbling for his keys, and lightbulbs seemed suddenly never to need attention. He believed it was people who didn't change, though their habits might in the way years ago he had stopped smoking the moment he decided to. After his undergraduate degree and before he began an undistinguished army service barely fitting in a tank, he had carried an untouched pack in his pocket for a year to challenge himself. He never ignited one. Still, Shai embraced a wide breadth of exceptions to his beliefs when they stared him in the eye. With that in mind, he mounted operations with the irrepressible hope they'd make more than a fleeting difference. In that vein, amid this current unremitting Syrian civil war, he had decided to attempt to maneuver the Americans and their occasional allies, the Russians, to join hands and rid Syria of their mountain of chemical weapons and, while at it, relinquish the missile delivery systems that might launch them. With age hounding at his heels, he had begun to dream bigger.

As Shai walked now from his car to Hadassah Hospital in Jerusalem, the persistent headache in his forehead jostling with each step, he propelled his thoughts away from fear about his health to the al-Assads, who were, for the most part, equally unmanageable. The *pere*, President Hafez al-Assad, had departed the planet in 2000, not too soon for hardly anyone, after thirty years of fire and brimstone deemed benign only now in the rearview mirror. Many Syrians longed for those good old days, given the unexpected ascent of Bashar, Hafez's second-in-line to the throne. Inconveniently yanked back from his ophthalmological practice in London in the quest to dethrone his meekness, Bashar al-Assad daily, if not hourly, sought to prove himself by leaving no opponent unstoned. This hunger for worth, like a tapeworm, required constant nourishing. In 1994, his older, flamboyant brother, Bassel, had coaxed his Mercedes through the fog to 150 mph towards Damascus Airport, late for a flight to Frankfurt and skiing the Alps. In his haste Bassel had neglected to buckle his seatbelt and, given the fog, did not see the barrier. After the funeral, Bashar was hauled back from obscurity.

In some areas, *pere* and surviving *fils*, shared a vision. This like-mindedness found expression at Institute 3000, a good way up Mount Qasioun. The institute's forty buildings and deep storage bunkers rose and plunged on the high mountain's barren flank. The not to be underestimated

Syrians—American cinema had all Arabs as terrorists, oil sheiks, or steering magic carpets, while Muslim women hardly ever left the house, Shai mused with disappointment —had manufactured military-grade pure sarin in impressive quantity. That was not the worst of it. Ingeniously they had overcome sarin's degrading over time, and the Middle East conflict, if nothing else, abided. Institute 3000 pioneered binary sarin. They housed the vats of isopropyl alcohol separately from the ones with the nastier goodies. Ready to mix immediately before launch, in this way, the sarin lost none of its might while hanging around, unlike he did, Shai thought with a sudden, slight grin.

Shai was more worried about Bashar raining sarin on his people than theirs—unless maybe he was on the precipice of a long fall when dictators were known to seek glory by conflagration. More likely, quantities of this nerve agent, and Syria had plenty to spare, would find its short way to Hezbollah, swarming across Israel's border with Lebanon. In 1982, the Israel Defense Forces invaded to drive the pesky Palestine Liberation Organization from Lebanon's south. The PLO guerillas or terrorists, depending on the international newspaper, crossed the border into Israel to launch attacks against schools and the buses full of noisy kids heading towards them.

As Israeli tanks crunched the highway heading to Beirut, the Iranian Mullahs whipped the southern Lebanese Shia into a new frenzied entity, Hezbollah, in a lack of creativity "Party of God," to snipe at the advancing Israelis from the rear. In Beirut, the fleeing PLO clambered onto boats bound for Tunis under the UN flag. The Hezbollah buds bloomed into an army sizeable enough to send combat units into Syria to battle for Bashar. Hezbollah added a political party, radio and satellite television networks, and Cabinet seats in Beirut along the way. Shai reminded himself that things indeed changed more than he cared to acknowledge and that pesky neighbors could always be replaced by something worse.

Despite the pain in his legs and his size, Shai agilely made his way through the lobby crowd. He typically wore unencumbering khaki pants and solid shirts yanked off a discount rack somewhere abroad where prices were more cooperative. He shopped in a hurry, the way he attended to most things, concerned not with the look but only managing the correct size. His graying brown hair had marched considerably back from his forehead. The whites of his small, brilliant blue eyes were red-veined from lack of sleep and relentless reading. He favored science journals and relaxed by collecting obscure facts that were occasionally useful. "I hear ninety percent of people die in bed," he often said with a colossal smile, "so I spend as little time there as possible." His mirth was equally inherent and a tactic to disarm.

Shai's recent fear had descended abruptly and unexpectedly, like a meteor. He became frightened the second time he slurred a word while speaking. It happened first in English. He said "accident," and "accent" departed his mouth. The following week "physician" emerged as "position." "Train" chose to assert itself as "twain." He felt nothing untoward, only heard the wrong word and, without embarrassment, quickly corrected. Then his frontal cortex began to throb slightly but unremittingly. He chose to start speaking slower, not his forte or fondness, and consciously enunciate. He had a lot still to accomplish and was frightened he'd be felled first.

An hour-and-a-half later, after the MRI in the basement of this Jerusalem valley rung by old, terraced olive trees, the neurologist summoned to the Emergency Room, Shlomo Infeld, accompanied Shai to his upstairs cubicle.

Infeld declined to hang his degrees: Harvard Medical School, Centre Nationale De La Recherche Scientifique in Paris, UCLA's Neuropsychiatric Institute. They would have left insufficient space for the photos of children and grandchildren, like a colorful mosaic filling the cork walls on all sides. With digital originals in the cloud, he punctured them with tacks as frames, too, stole too much room. When he needed to think, he moved them around. A row of pipes kept loose papers on his desk from being rearranged by the breeze from the open window.

"Lot of family," Shai said, inhaling a cursory glance. "I'm a little envious. Maybe a lot."

"Four kids, each has four. I can't decide if it's DNA, competition, or lack of creativity. I used to call them and their kids every Friday afternoon when I got home. Now I have to start on the way from the car."

"It's already occurred to you. Your kids thought it a model family, what they knew and liked. Two great-grandchildren so far," Shai added without looking again at the photos.

Infeld laughed, enjoying the observation which he had long shared. "I won't be surprised if they each have four too. Though there's always the possibility of a rebel slipping in a fifth. If we might digress, as for you the news is quite good. Your MRI's clear. Remarkably." Then with a playful smile he asked, "Any of your relatives in Poland marry each other?"

"Only all of them."

Shai suddenly craved a cigarette, an urge he had not battled for as long as he could recall. He believed he was on the wrong track in Syria, focused on the sarin, and hoped to shunt to a different siding quietly and outside his superiors' gaze. He thought about returning an unopened pack to his pocket as he was stubborn and that would ensure he resisted.

"Actually, one set of grandparents were third cousins," Shai added.

"Stretch your arm out straight ahead."

Shai obeyed. They both looked at the slight rhythmic shaking.

"How long have you noticed the small tremble in your arm and head?"

"If I was counting, a decade."

"See anybody about it?"

"It hasn't gotten worse."

"Until now, it appears. Could be stress, likely is. At

Hadassah, we refer to it as an East European tremor. The Americans call it an essential tremor."

"Genetic mutations probably aren't exclusive to inbreeding," Shai ventured. He was partial to *Science* magazine just behind *The Journal of Anthropological Archaeology;* both diverted his mind from wherever it wasn't resting.

"Let me hasten to the good news. It's benign. Not Parkinson's. I can tell from how you move. But I don't know what that ache in the frontal cortex is. But at your age, an essential tremor can begin to create havoc. I'd like to do a PET scan to rule out the onset of aphasic dementia. That's the word replacement. You have to eat lots of protein for a day before, so I can't do it now."

Dementia shook him like an earthquake. He looked down.

"It's unlikely," Infeld added. "You're recognizing the misspoken words. You won't like this, but if you rest some, a lot of this may go away."

"If I don't?"

"Episodes come and go. It will likely pass. It will likely return. But what's the harm in being thorough? You're having a fairly dramatic progression. I can't tell you how far it will go or when. We can give you something to quiet it. Of course, there are side effects, dull this and that. Might even calm you."

"I'd rather not."

"Maybe *some* exercise," Infeld pleaded more than suggested. "Doesn't have to be exhausting. Just regular. Body misses it after three days."

Shai's smile effortlessly returned. "I had a doctor here years ago. Cardiologist. Threatened not to treat me unless I took to walking."

"I presume you never saw him again."

Shai knew he'd be back to visit Infeld if only to see his latest photos. "I bought sneakers, used to walk through Shuafat, lived near there, then in Ramat Eshkol. I ended up having coffee with the villagers. I have a bit of Arabic. I had to go abroad, and the shoes never quite made it out of the closet. There is some exercise I do, on occasion, when I'm up early."Infeld's smile lifted his immaculate white beard, but unlike Shai's laugh, his mirth always telegraphed his feelings.

"Anything else I can offer? Given you're already here."

Shai decided to drop down one on his list, to Infeld's expertise in chemical toxins. "What's sarin manage to do?"

"Beyond clear, colorless, and odorless, so the perfect nerve agent. How technical?"

"Try me. If I'm not asking a lot of questions, climb from there."

"Neurotransmitters, the chemical messengers, think of them as passengers on a train in the brain. Once the train gets going, they pump up the muscles to do chores like lifting this pipe. After I do, the cleaning crew comes in with the name enzymes on the back of their overalls. They wipe up the mess from all this stimulation so you can put the pipe down. Sarin's a wall. The train crashes and can't get through. The nerves are supercharged, over stimulated. Muscle control ceases. Overstimulated, the diaphragm shuts down. The consequences of not breathing are no surprise. Death is at the doorstep. Atropine syringes can jump-start the heart. In lesser doses, it accelerates dangerously low heartbeats." Infeld now actually lifted his pipe. "If we're in danger of a sarin attack, please let me know. I'd like to take a bunch more photos."

"Let's consider this doctor-patient confidentiality. We've quietly distributed gas masks and atropine in the north. I think we're okay for now. The Syrian people, a good deal less so."

"Can anybody help them?"

"Yes. Or no. Bit uncertain at present." Shai unexpectedly stepped to the top of his list. "Here's a question. By sarin, by sword, or by barrel bomb. Does it matter how you die?"

Infeld cradled his pipe. Their news featured Syrian helicopters showering civilian neighborhoods with huge, explosive-laden metal barrels, which shook him.

"It does make a difference up until the moment they're

dead. Once they're dead, they don't have a preference about anything. But it matters to those who survived. Seems a lot's beating on your head," Infeld said gently.

"Given we're a speck of a people and in an awful neighborhood, is it enough that *we* survive? Can we just ignore what's happening in those neighborhoods? Or by returning here, claiming the right of history and unending moral values, do we have a responsibility on the world stage?"

Infeld tapped the pipe grounds into a glass ashtray. "You probably know the rebels leave their severely wounded at the bottom of the Golan Heights. Our armored cars go into Syria, leave food and medical supplies and bring them back. I've treated a number here with head wounds." He packed in fresh tobacco. "It's something, but if you say it's not a whole lot, you'd be right."

Shai stood and paced in the cramped quarters, even smaller with files stacked against the wall; a glance at the tabs exposed they were alphabetized. Parked cars filled the view out the window. Shai thought about the state's early decades when overwhelming import taxes on cars shepherded everyone to the herds of buses. They'd built a bounty, and it was high time to give back. He returned to his chair but held it from behind.

"Let's say, hypothetically speaking, we can stop the sarin. Get it all out of Syria. Then what? We sit on our rooftops and watch the barrel bombs drop."

"If the sarin's eliminated, you've managed some good. You shouldn't calculate how much. Or how little. If you try and measure, you will always conclude you haven't done enough."

"Little too reasonable for me, doctor," Shai said with his small smile.

As Shai opened the door, Infeld said, "Wait." He reached into his wallet, withdrew a business card, scribbled his cell number on the back, and stretched it out. "Text me if the head gets worse. I'll see you immediately, or some version thereof."

Shai's smile widened in genuine appreciation, and he snatched the card. He was gone quicker and more silently than

Infeld expected.

Outside, the sun comforted Shai, the pulsing in his head quieted for now by the release of his concerns. The multi-building medical center sprawled over a hill at the base of the empty valley, with newer appendages to the tall stone hospital. Shai quickened his gait and inhaled the fragrance of the pines like sentinels on the rising mountains.

Increasingly memories intruded. The statuesque trees reminded him of the Colonel, longtime head of the Service, prematurely pushed to pasture at his kibbutz near the sea and later buried there. The Colonel had sought not the CIA's 'brightest of the best' but the brightest of the aimless. The Colonel felt longevity in service lay in delivering purpose. His eagle eyes, Professor Anton Appelfeld, circled over potential prey. First-year law students at Tel-Aviv University all marched into Appelfeld's required Legal Research and Writing course. With a stentorian bellow, the tall, blonde-maned, red-bearded scholar laughed at their precious thoughts, berated them as borrowed, overheard, what others believed, and the eleventh plague— conventional. He demanded they defeat the first impulse of their brilliance: easily won. In those few days, he had taught Shai a lifetime lesson.

Shai learned later that Appelfeld spotted him on the second day of class in the back row from where Shai's questions often emerged. Appelfeld was certain he had not read the assigned texts. Two weeks later, the Colonel dropped down below Shai, who never again made his way to that lecture hall. He had no difficulty returning books he had not yet purchased. Instead, on the grass, he had slashed through the thickets of Dostoevsky, Pasternak, and Bulgakov, drawn to their quests for forgiveness. The way he charged through life, he sensed the future need. Frequently he looked up and scanned for women but was too shy to approach any unless he had a classmate cornered at a party and could ask about her, which all women liked.

As he arrived at his car, his cell phone rang. He groped

in his pocket, the keys in the way, and withdrew his phone. It slipped and clattered on the ground, all the while insisting he answer. He sat heavily on the hot asphalt between two cars in the serpentine lane, parked vehicles faced-in along the way like dominoes, and held the phone securely on his lap. He saw from the number that the babysitters demanded a hearing.

Shai listened. "I have an idea," he said, as his first words, and instructed where to meet him in Bethlehem.

Bethlehem, walking distance from Jerusalem for most everyone but Shai. In the West Bank so closed to Israelis for their safety. Not so vastly long ago, Shai's neighbor had shopped for lamb at a butcher there and brought them fabulous cuts. Shai stood by his car at the Gilo 300 checkpoint to the occupied territories and waited. Barbed wire curled across the top of the gray twenty-five food concrete separation wall. Soldiers lounged and stood by the busy checkpoint from the West Bank to Jerusalem. Partway up the high hill behind the security barrier, olive trees in the signature round stone terraces climbed in rows. Above them, Palestinian residential apartment blocks forged the rest of the way to the crest.

Soon he turned and saw one of the babysitters walk Lilia Wassaf toward him. To Daraa, he'd dispatched Yehuda, a descendant of the 150,000 Jews in Iraq at the 1948 founding of Israel. The 1950 to 1952 open window to flee Baghdad crushed property and business values as the Jews comprised twenty percent of the city and its commerce. Fifteen thousand chose to stay, as usual, those with the largest houses, Yehuda's parents not among them. By current count, four Jews lived in Baghdad. Yehuda taught Bible in a religious girl's high school in the poor Katamon quarter of Jerusalem, where he was so beloved that his not infrequent absences were overlooked.

Shai bustled out of the car to greet her. From their chats, he quickly noticed her eager curiosity. She'd be soon bored with the likes of the Church of the Nativity, where the tour buses swarmed like bees at the hive.

"Hi Lilia, come get in," he said to her excitedly in Arabic.

"Something I want to show you, bit off the beaten path."

She gave a tight smile and nodded.

As he climbed in beside her said, "Little restless, I'm sure."

"More than a little."

Shai drove quickly. "Great Palestinian-Belgian cafe not far. Cappuccinos, crepes. Probably had it to the gills with falafel by now."

A small smile broke the hardness in her face. "Actually, the food's not much different than ours."

"My point." He slammed the car to a halt. "First, want to see the most valuable block of concrete in the world?"

She laughed. "Not what I had in mind, but sure."

He had parked in front of a row of quiet shops, then walked back around the corner. They stood alone in front of an artist's work on a concrete wall, Lilia's mouth slightly open in surprise and awe.

"It's a Banksy," Shai explained. "British street graffiti artist. Nobody knows who he is. It's called 'Girl Frisking the Soldier.'"

She absorbed how nothing like this would be allowed to remain on a wall in Syria. The *mukhabarat* would obliterate it with black, like in Daraa. Lilia gazed at the painting of a schoolgirl in a pink dress sweeping her hands up a green uniformed soldier in a matching helmet, pistol, and handcuffs at his waist, back to the girl, his arms high in submission.

"For me," Shai said. "It's a colorful reminder that we were that little girl with other hands-on us throughout history. Banksy has flipped it on us. We're the ones now controlling children's lives."

"It's so pretty too."

"I understand Palestinian rage and the artist's empathy," Shai said with all his heart. "People hemmed in, delayed at checkpoints. Soldiers barging through their doors in the middle of the night to hunt for weapons or ransack because we can."

"What are you saying to me?" she asked, puzzled.

"Very little. You're my heroine, Lilia. I wanted to show you something out of the ordinary. I don't like to hide anything unless I have to. Banksy financed the Walled Off Hotel inside Bethlehem. Small art hotel for actual guests, with a piano bar, right across from the Separation Wall. Palestinian graffiti all over the barrier there, like the boy's work in Daraa, a bit more of Banksy's. Shall we have a look? Then coffee and crepes?"

She nodded and laughed. "*Yes.*"

He enjoyed these outings with her. And he had some time before he needed to cross their electronic mines and chain-link border fence into Southern Lebanon.

CHAPTER 3

HAMA, SYRIA

1982

In a sitting position, Dr. Hasan Masalmeh's arms and legs thrust forward through the car tire, his hands lashed to his ankles. His buttocks protruded through the rear, keeping the tire upright on the tread. Naked, his skin purple and patchy, some blood over his legs still wet, he rocked forward and back inside the tire, trying to warm himself. Muscles he had not known existed throbbed from days in this cramped position. Metal truncheons had sounded against his leg bones, but he did not believe any had fractured. An ophthalmologist, his glasses gone, he looked at the blurry nooses that lined the walls of the improvised basement prison in his city north of Homs and Damascus. Around him, buckets of water waited on the floor; above them, electric shock cords dangled from platforms. Bodies of two other prisoners had been carried away yesterday.

An artillery shell had collapsed a wall of their house on his wife, mercifully killing her quickly. It must have been three weeks ago, or two, maybe four? He squeezed his eyes and forced away the image of his son wailing in his crib. Neighbors had run with the crib to their home so Masalmeh could tend to those wounded nearby, the *crime* that landed him here. He tried to pull himself up from the weight of despair. In his delirium, he imagined himself in the hall of his wedding, heard the laughing, the singing. He had to survive for his boy, though he feared he would dangle from the wall before long, kicking fiercely and futilely against the plaster with his bare feet. The torturer had asked no questions, sought no information. He labored silently, a cigarette dangling from his lips. Sometimes Masalmeh heard the flick of a finger and then felt the ash burn his skin. They would display his lifeless body outside as a flashing beacon: dangerous shoals ahead if you sail from home under a defiant flag. Or bandage the wounded.

It had begun in February this year of 1982, Hasan believed, surprised at the clarity of his thoughts. For twenty-seven days and nights, thousands of Hafez al-Assad's troops surrounded Hama like hands around a throat. The whistling shells sent stone crumbling and dust rising as block after block tumbled. Hama was Sunni, home to the Muslim Brotherhood, fierce opponents of the Shia state of Hafez al-Assad. Two years before, the Brotherhood had nearly dismantled Hafez while he welcomed the President of Mali in Damascus's guest palace. Machine gun bullets penetrated only walls, and a bodyguard muffled a live grenade by diving on it. Hafez quickly executed a thousand in Tadmor Prison in the shadow of the stalwart columns of the Roman Temple at Palmyra.

Hasan was a physician of sight, apolitical, and belonged to no party. With no empty beds in the hospitals, he had thrown up a makeshift infirmary in what remained of his living room, the sky visible through the ailing roof. He screamed now at the memory, and the sound echoed off the basement walls and turned into laughing at him, but he believed that was his imagination. Tears wet his eyes. Where was his son? He ached everywhere. He focused on the pain to pull his thoughts from his boy, like shutting off the radio when a song reminded him of something awful.

That's right, he realized; it had begun at 2 a.m. He had

been up feeding Wa'el a bottle when mosque loudspeakers abruptly wailed for the people to rise in jihad. He heard later that the Muslim Brotherhood had massacred a Syrian army unit prowling through the Old City after one of the Brotherhood's organizers. Hundreds of the naïve and ecstatic, driven only by emotions, ran through the streets. They rousted government officials from their homes, trampled through police stations, grabbing weapons. They killed maybe a hundred at most, urged the populace to rise up, and declared Hama a "free city."

Hasan closed his damp eyes, and in that small motion, pain rippled through him like waves of acid flowing to shore inside his head. He wanted to recall these events to distract himself. Excited and hot-headed men. A free city? With no army, in a country of no freedom with an army set free to rampage.

How many thousand Hafez Assad troops circled Hama? 5,000? 10,000? 20,000? The coordinated bombardment began simultaneously from the air and ground, like dance floor partners confident of each other's steps. Wave after wave of jets screamed over the Old City, and the ancient stone walls shuddered and acquiesced. The loud, continuous tracks of the tanks followed through formerly narrow walkways. Artillery thudded from the perimeter. Minarets fell as if resting on a prayer carpet that was abruptly pulled away. Tanks climbed over debris until the ancient Hamra neighborhood disappeared. Women in long dresses with covered heads ululated as they ran. Fighters ducked into ageless tunnels beneath the Old City. Government tankers pumped down diesel and lit it, while tanks squatted at the openings. Tank shells blasted the crowds of burning humanity, bursting up for air. House-to-house searches commenced. Mass arrests blew across the city for two weeks like a merciless sandstorm. A row of soldiers executed sixty men in front of the Ma'soud Mosque. Lest anyone forget, *forget,* the doctor cried out the word— their unborn would remember that fingers were severed from lifeless bodies and placed on the mosque's stone walls.

The pain from Hasan Masalmeh's prone position was abruptly excruciating. His stomach muscles felt on fire. Hasan sucked in dank air through his nose and coughed, which hurt. He thought to pray to Allah for his son's safety and a good life and then laughed like a banshee. There was no good life in this country for Wa'el, not in the lifetime of the al-Assads. For a fleeting moment, he hoped his son had perished peacefully, and then he cut off that thought. How dare he wish he were dead? There always was hope, if not for him, for a future for his son he could not imagine.

The physician watched his torturer return, smoking. In the silence, he snapped his kurbash, a whip fashioned from the stiff hairs of a bull's tail. Hasan wondered if he had been foolish using his home to heal the broken. With his wife smashed, he had to attempt something, could not have lived with himself otherwise. He felt a metal pipe strike his leg and heard the bone crack, but he felt little, was drifting. He wondered with curiosity that brought unexpected peace as the slashing sounds grew distant, where he was going, if he would still inhabit this body, and most importantly, if he could watch Wa'el's growth and whom he loved?

The torturer's thoughts were less prosaic. Ten percent of the population of a quarter million was being eliminated to make a point to the remainder. When his arm grew tired and he saw the physician was not moving much and seemed unconscious, he removed his revolver and shot the doctor through the head. He hadn't felt like hoisting the dead weight to a noose.

Outside, block after block, neighborhood upon neighborhood, only partially remained standing, reminiscent of London in the Blitz, Berlin, Breslau, Hiroshima, what man does, the torturer who had studied philosophy at Damascus University but had soon become bored teaching children thought. Several of the seventeen *norias*, ancient wheels with boxlike wood collection compartments that raised the water from the low Orontes River to the city and fields were blackened from fire, struck by shells or otherwise silenced. The doctor was dumped in an unmarked mass grave not far from the grandest wheel, the Noria al-Muhammadiya.

The severed fingers at the Ma'soud Mosque waited on those walls for three years, fear pervasive that fingers that removed them might be freshly placed in their stead. Late one night in that third year, they finally disappeared.

Two weeks after the earth was bulldozed over Dr. Hasan Masalmeh, 219 kilometers to the south, Yussuf Fuad, in his uniform with green epaulets with a star, eagle, and a single red stripe of a *Muqaddam*, Lieutenant Colonel, left his Military Intelligence office in the Defense Ministry. He walked into the dry heat and sounds of traffic in Umayyad Square as if Hama was another planet in far orbit from Damascus, which it was. His success at orchestrating the cover-up of the operation there had already inspired talk of promotion. Fuad was more content than proud. Hafez had smothered the embers of rebellion before they flamed, and if Fuad had never been born, no fewer people would have perished. The breadth of the slaughter and the disappearance of the historic Old City shocked him, but the world's eyes on it would have changed nothing. So he committed late hours to making Hama a tree falling in the forest nobody heard, and bided his time. He was patient and prepared for the long game.

The stone Defense Ministry rose majestically in Ummayad Square, a multi-lane roundabout with a vast central fountain surrounded by two rings of smaller fountains and several circumferences of healthy grass. Fuad looked up at the towering stone Sword Monument, the depictions of flags on its face from the Seventh Damascus International Fair symbolized the glory of Syrian civilization, not to mention lest its citizens become restive, the might. The square stone five-story National Opera House directly across the roundabout from where Fuad walked, maybe to the West's surprise, was even grander than the Defense Ministry. A 1300-seat theater for musical productions and a drama playhouse half the size found partnership there with the Syrian National Symphony Orchestra. Fuad loved the operas of Mozart and Puccini.

Fuad had sealed Hama like a landslide over a cave entrance. Not a single photo of destruction and death brightened the nascent CNN screens that delivered up-to-the-minute disasters to a world jaded by the unremitting coverage. One American journalist escorted from Hama halfway through the shelling, his camera confiscated, had written of 10,000 murdered. Nobody listened when he soon doubled that figure. If a bomb shook the Middle East, Americans tallied only their dead in their headlines. Most of the planet could not point to Syria on a map and would be surprised that driving time to Jerusalem, if one could, was an easy five hours.

For what Fuad needed, he would drive himself to Hama without accompaniment or escort. Fatima had been unable to conceive, a tragedy for them both. She longed for a child, and in his abject loneliness, Fuad did too. Tough, deceitful without hesitation about his work, his concern for her happiness ran as deep as any underground river; she was a companion and not anyone he could whisper to. Five years his senior, the marriage had been bartered for advancement. Her father was a sheik from the Baggara tribe who commanded loyalty between Deir-ez-Dour, the largest city in eastern Syria, and the provincial capital of Raqaa in the north. Regardless of his motive, he would be blessed with a son and, if he was lucky, a friend.

Several hours later, Fuad drove through the outskirts of Hama and accelerated north towards the village of Ma'an. On a narrow road, water flowed to his right like a tributary. Soon he passed the cross in a field of the toppled stone church behind it. With the mopping up, the entire operation occupied three weeks, not very long unless you were inside Hama. Fuad was not often emotional, but unexpectedly he felt feelings he could not name, tight in his chest. To his surprise, two near-extinct hefty bald ibises with dull unfeathered red heads and long red beaks flapped loudly overhead breaking the silence. Emotional, he almost wished he was more spiritual and could see them as a sign of the continuation of a civilization. He returned his attention to the road and noticed most of the dead had been cleared from the streets. He sped past an arch, somehow standing despite jagged holes clear through on both sides. Dust spun from his tires on the otherwise empty asphalt. A map on the passenger seat rippled in the cross breeze from the open windows.

Soon Fuad was back in the countryside with familiar fresh scents, and he felt the emotion dissipate. In every direction, pistachio orchards—small leafy trees in rows— filled the dry earth blanketed by burnished yellow grass. These hardy trees lived to three hundred years in this desert climate; pistachios were one of a cornucopia of cherished Syrian exports alongside apricots and tobacco. At a crossroads, narrow dirt lanes in both directions, Fuad pulled off the road and consulted his map. As he lifted it off the seat, past the trees to his right, he saw a red-tile roof through the green canopy. He dropped the map and excitedly swung the military sedan towards it. Upon his orders, a French relief agency had turned this large home into an orphanage, with the owners missing and nobody looking for them. He slammed to a halt in a cloud of dust.

Fuad quickly walked through the open front door into an unspoiled courtyard with a mosaic fountain, to his surprise quietly gurgling water despite all the nearby destruction. Hospital beds filled with babies, some in bloodied bandages, ran in rows on both sides of the atrium. Children's crying rose everywhere in the house, one on top of the other, none singly distinguishable. Fuad felt the walls of equanimity inside him crumbling and his heartbeat hard at the agony of these children without parents. Then like slamming a bank vault closed, he sealed off that feeling. He would rescue one and maybe manage many more years from now. Maybe. He counted on nothing emerging as planned. A tall redhead in a long blue *aba* neared, a heavy cross on beads dropping between small high breasts. Her eyes were luminescent, green with copper accompaniment. At an earlier age, all would have stirred him to inquire if she strayed from God to man.

"*Muqaddam* Fuad," she said quietly, as was her nature, without fear or deference. "I am Margaret Eido. From the *Agence Francaise de Developpement.* We spoke." Knowing she could be struck by any one of various calibers of military shells, she accepted that if Her Maker chose to call her, it was her time. At twenty-seven and doing good works, she believed that in this brutal country she would be aiding orphans interminably.

He allowed a small smile at her ease with him and with this chaos. Her Arabic lilted from her native French, he knew, her father from Lyon, where she was raised, and her mother born in Beirut.

"This child must have a good home," she continued evenly. "I will not ask for your word to God." She gazed as if looking outside this place. "I have no time to ask anything of Him now. Maybe later? Maybe never."

"You know who the children's parents are?" he asked harshly. Then he softened, unsure why he spoke that way as he was drawn to her. "Or were."

"Some. I will only show you those that we do. As you demanded."

"I require a boy. The age is not important. Tell me about the parents, not their politics but what you know of who they were."

She gave a slight shrug. "I begin by telling you that you killed them all."

"Would it help if I said it was not my wish?"

"*Pas meme un peu,*" she said in French.

A small scream echoed from far back in the stone walls, high and prolonged. She watched the lines of his military eyes tighten at the sound as if he was squinting through a scope at a target. Only all the targets were gone, and she could not place what he was thinking. "We manage some small surgeries," she said.

"Can you send me a list of what equipment will help?"

"Of course. We've made requests. It's as if the phone rings and rings in an empty room."

"Write it for me in detail before I leave."

"As you wish." The tiny scream stopped. She slowly realized it was pain in his eyes. "Thank you. I see that you will fulfill it."

"Of course. I made the offer."

For a moment, she thought she would cry. Margaret walked ahead of him so he wouldn't see, down the hall into a bedroom. She strode in, her long dress flowing above her sandals, wholly composed.

He saw no doctors or nurses along the way, heard no footfalls. Children's sobs reverberated. Inside, the bedroom walls were newly whitewashed. A wood cross hung on bare plaster. The sounds of the fountain in the atrium suddenly became audible in a pause in the crying, then disappeared again as the misery reemerged.

"I have brought one girl," Margaret said. "She is the strongest." Margaret glided to a woven straw basket with a child. Fuad followed. The girl looked at him with wide brown eyes.

Margaret watched with surprise at the gentleness with which he lifted her. His lips moved silently in what almost seemed like prayer as he brought them to the infant's forehead. As he set the child back down on the blanket in the basket, the girl's eyes followed him.

"Her father was a structural engineer..."

"The boys?" he interrupted softly.

She walked with pique towards the only crib in the room. The boy was sleeping.

"Don't disturb him," Fuad said. "Tell me."

"He too is strong. Uninjured. His father drove a truck, brought vegetables and fruit to the marketplace. The mother made dresses in a small factory."

Fuad turned to another basket on the floor, the patterned blanket bloodied, a white bandage covering all of one arm. Tiny fingers protruded from a cast on his hand.

Margaret bent to the floor and lifted this boy, who began to cough and whimper. He was long for his age, perilously thin but with thick, curly hair. "His father was an ophthalmologist, Doctor Hasan Masalmeh. He was murdered for using his medical training to help those wounded from the shelling. You think men should be killed for bandaging wounds, *Muqaddam* Fuad? Or maybe if you kill enough, will you become a general in Hafez's army of Satan?"

He looked at her for a long time, admiring her courage; another would shoot her for such daring. "It would not disrupt my career path."

Her restraint abandoned her, and large tears formed lines down her cheeks. She quickly brushed them away and with the boy in her arms—strangely not crying—said, "The boy is very weak. I don't know his name."

"Margaret, do you think courage can be passed in the genes?"

She was surprised by the depth of the question. "We know evil can—drinking too much. The inclination to hurt. So if that is true, then the opposite must be also."

Fuad reached carefully to take the young Masalmeh from her, lifted his face to his own shoulder, and gently rubbed his back to quiet the boy's coughing. Fuad shifted his position and must have pushed the child's injured arm as the boy shrieked and shrieked. He gazed at the third basket, at a robust well-fed boy who was sleeping.

"His father too was strong, worked in the stone quarry. His house fell on him, and he still lived a week. One day the world will know what happened here."

"Probably," Fuad agreed. "But not soon enough to matter." He continued to rub the tiny boy's back until his crying soothed into whimpering. "His father was an ophthalmologist," Fuad more repeated than asked, as that training mattered more to Fuad than even the father's audacity and courage.

"We both know you have not forgotten. Are you hoping he will become a physician instead of a murderer?"

Fuad found himself laughing to cover his surprise at his sudden urge to have all of this woman, tears still silently descending reddened cheeks. If he repulsed her, he believed, she would not have shown the vulnerability of tears.

"No," he said truthfully and stopped there. Words, even in private, had a way of emerging later to wound or kill. "Prepare him as best you can for travel. I am alone. Something the seatbelt can secure. Bring me two bottles for the journey. And the list. I will wait for you outside." He reached into a front pocket and removed a thick of cash in a gold clasp. He freed the money and held it towards her. "Not for the boy. For the others."

"You are kinder than they say."

"Not true. You are right. Whenever I order a trigger pulled, I'm the murderer."

"Men most are far less than they appear. You may be considerably more. I can accompany you and hold the child. Whatever more you like, if you want, once there. I want to forget the suffering for a long breath. I will wait for what we need and return with it."

"You do not need to safeguard the medical supplies. I will send them regardless."

"I know. That is why I am coming."

She wiped her tears away with both hands in one fast swipe. "God has abandoned this place. So I can abandon Him for someone completely Godless. It's what God deserves. One week. I want the supplies ready then."

"You will be a big help on the drive back." He sensed an athletic build beneath her loose garment. "Do you like to swim?"

"I enjoy few things more. You have a file on me?"

"No. Not yet."

With young Masalmeh on his shoulder, Fuad walked quickly outside to escape feeling more in the house of tears. He must be losing his mind, he thought, because he already loved this small warm body whose tiny fingers on his good hand strongly gripped his epaulet. As for the woman, he was a little afraid of what he could feel for her.

Soon she emerged carrying a small valise. "I want you to call him Kassem," she said. "After a boy who died here yesterday."

* * *

When Kassem Fuad was seven years old, at 4:30 a.m., two familiar words pulled Yussuf from sleep.

"Dad, come."

Small and round, Fatima knew her husband preferred to go and had trained herself not to wake at these outcries.

"What's the matter, son?" Fuad was standing barefoot now on the cold stone floor in the dark hall, hoping not to wake his wife.

"Come."

"Okay. I'm going to the bathroom first." Yussuf had forced himself to no longer run down the hallway, felt it was better for his son not to. Encouraged, he could not remember the last time Kassem had summoned him in the dark.

Half awake, Yussuf collapsed down beside his boy; the springs sang.

"I had a *really bad* dream."

"You want to tell me?"

"I don't know." He hugged his father with all his small might. "Maybe in a minute."

Yussuf ran a hand through the boy's thick black curls.

Kassem said, "Remember the dream catcher we used to have?"

It was round, Fuad remembered, blue with Arabic calligraphy. Four hawk feathers dropped from it. "Yes, it's in the closet in my bedroom."

"We took it away because it *made* me have bad dreams."

"I don't think that's true, but it didn't help. Remember when we put the bad dream in your hand, and you blew it up to Allah, and he stuck it in his robe pocket? That worked."

"That was when I was *little*."

"That's true. You're big now."

"You want to hear the dream?"

"I've been waiting."

Kassem punched his father's arm with a powerful clenched fist. "Listen Dad, two wild men wanted to kill us, and they put us in chains in a cell and acted like we were pets, gave us food. Somehow you escaped, and they said, 'now we have to kill you.'"

Yussuf was startled by the ferocity, but Damascus children often heard of people in cells. "What happened then?"

"Nothing. It was over."

"I would never leave you. I have guards that would be near. Nothing can happen to you. Go back to sleep now. I'll stay."

Kassem gripped his father's forearm with both small hands. Yussuf wondered if the baby might have breathed in the thunderous artillery shell, the wall toppling over his mother, his father's disappearance, the round-the-clock crying at the tossed-together orphanage. He had felt confident their love would erase that past. Fuad realized he had been naive. Kassem was more frightened than his classmates and covered his eyes during the scary films the boys watched. Still, though quiet and shy, he had a dogged determination and humor. Fuad was not certain which of his fathers delivered that, maybe both. He was not jealous of the physician but had not told the boy about him. He would do so strategically, and he pretty much knew when. Soon Kassem's breathing deepened rhythmically.

In the morning, Yussuf entered his son's room holding

a bag. Kassem remained intent on his Japanese Game Boy machine. Kassem was tall for his age, reed-thin and round spectacles fitted over his ears. Kassem preferred to play alone and loved Aretha the Famicon. A ten-year-old girl had to forge through the forest of Nineveh, just across the border in Iraq, and improve her magic for the ultimate battle against evil. He found the game surprisingly prescient.

Kassem flicked buttons and didn't look up as he spoke. "Father, I do not want to play polo anymore. Those boys are not my friends. I'm afraid of being hurt. I'm afraid of a lot of things. Is it important to your position that I play polo with them?"

Fuad felt excitement on his skin, like a lover's touch. He imagined having a son would be great, but it turned out even better. Fuad did not care that Kassem frightened easily. He still felt certain their love had formed a foundation for his life and eventually he would leap from it to his own solid ground.

"You can stop polo. My position is gratefully such that you may do as you like. I will explain to your mother. The only thing that truly matters in your life is whom you help. I may have something here you may enjoy more than hitting a ball from a horse."

A dry, spring breeze wafted through the open window rippling the half-drawn curtains. It was cooler here midway up Mount Qasioun. Fuad approached the window and looked out. He loved this country and this people, who never refused a request from a friend and readily traveled distances to return a favor. It was not uncommon at a barber or a restaurant to discover that the previous occupant of his chair or the family at the next table they had chatted with had paid his bill on their way out. He pulled the curtains wide open. *Iris Damascena* covered the eastern slopes of the mountain above him and rose from the dry ground only here in Damascus at 1,100 meters. Two white or sometimes gray flowers, both purple-edged, budded from each small stalk. He often had to remind himself of the breathtaking beauty in the world as he spent his time trying to control the opposite. More restaurants were opening lower on the mountain with views for the blossoming middle class of the stone city of two million below.

Fuad turned and pulled a large box from the bag. "This is for boys a little older, say eleven. But you can do this. It came from England."

Kassem jumped up, grabbed the box, and looked at the pictures of beakers, test tubes, gloves, goggles, balloons, the writing in English.

"What does it say?"

"Complete Introduction to Chemistry Kit."

"*Tzababa*," Kassem said. Arabic for great, excellent. "What can we make?"

"It has twenty-seven experiments. We will learn about the safety equipment first. Arabs invented chemistry."

"Really. You sure? Who, when?"

Yussuf pointed to the English word on the box. "In English, "chemistry." From our Arabic *khemia*. In the ancient Egyptian writings we see they attempted to turn black powder into gold. It did not work, but like many wrong paths, it led to great discoveries. There is another word you will learn in this set. In English, *alkaline.* It comes from *al-qali.* There is a plant that grows by the Mediterranean called the glasswort. They are highly salty. Thousands of years ago, the Arabs made glass from them. The material from that plant is called *al-qali.*"

Kassem wasn't listening but didn't like his father's teachings, well, most of the time. Some were okay. "Can we blow up things?"

Fuad laughed. "Not in your mother's house. I do not know about chemistry, but we will learn together. We can begin by placing *al-qali* metals in water. I read from the instructions yesterday. Each will burn a different color."

"That is so great! Dad, I love you so much. Even more than Mom, but don't tell her."

They hugged. He knew it was petty, but Fuad liked that he loved him more. "Of course not."

Fuad thought about how many secrets he carried, often feeling like a mule with increasing furniture lashed to its back. He drifted back to the window. Wondering what might have penetrated and solidified in Kassem's bones at the orphanage had brought memories of Margaret Eido. He had ensconced her in the Cham Palace, one of the city's oldest, with its inlaid mosaic furniture, incandescent chandeliers, and ivy dripping from the many floors of walkways surrounding the high lobby. While he labored a few early hours at the office, she swam in the indoor pool.

They spent two weeks of afternoons in her room on the top floor with views of the city and Qasioun. In coupling, she constantly moved like a butterfly and was entirely silent, even as she arched. Then as satisfying–even more–they talked. He had joked about her lovemaking, "You don't want God to hear." She fired back, "He knows, is laughing. Anyone who'd create this world and then step aside and let us destroy it has to be a jokester. You're on the side of the destroyers." He knew, because she challenged him, that he could love her in a way he did not the deferential Fatima. After six days, she said, "One more week, and it's not because I like the pool so much." As the sun set, they explored the city.

Twice he returned to the orphanage, which with his personal funds had become a permanent edifice with a doctor who visited several times a week. The first time she refused to see him. On the second, she was gone but had left a note for his inevitable return. When he lifted it to his nostrils, it carried the Damascus Rose perfume he had bought her. It was like ripping open his heart as he broke the red wax seal. In block letters:

DON'T UNLESS YOU ARE PREPARED TO NEVER LEAVE

On occasions like now, he dreamed at the window of them walking again through the lilies on Qasioun. Today he had ratcheted up his betrayal of Kassem with the premature chemistry set. Betray Fatima, well he already had, hadn't he, and was doing so again in remembering Margaret in the lilies. Margaret was now in the small village of Saydnaya placing orphans with the nuns in the vast mountaintop Our Lady of Saydnaya Convent. She was thirty kilometers north of Damascus and in his hubris he liked to tell himself she wanted to be near though he doubted that was true. He could not abandon Fatima, his plans, and especially Kassem, so he loved her in his memories and followed her life from afar.

* * *

Two years later, Fuad and Kassem hiked slowly up a steep incline on Mount Qasioun.

"Dad, this is hard. I'm tired," Kassem whined.

"Okay, ten minutes rest, then higher."

Fuad followed Kassem off the trail into the dry brush, letting the boy wander while he absorbed the view. Most of the city slept in houses of one and two stories, stone or white stucco. A few tall office and government buildings and slender minarets reached higher into the hazy sky, the air hemmed in by low brown hills to the south and this northern range. Nearer clusters of newer tall stone apartment blocks, mostly ten to twelve stories high, formed long rows. The only trees clustered along the base of the mountain. Fuad turned. Housing gradually had crept up the mountain covering a third of the way, all low structures that blended into Qasioun's flank. Higher was brown, with long stretches of white stone, the flat peak at 1,200 meters sprouting the tall red and white antennae of Syria's television and radio stations.

Kassem called out with excitement, "Dad, I found you a great discovery. A rattlesnake hole."

Fuad hurried towards him; this time, he was the one frightened. "Show me."

Kassem bent and thrust his forefinger near the mouth

shaped like a tiny tunnel with small pebbles and loose dirt pushed from the inside camouflaging the entrance. Surprised and pleased that the boy was not scared, Fuad did not grab his hand and said softly, "Let's move a little bit away and not offer him that finger for lunch."

Kassem laughed hard. "I couldn't possibly taste good. Mother wouldn't let me have dessert. You think if we wait, he might come out?"

The spring sun beat down, the air dry. "I think he'll wait until it's cooler."

"All right. Let's see what else I can find."

Kassem skipped up the narrow trail. They approached a bulldozed road cut horizontally in the face of the mountain like a fire road. There were no structures here to protect from a blaze. Beyond, government construction rose. Two armed soldiers stood near them at this end of the wide dirt path.

"Why can't we go there?" Kassem asked. "It's flat. I'm tired."

The domain of Air Force Intelligence, even Fuad could not pass without prearrangement. "It's a fire road," Fuad lied. "To protect homes and forests so the firefighters can get in."

"That's good," the boy said.

"Look around and tell me why what I just told you doesn't make sense."

Kassem was puzzled, then his face brightened. "No trees grow this high. It's all like rock."

"Good."

"Would soldiers guard houses that aren't built yet?" Kassem asked.

"Maybe if it was the president's palace, but otherwise no."

"Dad, I don't understand what you want. I'm a nine-year-old kid. Can't we just hike?"

At such moments Fuad slowed and made a turn. "Of course. I want you to challenge what you think you see and what you're told."

"Even if you tell me."

"Even what I tell you."

"*Tzababa*, I can do that for sure."

"We're almost at the lookout. Want to go? We'll be alone there."

"Yes!" Kassem thrust a forefinger in the air. "I like being alone. I think it's important."

"Why?" Not that Fuad disagreed.

"Gives me time to think, and I'm away from the dumb things the boys say. They talk about what girls do with sex. It's all lies."

"How do you know?"

"The girls are good. They wouldn't do such things. And they're too young. The boys try and be bigger than they are. It's stupid. But I don't care. Anyway, when's my new chemistry set coming? It's taking like *forever*."

Fuad had not told him it arrived this morning because he had been eager to move his legs and feared the boy would refuse to hike.

"Soon," he said. "I'm certain."

"Can I throw stones down the mountain where there are no people?"

"Of course."

Kassem bent and ran his eyes along the terrain and looked for flat ones.

Fuad eyed the compacted dirt road. Long ago, Hafez had initiated chemical weapons research. A few buildings already rose in this division of the Scientific Studies and Research Center. Fuad was monitoring the progress of Institute 3000, the new center here for the development and manufacture of chemical and biological weapons. Air Force Intelligence had begun simultaneously to court the China Precision Machinery Import-Export Corporation to obtain missile components for their delivery as part of a broader affair.

Fuad's eyes moved to the new construction. Since Hama, he had observed as few others the aphrodisiac of annihilation.

He watched the boy start back down the mountain

without asking. He watched the boy stop, put two feet together and leap over admittedly a very low and short boulder. Fuad felt little guilt at what he was doing thus far. Though how far Kassem would run in rebellion when it all spilled out worried him.

CHAPTER 4

A GIRL'S BOX

2011

On foot from the north, in his general's uniform, Fuad approached the Bab al-Salam, The Gate of Peace, one of the seven still trod Roman portals into the Old City. The Romans had called it the Gate of the Moon for the way the orb hung over Qasioun. A semicircle of alternating black basalt and white limestone curved along the entrance passageway in the formidable brown arch. New white stones smoothly replaced the crumbled brown crown, new by Damascus reckoning, these from the 12th Century Ayyubid Dynasty. The towering wall of Old Damascus continued to his left. As Fuad entered, he ran his hand along the dark arch, the stone smoothed with age, maybe a bit like him, he hoped. Fuad felt rudderless, unable to steer in this civil war that flooded the country everywhere beyond the bulwark of Damascus. With whole suburbs flattened, the finest fleeing, and the rest gasping for breath in these waters, despair nearly pulled him under too. He was headed for a buoy.

Inside the deep arch, long dresses, small carpets and leather purses hung from rope stretched inside the venerable gate. He emerged into a slant of light in an open space and entered the covered marketplace. He reached the eastern section, the oldest part of Damascus, farthest from the cooling Mediterranean breezes; the temperature rose as the sun beat on the arched tin roof high overhead. Fuad skirted around a donkey laden with twin burlap bags of apricots, hooves in clacking harmony on the stone.

A small trowel in his pocket, Fuad wove through a maze of tiny backstreets onto the narrow and dimmed Tal Elhijara Street. He stopped at an old door with metal workings. The same alternating white and black rectangles of the Bab al-Salam circled the wood. Two lanterns, one on each side, remained on in the parsimonious daylight. As Fuad entered, the heavy door opened quietly on greased hinges. The 300-year-old house, once the fiefdom of one of Damascus' most prominent Jewish families, had been stripped bare but resuscitated into the 17-room Talisman Hotel over time.

Fuad eased into the remarkable open-air courtyard, silent now; since the uprising, tourists wandered elsewhere, in streets where they needn't be concerned about what might descend from a helicopter. The upper half of all the walls had been reinvented a deep red. From there, alternating horizontal lines of black and white stone descended to the ground. A row of tall windows with glistening wood frames marched all around. A low white wall circled an active fountain. Iron tables and chairs painted white rested on a sparkly white marble floor, red diamond shapes matching the upper walls set in alternate stones. Fuad had to hand it to Bashar and Asma. Who popping over from Washington wouldn't think them an up-and-coming couple?

In 2007, Bashar and his British beauty, who knew how to throw a party on any continent, swept Democratic star Nancy Pelosi and her Congressional bloodhounds, distracted by the redolent scents of the Old City, into this courtyard. At lunch, either from the elegant table or later tete-a-tete, Bashar reminded the Americans that post 9-11, he had honored their rendition requests and introduced *their* terrorists to the age-old Syrian traditions of persuasion. With feigned hurt, he told the politicians that he did not find it *fair*, after welcoming these terrorists and rushing over all they could no longer contain, that *he* was being pilloried for assisting resistance movements like Hezbollah and Hamas.

"Syria wants a long-term dialogue, not a one-two-three-four solution," Bashar, master of speech that sounded like he was saying something, intoned in his British English. It seemed Americans believed it was impossible to lie in a British accent.

"Of course, we too," the politicians responded rather than observe.

After dining, Asma, who had strategically selected this venue, provided the perk of a personally accompanied tour of the ancient Old City, from the pounding of metal workers on the dark-covered Street Called Straight to the leather goods alleys where they picked up souvenirs for a song.

Asma had arrived with the intent of holding hands with Bashar in spectacular change, the Princess Diana of Damascus. He too genuinely pledged a Syria better than his father's. But Bashar cowered in a dark cave of insecurity, vacillation, and meekness. When the regime jackals circling him came near, he threw them red meat. The anointed brother, Bassel, had parachuted from planes, commanded an armored brigade, and shined at a Soviet military academy where he learned the language at night in his room from atypically beautiful instructors who frequented the local bars. Known as *The Golden Knight* of equestrian fame, sans a lance for now, he rose to command presidential security early on. He had been groomed with all the fine brushing given to Syria's prize-winning Arabian stallions.

Bashar escaped the army altogether. Only when hauled back from London after Bassel's recklessness was he escorted into the military academy at Homs to print credentials for the influential martial class. Since Hafez was 64 and not getting any younger, in a lightning five years Bashar ascended to colonel in the elite Republican Guard. The following year, in June 2000, Hafez's thirty-year iron grip on the Syrian presidency was released with his death. Bashar stepped immediately into the general's sizeable shoes. To silence the grumbling of those who required talent, old commanders were escorted into retirement and replaced with young Alawite officers, who repaid Bashar with unflinching obedience.

A graduate in economics from King's College in London and in 2000 about to enter Harvard for her MBA, Asma met Bashar that year and instead lashed her star to his. She told everyone, and meant it, that she turned around from crossing the Pond to reform Syria with her husband. In November, she packed up and headed east. The following month they married. Rumors swirled of her private frustration and anger at the brutal response to the uprising, but none surfaced about whether she regretted jettisoning Harvard. Though of Syrian heritage, she had arrived wide-eyed and naive. In her designer suits and Christian Louboutin's, she was eager to reach out to the people. She shed those heels to enter rural homes, sat on the floor and ate from communal plates with her hands.

Early on, she was genuinely perplexed. On a visit to the ruins of previous conquerors, those Greek and Roman, at Apamea near Hama—when Syrian reporters hastened to her press people for instructions on what to print, she was speechless. She learned the ropes and steadied herself on them. During one of her interviews at the presidential stronghold, she sat smiling as Bashar interjected to *Vogue Magazine* that he had chosen eye surgery because there was very little blood. Fuad felt there was a lot Bashar preferred not to face.

In a second courtyard, Fuad passed the sizeable swimming pool with the same red and stone facades and iron tables and chairs. White tablecloths dropped gracefully from these. Brass lanterns sat on the two long lengths of the low marble wall surrounding the pool, leaving the width unobstructed on one end for children and the other for diving. Bashar wasn't going anywhere other than to the annual Al-

Sham Arabian Horse Festival at the Old Damascus Show Grounds, their hooves commemorating the trampling of the French Mandate over Syria in 1946. Fuad believed they'd have been better off with Bassel's fortitude in the palace.

Fuad had yet to see a guest or anyone at all. The war propelled dignitaries, observers, the press, and the UN chemical weapons inspectors—when allowed in and then stymied with Arab delay, more coffee, and further profuse apologies—to the Sheraton in Ummayad Square and the nearby Four Seasons Hotel. Both offered the westerners familiar whiskeys in all the bars, expensive beds, and the added comfort of military guards stationed around the new perimeter fence at the Four Seasons.

A small garden remained at the back of the hotel ringed with rose bushes and, as Fuad knew, untouched in the renovations. Long benches completely adorned by blue and yellow mosaic tiles awaited guests seeking privacy, contemplation, or respite from a partner. Fuad counted to the fourth from the left of the gnarled red rose bushes and sat next to it. Just then, the tinny voice of a muezzin called through a minaret loudspeaker for afternoon prayer, followed by one after another in harmonious cacophony. For a moment, Fuad, already on the ground, had the urge to touch his forehead to the marble floor to leave everything whirling inside him and join not God, without doubt Margaret's jokester, but the long tradition of his desert people in worship.

Again, Margaret had arrived, like an old friend unexpectedly knocking on his door. For a moment, he let himself wonder if something more with her was conceivable? Fifteen years ago, she married a French orthopedic surgeon from *Medecins Sans Frontieres* in Beirut. Sometimes she accompanied him to postings abroad, and others worked and waited in Lebanon. A decade ago, though that civil war had long quieted, an errant Christian shell exploded their apartment while she was delivering a child to adoptive parents in the coastal city of Batroun. Shattered, she soon returned to

Lyon but not before agreeing to see him. They met equidistant at Baalbek in the grape region of the Bekaa Valley. The long fertile depression stretched between the pines and plunging rivers of the Lebanon Mountains and the taller snow-covered parallel Anti-Lebanon Range to the east, the border with Syria mostly running along the crest of the range. Mount Harmon in the Golan Heights rose imperiously from the southern end of the Anti-Lebanon Range. She had always wanted to see the imposing Roman ruins at Baalbek.

Her cross no longer swung from her neck. This time, in mourning, they did not touch other than to embrace at the fore and aft of meeting. They trod up the hills and down to the 2nd Century ruins of the Temple of Bacchus and Temple of Jupiter, intact Corinthian columns with Ionic bases, not unlike the Acropolis in weathering the storms of man.

"I think of you from time to time," he had said with considerable understatement as they sat atop a toppled Corinthian column crown at the entrance to the Bacchus temple, legs dangling.

"Only from time to time?" she asked, and at that moment, finally smiled. She had let the gray seize its lined place in her hair, averse to any artificiality.

"If I said all the time, I'm afraid you'd bolt to the sea." He looked away to avoid her eyes. "Often would not be exaggerating."

"How is your wife?"

"There is early dementia in her family. I see some of it already. She denies it. It's worsening. Her mother and several aunts ended up early in treatment hospitals."

"I can never come back to the Middle East," Margaret said. "The suffering is bleeding from my eyes. I will find something else in Lyon. Maybe teach young children. I have loved twice in my life. Maybe, it is enough. Since I've been around children so often, I didn't want to have any. Needed the quiet at home. Maybe I should adopt an orphan myself?"

"I'm not sure there's ever any real peace. My son is my

reason to go on when I am uncertain and weary."

"I thought that might happen," she said.

"You're the only one."

"So you chose well in us both."

"May I write you?" he asked.

She looked at the dancing Maenads on the stone parapets, literally joyous raving ones, the female followers of Bacchus. She was not sure she would ever feel ecstasy again though she supposed most of this suffering would eventually escape from her to land on and torment another.

"Yes. But not often. I will give you my mother's address until I'm settled." She turned to him. "He was not like you. He wanted to tell me everything, even when he was exhausted after a whole day of operating. Sometimes, it was exhausting. Your secrets are a respite. I want to know as little about what you've been doing as possible."

"That day in the orphanage was the most important of my life."

She laughed again, this time with abandon and release. "You are almost saying I am important to you."

"I was certain I had."

"So you are completely *fou*," she said, switching from Arabic to French.

"Forgive me," he said. "For loving you from afar."

She eased off the column and jumped to the ground. "Let's steal some grapes. Like when I met you, I am *fou* from being so good."

He lowered himself carefully from the column top, his arm shaking from all the emotion of being with her, as he dropped down.

"They're mostly French origin Cabernet Sauvignon," he explained after he landed easily. "So a good transition for you. Afterward, a glass of the real thing?"

"Maybe two." She smiled. "But it won't make me take my clothes off. I cannot, Yussuf. I can't have all these feelings inside me at once. I might not survive it. Though I am glad to see you."

"It's enough to have this time." Her scent was exactly as he remembered. He did not add that any more would be too much for him too— if then they had to part. "There are old, indigenous vineyards not far to the north in the Bsharri Mountains. Merweh grapes. Resistant to disease and civil war, it seems. What remains of the Cedars of Lebanon are there. Bsharri is Khalil Gibran's birthplace. We could take a drive if you have time."

"Today, I have nothing but time for you." She ran towards a hillside of vines and turned her head back. "First, we do some work here."

Fuad wrote her every first of January and July, a structure to harness the desire to be with her more often. Always just a line or two or three. *Kassem and I hiked through the irises today. It's been a very cold winter, making it harder to be hopeful.* She had not always answered but overwhelmingly had in kind, with images of her day. She had not adopted and was teaching children under five. From her: *I watched a hummingbird build a tiny nest outside my window and finally felt excited.*

Anyone who wandered to the back of the Talisman would certainly retreat. In the al-Assad's Syria, questions were dangerous and rarely risked other than among intimate friends, if then. People disappeared for less. He dug deep with strong, swift strokes and piled the dirt carefully beside the next bush so none would spill on the marble flooring. He hit the sound of metal and for the first time looked back. He heard only the splashing of the second fountain from the direction he'd come.

He unearthed the small, rusted box and slipped it into his pocket.

* * *

Shai stepped down from the army helicopter into the northern panhandle of Israel that jutted into Lebanon like a forefinger. To the west, it was sixty kilometers to Lebanese Tyre on the Mediterranean. To the east, Shai looked out at the lush, formerly Syrian Golan Heights, overrun in the 1967 Six-Day War that the Arabs called The June War. Fought from June 5-10, understandably Israel's neighbors were less than eager to be reminded of the humiliating loss of the Golan, West Bank, and Sinai in under a week. He took in the snow and multiple lines of chairlifts at the Israeli ski resort on Mt. Hermon; for the last long length they seemed to run vertically to 2,814 meters. The Hermon highpoint and the range running northeast blocked the western rain-laden winds from even glimpsing Syria. They fell instead on Israeli vineyards in the heights; the abundant volcanic soil yielded a bounty of wines when wild pigs had not broken through the barbed wire and declared, "dinner time." Past the peaks, the hot breath of the desert blew all the way to Damascus. In this small land, to the north it was not much more than a stone's toss to the Lebanese village of Kfarkila that he'd pass through at first light.

With the thunder of rotors and Shai's few remaining hairs rising in salute, the helicopter lifted and soon shrunk in the distance. Shai walked slowly and peered down on the green fields of the Hula Valley and the archeological site from the 6th century BC. It was still hard to plow anywhere around here and not unearth dark burnished ware. Shai noted that when distracted, his head forgot to bother him.

He soon trampled through the immaculate grass by the large swimming pool in Kibbutz Kfar Giladi. Under the British Mandate, the Mossad had spirited twelve hundred Jewish children from Damascus across the then porous border and hid them in the chicken coops and horse barns here from Whitehall's fiat against the Jews escaping persecution under their raised noses. Shai was long acquainted with the Kibbutz Secretary, head of the equals in this communal settlement. Periodically Shai turned up for the night at their Guest House hotel and paid in cash. He then disappeared into Lebanon, the

Secretary knew, because he drove him personally to the once optimistically christened, The Good Fence. In 1978, Israeli wire cutters opened a portal into their neighbor's backyard. Maronite Christians regularly passed through the crossing to work in Israel, export through Haifa port, and go under the knife in Israel's northern hospitals. In 2000, an endless line of returning tanks and armored vehicles kicked up dust and despair, losing so many of their boys without a clear strategy to disrupt Hezbollah across the border. The grand gate was welded shut.

A short man with a hedge of white hair and a burnished head, the Secretary led Shai to his quarters. The wood two-story guest houses with a triangular terra cotta roof had been varnished a new darker brown since Shai's last overnight here.

"Right to the old Fatima Gate?" the Secretary asked.

"Nothing like hiding in plain sight."

"Transport requirements?" the Secretary asked as he preferred preparation, both by temperament and to minimize inquiries.

"Anything big. A couple of cows. Or horses, whatever you can spare for half a day."

Shai loved Lebanon. The beauty of northern Israel continued beside the rushing Litani River as if the maker had not thought of borders. After King Hussein of Jordan had enough of the Palestine Liberation Organization hijacking commercial jetliners and setting them down in his desert, in 1970 he drove them out. When the sands settled, they had set up shop across the border in Southern Lebanon. Before the PLO overran the Crusader Beaufort Castle, built atop a mountain to survey all in its domain, farmers from these northern settlements had crossed into Lebanon daily to farm in the Ayoun Valley, about a kilometer northeast of the fortress. Shai thought of the arrangement as what the region could still manage.

"Time?" the Secretary inquired.

"Five a.m. should about do it. The dining room open

then?"

The Secretary laughed. He was certain Shai knew they started serving at 4 a.m. There was always something, lashing kicking turkey legs together to ship to slaughter, pulling fish from the ponds to get to Tel-Aviv restaurants fresh for tonight's mixed grill.

In the morning, after Shai had restrained himself to two hard-boiled eggs, salad of tomato and cucumber, and stuffed some pitas in his pocket, the truck with the Secretary behind the wheel barreled north on the single-lane road west of the Israeli town of Metula. Two horses neighed in the back, and horseshoes protested on the floor. Shai wondered if they, too, had been woken early.

"Horses make more sense," the Secretary said.

"Not a lot of reason to bring cows over the border, I suppose."

"None. I would have told you if you insisted."

Shai felt buoyed, preferred the field to the tyranny of office committees and oversight. He did not wait well, and finally being back in the thick of it energized him.

"I hear we are graced with more Hezbollah checkpoints?" the Secretary asked, both from curiosity and concern about his proximity to their missiles.

Shai pictured the Hezbollah checkpoints. Tires flat on the road encouraged approaching vehicles to weave slowly around. Young men watched, for the most part fingers too tight on their machine guns. Always from the guard tower, fluttering or subdued, that rallying yellow flag with green writing; the first letter of Allah reached up and grabbed a rifle in its fist. Shai found it artful and compelling.

"They're a problem, no doubt. Spring up everywhere, like wildflowers after a wet winter."

"You scared there?"

"I bring a bona fide Christian general with me. They wouldn't dare shoot *him*."

An Israeli sign in green said KFARKILA in Hebrew with

an arrow pointing ahead. Above it in Arabic and English, a more welcoming blue sign with white lettering: WELCOME TO KFARKILA. They reached a sprawling Israeli military base, tents long ago replaced by hardened structures, with enough antennas to hear Fairouz in Beirut and likely Cairo too. For fifty years, she reigned as the musical icon of Lebanon, belting out patriotic ballads of peace and love. Every radio station in the Arab world began its morning with a Fairouz song, the greatest unifying force on the planet.

They halted at a low metal gate across the road. A pockmarked 18-year-old soldier approached, Uzi loosely gripped. Shai leaned over the Secretary and handed the young recruit ID. He motioned to another soldier to stand ready and near, which he obliged while the boy trotted inside. The horses quieted, seemed to like stopping.

Soon the boy rushed back. "*Ain baayah*," no problem, he said in laconic Hebrew, often the country's temperament, abrupt and feigning carefree. He came around and handed Shai his papers.

"Keep them for me as usual." Shai opened the glove compartment and slipped them in.

This time the horses ignored the forward acceleration. The gate was suspended in the air with hinges on one side, maybe one meter in height. An Arab sat on the ground, and his keffiyeh headdress about touched the lower bar. Christian soldiers to one side waved casually at the yellow Israeli license-plated truck, and one swung the gate open without inquiry. If Israeli soldiers allowed passage, they would.

The truck rumbled through the Arab village of 10,000. Olive trees and grape vines climbed low hills terraced with small stone walls of various sizes made of round rocks. Shai saw a large beekeeper's farm on the nearest rise, like those not far back across the border. Seventy meters above sea level, the temperature was mild and dry. Just up ahead, Shai saw a parked jeep and General Jean Lahoud standing outside it, smoking impatiently. Shai felt a burst of kinship and hope.

"Pull over here, if you don't mind," Shai requested.

The horses didn't seem to mind the lurch or the squealing brakes and remained quiet. Shai gripped the Secretary's forearm.

"Thanks, old friend."

"Do make it back," the Secretary said. "Too much I don't want to have to explain."

Shai squeezed his hand and deftly climbed down and out. Lahoud neared, and they hugged and kissed on both cheeks. Then Lahoud tossed his burning cigarette in the road, went to the back of his jeep, and pulled out an ironed uniform.

"I made you a general this time," Lahoud said. He slapped Shai on the back. "Since we're both generals, you can tell me everything."

"I can't tell you anything," Shai said jovially. "As always."

Lahoud shrugged. "Ah, but I watch. Where to? Will I be home for dinner? My wife does not like to be kept waiting. She throws things if I'm late. She is not impressed with generals, says we have too many. Of course, she is right."

"You won't be late," Shai said, unbuttoning his shirt. "I promise."

Lahoud whistled to two soldiers waiting by another jeep down the road to come to take Shai's clothing.

Lahoud turned back. "You always promise. I will wait to see what transpires before I dare call her."

* * *

Behind the wheel of his Peugeot, Fuad waited in a long line, dark exhaust noisily departing most of the old vehicles. He had chosen to join the horde of day shoppers queuing to enter Lebanon from the northwestern village of Jdeidat Yabous. The car ahead of him moved forward, and Fuad weaved around black and yellow cinderblocks at the Syrian checkpoint. A row of soldiers stood rigid, rifles diagonally across their chests, to discourage the rag-tag from fleeing the bombing.

Two high twin stone arches like crab pincers marked where troops poked their heads through windows and opened trunks looking for stowaways that caused this merciless delay. Jdeidat Yabous sat in the sparse hills, and Fuad watched a stray donkey pick at scant spikes of yellowed grass. Fuad was patient by nature and profession.

Finally, past the pincers and freed, he followed closely packed vehicles through the steep gorge and rugged parched mountains through nine kilometers of no-man's land. On the other side, the practical Lebanese readily welcomed anyone with bills in their wallets.

At the international Masnaa Crossing, twin red terra cotta roofs, each supported in the open air by four metal poles, supplied shade for the Lebanese border guards, if any had been in sight. The low gates were open. A lone soldier sat in a red guardhouse like a British phone booth. Farther ahead, a stone red-roofed building offered passage through square tunnels in both directions. Unimpeded, the line sped up. Fuad entered not only a different mentality but abruptly, as often as he'd been here, still a shockingly green country. Unlike on the Syrian side, pines climbed these hills, a soft blanket of grass stretched between them, and Fuad heard a churning river through the open window.

He eased cautiously through the street vendors and along the small stone shops with the same signature roofs, people hawking everything from cell phones to fresh beets from the nearby Bekaa Valley. Hashish and opium, which shared those fields, were available in the back of stores at discreet inquiries.

Past the shopping, Fuad accelerated into a black highway that sparkled in the sun. Soon at the crest of the mountains, the ribbon of granite wound and descended to Beirut, which shimmered at the sea. War always churned up a tidal wave of profiteers. When the Lebanese civil war exhausted itself in 1990 after fifteen futile years, the pockmarked and crumbling became shiny anew with investment cash from the Gulf that often passed under the table.

Checkpoints and tent cities swollen with Syrian refugees who had managed to circumvent the border crossings alternated on the road, as did Muslim and Greek Orthodox villages. Tens of thousands huddled in flimsy tents at the Syrian refugee camp directly west of here near the port of Zahrani. When the cold opened and rained, they burned clothes, plastic, and sheep manure for warmth. Those in the Arsal Camp, huddled in low white tents provided by relief agencies in the mountains above the Bekaa Valley, endured snows that at the same time blanketed Mount Qasioun. Someday they might return, he hoped, though he did not really believe they would.

Fuad hugged the eastern flank of Lebanon and drove south towards Marjayoun, the headquarters of the Christian South Lebanon Army. The Israel-backed militia controlled the border region mostly, as Hezbollah, like the roots of a giant Cedar, perpetually reached for more territory. Though Shia villages dotted the surrounding mountains around Marjayoun, in patchwork Lebanon the town itself was Greek Orthodox. Before long, he saw the two-story limestone structures with red tile roofs reaching on all sides to the base of the hills. He smiled that the checkpoint to the city was temporarily abandoned and empty.

As he drove into Marjayoun, individual thick and twisted olive trunks with silvery-green leaves crowded everywhere in private plots between the houses. Crosses topped the many church domes above the low red roof skyline. Cows grazed along a Litani River tributary as he continued on the two-lane road. Farther south, the snowcapped Jabal al-Shaykh, The Mountain of the Sheik, which the Israelis called Mount Hermon, towered in a cloudless blue sky, like a calendar photo of the Swiss Alps. He was tired from the drive; he wore out faster these days, which frustrated him.

The Marjayoun Maronite Church was empty and not at all by chance. Fuad entered and took in the several dozen rows of wide wood pews. A great glass chandelier descended from the ceiling illuminating the two-story interior, with the half dozen arches on both sides supported by Corinthian columns. The Romans had quarried and raised temples across Lebanon and Syria, which became building blocks for Christian and Islamic edifices. Wood crosses looked down from the walls, and a large painting of a bearded saint surveyed the empty house from behind the brilliantly lit altar.

Shai sat in the front row in a general's uniform of green khaki and red epaulets.

Feeling energized, Fuad slipped down beside him.

"You got a promotion."

"I guess I'm getting so old, they're worried people will be suspicious I'm still a Colonel."

Fuad smiled. "I've been a general for a long time. It's easy."

"Yes, I've taken to it immediately."

Fuad asked in quiet Arabic, "Who knows you're here?"

"Nobody in Jerusalem. Just the kibbutz Secretary. The helicopter pilot that dropped me filed a flight plan to Haifa. Sister's a friend of a friend. Wouldn't want you dangling from a rope in Marjeh Square. Our border patrol is used to a variety of unorthodox individuals coming through. No questions asked. I used documents with a work name."

Fuad was concerned his country's surveillance systems, taken over by whiz kids whom only yesterday had manned video game consoles, could hear a pin descend.

"I've trashed the radio transmitter, scattered it in the desert. I can't communicate with you directly or see you again. This is the last time, as we discussed. They find me. They'll grab Kassem." Fuad reached out and set his weathered hand on Shai's. "We've done this for a very long time. Longer than we should have been able to. I'll miss you."

Shai squeezed Fuad's hand and held it, eyes filling; to pull back from the emotion, he gazed at the glorious frescoes across the arched ceiling here in a remote town of 5,000 Christians. Angels with wings held a shawl on both sides where the heavy chandelier gripped the plaster.

"Well, that's why we're here, isn't it?" Shai said, trying to shed the shaking from his words. A loyal Syrian, Fuad was his longest-standing relationship in the field, an attempt to toil together for the greater good when an opportunity poked its head above ground. His wife Tami hadn't even been born when they first met in London. "To pass the torch and hope not to burn the replacement," Shai said, the emotion winning and rumbling in his voice. Shai stood, marched towards the altar to calm himself, and then turned. "How's your boy?" he asked.

"Wonderful, self-conscious, even more scientific than we'd planned. It's a mask sometimes when he's unsure of himself." Fuad rose and joined Shai, his firm footsteps echoing in this cavern. "I love him more than I imagined possible."

"In certain areas, you lack sufficient imagination."

Fuad laughed. "You're not surprised."

"Takes someone who knows how to love the whole way to do what you are with me. How's Margaret?"

He remembered somehow having a similar discussion once with her at Baalbek. "She's not answered my last two notes," he said calmly, though sadness at the likelihood he would never again see either of these two people, so long in his life, moved through him like a tornado. He changed the subject. "As a boy, Kassem frightened easily. It's not all gone. But he's worked his way out of a lot of it."

"All one can ask for. Especially given how he started out in life. How's his attachment to you?"

"Deep."

"Do you play in your mind what will happen when you reveal his history? Angry, enraged at you for the lie?"

"*Lies*. I think about it all more of late. Maybe rage would be better. Get it out. A chance to eventually send it into the winds. Silent and festering might cause us problems later on with what we're attempting. Resentment, rebellion. Follow *his* own path."

"The closer you are, the more he will feel. You kept the

secret his entire life. He will not immediately care about why."

"He's patient. Deep thinker. Studies problems carefully before he jumps at them. I think it will be like that. I hope. Remember that first chemistry set?"

"I worried that you were pushing it on him too soon, at seven," Shai said. "Unlike your boy, I struggle with patience."

The memories of Kassem's childhood filled him with joy. He'd truly enjoyed those science experiments together. "I had the instructions translated, and Kassem sat alone with them for two days. Wouldn't let me in his room. He figured out how to float bubbles on carbon dioxide gas. It was the happiest I'd seen him in years."

"You won't lose him, Yussuf. Maybe for a minute, but not longer."

"Chances are a good deal longer."

"I was speaking in tectonic minutes."

Fuad chuckled. "What you're trying here is...unlikely."

"Yes, exactly. Agree wholeheartedly. Why it might work. I have another old friend, an oligarch in Moscow. He might rally to our flag. He's drawn to the absurd—big fan of American movies."

Everything felt like a painful loss to Fuad now, Shai the latest apparition from the edges of his life disappearing. He was unaccustomed to these swirling emotions and didn't care for them. Fuad was more afraid of Kassem charging away from him than he dared speak.

Fuad removed the small box he had unearthed at the Talisman Hotel. Shai launched a large paw, and the box disappeared into his pocket.

"Not sure of the impact it will have," Shai said. "But I'm ever hopeful."

"It will matter. We're all sentimental. I'm finding, even me."

Shai approached and pulled Fuad to him in a bear hug, kissed him on both cheeks in the Arab way. "Don't want my friend outside missing me too much," Shai said, a bit angry at himself that he didn't want to show his tears.

"*Bisalama*," Fuad said, himself near tears, in the simplest of Arabic departures, *Goodbye*. "Though God's a jokester," he found himself adding. "He may want us together, so we have to do this all over again."

Shai laughed, unexpectedly joyful, started to leave, and then turned.

"If it all blows up, want us to take Fatima out with you? Kassem if he's in danger?"

"Fatima, yes. Kassem only if he's near the noose."

Shai nodded and hurried out, thinking it better not to highlight that's where they were placing his son.

CHAPTER 5

AFRA

THE GOLAN HEIGHTS

S hai woke panting and gasping for breath. An hour ago in the dark, Tami had bolted up at his stirring. Since then, eyes open, she watched and worried. The first stretch of dawn, yellow and pink over the Jerusalem mountains, peeked through the curtainless window. Tami always needed to see the sky.

"Two breaths through your nose, then four slowly out through your mouth," she said, her voice steady in a crisis. She panicked privately.

A child of two Holocaust survivors, an accidental birth late after their inability to conceive, Tami's vigilance was born of a mother who feared the loss of every shekel, criticized with nearly every utterance, and envied everyone who had more, which was a small population. At sixteen in May 1944, her mother had stood against the Beregszász Ghetto wall in Czechoslovakia, a former immense brick factory, as a Nazi placed a bayonet to her mother's throat. Her wedding band clanked into a bucket. As they stepped from the transport into Auschwitz, those reconfiguring Europe in their own limited image ordered three girls to one side and Tami's grandmother to the other. Tami's mother said to her youngest sister, thirteen then, "Go stand with mother so she won't be alone." Those two disappeared into another type of brick building, the only exit from the chimney. Tami's father, a wealthy builder, dynamic in the streets, joking with everyone, darkened as he crossed their threshold; he was frustrated and not quiet about his wife's fears.

When out that door, young and on her own, Tami drifted through hippie-ish, hashish years with various men and without her clothes. The revisionist history in America about the 60s being vacuous years puzzled her. She still had wonderful girlfriends from that time, suspended in a chrysalis, from which she emerged reborn and flew free. After the second man sobbed that he could not live without her, though unimpressed by his ardor, as she'd been an indifferent partner out of bed, she decided to turn to a new chapter. She changed residences and charged into a life of service unadorned with possessions. Twenty-two years his junior, she met Shai when hired as his boss's girl Friday. As she sat beside him in bed, she was dismayed that as she grew older, the well-being she'd massed in her rebellious years had weakened into worry, not like her mother's, but more than she cared for.

"Should I bother and suggest a quick vacation? The Dead Sea? One place you won't sink."

Shai patted his ample belly and swung his feet off the bed. "Sure, let's go now."

"You're joking, right?"

"I could use it," he said, as often with Tami he lifted the veil on truth he left down elsewhere.

"What? Now I am worried. You're going to take the day off?"

He headed towards the bathroom, afraid she might read the exhaustion in his face. "Only the morning. You'll need to drive back. If I steal the time, you'll have to endure a helicopter landing."

"I wouldn't care if a tank battalion rolled in." Tami

hurried out of bed, wary. "I'm packing some things before the phone rings. I'll tell Asher to go to a friend's after school. I might take my time since you won't be rushing me to get back." She had vacation time amassed, as he usually said he was away too much as it was.

"I'll tell him."

Shai padded into his son's room; he had shed weight ten years ago at his birth to attempt longevity for the boy but then succumbed to the comfort of old habits. In bed, Asher had two copies of *The Golden Compass* open, one in Hebrew and the other in English. He was reading them simultaneously.

"You practicing your English reading?"

"What for? I read fine. I'm checking where the Hebrew translator made mistakes."

"How's he doing so far?"

"Not so bad that I have to write him."

"Mom and I are going to Ein Gedi."

"Can I come?"

"You have school."

He kicked from under the blanket, and both books tumbled to the floor. "That's what I thought."

"Can you go to Dror's or somebody after school? Mom can call his parents."

"Dad, don't be stupid. Nobody needs permission to have a friend over. I don't know where I want to go yet. I'm not even up."

"Tell Mom before you go to the bus."

Asher climbed out of bed and yawned exaggeratedly. "Maybe."

Back in the bedroom, Tami had her long dark hair in a ponytail and was already packed. She favored short, colorful dresses that revealed her exercised legs. Everywhere she wore her brown ankle-high Blundstone boots not for the smart looking leather but for the pull tab loops front and rear and the ribbed soles grip on hills and sleek streets, particularly in the occasional snow that paralyzed Jerusalem. Shai somehow knew that the low boots had been devised for versatility in the Tasmanian outback. Tami loved his random knowledge. She felt safe that his crowded mind would always have a pathway out if needed.

As he dressed hurriedly, Shai's thoughts were already on his afternoon flight to the army base on the Golan Heights. He had planned to drive, but he could use the leisurely morning.

He said, "For sure, he's your kid."

Tami didn't want to waste any time asking what Asher had said and glared impatiently at her husband for being ridiculous. Instead, she threw a pillow at him. "You're the one who taught him to say what was on his mind."

"It seemed a better idea when he was younger."

"You like it even more now."

He smiled in capitulation. "Shall I make breakfast?" Shai said, noticing his speech was steady, and he wasn't slowly forming the words so they would emerge without notice.

"No. Stuff some cheese in a pita for Asher and let's go before your phone screams. Consider it dieting."

At the freshwater nature reserve of Ein Gedi, just inland from the Dead Sea shore, Shai and Tami sat on a boulder downstream from the waterfall that filled a pool where people played noisily. Tall reeds with purple plumes reached into a cloudless sky, date palms behind them. King David had galloped here from King Saul and scampered by foot up the mountains accessible only to goats. Shai loved the Bible, though his relationship with God was on less solid ground, which he solved by not walking there. Ein Gedi meant 'spring of the goats.' Curve-horned ibex clamored higher in these hills and on occasion could be seen drinking in the stream after the bathers had gone.

Shai splashed with his legs as Tami sat still beside him.

"How's your head?" she asked, trying with some success to hide the terror from her voice.

"The stubbornness or the headaches?"

"The stubbornness is not news. Let's do some breathing

exercises."

He turned to her and grinned. "How about we consider my actually being here enough for now." He lifted the water soothingly cold with one foot. "I'm better."

Tami wondered what beyond his health was worrying him. She felt it like a pebble in her boot that she couldn't dislodge. He wasn't telling her something, not the operational details, which he never divulged, but something squeezing his heart.

Shai watched two goats with straight horns scamper over rocks high above them. Small stones skidded down, some splashing into the stream. Above the goats, a helicopter abruptly rose from behind the mountain and hovered noisily. Shai thought about how only hummingbirds could fly in place. Like a hummingbird, the chopper abruptly veered toward flat sand beside the thick salt crystals massed at the Dead Sea shore.

The disappointment *already* formed on Tami's lips, but she caught herself and said something she felt more profoundly instead. "Thanks for the morning."

"We'll have a guest for dinner, just the three of us. See if Asher can sleep out. Make a reservation for eight p.m. Maybe Sushi Rehavia. Let's walk. I'm considering doing something about my weight."

"Sure," she said. "Just when you have so little else to do."

"I get more done everywhere when I'm busy."

She felt him hug her close but not tight the way he did before he disappeared abroad. Silent, Tami bent to her carryall and tossed his heavy jacket to him.

Snatching it, Shai walked quickly to where the small Hughes light utility helicopter waited. The rotors beat the air louder as he approached, and the transparent door popped open. He hoisted himself in, excited to meet this young woman he had to win over. Last night he had reread both her military record and the more comprehensive file he'd commissioned. As expected, Shai learned nothing new, had remembered it all.

* * *

Less than an hour later, Shai sat on the boulder-strewn plateau of the Golan Heights looking at the Syrian valley below. Shai wore his heavy jacket in the cold and smiled that, as usual, Tami had been correct. Near him, small patches of snow speckled the landscape. Peaceful green fields spread across the nearby valley below. Just beyond, low stone Syrian villages blended into the semi-arid steppe where trees rose only along rivers. In the unblemished distance sixty kilometers away, Damascus sat between high brown mountains like a bright diamond.

A jeep sped at unsafe velocity towards him on the dirt road, the engine the only sound anywhere. Shai took in the listening post it had departed. A single space-like antenna reached toward the stars. Below it, on iron legs, crouched five domes with forward antennae like beetles. He wasn't sure how far they could hear, but Tehran wasn't a stretch. On the rim of the front line, these listeners huddled in reinforced bunkers deep below ground. Not any place he'd want to spend more than afternoon tea, Shai thought, and added to himself that hopefully, he wasn't alone in that view.

The vehicle approached, empty save for the young woman behind the wheel. Shai didn't show his smile, liking that she had declined to be driven by subordinates. The jeep slammed to a halt near him with a squeal of worn brake pads against metal rotors; he didn't flinch.

Early thirties, jet black hair severely pulled back in a ponytail, revealing a naturally beautiful face unfamiliar with makeup and a perfectly shaped nose as if it had been sculpted but had not. He took in the three silver leaves on a blue background, *seren*, the Air Force captain's insignia. She trotted towards him, ponytail swinging. He rose like an eagle taking flight, fully in his element.

"Afra," she said without reaching out her hand. An Arabic name, sister to the Hebrew *afar*, the color of earth.

"You didn't change it to Afar?"

"Obviously. Shai your real name?"

"I have others, but yes."

"I was ordered not to ask questions."

In a glance, he took her look in without inappropriate lingering. She was small everywhere and perfectly proportioned. He said, "That didn't last long."

Her lips parted in a small smile, then it retreated. "Hasn't ever. So far."

He took a step towards the edge and gazed down. Syrian armor was absent. "The tanks seem to have found greener pastures."

"They know we won't attack. Down there, that is. They've left to blow up neighborhoods in Homs and Aleppo."

Shai nodded wearily. Israeli fighter jets controlled the Syrian skies when inclined and not merely to starve Hezbollah's hunger for more missiles. They recently turned an anti-aircraft missile battery that ISIS had carted away from internecine Jihadi shelling in al-Shajara into scrap metal. Israel made it known they would visit their displeasure on anyone on any side who encroached upon the Druze villages of Hader and Arneh on the Syrian descent of Mount Hermon. The Arabic-speaking adherents of the seven prophets, Adam, Noah, Abraham, Moses, Jesus, Muhammad, and Muhammad ad-Darazi, the Druse were a million strong in the Levant. Some Israeli Druze fought ferociously with the IDF. Shai felt neither pride nor joy at the bellicosity; it was simply a necessity here, like getting dressed.

Shai said, "I gather the regime's fallen on its face along the Jordanian border between here and Jabal al-Druze."

"That was not a question. Why don't you head toward what you don't know?"

"Al-Nusra," he asked, thinking she was perfect, headstrong, and quick on her feet while stationary. "From your close view."

"The regime's left only one contingent to control Daraa and the road to Damascus. They're stretched thin. Bashar's nowhere near invincible. With help, the SLA can take them. The jihadis come together, regroup, and split apart. Different aims other than hating Bashar and us with undifferentiated fervor. The flavor of the month is LSY, *Liwa Shuhada Yarmouk.* They control what's left of Quneitra City on the Syrian side of the Golan."

The Martyrs of Yarmouk, named for the Yarmouk River, the mightiest tributary of the Jordan River that irrigated the nearly fertile valley by overflowing its banks. "Mostly without ideology," Shai breathed, sometimes a bit overwhelmed by the variations. "Local and extended family ties."

"They kidnapped seven UNDOC soldiers from the demilitarized zone." She nodded towards no man's land, and her hair bounced. "United Nations Disengagement Observer Force, a thousand or so mostly Filipinos. Poor guys just trying to help. LSY believes the UN is silent about the regime's crimes against the Syrian people."

"They have more than a point. Aren't we all?"

She looked at him, figuring he must be security of some cut, internal or globetrotting. "Some world when we agree on anything with them. Somebody in the Gulf paid the ransom."

"Qatar," Shai clarified. "I don't sleep well, so I read."

She laughed. "At least you sleep. Al-Nusra's active nearby. Swarming and promising on the lives of their mothers to liberate the Golan as soon as Bashar is buried." The best trained and fastest on their feet of the howling pack, Al-Nusra, the al-Qaeda gang in Syria, deeply worried Shai.

Bashar wanted the West to drink like soothing, nighttime warm milk, that *he* was the stabilizing force. Bashar topples, and this bubbling cauldron of Hezbollah, al-Nusra, and ISIS with seasonings of smaller factions boils over, he pontificated at every opportunity. With Bashar riddled with bullets, it's open season on shooting the Syrian Army, the Free Syrian

Army, and each other while scooping up abandoned chemical weapons to launch or sell to the deepest pockets. Bashar's a school marm in comparison, he wanted everyone to conclude, pulsed in Shai's head. Yet Fuad felt otherwise. He was certain the strong middle class, the existing Council of Elders with far-reaching tribal ties, and the lesson of Iraq not to gut the military but choose someone moderate from its ranks would deliver stability. The FSA could then send the jihadis packing.

"Any mention of sarin?" Shai asked matter-of-factly. "Among the jihadis? Hezbollah? Anybody, actually?"

"No. Not even in the typical boasting about how they're going to barbecue the regime and, for dessert, flambe us."

Shai was not comforted. "Mind if I sit? These legs."

"Your party. I'm enjoying the fresh air."

He moved to a nearby black boulder. Yellow bulbous wildflowers peeked out from around the edges, capturing moisture dripping down the rock. *Halmonit,* in Hebrew, the same as egg yolk. They had arrived in Israel with the vocabulary of petrified Biblical Hebrew, so those who sat in a stuffy room and grabbed words from the air snatched *halmonit* with its identical color for these wildflowers. He sat heavily, and she drifted down onto a smaller boulder opposite him with the familiarity with her body of a dancer.

"How's this posting for you, below ground? Miss stretching your legs?" She was second-in-command.

"I'm sleeping with the commander. You likely picked up that I could like him more. He's from St. Petersburg. They're all bloody Russians singing childhood songs after dinner. I imagine it could be worse, say, if they were drunk. But not by much. The air chatter had been all Russian. But I'm hearing more Syrian in the last few months. A lot more."

"In Damascus or near the border?"

"Across the country. The Syrian pilots have been just competent enough to barrel bomb civilian streets. Though from the practice, they're gaining ground. We see it in the maneuvers. They only fly the old Su-24s. Russians jockey the MiG-29s. We don't bother much with what the Syrian pilots are doing. It's ugly, just not important from a security standpoint."

"Tell me about the Russian pilots," he asked so evenly that it seemed to her this was where he had been headed all along.

"Less competent than you'd think. A lot less. Haven't fought a war in thirty years, since Afghanistan, and that one they lost. We sometimes have a little chat with them beforehand and go up against them. Fingers off missiles. If we had to, we could take them out pretty easily. That what you're looking for?"

He gave a small smile. "We took down an Il-20, was it? Without much noise afterward."

She looked at him, unable to grasp what he was after. "More like it fled from us into Syrian air defenses. They downed it. We expressed condolences on the death. I suppose if needed, we could do it on purpose."

He took a turn without slowing. "I understand you spend a good deal of time listening."

"That's why I'm here. Rank doesn't matter. I might hear something significant in local slang. Boys bragging. Or scared. The way boys always are. Both."

"I know the Canadians got you out of Damascus. We erred not being more focused on those Jews. Excuses about borders to defend and such are nonsense. I'm sorry."

The Jewish quarters of Damascus and Aleppo once bustled with 75,000 Jews. In his longstanding chess game with the West, Bashar held the remaining thousand as extra pawns, always in his hand below the table. Foreign statesmanship and brute threats had done little to pry these Jews out. With bravado, a lone Jewish woman in Canada, Judy Feld Carr, had realized with an elegance alien to the diplomatic class that she could bribe officials to slide out hundreds upon hundreds of Jews on an escape route greased by others who had traversed it. It brought Shai hope of what an individual might manage.

She noticed the "we" but said nothing. As if responding now to his earlier question, Afra stretched her short legs, crossed them, and they disappeared gracefully under her. Resentment climbed in her voice, like the horns pushing away the violins at the close of Haydn's Surprise Symphony. She often escaped with classical music in her headphones. "Sitting in Toronto, she bought us out one by one. When I met her in Tel Aviv, she told me that she felt disgusted doing it, that it was like haggling over the price of cattle. I told her the cattle didn't mind." She leaned forward, and her large black eyes looked cat-like as they filled a great deal of the white. They stared straight into his. Everything I'm telling you, you already know."

He smiled. "Only most of it."

"You didn't have to pull me outside to ask about nerve gas and Russian pilots."

"Correct. Could have gotten a status update on the phone with a lot less wear and tear on the old bones." For once, in person she matched the file. Usually, people looked better on paper, like most neighbors.

"You going to get me out of here?"

"There's someone I'd like you to meet," he parried.

Three two-seat Israeli F-16Is streaked loudly overhead, hugging the border, the sound through the valley below like rolling thunder. Since Lebanon was seconds away, they immediately arced back toward the heartland. Occasionally, she went up in the tandem seat, but nobody would accede to her requests to veer into Syria. The Israeli F-16 adaptation, hence the *I* added the extra seat. Their Popeye missile guidance system required a "man in the loop."

"We log five hundred flight hours a day," she said to fill the space, unlike Shai on poor terms with silence. "Most of the time, going nowhere." She smiled. "Never know when we're called on to go somewhere."

The white jet entrails began to dissipate in the high thin sky. Shai's mind drifted to the barrel bombs. They whistled down from helicopter gunships and fixed-wing aircraft, indifferent to precision, their payload equal to seven mortar shells which left nothing standing in a considerable circumference. Shai tilted the scales of justice and sarin rose again. He reminded himself not to underestimate how far Bashar might go to continue atop a bucking stallion about to pitch him into the mud and then trample on him.

"You're not Air Force or Army?" she asked, fishing to hook what she suspected.

Shai smiled. "You're correct. I can't issue you orders." He gazed into Syria. "How did you find the people, your neighbors in the Old City? Enjoy being around them, all of us Semites and such? Or were you *the other* and hated it? I appreciate you were only a teenager."

"The people were like here," she said. "Most of them are great. Some of them are assholes. My older sister told me Syrian men think sharing is both of you taking off your clothes together. Just like here. When anybody's in need, neighbors can't get there fast enough. Just like here too." Memories tumbled through her that she typically thrust aside. "Even though we slept in the Jewish Quarter, we shopped and lived among everybody. Guards at the ghetto entrance rarely bothered us. Unless we wanted to go to the airport. It's not home. But it's not, not home."

With that, Shai dug a hand into his voluminous coat pocket and withdrew the metal box. He watched the lines around her eyes tighten, tears rise in her eyes, but he saw she willed them not to descend. She swept them away with simultaneous elegant twin motions of first one hand and then the other.

She came close and grabbed it from him. "How'd you fucking know?"

"You gave a talk at your high school graduation. Top in your class, if I'm not mistaken."

She laughed, "You probably know my fucking shoe size. And certain other sizes too." She held the box tightly but did not open it and looked up. "You have listening devices in high schools?"

"Not usually. We do keep a periodic eye on people we admire who have the right language skills—Arabic's no problem. The exact accent, on the other hand, is challenging. Usually, we have to make up some nonsense that the family went to the Gulf and the father worked in the oil fields when the kid was very young to explain why it's off. After a few dozen times, people catch on."

She tried to open the box that had been welded tightly underground and wouldn't give. Shai withdrew a screwdriver from his other pocket and tossed it toward her feet. "I try and be prepared. In truth, I often don't manage it."

She started laughing and this time allowed her tears the freedom to drip down her cheeks. She set the box on the boulder she'd been resting on, pried the tin lid, and soon it popped off to reveal a small silver Star of David with tiny turquoise stones on each point. She took the necklace in both hands and let the box tumble; it noisily hit the rock.

"I wanted to leave part of me there. A friend lived in that house. I was highly emotional. I believed I would be able to return to get it."

"Peace happened unexpectedly with Egypt and Jordan," Shai said. "Maybe with Syria in a future we can't yet see. So, now that the gifts are opened even before the party's begun, we need a liaison to someone in their chemical weapons facility. I'm asking you to go back. We have a legend for you, an actual identity to step into is always preferable. In the chaos of Syria, it will hold. A teacher from Daraa. You'll be enrolled in advanced education classes at Damascus University. If I may intrude, are you surprised you never married?"

She laughed. "You mean do I mind being expendable?"

"Obviously, it is on the dangerous side."

"To answer your question, I am, but only somewhat. I left a couple of great guys. There was a lot of excitement which I relished. But I tend to get restless. You know that about me."

"Yes."

"When?"

"You might go back and pack. Your replacement's on the way."

"You were sure?"

"I'm never sure. I had a hunch."

She reached behind her neck and put the necklace on. It dangled over the loose uniform and fell between her breasts, the silver tarnished.

"May I suggest too that you don't tell anybody where it came from? Since you'll have to leave it behind, I thought I might hold onto it for you. Prefer your sister doesn't know you have it, if I may trample further into your life. Safest to keep the circle small. For your safety, actually."

"Can I have it until I leave?"

"Of course. I've taken the liberty of having your things packed. Unless you prefer to say your goodbyes. Nothing secretly hidden under the floorboard I might have missed? Poetry from your Russian? Many can raise a Pasternak or Osip Mandelstam verse for any occasion. Though Mandelstam's poetry is for the more complex at heart."

"He is definitely not one of those." She laughed deeply, feminine in it, a woman who was accustomed to influencing men, Shai confirmed. "How'd you know I'd just leave without going back inside? Don't bother. That's just fine. Maybe I'll just toss everything there and start over. I presume you have clothes without Israeli tags for me?"

"Some of our boys picked up a few things over the border in Daraa for authenticity. I'm afraid I can't vouch for the taste. Don't think they're much accustomed to shopping for young women."

She laughed again, louder, with real joy in it. "The jeep?"

"You might leave the key on the seat."

He watched the grace of her movements as she seemed to lift with each step toward the army vehicle and bet her commander would be laid flat.

Afra felt a swirl of emotions, thinking of the sea outside

the grottoes at Rosh Hanikra that broke against the offshore rocks in furious writhing foam. She liked to test herself swimming alone to the flat boulders. She was shocked that she would be back in Damascus but not surprised that she had readily agreed. She had no vague feelings to find peace with there, nobody to see, already knew before they told her that she could not gaze upon her childhood building not far from where she buried the chain she clutched with one hand. She thought she should be feeling more fear but suspected that would shake her later. For now, she was a soldier, not calm, not excited, but resolute, and she did not want to tell him she was grateful.

Afra floated back briskly from the jeep. "I hate this shithole. Stinks of cabbage and cologne. Who the hell wears cologne in a bunker?"

I don't own the stuff myself," he said truthfully. "Someone I'd like you to meet now, if you don't mind?"

"Here?"

"Yes. Let's have a stroll."

He led Afra on a small path, hard snow patches between the rocks on both sides, occasional yellow flowers peeking out and searching to be warmed by the cold sun. On the next rise, a woman sat on a large square flat cinderblock atop some others, legs dangling, looking out at the Syrian plain. Shai supposed she felt a longing, which didn't worry him. In the near ground below, green fruit trees fanned out across the valley inside Syria.

As they approached, the girl stood. She was about Afra's height, same black ponytail, maybe a little thinner. As Afra hurried along the cinderblocks leaving Shai in her wake, she took a small jump onto the wide flat block where the woman had risen quietly.

Somehow she just knew to address her in Arabic, "Ignore the uniform," she said. "I'm Afra."

The young woman, too, felt something she had not expected, a sense of home in this woman's dialect and manner.

"Lilia. Lilia Wassaf."

When Shai arrived panting, it struck him as the young women were chatting and pointing into Syria, and a laugh burst from a cooped-up Lilia that he was entirely superfluous, which he enjoyed. Whenever possible, professionally and elsewhere, he preferred to disappear.

"I'll tell the helicopter to give you two an hour."

"Come, we can get to a great view of *Jabal al-Shayhk* and back by then if we leave this fat guy behind," Afra told her, using the Syrian name for the crowning height. The Mountain of the Sheik. When the pressure built, she often hiked there alone to relax, like releasing air from an overinflated bike tire. Her commander ordered her not to wander there by herself. It was easy to say fuck you to a superior you were fucking. What the fuck was he going to do?

"Afra, you're going to stay with Lilia in Jerusalem, but the briefers want to have a go at you as soon as we land. You'll have time to get to know her."

The second she saw Lilia, the similarity was the puzzle piece that revealed the picture. "You mean *become* her," Afra said easily.

"Well, as close as you can is all we ask."

"What if I said no?" Afra challenged. "You have another one of us?"

"We are not so blessed. Back-up had not yet been addressed. I was hopeful." He turned to Lilia. "Ever had sushi? The Hanabi Sushi Bar in Damascus has quite the reputation. Smart plopping it down across from the Japanese Embassy."

Lilia shook her head a tight no. Everything was hurtling at her fast, and she was a little afraid of coming apart and crying like a silly girl. She missed her brothers fiercely but would have made this same decision again for a chance to do something bigger than being driven out of the Omari Mosque courtyard. Shai had explained that this woman would step into her shoes if it were okay and asked her to help with the fit. She had said little, simultaneously upset and proud. For sure she had *not* expected to like her but then immediately had, and, very alone here, needed to.

"We'll fix that omission tonight and bring back some sushi for Afra," Shai promised, buoyed by both women. "Sometimes they're missing an ingredient or two but then as close as one can manage is usually good enough in most things."

The sun slanted Afra's image across the concrete blocks, and Lilia moved into that shadow and felt protected. Though it might have been the other way around, as Afra would walk in hers. Lilia took her hand, stretched it out horizontally, then flipped it vertically with a slight upward shrug. "I do this a lot," she instructed Afra. She gazed at Shai, who knew what was coming. "Especially when I don't want to answer a question."

The civil war was like two rams bucking heads, Fuad thought as he sat alone atop the bathroom seat in his home, wanting to be alone, frightened about what he was about to risk with Kassem. Neither side gained much footing, but the trampled dirt ran with blood. Sparked by the iron fist that hammered Daraa shut, the uprising raised its own fist across the country. They did not initially demand that, like Egypt's President Hosni Mubarak, Bashar attempt to fall asleep in a dank cell. Hopeful, even optimistic, the opposition advanced a call to shred the state of emergency, empty the jails, and stop the *mukhabarat* from pounding on their doors and sitting at their dinner table. Many of the elders remembered and feared that it would all end like Hama, or worse, and shaking lined up behind the regime or sat silent. They tried to school the younger in the danger of defiance, with the expected lack of listening.

Fuad stood and looked out the small window in his home on the eastern slopes of Qasioun in search of the irises. He longed to see some beauty in the barren landscape of his thoughts. He saw no end to the carnage, and from this angle, none of the irises either. Unlike Mubarak, Kaddafi, and Ben Ali in Tunisia, all on the trifling northern expanse of Africa, Syria had risen at the crossroads of the Middle East, which is why Damascus was the oldest continuously inhabited city on the planet. Her patrons, Iran and Russia, had their talons in Syria's flesh.

Like a chameleon, Russia tried to conceal its true colors. Putin's inner circle pulsed with Orthodox Christian mysticism, anti-American conspiracy theories, and extravagant living. The Russians treasured their warm-water Tartus naval base at Latakia on the Syrian Mediterranean. To the southeast, the Bassel al-Assad International Airport sat mostly silent. The Russians planned to smooth the vast nearby fields into a behemoth Russian military airfield for their invading troops and fighter jets. Ever practical, they would share some runways with the al-Assad field. For them, Syria was a warm-up to right the wrongs of history that pried a long line of republics from the motherland.

The Iranian mullahs too hankered for a land corridor to the said sea and were a good way there given that the Americans had made Iraq an open thoroughfare. To Iraq's west, Syria waved the go flag to the mullahs like officials at the Sahara camel races in Niger. Someone, somewhere, had to do the right thing, though hope was not an emotion Fuad was on comfortable terms with. Doing the right thing, too, seemed an outdated concept in today's world.

Late that afternoon, with Kassem in the passenger seat, Fuad drove north to Hama on the M5 motorway that ran due north to Aleppo in the shadow of Turkey. The regime sat comfortably on the major arteries. Though in places, such as midway between Hama and Aleppo at the Saraquib junction with the east-west M4, no government vehicles dared wander west towards the rebel bastion of Idlib.

Now that the long-awaited hour had struck, Fuad was calm and, he feared, maybe overconfident. Subdued by regime troops, Hama was quiet though protests occasionally surged into the main squares like the tide surging over the tank breakwater. Such as the April 29, 2011 'Day of Rage' when anti-government protestors, prudently masked, climbed from the crowd and ripped down twin portraits of *pere* and *fils*, equally mustached, though only Hafez's upper lip bore any gray in these immense side-by-side photos. Then Bashar was only forty-six.

Soon Yussuf and Kassem sat on a stone wall over the Orontes River. A considerable distance below, thriving shrubs lined both banks of the green water. As for the 1982 leveling of whole neighborhoods, as with most massacres, unless there was groundswell to honor the site, and here Damascus demurred, new construction obliterated the evidence. When the internet flashed to life, long-secreted photos of the 1982 deaths anonymously appeared online, to little outside notice.

Below them, two of the ancient wood norias turned slowly in the flat water, emitting wood song.

"We don't know precisely when most of these waterwheels were built," Fuad told his son. "This one, the Noria al-Muhammadiya, is from 1361. There's an inscription. Some are considerably older."

"We come all this way for a history lesson?" Kassem said, smiling. Though his father wore civilian clothes, he was puzzled why they embarked without armed escorts into Hama, where the uprising had fanned long-smoldering embers into fire.

Fuad glanced at Kassem and felt a sourness in his stomach; suddenly realizing he had been fooling himself, in the same way, he believed he might love Margaret again in more than memories. He foolishly saw the world the way he desired it to look. Kassem would see every day of his life as a lie. A rift would open in the earth between them that Kassem couldn't cross.

"In a way, yes," Yussuf said quickly, accustomed to hiding his feelings from Fatima, from his underlings, and often from himself.

With intense interest, Kassem followed, the water

carried high in the boxlike wood compartments. Each splashed rhythmically into the stone aqueduct supported by ancient arches along the entire length. He observed that the massive axles and bearings were hard walnut; he eyeballed this wheel at 17 meters high and 21 meters in diameter. Below, the wood boxes dipped into the river. Kassem closed his eyes and listened to the soft lift of the water, the groan of the giant wet wood axles rubbing against their wood supports, and the water spilling into the aqueduct.

Most of the city pushed back from above the low river. In 1982, Hafez's errant but effective shelling caved in the dome of the 8th Century Great Mosque of Hama, along with everything below it. The stone Old City, though proudly erect for millenniums, had been no match for mechanized tank treads. Mindful of local sensitivities, the government's Antiquities Department restored the two minarets and the various mosque buildings. While at it, they dug up and utilized some of the Corinthian columns from the subterranean Roman basilica. About a third of the Old City rose anew. More efficiently, rubble disappeared below mounds of dirt, planted grass and landscaping. After repair, the giant wheels rotated and sang again, all seventeen of them.

"This one was built to supply The Great Mosque and the nearby area— the bathhouse, irrigation," Aware he was stalling, Fuad finally said, "You've been to Hama before."

"I don't remember. Did we come when I was very young? To see the norias?"

"You were, in fact, born here."

The old story finally coming out was like a reunion with a close friend he thought about often but had not seen in a very long time. Fuad felt oddly excited.

"We moved to Damascus?" Kassem asked, puzzled. His eyes blinked rapidly. He was frightened but couldn't grasp why.

"No, only you were. I chose this spot to sit for a reason. Walk with me, and I'll explain."

Kassem bolted anxiously to his feet. "*Please*, Dad. I don't understand. Your stories always take too long to get to the point."

"You will understand. I promise. In a few more minutes." He wanted to say 'trust me' but stopped himself at the conceit.

In this rebuilt part of the Old City, they walked across the river on a new low stone bridge wide enough only for pedestrians. Yellow wildflowers covered the hill to their left where Fuad remembered houses crowded against each other, surfaces dark with grime. Red cyclamens pushed up occasionally between the yellow. The emotion spilled gently through Fuad like the water from the noria, from the irony of all this beauty here, from finally stepping into this moment with Kassem he had played in his mind so many times.

They reached an old domed mosque; a rusted iron fence surrounded it, the black paint peeling. The entrance hinges were loose and squealed as Fuad moved through the gate. Palms and pines rose in the small area. Behind them, back on the far side of the river, they could see the Great Mosque with its clock tower minaret, raised in the image of its 12th Century predecessor other than the bullhorns in every direction at its crest. As was common, the facade alternated bands of black basalt and limestone. In a few decades, the three adjacent white stone domes were considerably blackened by city exhaust.

Grass covered this open ground, a small plaque in the center hidden in the blades.

"How much do you know about Hama?" Fuad asked.

"There are Facebook pages about what happened. I saw photos of a bulldozed field with individual graves. Each surrounded by cinderblocks."

"With no internet, it was not hard to keep from the world."

"This is a mass grave?"

Fuad nodded. "I came to Hama, actually to an orphanage just outside the city. It turns out I cannot bear children. It is me, not your unfortunate mother. At first, it was not easy to accept. Your mother did far more easily. She believes Allah caused my infirmity to bring you to us."

"What do *you* believe?" Kassem said loudly, with abrupt anger. His face hardened. "Who's buried here? My father, mother, brothers?"

"I believe when men become frightened, they destroy. Sometimes with a little luck, good things can rise from that. Usually, they don't. You were one that did. Your father is here. He was an ophthalmologist. I cannot locate your mother. I tried for many years."

"Is my name even Kassem?"

"No. Wa'el, I discovered later." Fuad was calm. "A French aid worker named you for a child who died in her care. She wanted him to endure through you. I took you from an orphanage in the pistachio fields after the massacre. It was for your mother and me. If it improved your life, we will never know for certain."

"So the regime, your regime, my regime, murdered my family."

Kassem stared down and then strode towards the plaque, face red, almost choking, shattered, and desperate to be whole again. The plaque read: PEACE TO THEIR SOULS, the Syrian wish for the dead.

"Why bring me here now? You never do anything without a reason. Why didn't you tell me? All this time. How..." Tears slipped down Kassem's cheeks.

"You are right, as always. There is a reason. The hospitals were beyond full. Your father used his medical background to help the wounded. In your house, not far from here. He was arrested for it."

"And tortured. Do you know how he was tortured? Were you there? Did *you* order it?"

"I did not order it. Though I was instrumental in keeping what happened secret. That success furthered my career. I never met or saw him. I first heard of him at the orphanage when I chose you. You were small and quiet, as you've always been. It was not certain you would live. There were stronger boys. I took you because of your father."

Kassem walked a few paces away and spoke without looking at Fuad. "Because of his bravery? Or do you consider that stupidity, helping the wounded? He must have known what might happen, defying the Assads."

"Some people are absolutists. They do what's right, always. They are personally injured when people close to them do not. I imagine he was like that. In the real world, it's both a gift and a curse."

Kassem spun back. The sound of a motorbike on the street rose and then fell. In the sudden silence, the groaning chant of the enormous wheel returned. "So they're always hurt?"

"Yes." He approached his son but resisted the urge to place a hand on his shoulder, which he needed now while the boy required time. "Though I'm not at all that way, moral absolutism appeals to me. Reminds me I could be better."

"And dead."

"Well, yes, there's that drawback."

"What does mother know?"

"That you were adopted from an orphanage. Not that it was here. She's used to me circumventing regulations."

"You lie to her."

"To mostly everyone," he confessed.

Kassem collapsed to his knees, attempting to be closer to this father he never knew. He dropped his forehead to the grass, more to try and touch him than in prayer. He lifted his head. "I felt none of this. I've always been whole. You were a better father than any of my friends had. Was it all an act? You want something."

"I do. There were lies, more than a few. They never interfered with who we were together, how I felt. My unconditional love for you."

"I should believe that?" he shouted.

"I think you know it. You will see how you feel when all

this settles."

"Why bring me here? Why tell me now? Whom do you want me to hate? Hafez? Bashar? The torturers? Or you?"

Fuad eased down on the grass beside him and said nothing. Like a coiled snake, Kassem needed to strike, with venom or not remaining to be seen.

"You chose me because of my father?" Kassem covered his face with his long, slender fingers and then parted them. "*Why?* You want me to be a hero like him? I'm not. I don't know who I am!" he wailed.

Fuad rested a firm hand on the boy's shoulder. "Everybody likes you, Kassem. That's not a small achievement."

Kassem wiped his face on his father's shoulder. "I always felt you wanted me at Institute 3000. That true?"

"Yes."

"*Oh no,*" Kassem said with a sudden clearer view of his life. "The chemistry sets. From when I was so young. You planned from then? Is that even *possible*?"

"Even earlier. I chose the son of a courageous man of scientific aptitude. I hoped that I would love you. I found I did from the moment I lifted you to my shoulder in that orphanage. It was unexpected. Everything I've achieved in my life is secondary to how you turned out and who we've been together. And I thank your father for whom he bore."

A small smile slowly crept up Kassem's face like sunlight moving past clouds.

Fuad said, "I want you to be who you already are. Just maybe look a little deeper. I want you to help protect the Syrian people. Maybe the entire region."

Kassem laughed, a deep, loud bellow of release. "That all?"

"Like the man who bore you, you're in a position to do something important, only on a grander tableau. You could save thousands of lives. Maybe many more. There's potential for a mass chemical attack in Ghouta in East Damascus and in Dariyya in the Western suburbs because they oppose the regime and are so near. Even one with our sarin in London or Washington."

Then as if the sun went behind a cloud, the shadow returned over Kassem. "I'm in great danger."

"You're tied to me, so you've always been. Only now you know it."

CHAPTER 6

McE

GEORGETOWN WATERFRONT PARK

S hai sat with Paul McEnnerney on a bench in Georgetown's Waterfront Park near the green switchbacks painted on the cement leading to the black center. Almost at arm's reach, the Potomac was flat and unmoving.

"Want to give the labyrinth a try?" McE, as he was known inside the corridors of Langley, asked. "The journey, as brief as it is, is meant to help one disconnect from the present world."

"And go where?" Shai asked with amusement.

"That is the question, isn't it? Nirvana. A place where there is no suffering, desire or sense of self."

"Might be longer lasting to become someone you like."

"Like us both," McE quipped, meaning it.

McE wore a beige linen suit and expensive sunglasses. He gratefully did not depend on his CIA salary. McE's prescient ancestor arrived a century ahead of those scurrying from the Irish Potato Famine of 1845. Angus McEnnerney received a 1,100-acre grant at the fall line of the James River destined to become Richmond, Virginia. The same fortune, albeit blowing in the opposite direction a hundred years later, left the now

160,000 acres in ruin by a McEnnerney prone to booze, cards, and attempts to recoup losses by sinking what remained in proposals of grandiose promise. His son fled to the western ends of Virginia and, in the Shenandoah Valley, cultivated a dozen varieties of apples from Red Delicious to Ginger Gold, land McE held onto, despite obscene offers to Houdini to turn the trees into condos and, of course, a golf course. McE often escaped Washington to trudge through his fields. Forged in the crucible of the family fable, McE was a cautious investor, sinking a fortune early on into equal mountains of Microsoft and Apple stock, which required less of his time than his apples. Unlike Shai, he was a profligate spender, but he did not need a compass to head true north like him.

"Nice glasses. Are they the new Persol649s?" Shai asked, squinting in the sun and noting that he should yank some shades off a drugstore rack. Shai inhaled details and in addition to science journals, perused fashion magazines for anything useful for the field he might acquire. In his nightstand drawer, he kept a copy of the *French Vogue* editor's lengthy profile of Asma al-Assad. "A Rose in the Desert" lifted eyebrows, mascaraed and many more not, for heralding the first couple as "wildly democratic." While standing by it, *Vogue* erased the piece from its website and everywhere else on the Internet within its influence; so quite successfully.

Helmeted cyclists and skaters glided by on the bike path cleaving the deep green grass along the river. McEnnerney pulled a cigar from an inside coat pocket. He didn't offer Shai one, given that the Israeli always refused them. He lit it and inhaled softly. McEnnerney was practiced both at unearthing small pleasures and enjoying them.

"So, what can I do for you that we haven't yet managed? Parting the Red Sea's been done. We've already saved your firstborn multiple times, from Phantoms to F-16s. You're head of the queue for the F-35s. Your lot is worse than my spoiled kids."

"And you love us all."

"True, but not at all equally." He pulled hard on the cigar, always enjoying Shai up to a point, depending on how high the price was.

"Small favor, actually."

"For *now*, you mean," McE said with menace.

"I do have some greater aspirations," Shai admitted, not entirely sure how much he was going to jettison now. "All of a sudden, things have tightened up considerably at the Nasib Crossing."

"I have a passing understanding of the ins and outs there."

"Sooner or later, the Free Syrian Army will have to make a go to take it, to have a chance at winning," Shai said hopefully. "I think they'll manage it. My problem is as it stands now."

The Nasib Border Crossing on the Amman-Damascus Highway was a vital egress for Syrian exports to the GCC, the Gulf Cooperation Council. The CIA smuggled weapons to the rebels there while the sympathetic Sunni King of Jordan strolled in the other direction.

"Bashar's rushed in the Republican Guard to fortify it," McE said. "I have that, right?"

"We allot them the respect they're due. Would appreciate a little help working up some papers. Important enough, we'd like them legitimate. On the off chance the Guard decides to look deeper. An American aid worker from some NGO. The American Relief Coalition for Syria might play. Early 30s, female, just happen to have a photo for the documents with me. Syrian background as a reason for being there with all the bona fides appreciated."

McEnnerney laughed. "I thought you were going to ask me to get Obama to invade Syria."

"That comes later," Shai said with a smile, sincerely meaning both.

McEnnerney tugged on his cigar and released the smoke in a storm overhead, trying to gauge Shai's seriousness about invasion. He rose and motioned his head for Shai to accompany him toward the Potomac. Shai followed, appreciating an outlet for his restlessness. A scull crew slid by on the water, six men in a harmony of arms, the shell yellow, each with a yellow cap, oars yellow too. America did the little things too well, Shai thought, at the expense of the bigger picture.

McEnnerney's encrypted phone rang. He looked at the number and scowled. "They think I'm out buying wine for the house. I like to do that."

"Do they know you're meeting me?"

"Who the hell cares? You're an ally these days, I believe. Though your Prime Minister's a bit cozy with the Russkies for many people's tastes around here. Including mine."

"It really doesn't do us much good," Shai agreed.

McE delayed answering the phone and put a hand playfully on Shai's shoulder. "Papers are easy. Come to dinner. 7 p.m. Don't you dare bring anything, the wife won't have it from friends. Okay, daisies for her. We're not *that* close. She adores your visits because you devour everything. Says it's a chance to get rid of the leftovers in the back of the fridge. When I'm sufficiently soused, you can step up to the pitcher's mound and show me what you've got. Straight in the strike zone, my old friend. The fun's over."

McEnnerney stubbed the cigar on the side of a trash receptacle and threw it in. "Papers, my ass. You guys have the best forgers anywhere, dating back to those in the Warsaw Ghetto."

"Legitimacy never hurts."

"Sure. Why not."

* * *

After dinner, where Shai did his best to inhale as much food as possible for Mrs. McE's sake, the two men sat on rattan chairs on the outside patio. Behind the immense black BBQ, a short spurt a few inches high rose in a tall round fountain, and water from the brimming fountain trickled over blue Mexican pebbles. McE lit a cigar and then ran a hand through his reasonably full head of hair, still red enough to convince him he had some youth left there, if not in his gait. Early on, the older Israeli had been a mentor on recruiting agents when McE found himself in Cairo.

"Let's dispense with the curve balls, shall we," McE said, "since we're on the same team and all."

Shai had obliged McEnnerney by drinking a glass of some dark violet wine, which he believed was intended to nudge him slightly off his game. As Shai never imbibed, it had succeeded.

"The Free Syrian Army," Shai began.

"Courageous boys."

"Hundred and fifty thousand strong. They have a chance, as it happens, not just my assessment. All the way up to our top, utter believers. Shared even by those watching the ants scurry around below from the Golan lookout."

"Don't disagree. Though they'll need a bit of help, we think as we crouch on the sidelines and occasionally stand up and wave our pompoms."

"And then sit back down again," Shai said evenly. "

McE smiled. "We are a people who prefer being comfortable."

"Since the war at the moment is pretty evenly matched, time is on Bashar's side. With Russian and Iranian reinforcements flowing like your mighty Mississippi, if he's patient, he can grind them down."

"We don't have him as the patient sort." McE lifted a delicate green hand-blown wine glass from the Italian island of Murano and saluted Shai with it. "These are a great story. When the wife and I go through, I see only aperitif glasses, maybe a dozen colors. Our salesman says he had wine goblets. I ask how much more for those. He purses his lips and blows. Says, 'Same price. We don't charge for the extra air.'"

Shai laughed, as always enjoying his time with McE. "All

right. I'll get to the point. We think Bashar's likely to use his sarin on civilians and maybe in an impressive way."

"For the mayhem? Panic people to flee from suburbs uncomfortably close to him? Fill it with his tried and true."

A little lightheaded, Shai breathed heavily. "Yes. The thing is, it will work. Even magnificently."

McE sipped some more and waited.

"If anybody's ever going to do anything to tilt the odds for the good guys when he does, that'll be the opening." Shai rubbed his head. The wine, rather than relaxing his muscles, tightened his temple. "At the end of the very long day, what will win this war are these barrel bombs Bashar can produce without relying on his foreign friends. Fertilizer and diesel sent screaming from a helicopter takes out quite a number of square blocks, and the pilot's back in time for morning coffee."

"How many airfields and the surrounding hangers would have to be flattened to give the FSA an opening?"

"A dozen, give or take."

"Not a lot. We flatten it all. What's to stop our upset young lad from hauling the sarin out of its deep bunkers and shooting it off everywhere there are people who offend him? Which surely includes you folk."

"What stops that? The threat that cruise missiles next visit the presidential palace and a lot of similar addresses. And maybe follow it with boots on the ground. That threat should be sufficient."

McEnnerney drained his glass. "You sure you don't want another while I get a fresh bottle?"

"Entirely."

As McE headed to the sliding glass door, he stopped and turned back. "Anything else? I want to know how expensive a bottle I have to open."

"If you get the really good stuff, I'll risk a glass. We're also going to get all the many tons of sarin out of Syria. Bashar's going to give it to us voluntarily. Eventually, I'm going to need you to go see a Russian oligarch with me."

McEnnerney chuckled, enjoying himself, slid the glass open and shouted, "My dear, get me the keys to the kingdom. I must descend to get something reserved to toast to the impossible."

Shai wondered which part he deemed impossible and decided not to inquire.

A little over two weeks later, Shai drove Afra to the Sheik Hussein Bridge Border Crossing into Jordan. As he sped up, he said, "Don't let an easy passage through the Nasib Crossing dull you about the danger."

She found herself surprisingly open with him. "If nightmares are a sign. Then I'm sufficiently scared."

"Have them myself. I think they help me manage the stress of the day."

"I can do without them."

"Usually, it's easier once you're in place."

Inside Jordan, everything was lovelier, which she had not expected. She caught herself that condescension could hamper her in Damascus. Stately frond-crowned palms lined both sides of the road in precise rows, like soldiers at parade rest. Lush yellow and red flowers poked up from planters. Immaculately trimmed bushes stood before a Jordanian building with black lettering in Arabic and English: SECURITY AND CUSTOMS CARS. Their border police officer was interested in nothing about them as Shai drove through with a broad smile, a wide wave, and without slowing.

"The young woman SLA officer undercover at Damascus University," Shai said. "Meet her in case you'll need her later. But just the once for now."

"So you've said."

He smiled. "How many times?"

"I got it several times back," she said with a laugh.

Soon they were on the bridge over the Jordan River, narrow here with marshy weeds on both banks. Beyond, she saw the rolling brown hills of the desert, which oddly felt inviting.

"Probably I shouldn't be excited," she said, "But I don't give a damn. I am."

"Good deal better than dread," he replied offhand. "I'm better myself on the hunt. Otherwise, it's a caged tiger. I have a very patient wife."

Afra gazed out at the desert; the sandy tops of the mountains were beautifully white. She turned to him and slowly released a smile. "You're the perfect husband. You're gone a lot, and you don't cheat."

"My wife actually likes me around," he said sotto voce. "I hope you'll find that someday."

Up ahead, Afra saw a white Toyota van with lightly tinted windows to allow suspicious onlookers with rifles a clear view in. It was parked off the road near reeds bending in the hot wind. On the flank and both sides it had, in bold black, *UN*.

As Shai pulled behind it, Afra looked down and then at him and said, "Me too."

*   *   *

After an hour due east, then another twenty minutes north past the Jordan University of Science and Technology and the city of Ar-Ramtha, the single-lane highway in both directions completely emptied on the last fifteen minutes to the Jaber Crossing. They stopped, the only vehicle before the black iron gates. Beside the gates, two posters towered: one a crown, and the other a painting of King Abdullah II of Jordan in a business suit, tie, and a red-checkered keffiyeh headdress. Her driver, an Egyptian with parched, darkened skin, said, "I think the Arabs got this huge picture idea from the poster-loving Soviets during their various unending stays."

Two Jordanian police officers in blue short-sleeve shirts and matching berets approached. After a cursory check of their documents, the gate rattled open.

Half a kilometer inside Syria, the now dust-coated van,

with Afra in the passenger seat, approached the austere Nasib Crossing. Armed soldiers stood on the parapet of a tall, concrete bunker painted green. Atop it, a tricolor Syrian flag danced in the hot wind. Near the ground, sand lifted and sailed. A high arch of multiple metal rods, offering neither utility nor aesthetics, spanned the highway. Concrete barriers in sections parallel to the road along both sides stood ready to block the Amman-Damascus Highway. Each sparkled with fresh paint: the green, white and black horizontals of the Syrian flag with three red stars equidistant in the middle white. Afra thought that apparently, Bashar wanted it known that he controlled the concrete.

Everything everywhere around Afra was brown and flat, other than twin lights atop tall metal poles at intervals on the hour-and-a-half to the capital. Shai had outfitted her in black western pants, a dark headscarf, and no sunglasses; after all, she matched McE's travel documents and was in a legitimate UN vehicle, so no reason to encourage further inquiry. The sole vehicle at the checkpoint might give the bored guards occasion to linger and examine a woman's papers and, in the concrete bunker, maybe more.

As two helmeted soldiers reached her side of the vehicle, Afra lowered the window. The unrelenting sun and heat blasted in. She passed them both their documents. Afra's heart jumped as they squinted at hers in Arabic and ubiquitous English. Her mouth dry, she reached for the pack of Jordanian CLARA WATER on the seat floor, grabbed two bottles, and thrust them toward the soldiers. She knew it was irrational, but she believed it could not end here before she even began. They returned the documents to twist off the blue caps, as Shai had suggested might be the case.

"*Shukran*," both chorused.

"*Anah min dawaei sururi.*" She kept it brief. My pleasure.

Water in hand, smiles under their helmets, they waved the van on.

CHAPTER 7

DAMASCUS

After so long sealed below ground, Afra felt the thrill of freedom, even of homecoming, but the excitement that rippled through her was unexpected and alien. She stood in the dark pedestrian Street Called Straight and gazed up. Sure, the towering walls above the shops and below the arched roof had been freshened white, but the rise and fall of bargaining, the women carrying black plastic bags full of fruits and vegetables, the competing perfumes of sugared candies, coffee, cardamom seeds, dates, figs, spices and the rest —and above all the jasmine spilling from the shops, tumbled her back in time. She almost felt like that child who had darted through the Old City.

Beyond everything here, she had always waited impatiently for the annual jasmine festival—she seemed to think it was in April—when the sweet scent of the white flowers floated in all the marketplaces. One of the briefers had mentioned that to defy the uprising, Bashar had ordered every Damascus resident to plant a jasmine bush. The briefer had added: he wants to hide the stench of death. Despite her rage at the ploy, the memory of the sweet floral fragrance made her emotional and filled her with a sense of loss she did not completely understand. She suddenly felt a little out of control, which she didn't like. She stomped with short, fast steps towards the rendezvous.

Half an hour later, Afra sat at an empty park picnic table and waited calmly. She felt fine now, the Afra of the Hermon lookout. She absorbed her environs. In the northern suburbs below the broad 6th Tishreen Street, Ibn al-Haytham Park filled a square block. At one end below the northern hills, balconies in the high-rise apartment blocks peered down on the fountains. Jets sprayed from the dark green serpentine lake. She had never been here as Jewish children rarely ventured far from their Old City quarter. She admired its beauty. Inside Damascus, only occasionally did opposition mortars whistle and explode, or their bombs noisily lift cars. In the quiet, she found the scent of jasmine in the park a joy.

* * *

When his father sped them home from Hama, Kassem had felt the heat both from the desert and radiating from inside him on his face. Like a puppeteer, his father had controlled his every move. He was nothing, someone who danced as the strings were pulled, not even a man. He had felt alone and bereft.

Finally, in their silence, his father had said, "When you pour out love, unlike with water from a pitcher, there's no less left inside. If you love the man whose seed birthed you, you have no less water in the pitcher."

He grew angrier and felt they were more words to control his feelings. Dreams that night tormented him, men's faces dissolving into each other, coming one on top of the other faster and faster. Then he was below ground in that cemetery, being beaten inside a tire, and gasping for air. He woke, his eyes closed, in some netherworld between nightmares and reaching for the morning.

Deep in Mount Qasioun, as Kassem rose alone in the huge lumbering below-ground elevator, he saw the house where he was born and what happened afterward as if it was on a film screen. He felt swelling love for this ophthalmologist who wrestled with *Azra'il*, the angel of death, with his 4,000 wings, many eyes and tongues, to treat the wounded. Kassem saw too that if he felt this way, it was because he had become the man of breadth, unlike all those others at Institute 3000, Fuad had guided him to be. He was furious at his father, but he loved him fiercely. He was whole now without ever realizing he had not been.

"So why, all of it? *Why*?" he had screeched to his father in the car as he first saw the minarets of Damascus on the horizon.

"Chemical weapons. The program began very early. Qadhdhafi in Libya had them and passed them to Iran and to Hafez to strike at Israel. That's how it started. There's no lock on the gate. No stopping what the desperate might do. There is a Council of Elders I will come to tell you about. And some others, in particular one friend. We felt a check was needed. You are that check."

In an instant, Kassem saw what he would be called to share, reveal, and betray. He was so overwhelmed that he could not speak. He welcomed that there was much about his father he had not imagined, a world vaster than Kassem's daily job, meals, and insecurities. He said nothing more that entire day or the next, but in bed the second night, a quiet enveloped him like a soft blanket.

Picnic basket in his grip, as Kassem left the many stone buildings that almost disappeared into the brown flank of Mt. Qasioun, part low Arab architecture, part security, he recalled as a boy when, with his father, he had first seen the early construction of Institute 3000. He could not grasp the view through an astronomy telescope to find him in the heavens and then drop him here like an unrecognized alien. He had always felt his work vital, the sarin secreted around the country, a protective umbrella against an Israeli nuclear sun. Though scared for his own life, he felt freed, as if he'd escaped from a locked room, from the terror that he would deliver mass murder. He might now be the hand that halted it.

In Ibn al-Haytham Park, Kassem headed towards the blue metal tables and peeling blue-painted benches on the south side. The brown and inhospitable northern hills dipping from the Qasioun peak continued this far eastward. He hurried past the empty multi-colored children's area, along the paved path, and onto the short-arched bridge that crossed the lake. Nervously he switched the basket to the other hand and wiped his damp fingers on his pants.

Two weeks after their return from Hama, while hiking as usual on Qasioun with his father, Fuad had said there was a woman from Daraa, a teacher just arrived at Damascus University for an advanced degree in the Faculty of Education. They were to date as cover for the launch to some great unexplained star beyond. She would be content to sit on his couch and read and, in time, probably best for appearances if, on occasion, she slept on that couch too. Kassem realized there was no path down this mountain, only a plummet off a cliff, and he wished he was meeting a man rather than a woman. No women dropped below the clerical ground level of the Institute. He had business only in the secret bowels of Qasioun, where they stored the chemical ingredients and married them in gleaming steel vats when ordered.

Not always, but horribly sometimes, he had stuttered at Damascus University in the greatness of Syria, free to all accepted students. It always happened when fate forced him to make small talk in the cafeteria after a girl lowered close beside him at the crowded long tables. A student, holding her tray as she balanced to sit, her leg sometimes brushed against his sending shivers to places unfamiliar with that arrival. Women guests at their home flitted to his father like butterflies to a stalwart sunflower, and from this alone, Kassem should have known he was not Fuad's issue. This morning, his father presented a cell number and his mother an unwieldy picnic basket, believing that the girl was the daughter of prominent political friends. His mother was beginning to slip into dementia, and he walked fast to outrun the worry.

Kassem quickened his already fast steps. High branches fanned overhead and rested on the row of narrow metal arches, a green canopy over the bridge. Patches of light struck the stone steps. On this side of the lake, under thick date palms, picnic tables beckoned, the tables empty, save for her at the last. Her black hair was trapped by a scarf, a few errant strands escaping over her forehead. Again, he ached for another scientist as this subterfuge was terrifying enough without attempting small talk.

He nervously set the picnic basket down. She was attractive, not anyone he might stop and gaze at from across the street, if unseen, But with large alluring almond-shaped black eyes. Unsure how to proceed, if he should introduce himself or if it was assumed they had met, he said hurriedly, "The park is named for Ibn Al Haytham." He felt stupid; she would realize that, but halfway across this river, he paddled hard lest he capsize. Al Haytham was Iraqi and might not be known to many Syrians. "In the tenth century, he built the first camera obscura. In his *Book of Optics*, he created the term *Al-Bayt al-Muthlim*."

"Darkroom in English," Afra said.

He sat a little clumsily, his long legs hitting the tabletop from underneath. "You know about cameras?"

"A guess. Literally what he called 'dark house,' I presume would mean darkroom."

"He wanted to prove that light travels in time and with velocity."

"How'd he do it?" She wanted to understand and found his awkwardness cute—as long as he overcame it quickly.

"He posited that if a hole was covered with a window curtain and the curtain was pulled away, the light traveling from the hole to the wall would take time to arrive. He introduced the camera obscura by studying the sun's half-moon shape during eclipses." Kassem grew excited. "He made a small hole in window shutters. When it hit the opposite wall, the light projected a moon-sickle."

She found the explanation illuminating and clear. She wasn't sure if he was nervous or if this was how he talked upon meeting a woman. She suspected the latter. She smiled softly. To calm him, as with most men, she only had to talk about what they already knew. "I think some of the great masters used looking through the pinhole Obscura. Some believe Vermeer used it to create the sparkling highlights in Girl with the Pearl Earring. A box with a hole in it captures the image so it can be drawn precisely."

His mouth dropped. She figured he was a goner now. She admired the risk he was taking, as the Eurovision song contestants annoyingly always mouthed, "for world peace." By chance, she had taken a class in the Old Masters at Tel-Aviv University. Her father had hated her staring at paintings, hounded her heels with his rapid retorts that she was smart, could be so much more than a teacher, that she was a disappointment. On the two occasions she told him his words hurt, he replied, "Why? It's plain truth." She had wandered into the military for his applause and was aware she was angry at about every male who crossed into her sights for acceding to him. Not knowing where she would have marched on her own rhythm had left her underground and not only on Mount Hermon. Then with the snap of a magician's fingers, she reappeared in the Damascus sunlight.

"Al Haytham was under house arrest in Cairo when he rewrote what the world had understood about the properties of light," Kassem said, leaning forward eagerly on both elbows. "In an instant, he created the scientific method, hypothesis, then experiment. Accept or reject." Suddenly he felt like an unpopular schoolboy trying to impress the new girl in class. He spoke quietly, "What do I call you?"

She found him charming, had been assaulted by every smooth and suggestive line males could conceive, so had often favored quieter men. She felt only a little guilty that she had known nothing of camera obscura until Shai walked through it chapter and verse to facilitate his comfort. It had not arisen in her art history courses.

"Lilia, Lilia Wassaf," Afra said. "What's next? Lunch or saving the world?"

"Lunch," he said, and then with an uneasy smile. "But only first."

Heavy whispers of the intent to explode gas on opposition suburbs in the outer flanks of Damascus, both Ghouta in the east and Dariyya past the presidential palace in the west, had dropped though Institute 3000 like a black cloud of sarin itself. Even before his awakening, he had shrunk in horror at the prospect.

Kassem reached for the basket and removed manakish, *round bread topped with cheese, zaatar, and tomato sauce.* Next came yabrak, *stuffed vine leaves,* and Syrian shawarma, *lamb encased in pastry dough.* He tried to grab hope about his mother that she could still cook.

"You make this?" she asked.

He reddened. "No, my mother. She insisted."

"I appreciate that kind of mother."

"Yours was?"

"She died when I was a girl. Overprotective. Worried. One picnic basket wouldn't have been near enough."

He laughed, the sound rich and deep. "I know that kind of mother."

She liked his sound, and as with Shai, she suddenly felt the urge to unburden. "I always felt chained. Didn't appreciate her then. I apologize for that tired cliché. In other areas, I'm more creative."

Which blew right past him. "When one dies should be completely random, like your mother," he said passionately. "Sometimes we can do something about it. I believe that's why you and I were placed here."

He was a bit too spiritual and "world peace" for her. Though she abruptly wondered if he might pare some of the thorns from her rose.

After lunch, Afra asked, "Can we walk? Do you have time?" She was uncertain whether she did not want to return alone to her small apartment or found herself drawn to this tall, curly-haired, awkward scientist? She sensed no guile in him and despaired for his safety.

"I am happy to make time," he said.

Beyond the park, they walked in silence. She pointed her head towards a newspaper stand, grabbed his hand, and skipped towards it. He assumed it was all cover, yet still, her small hand clutching three of his fingers was such a surprise that he feared she could hear his loud heartbeat. With this boldness, he would never have walked so near her.

Afra studied the horizontal strings above the rotating postcard rack, the untouched offerings yellowed by the relentless sun. Clothespins clipped magazines and newspapers face out for passersby. The top row featured two Arabic soccer magazines and the weekly sports rag *Al-Mokif Riyadi*. The next row advertised the Syrian national daily, *Al-Watan*, the Baath party al-*Thawra*, the local *Qasioun*, and *Al-Jamahir*. Next marched a row of full-size identical lottery magazines that made her think of that novel *Love in the Time of Cholera*; escape in a time of dying. The largest selection, women's fashion magazines, wafted from a bottom string. There were more than twenty of them, all with smiling western-dressed Syrian models, waves of blonde and dark uncovered hair cascading below shoulders, several above bare arms and plunging necklines. Bashar might point to them, she thought, as signs of his reforms. She had talked to a girl in the Damascus University café with platinum hair, who, with tears in her eyes, confessed that she changed her hair color with every meltdown. The month before, fifteen students had died when a rebel mortar screamed into an outdoor cafe at the College of Architecture in Baramkeh, near government buildings and the Defense Ministry in Umayyad Square. The woman had shouted that the pro-government al-Ikhbariya television showed a woman walking to the hospital with blood dripping through her hair, so she dyed her own red in sympathy.

Afra saw that nothing in a foreign language was offered, not even the English *Harper's Bazaar Arabia*. Well, one, *The Syria Times,* consoling any Anglos concerned about Spain's standing: KING CARLOS STRESSES RELATIONSHIP WITH SYRIA STRONG.

She still held his hand, which felt strong and dry. She thought Shai might be unhappy with what she was about to suggest, but if their relationship was cover, she thought, let's make it airtight. She was more emotional and needy in Damascus than she'd expected.

"I think we should go back to your apartment." Then she looked up unwaveringly into his eyes and advised. "I'm more experienced than you. If that's a problem?"

He had no inclination to feel shame because he was certain it was true. "My father taught me to think highly of another's talent."

She smiled, and as they walked, she took his entire hand. "I'm generally with men whom I liked just enough. On occasion with one..." Her voice had softened. "But I really want to. I've been thinking about it longer than I'd like you to know."

He was charmed since they'd known each other for two hours. "Keeping secrets already?"

She leaned her head into his shoulder. "I'll try not to. Other than the really big stuff," she joked, to hide that it was true.

"I don't care what you tell me or don't," he said. Overwhelmingly now, he cared about stopping the mass death of his own people. There was no way to know if what they would shout to the world about Institute 3000 would be heard or drowned out by the drone of traffic heading to work. And even if it ascended to Mount Olympus, would the Gods care enough to throw thunderbolts? Any pleasure while he remained alive he felt were stolen moments. He stopped and said, "Only one question, and I want the truth."

"I'll try."

"Were you asked to do anything more than sleep on the couch?"

Her head against his chest, he felt it move in a no.

Twenty minutes later, after he finally found a spot on his narrow car-lined street, they approached the dense cluster of two- to five-story stone apartments rising on a hill below Qasioun. Gray satellite dishes crowded every roof.

"What do they watch?" she asked.

He was surprised she didn't know. Maybe it was because she was from a small city in the far south, he told himself.

"Three satellite channels. Two conventional ones. The pro-government *Sama* TV has the highest viewership. Percentages out of loyalty or fear cannot be tallied. Because we get real reporting from Al-Jazeera and Al-Arabiya, the government began to install controlled cable systems in every building in the capital. The excuse, a call for public decency."

She laughed. "I suppose there is a lot indecent about dead civilians."

The people would not easily relinquish their satellite feeds, Kassem thought. *Al-Jazeera* and *Al-Arabiya* reached their dishes from Qatar and Dubai, respectively. Syria TV reached them from Istanbul, and the Kurds' Zagros TV from Erbil in Iraqi Kurdistan. Both cheered the rebels and rushed reporters into opposition-controlled territory. He thought with unease how his father had so easily stolen the Hama images from the world.

Inside, they climbed stone steps along white walls to the fourth floor. "They better not try and stop the Turkish soap operas getting here," Afra said.

"They know better. The government would be toppled in a week."

As Kassem opened the front door, he said. "I apologize. It's not much."

She loved Syria's simultaneous embrace of the ancient and accelerating worlds. Shai had found her tiny apartment through Erasmus online student bookings, the way a spy might set up shop in New York or Paris.

Kassem led her past a small round table with cheap metal legs mostly hidden by a drooping white tablecloth. They arrived in the kitchen through an entranceway with leather straps hanging from the top of the wood frame. Cupboards above and below the stone counter shone and were a pristine plastic wood substitute.

"Something to drink? I don't have much. Coffee?"

She took his hand. "We just ate. No."

Below a wood-framed window, a small bed precisely covered by a green bedspread was pushed against one corner. A pine dresser, tall like the original tree, with a full-length mirror, rose beside a lamp on the end table. The round wood table in the center of the room was empty and gleamed. She looked at white, naked walls.

"You do live here?" she laughed.

"I work a lot. I like to eat with my parents when it's possible."

She stood on her tiptoes, put both hands around his neck, and before kissing him asked, "Out of obligation, or do you like them? Or you're lazy?"

He lifted her from behind by her buttocks. "Do you care?"

"I do. Though I usually don't, I want to know everything I can." She hinged her legs around him. "It can wait."

Above him, she was like a butterfly, continually moving, almost silent, her face near his neck as she kissed him only there, maybe afraid of feeling too much, he thought, worried for her. Lest he miss, he let her lift herself and descend. Embarrassed as he quickly convulsed, her wings flapped faster. She brought her mouth to his neck again, and with that, as his sounds reverberated off the walls, she tightened quietly and then melded into him.

Amazed, this entirely unlike the two self-conscious women he had been with before, he said, "How'd you do that?"

"Practice."

He felt no jealousy and was excited at how much he would learn from her.

She rolled off him and sat on the edge of the narrow bed.

"I don't sleep naked. I need a clock in the bedroom. I get nervous if I wake and can't tell what time it is."

"Digital or analog?"

She punched his arm. "Luminescent."

Her vulnerability, he thought, was like an open wound bandaged with bravado.

When the sun began to set, they sat on the tile roof outcrop. Long ago, Kassem had removed the screws that held the window glass in place to slide one side behind the other. Though the falling sun was unseen behind them, yellows and oranges silhouetted Qasioun. A few stars winked in the darkening sky. She sat a little away from him and then bent her head to his shoulder.

He believed that he could provide steadiness to help her let go.

CHAPTER 8

INSTITUTE 3000

EARLY AUGUST 2012

Kassem drove into Institute 3000 and what he saw shook him. Camouflaged transport trucks and jeeps, not usually seen inside the chain-link fence, waited everywhere. Soldiers were loading steel vats of the DF, methylphosphonyl difluoride, the mother's milk of the sarin, into the back of the trucks. Other soldiers carried wood barrels of isopropyl alcohol. No mixing vehicles sat inside the perimeter. Worried, Kassem jumped out and ran. Underground storage caverns hewn deep into the earth dotted the country. Nobody had foreseen that the array of bunkers in the hills to the east of the city, above the rebel enclave of Ghouta, could conceivably fall to the Syrian Free Army or al-Nusra. The latter, along with ISIS massing in the north, attached octopus tentacles to everything and yanked down. Since their storage bunkers were heavily supplied, this had to be preparation for widespread chemical launches from multiple locations.

Below ground, through the thick oval glass in a metal door, Kassem saw men in white disposable protective suits, heavy plastic reaching from their shoes up over their heads like a sweatshirt hood. They breathed through masks with twin purple respirators. Kassem quickened his pace. He passed through the room with broad metal tanks shining in the fluorescent lights, each holding two-thousand liters in precise rows like soldiers awaiting orders to report to the field.

He found his friend, Sami, on the phone in his office, panic in his eyes and gripping the edge of his desk with one hand, muscles straining. A photo of him with Bashar at the horse races sat on his cluttered papers. A massive map with string and red pins to mark sarin storage facilities as far north as Aleppo and south as Tadmur covered an entire wall. Sami, a logistician and the civilian head of the underground facilities, reported directly to the *mukhabarat* Air Force general, Muhammad Mitqal, perched atop Institute 3000 and Mount Qasioun like Zeus.

Sami hung up and looked at Kassem. They were both loners, their lives not so much subsumed by work as moderated by insecurities that paired naturally with a solitary life. The tall, reed-thin Sami with a slim mustache was bookish, read ancient history, and longed to have lived in the time of the Romans with the beauty of their building and colonnades. All above ground in the warm sun.

Sami motioned with his head for Kassem to close the door behind him, not realizing that Kassem had already shut it.

"Practice? A drill?" Kassem asked.

"No," Sami said softly. "They're ordering the mixing trucks to a variety of locations. Our people will follow."

"Where?"

"Different bases around the country. Ten."

Sami wiped the sweat from his hairline. He was an academic, a research scientist. His predecessor had foamed at the mouth and ceased breathing after a spill accident, and Sami was pushed into his organizational place.

"The targets?"

"Nothing's been said to *me*," he said too loudly, both

frightened and feeling bypassed.

Several times deep, deep in the night, they had confirmed that no listening devices had burrowed into Sami's office like unseen rodents.

"What can we do?" Sami beseeched his friend, turning to Kassem for guidance as he often did. "They're sending it everywhere."

Kassem was silent for a long moment. "Nothing," he said finally and firmly. It was the first lie he had ever told his best friend, and he knew it would not nearly be the last.

He had to meet Lilia immediately as the world's beaming light on this might possibly stop Bashar from asphyxiating his own people.

* * *

Afra approached the Pop One Cafe in the Alassad suburb north of the Old City, worried that Kassem had called to meet during work hours. He struck her neither as histrionic nor a puppy dog needing a female hand on his brow. A cheap imitation leather bag befitting her station dropped from her shoulder on plastic straps. Her encrypted laptop boasted a host of fictitious emails and volumes from the Noor Library, the digital skyscraper of Arabic eBooks. It was sheltered on both sides by course books of actual paper from the Damascus University bookstore.

Illuminated in yellow neon even in the startling 3 p.m. sun, the outside lights read CAFE RESTAURANT and below that POP-ONE, both only in English. Everyone in the world emulated America after first vilifying her in envy. The exterior was all glass, the frames painted dark blue, the traditional color to close the Evil Eye. Heavily, she mounted the white marble steps. The inside was what she imagined a hipster cafe to have looked like in the American 60s. A cubist painting in browns and purples of skyscrapers in Manhattan covered one wall with C-I-N-E-M-A in vertical letters. To the left, FUZZ shouted. Heads of men in sunglasses filled several pop-art squares. In one, a baseball player swung a bat. Below FUZZ in smaller letters: ASSASSINATION.

A large sign on a brown wood pillar offered: HOT CHOCOLATE and BROWNIES in English and Arabic, a steaming red mug between the two languages. Long tables with cushioned wood chairs filled one side of the room. Several young men smoked shisha molasses tobacco from hookahs. She smiled. Two had laptops open, so Kassem had chosen astutely for a young, hip couple. The shisha scent was heavy and sweet. A wall featured photos of fare described only in Arabic. The food was a collision of the West and the Middle East: sandwiches in long Syrian rolls, pizzas, potatoes swimming in melted cheese, deep-fried chicken rolls, and french fries with sides of spicy red dipping sauce. A small chalkboard on the counter displayed the Wi-Fi password.

To her left, vinyl-cushioned chairs circled small square tables. A kind of despair weighed on her as she waited, not knowing what had happened. She adored this café, but so much of Damascus pretended the country was not being ripped apart like a fine garment.

She approached a waiter, ordered black coffee, and asked, "What does Pop-One mean?"

"It is inspired by the English word *popular*. It means the popular one."

She smiled. "That's why I'm here. My boyfriend heard from friends this place was something to see."

Shai had told her, "Plain sight is the ticket. Don't sneak around. Meet him in public. You want to hold hands. I'm sure he won't complain. Nobody will pick up this signal the way it's configured, but don't send from the apartment as a precaution."

Afra eased into one of the corner soft leather chairs, gracefully tucked her legs under her, and set up shop, first the books and then a pad and pen to dash off a student's thoughts.

She logged into the Wi-Fi to tap into the antenna array in Herzlia on the coast north of Tel Aviv.

Kassem hurried in, distraught and even a bit disheveled, she realized. Though not known to cafe goers, to appraised watchers, he was undoubtedly a face in their files, Shai had warned, and there's no shortage on their payroll of watchers.

As he reached her, which was soon given his velocity and long stride, she rose, threw her arms around his neck, and had to pull herself up to reach his ear. "We'll handle it. Whatever it is." She kissed his neck and ruffled his hair giving its disarray provenance.

At that instant, he saw her flashing warning lights and pictured how a young Fuad would have entered to greet a contact. He laughed out loud at himself. "I'm just excited to see you again," he said by way of cover and newfound courage, placed both hands on her waist, lifted her, and kissed her. She circled her arms around his neck, pulled herself tighter to him, and found herself shaking a little against him, her lips remaining on his.

He set her back in her chair without her feet landing. "I'll order," he said, meaning before I tell you, I see now.

"I have coffee coming."

"Something else?"

"Whatever you choose."

While he ordered, she opened a book. Soon he returned with a tray bearing a *kanafeh*, a cheese pastry with lines of rose-scented syrup back and forth across it. His mouth was dry, and he didn't think he could eat. She set the book upside down, pages open like a fan. She had loved *kanafeh* as a child. She often inhaled sweets when off-center, which was often, and the next day ran long distances outside to destroy the calories. While sprinting, she often shouted out loud at herself.

Afra reached across the table, lifted his fork, and stabbed into the square pastry. The *akawi* cheese came away in strings, smooth and chewy. They truly were one region, cleaved only by the machinations of men; *akawi* was named for the port city of Akko in northern Israel. A little salty, not overly sweet, a bit like her, Shai might have said. It was heavenly though she doubted he'd go that far in any comparison, though maybe he would.

"I can share," she said.

"No, please. I don't want to deny a moment of your pleasure."

"Good choice."

He watched her demolish the dessert. Her coffee arrived, and she made no move for it. He had never met a girl—a woman, he reminded himself—like her. She was less afraid than he, did as she pleased without concern for how it looked, and even less for what he and others thought. He wondered if what he felt for her, the excitement, was real or a fantasy flight from all the horror, danger, and now increased isolation.

When she was done, she drained the coffee, which had cooled, in one long pull.

"I'm going to the bathroom," she said. She slid her notebook and pen towards him, and he understood he should write it to circumvent any unlikely electronic ears here.

When she returned, she said, "Just let me send a quick email to my partner on this paper." She pushed a book toward him on the importance of education in the medieval philosophy of Al-Jahiz, Al-Farabi, and Avicenna. She launched the email to her workmate first.

* * *

Shai sat in his office watching a recorded replay of a CNN broadcast ten days before, August 20, 2012, worked up for him by the burrowers in Mossad headquarters in Herzlia. Obama was answering reporters' questions in the press briefing room, a superfluous American flag as always at his side. In a non-scripted answer, Obama spoke with offhand elegance:

"We cannot have a situation where chemical and

biological weapons are falling into the hands of the wrong people. We have been very clear to the Assad regime and to other players on the ground that a *red line* for us is that we start seeing a bunch of chemical weapons being moved around or used. That would change my calculus. That would change my equation."

Kassem's warning had bounded across the globe from Damascus to Herzlia to McE in Washington and emerged from Obama. Shai could not have scripted Obama's words better and marveled at the majesty behind the restrained threat. Shai saw the seismic pressures bearing on the American president, how his conscience wrestled with the daily slaughter in Syria while bearing the burden of the continuing war in Iraq and American boys exploded in IEDs. Shai felt Obama's frustration as he absorbed the clarion call from his closest European allies not to involve them in another U.S.-led adventure in the Middle East. Previously failed forays in the region, the only kind Washington ever launched, had yanked the teeth from Obama's tiger. Yet standing still in full view of the carnage challenged everything Obama believed in.

Shai walked into the Mossad chief Levi Goodman's Jerusalem office to share McE's phone conversation of an hour before. The discomfort in Shai's frontal lobe was more like an unwanted guest than a headache, not shouting but someone often in his house he could not easily dislodge. He reluctantly admitted that Tami's breathing exercises helped. In Shai's long sojourn in the Service, Goodman was his third chief, not much younger than Shai himself. Born in Johannesburg, Goodman had skied down Tiffindell, the highest peak in Cape Province, and plowed up the intelligence ranks with backroom deals across the variously hospitable Maghreb—literally "West" as the Arabs referred to their own in North Africa. With word whispered to the sheiks, Goodman landed in the Gulf to barter security technology for unannounced trade accommodations. He spoke Arabic, French, and a guttural English that always required the Emir of Qatar to summon a translator, despite his graduating from Britain's Royal Military Academy at Sandhurst. Short and bald, clean-shaven with expensive cologne, Goodman exercised even less than Shai other than carrying his skis to the Mount Hermon lifts.

"If possible, you look even worse than usual," Goodman said as Shai unleashed his large bulk into the small chair opposite Goodman. "Your eyes are swollen. And don't tell me you're up late reading."

"I *am* up late reading."

"Of course you are. But the thing is, you always are. So, what's this?"

"Don't know. The doctors aren't worried, so I'm avoiding any tests that could change that."

Goodman lit a pungent, unfiltered Gauloises. He was a French Resistance aficionado. In the early years of the State, with every neighbor eager to set Tel-Aviv ablaze, he felt common cause with the French Resistance pluck.

"Why don't you tell me if and when I *should* worry?" Goodman said, stomping his fresh cigarette into an ashtray with restrained vehemence.

To shift the subject, Shai nodded at the legendary Gauloises pack smoked by Camus, Sartre, and even Picasso. "Hard to believe they're made in Poland. God bless the fall of Communism that made this possible."

"Just in time," Goodman said. "Couldn't get enough of the dark Syrian tobacco for them now. Refugees clogging up the trade routes, not to mention farmers busy chasing the army with their scythes." Goodman lifted matches and slowly lit another small cigarette. "Shai, Bashar's not building gas chambers."

"Exactly. He's going to do it without the bother of herding them into fake showers. Get them at home, right in their own."

Goodman smoked and waited, always interested in what Shai's volcano bubbled up.

"There are options," Shai said. "There's a Council of Elders. They meet in twos and threes, so they won't be carted away for conspiracy. Most were in power under Assad, the father. They look to a model of a Confederacy, religious power-sharing like in Lebanon. There's a future there. The Council of Elders studied Iraq after the Americans swept all the Ba'athists into the gutter like dried leaves and stomped on them. In science, in a vacuum all the sparks are invisible. The free Syrian northern alliance is very strong around Idlib, Aleppo. Their political classes are camped out in Istanbul, waiting to go back if Bashar's cleared out. If the fifty or so crazies around Bashar went somewhere, like the Black Sea, they'd be happy to live with another military leader. Only so much tradition one can defy—successfully."

"Not our patch, regime change," Goodman breathed. "Fell on our face when we tried to redraw Lebanon, didn't we? Twice, as it were. Talk to your buddies, the Americans. Maybe they can get it right this time. This would seem to be the time and place. If we can help here and there, my ears are listening to whatever music everyone else is playing. Ready to blend in unheard where we can. Right now, the sarin is project one."

Shai did not say what was on his mind, that this time regime change in Syria was imperative, and not only for the Syrians.

Goodman stood, paced to his window, and inhaling hard on the crackling cigarette, looked out at the park of roses next to the Supreme Court without seeing either. With the present sarin threat, he leaned his forehead against the warm glass, his mind hurtling back to January and February 1991, when Saddam Hussein's Scud missiles dropped into the heart of Israel. Forty-two of them, for starters. Saddam boasted that he would exchange the explosives for chemical weapons if the Americans were near banging on *his* door. Every Israeli apartment erected a "gas room" with impermeable plastic sheeting. People hauled their gas masks everywhere, he remembered angrily.

Goodman turned. "Let me tell you a story. During the Gulf War, my grandson broke his arm." Goodman continued as evenly as he could though his voice trembled. "I took him to the hospital, and as we were walking in, the sirens sounded. I had to fit his gas mask over him. Not only was my grandmother gassed in Auschwitz, but now I'm putting a gas mask on my grandchild so he won't be. It was wrenching. I was emotional, felt it personally."

"It doesn't matter that he never launched sarin," Shai whispered. "When it comes to gas, it's in the gut. Here we go again."

"Shai, I'll tell you something that I'm going to shout to the newspapers when my time here is up. The concentration camps did something to us as a people. Entered our consciousness, genes, psychology, and bloodstream. Look whom we've become. Settlers uproot Palestinian olive groves, and the army stands by and checks their Instagram. Or they watch. Or silently applaud. When they're done with their daily prayers, the Hilltop youth attack and bloody those Jews trying to help with the Palestinian olive harvest. Old women draw knives at checkpoints, and our boys shoot them. Not long ago, in generally peaceful Husan, they shot a woman in the thigh when she wouldn't stop, hit an artery, and she died while they attempted first-aid. She was unarmed. We cannot manage to equip these too-young soldiers with tasers, a chemical irritant, or *anything* so as not to continue to kill old women? Then we blow up the family house and charge them for the demolition. Charge them our cost for destroying a family's life. Deterrence? My arse. When did ratcheting up more rage ever do anything but help it run over? *Our* soldier kills a shackled prisoner on the ground and launches a national movement. Not for accountability but for leniency for our killer. This is what marching a *people* into the gas wrought. It's shut our eyes. Hardened us. Anybody protests what *we* do, we bark anti-Semitism. We're the only democracy around here, even support LGBTQ rights, we say, to do a Three-card Monte to hide what we *are* doing." Tears crept down Goodman's wrinkled face, plunged off his chin, and disappeared into his dark plaid shirt.

He continued suddenly quieter. "How many people are we holding in administrative detention with no trial now or ever? With our long history of being locked up and the key tossed in the sea."

"Three hundred give or take," Shai said uncomfortably.

"If only the Palestinians had taken the Oslo Accords and gotten their state. We gave them everything and the kitchen sink, and they wanted to keep stockpiling weapons under that sink and put anyone who attacked us on a revolving prison sentence. They're taking compromise seriously; would have saved us from ourselves." Goodman's tears were running full stream now, and he made no move to wipe them away.

"Never again," Shai said, his face tight. "Should be for the Syrian suburbs, not just us."

"Of course. But what can *we* do that won't cause him to rain sarin on us?" Goodman lit another cigarette, set it down, and smoke rose from two in his ashtray. "Shai, right now, we're presented with this unique opportunity. Greatly because of handiwork getting the murdering gas out of Syria. For us, for their suburbs, and maybe for some American kids mostly minding their own business on the Washington metro." Goodman collapsed in his chair like a rag doll. "So where are we with *our* kids?"

What they had taken to calling Kassem and Afra.

"They got to us just in time," Shai said, emotional, worried, and irrationally hopeful. "Obama launched his own preemptive strike, Deputy Secretary of State William J. Burns. Struck a direct hit on Syrian foreign minister, Walid Muallem. Then Hillary and Obama, a tag team as passionate as "the kids," with significantly greater field time, hit the airways and didn't bother to merely hint at the doom coming from the skies if the sarin did not scurry back into its rat holes post haste. The trucks have turned around, the poison back in its lair," Shai continued. "Confirmed by a few pictures McE's satellites took once the kids told us where to point them."

"Seems enough of it was headed to Hezbollah. So, we have a finger in the dike," Goodman said, lifting the fresher cigarette. "Not overly reassuring."

"Bashar blinked. This time. Obama's *red line* speech was extraordinarily helpful. Without knowing, it's what I've been waiting for to get the sarin out. As things get worse for Herr Bashar, and what doesn't get worse in this world, he will feel the lack of options."

"You're convinced he'll hit Ghouta or Dariyya? One or the other. Both?"

"Yes. It's the easiest way to clear out those neighborhoods, fill them with his backers. And feel powerful."

"If he does, you really think you can get Bashar to give up all his sarin? That's a tall order. Even for us who have counted on miracles."

"If I can get the Russians and Americans to play doubles on the same side of the net, I think I can make it happen," Shai said too loudly, his head throbbing. "I'm counting on a sarin attack of muscle to get everybody to the court."

Goodman collapsed back in his chair. Now a headache tormented him, pounding at the back of his eyes. "Want to whisper what's eating you? I won't repeat it to a soul. Promise."

"There's the matter of the barrel bombs, the secret prisons, the tens of thousands disappearing. Maybe I get the sarin out and everybody says, 'Great tournament. Help the poor Syrian people? We just did. Mission accomplished. Lot on our plates. Don't call us again. In fact, lose our phone numbers.' Maybe I ensure uninterrupted slaughter by lesser means?"

"What, by chance, did we just see? Sarin rolling out to military bases far and wide. Convinced me he could let it loose from everywhere. Shai, just get the fucking sarin rendered inert will you, *please*," Goodman said, elbows on his desk, propping his head in both hands, smoking curling from one. "I'm letting you run with that and only that. You're on a very short rope. The smallest misstep, and you're sure to get mauled. If not by something in the savanna, by me. There are too many loose ends, the Wassaf woman in Jaffa, to commence a long list."

The magnitude of the potential results had propelled Shai to mobilize the unwashed. He could not be sure how Kassem or Afra would behave in the eye of a hurricane of death spinning around them or what Lilia, torn from her family and her cause, might abruptly try. The service ironed out sentimentality like creases from a shirt. Though over time, Shai knew, his own shirts had wrinkled and remained that way.

"Afra trusts her. So do I. She's a hero."

"She should be under lock and key. Too many goddamn ways in this new world to call Mommy and say, 'I'm fine, and this very nice girl is running around Damascus as me. But you mustn't tell.' Fuad told us what we already knew. The Iranians are showing the Syrians their bag of tricks. I presume you saw Damascus hacked into the *60 Minutes* Twitter feed to enlighten the world that: *Obama's in bed with al-Qaeda.*"

Shai said, "It showed a reach that caught my attention."

To slap down the uprising, the Syrian Electronic Army had risen openly like a sub breaking the surface. They defaced websites. They released Blackworm to crawl into and eat antivirus programs and spawn a grumble of maggots on the third day of each month. With the nimblest of mall shoplifters, they did grab-and-goes in U.S. defense contractors' systems.

Shai sucked in a breath. "She's happier in Jaffa, sea air, a lot of Arabic about. Set up in a small apartment where she can cook for herself. Even though she won't stay, she wanted a Hebrew tutor. She's followed around the clock. She even approaches an internet café—anywhere that sells phones—we grab her. Back to the safe house here. Let's let her breathe. Please, Levi."

"I'd say you were going soft. Except you've always been too flabby. And I don't give a damn how much your teams like you. I don't want a necktie party in Damascus. I never sleep well. Now I don't sleep at all."

"You've told me you sleep easily in the worst of times. I admire it."

"I'm lying," Goldman said loudly. "Doesn't matter which time."

Shai felt pressure in his right eye from the pain above it. He needed the Russians. At their all-you-can-eat buffet, they laid out Bashar's planes, tanks, and Kalashnikovs and, as such, held the Syrian president on a leash.

Goodman abruptly mashed out both cigarettes. "You trust the Americans?"

"They're always first in line for anything that makes them look good. Getting the sarin out will. I just have to get them not to mind that it's the Russian's idea."

CHAPTER 9

DAMASCUS

SOUQ AL-BUZURIYAH

AUGUST 2013

Fuad waited in the Souq al-Buzuriyah for Muhammad Mitqal, deputy head of the mukhabarat Air Force Directorate. Inside the Old City walls and just south of the Great Ummayad Mosque, Fuad inhaled the spices trapped under the arched roof that kept the dim lane cool. The summer sun beat down a hot but not oppressive 30 degrees Celsius. Electric bulbs threw small patches of light on the stone walls outside the ground-floor shops as little sunlight penetrated the towering black ceiling. In an endless row, every ten meters, circles in thin iron arches supported the roof. Maybe because the walls of danger pushed in from all sides, as if he was in a shrinking room, his love for the Old City felt fiercer. Windows and rusted iron balconies lined the second floor on the crowded, wide black-stone walkway. Tall burlap sacks nearly overflowing with dried apricots and almonds rested on the sidewalk, one step up and of the same basalt. In stacked wood boxes inside, crystalized fruits rose beside jellied cubes and almonds that too had whiled away days swimming in sugar water. Sometimes when Fuad felt alone and uncertain, as he did now, slow steps in this enduring place softened his worries.

Fuad saw Brigadier General Muhammad Mitqal heading towards him without his uniform, the way they met privately. Mitqal reminded Fuad of the copper horseman weathervanes that topped the *qubbat al-khadra* green domes in the palaces built in the 8th through 10th centuries. In addition to predicting storms, the caliph believed that if the rider's lance pointed in a given direction, it was from there that rebels would appear. Fuad thought of Mitqal as a weathervane who turned and joined the prevailing wind—which might make him useful.

By prearrangement, Fuad entered the open glass door of the perfume shop. Grasse and Nieuw perfumes from France and Amsterdam no longer graced the shelves, the civil war also strangling the tourist trade, and the space abandoned to Damascus Rose Water. Even in calmer times, the essence of crushed petals, once dabbed on the throats of Assyrian queens, brought the shopkeepers twice the reward of their counterparts from Grasse. Workers sacrificed legions of flowers for their resilient scent.

Of course, he had come here with Margaret in a late 19th Century dress he had pressed upon her despite her protests, beige and floor length with Syrian red stitching around the cuffs, her cross dangling below a red string neck. In her two-week escape, she rejoiced in everything sensual, from him to Mansaf al-Melechi, lamb, bulgur wheat, and yogurt; to the sweetest Kunafah, cheese-filled crunch knefe dough drenched in sugar syrup and flavored with orange blossom water. An hour-and-a-half each morning in the indoor pool, her long arms like a windmill, she actually shed weight. She had snatched the expensive rosewater in her hotel room, laughed like a sly child, and splashed it empty on both of them. Then she wrapped her petals around him until they were one rose. He tried to wiggle free of the painfully perfect memory now, like a snake shedding its skin, leaving the past behind, with considerably less success.

Fuad pushed his attention to the shop. On the shelves, corks plugged small bottles. Had the proprietor not known his guest, he would have whipped some onto the counter, freed the scents and dabbed musk, sandalwood, jasmine, and the orange blossoms of this oasis. Most among Syria's ruling military shrugged that in sealed-off rebel Ghouta just to the east of the fruit orchards that surrounded the city—to hold a single almond was a banquet.

Muhammad Mitqal, like much of the foundation Bashar stood on, was the issue of the elite. Mitqal's father, liege of a prominent Aleppo tribe of Turkish and Circassia intermingling, had plundered as Hafez al-Assad's defense minister. Mitqal, the *fils*, had staggered along in the drinking cohort of Bassel al-Assad before Bassel discovered the consequences of considering a seatbelt unmanly. Mitqal slid over to become the younger lost son's confidante in their mutual grief for the heir to everything.

When Bashar mounted the high step to the throne, Mitqal sought to expand Bashar's paper-thin support among the Sunni majority. To help shepherd this wayward flock, he lured the Finnish manager of the Four Seasons Hotel and his Czech wife. The Four Seasons had strung a sticky web across the Syrian government that caught sizeable deals, and Mitqal hoped they would promote abroad that the doors of Damascus were wide open for business under the reform-minded Bashar and his business-savvy wife. Mitqal lured the guests for lunch in his vacation home in the mountains near the Lebanese border. The stone house was simple, tucked in just below the crest of a high peak. Visitors had to park near the base, hike up to the two-bedroom house, and shed their shoes lest they track the mountain onto the Bedouin rugs. The view from the terrace of the often snow-dusted anti-Lebanon peaks and the plummeting pine valleys, where Mitqal's wife served drinks in western attire, set the stage for the soft arm-twisting given that the Sunnis comprised 74% of the populace and were showing of late they could punch back.

Fuad headed through hanging beads that made a noise when parted to alert anyone in the rear vestibule. Turkish coffee in two porcelain cups was set out on a hexagonal wood table inlaid with geometric designs of teak, mother-of-pearl, and ebony. Mitqal followed, and the two men sat on the leather cushions at either end.

On Sundays, Mitqal meticulously trimmed his gray beard. His parted, silver hair seemed to lay casually across his head, but that appearance required his close attention. Hints of black remained only in his mustache. A weak muscle loosened one eye to perpetually drift towards his nose, creating the illusion of vulnerability.

A practical man of unusual elasticity, Mitqal had been the first to attempt dialogue with the rebels in Douma, al-Tal, Homs, Daraa, and his birthplace, Rastan, to advance a political solution after what he felt was an overreaction to the Daraa schoolboys. It's only writing on a wall, he argued to his superior, *Feriq Awwal,* the General at the apex of Air Force Intelligence. There was entirely too much scribbling on walls from Mitqal's view. Their own *Shabiha* militias scrawled on buildings everywhere, *Assad or We Burn the Country.* He both loved this land and preferred that a country remained for his cohorts to control. Mitqal noticed two extra cushions—without coffee set yet—but said nothing.

Fuad wondered why Mitqal had asked him here, though Fuad had exploited the opening to invite two colleagues. After the round of pleasantries and flowery well wishes, Fuad opened quietly.

"In time, we can destroy the rebels."

"Of course, but they are our people. Their blood is our blood." Mitqal held the small warm cup in both hands. "But that discussion is for another day."

Fuad enjoyed Mitqal turning the table on him. As Fuad had surmised, he and Mitqal were closer in their aspirations for Syria than they had revealed to each other. Mitqal, the weathervane, always rotated with the shifting sands of power, the way he had rapidly placed an arm around a bewildered Bashar's shoulder after Bassel's death. Above all else, Fuad calculated, Mitqal sought to survive.

"As you wish," Fuad said.

A one-star general, but in the Air Force stratosphere of the *mukhabarat's* four directorates, Mitqal oversaw the Republican Guard. To discourage defections from the conscript Syria Arab Army, whose brethren were being mowed down often inside their homes, with Bashar in charge, they cleaved the Guard and set watchful eyes atop army battalions and companies. The Guard was blessed with ample personnel for the expanded assignments. Mitqal also oversaw Institute 3000.

From a long-handled brass pot, Mitqal carefully poured each of them coffee so the fine muddy grounds would settle at the bottom of the cup. Satisfied, he looked up. "Somehow the Americans found out as soon as we began to move the sarin."

"Satellites? Drones?"

"Possible, of course. But how over so many sites? It is suspicious. The trucks were well camouflaged and moved from multiple depots. We may have a very big problem which is why I've come to you."

"In time, most problems can be solved," Fuad said to camouflage his worry with the truth.

"It has to do with Kassem."

Long practiced at disguising his emotions, Fuad reached casually for his coffee. He calmly spooned in sugar, said nothing, sipped, and waited, though his hand was damp against the warm porcelain.

"Could have been spies on the ground, but it seems highly unlikely they are *that* close," Mitqal said quietly. He was concerned equally about a leak and being blamed for one in his domain. "Still, nothing is impossible. Might someone sell information now to secure favor if Bashar falls? I want to examine all avenues of how the Americans knew what they did."

"How precise was their information?"

"Too precise. Unfortunately, there is great belief in the Air Force that the knowledge surpassed aerial observation."

"That is of concern," Fuad said, with long experience controlling his feelings, whether fear or its obverse. The worry that Mitqal suspected Kassem echoed through him like a scream in a cave.

"I have been watching for signs myself," Fuad lied, "of anyone who might be looking to sell themselves for a place in what could quite possibly come about."

"Exactly. As your son Kassem is the most trusted scientist in Institute 3000, the inventor of binary sarin, the cream of the cream. I have come to you."

"I am honored by your words, Muhammad."

"If it is not an imposition, I would ask you to speak to him —both about what he has seen and to look for what he might. The Israelis, the Americans, and the British could all have eyes here, not to mention our former landlords, the French, who sprinkled seedlings before they departed. Some have grown into trees they climb now to look over our walls. If there is anyone disloyal, I don't want him to become suspicious that I am speaking to Kassem. I am not sure how your son will react to being asked by me to report on others. Better if it comes from you. When will you next see him?"

"We sometimes hike on Fridays. I can ask him to come this Friday."

"If he suspected someone already, would he have come to you?"

"Maybe. But likely not. He's fiercely independent. If I offer advice, unless he has asked for it, he's curt. Voice hard. I find it highly hurtful. It is an area of my life where I cannot relinquish my self-delusions." Not the only, Fuad thought, as his thoughts continued to land on Margaret as if he would be truly alone without talking to her in the empty passenger seat. "Kassem and I were so close when he was growing up. I thought that we would never argue. That it started in his twenties was a shock."

"Maybe he only began to feel confident then?"

Fuad smiled at his friend's astuteness. At fifteen years old, Kassem had sat on the prayer rug in his room, tears rolling down his cheeks, his father on his bed. Kassem had said, "I don't know where you end and I begin." Driven by newfound emotions, Kassem was on his own path, and Fuad was a little worried that all the newfound emotion might make him reckless.

"I have delusions, too," Mitqal said. "That we can bring the country together without burning it. I am trusting you, old friend, saying this."

Fuad wondered again if Mitqal might be swayed into becoming an ally to save their wonderful people and the Syria they loved so deeply.

Fuad said, "I am trusting you too. I have taken the liberty to invite some mutual friends to join us. Otherwise, my friend, I am, in fact, old. My ears hear nothing but your praise for Kassem."

Mitqal laughed. "You will not be insulted if I say he is your greatest achievement?"

"Then my short time on this earth has been well spent."

"If you ask, Kassem will answer you truthfully?"

"Yes. He will."

I am the only one who lies, Fuad thought, and sudden regret sank through him. He imagined how bearing a son elsewhere would have been—without the subterfuge, the steering his life. To his surprise, he realized that, with their mutual love, he and the boy would not have been much different.

"Will Bashar use the sarin?" Fuad asked, wanting his own opinion confirmed.

Mitqal spoke without hesitation. A slight sadness hung in his words, like watching an animal die while punctured in a snare. "It is inevitable. When and how is uncertain. Whether it will be more strategy or pique?"

"And Obama's *red line*?"

"It will delay him for a time. Maybe a long time. But those who hide their terror from themselves are inclined to arrogance."

The curtains parted with the clicking of beads and two men entered together, both in slacks and short sleeve shirts. Mitqal brought himself to his feet and Fuad joined. In the rarified air above the city exhaust, all the military elite were acquainted. Nazem Rifai and Ammar Khani, men of different eras and histories, ceremonially greeted Fuad and Mitqal with hugs and cheek kisses. Nazem Rifai, born in 1935, and Ammar Khani, born in 1950, had both slipped from the heights of power. Seen as a charismatic threat to run against Bashar for president, the young Turks drove Rifai out to pasture in February 2000, a few months before a fading Hafez's death. In 2012, Khani walked away as Ambassador to Paris, ashamed of the regime's breaking bones in the streets.

Rifai had sat atop military intelligence before Fuad. From a small land-owning Alawite family outside Aleppo, Rifai had entered the army in the 1950s. In the following decade, his eyes were opened to the larger world; he served as military attaché at their embassies in Rome and then Poland. He was at Hafez al-Assad's hip, as he would remain for the rest of the president's life, during the November 1970 coup. In December 1983, when Hafez lay dangerously ill, Rifai led the small committee steering the state. Tall, with his full head of black hair, shot through regally with gray, he and Hafez shared a love of literature and the sentimentality often found in casually brutal men. Then early tragedy sanded Rifai's sharp edges. In his twenties, a dog ran into the road; a tractor driver swerved and ran over his wife and firstborn son. Rifai's men surrounded the farmer's house, the tractor driver and his family inside. As a newly minted officer, Fuad had stood there and said to Rifai: what you do now will decide everything you will be for the remainder of your life. After a long silence, Rifai had hugged him and withdrawn. He remarried and bore five more children, but Fuad had never seen him loosen his love for his first family. In a bond woven outside that farmhouse, Rifai and Fuad sought each other when in need of counsel or silent company. The four men settled onto the bean bags around the low table.

Ammar Khani had studied mechanical engineering and finance at the Sorbonne. His family-controlled Honda car distribution throughout the country as well as the International Islamic Bank. He still advised the country's banking industry and had not yet been catapulted from the board of Syrian Arab Airlines.

The perfume proprietor, the son of one of Fuad's oldest friends, entered with a brass tray and two additional cups that he set down. Then he quickly departed, the beads near silent at his soft passage.

Rifai turned to Mitqal and said, "Due to the current circumstances, the Council decided to expand in greatly unexpected directions."

Mitqal knew of this informal group of elders from various families, tribes, and communities. Its heartbeat with former confederates of Hafez pushed from power, who found the son's handling of complexities at its politest, lacking.

Mitqal looked at Fuad. "You are part of this?"

"I am Syrian. For now, I listen."

Mitqal held his cup in his hand to feel its small heat. It was not certain Bashar would remain in control, so he too was happy to listen.

"I am no longer the young one," Ammar Khani joked. Bald, his large tortoiseshell glasses seemed to shrink his brown eyes. "We have a young religious reformist thinker, the son of a sheik from the Milan Kurdish Tribal Federation," Khani said excitedly. "A woman judge from Aleppo, who is a member of the Syrian Constitutional Committee. A Christian lawyer from Homs. A political activist and digital wizard from Damascus."

Rifai added, "The prince of the Fawa'ira tribal federation and sheiks from the Uqaydat, Al-Bukamal, Shammar, and Annazah tribes. Of course, among others."

Khani became agitated. Mitqal could not ascertain whether it was excitement or fear. Khani added, "We are writing a new social contract. A 'Code of Conduct for Syrian Co-Existence.'"

"That we must all come together, Bashar would agree," Mitqal said and turned to Fuad. "Why me? Why us? Who, if I may speak as I feel, have much to lose?"

Rifai drained his cup in one calm pull. "As we do in coming to you. But we are opening ourselves to you both because of what we hope."

"It is uncertain which way the winds will blow," Khani added quietly, inching forward as if there was safety in whispering. "We are planning both for a Syria with and without Bashar in the near future."

"We want to anchor Syria in these heavy winds," Rifai said. "Keep the jihadis and ISIS away. There will be an opening. We do not know exactly what it will be, but it *will be*. To step in and stop the killing. End the chaos. For national unity. When that opening happens, the future of Syria depends on our moving decisively to prevent disintegration. The stronger we are, the more stable the new Syria will be."

Mitqal nodded non-committedly. He understood. If Bashar fell or fled, they would quickly step in and fill the void.

"For now, we offer to help solve small regional conflicts as we recently have with the Druze and Greek Orthodox in as-Suwayda," Khani said.

"Obviously, I cannot join you," Mitqal said, with considerable interest. Settling secondary disputes signaled both their powerlessness and potential.

"We would not ask to put you in such a position," the elder Rifai spoke with deep passion, his baritone quaking. "But when this opening comes, if *inshallah* it does, we would like to have you with us. I do not care about who becomes the next President. It does not have to be me. My time has passed. Maybe I can offer my service as a brief caretaker. Maybe it should be Fuad."

"We would simply like to call on you two from time to time," Khani said. "For coffee and the honor of your company. And to discuss developments."

Mitqal liked options. They would benefit from his far reach and influence in winning over the military.

"Maybe the only certainty," Mitqal said, "is that we face grave challenges. I am always available for such private conversations. Your work benefits us all. Please consider me a friend. Yussuf?" He turned to Fuad.

Fuad felt like a juggler with one too many balls in the air and was afraid they all might drop. "I am honored to drink coffee in such company," he said.

"I am worried," Rifai said, the sadness he usually could keep at bay washing into his voice. "With the death of my firstborn, I saw it can all crash in the blink of an eye. It can happen to all of Syria." He looked at Fuad. "It can happen to you."

An hour later, Fuad walked alone in the dusky *souq* brightened by patches of electric light on the walls. Rifai's warning had penetrated. Fuad's fear for Kassem was dry and palpable on his skin, as if he'd wandered too long in the desert. Fuad hoped that if Mitqal could be edged closer to the Council, he might shield Kassem if Kassem was exposed and without protection. He knew too that the stronger Bashar grew, the closer Mitqal would march beside him.

He stopped to slow his breathing which took longer recently, which somewhat worried him, and peered behind the glass windows. He took in the brooches, rings, and necklaces, all cheap metal and heavy turquoise, among them an occasional vintage coin pendant from the 1930s or shinier newer coins depicting the Euphrates River dam that had finally brought power to the northern villages. He headed into the shoe seller's bazaar and saw one of the porticos with its Roman columns that led to the Umayyad Mosque.

Damascus was thus far greatly unscathed other than from the bold Operation Damascus Volcano. Last year, in July, thousands of rebels eased into the capital. They swarmed over half a dozen quarters and sent four high officials higher into the sky in pieces via a car bomb, including the defense minister, Daoud Rajha, and the Deputy Defense Minister and Bashar's brother-in-law, Assef Shawkat. For the first time government tanks rolled noisily through the streets. Helicopters lifted from the Mezzeh Military Airport on the western outskirts of the capital. They thundered low on their way to releasing barrel bombs into the southern, western, and eastern suburbs. Shock waves rattled buildings everywhere; dark smoke rose and hid the sun. It took an interminable three weeks of bombs and bullets to send the rebels scurrying back to the countryside. For a time, rebel fire closed the main highway to the airport located in the south.

Fuad worried that it was a foretaste of even more devastating destruction. At the same time ISIS was marching from the north and would destroy all this history, even the Great Mosque, the fourth holiest shrine of Islam. His fear for his country was like an electrical shock jolting with each step as he walked faster. The Council was correct. There would be an opening, a moment when Bashar's juvenile rule by tantrum could be crushed. He had not known the Council had welcomed younger and modern thinkers, and women, which added to his hope. It did little to penetrate the dread that darkened him. Kassem was too near Mitqal's gun sights.

* * *

Five days later, on August 20, 2013, Kassem felt colorful emotions turning in him like the kaleidoscope his father brought him from London when he was a child. Mixing trucks must have arrived early and stood inside the gates. He felt everything in his life, except for Lilia, fragmenting into those sharp pieces and spinning. She slept with her back to him, her small fingers holding his hand wrapped around her, as he remained awake deep into each night until finally unaware when he was no longer thinking. He woke tired, as if he drifted under the surface of sleep.

His beloved sarin, the return to Arab scientific stature, designed as a deterrent against a nuclear cloud, was being used horrifically. It began two months after Obama carved his *red line* in the sand. In the Bayada district of Homs, a hundred had gasped for breath and found none, delivered by a tank shell. A small gas attack in Saraquib, three canisters whistled to earth from a single helicopter onto the road to the rebel province of Idlib in the north, killed one woman and hospitalized many. Then twenty, covered with sheets, lay on slabs outside the Khan al-Assel neighborhood of Aleppo, including government soldiers. Sarin was not so heavy that it did not ride on the wind, which had a mind of its own. He had shared with Lilia the development of new technology: sarin gas grenades and small rockets. Kassem tried to console himself that the number of deaths was still small.

The American president must have considered these incidental crossings, like an occasional lone eagle that flapped across borders and pitched a mountain goat off a sheer rock wall with its yellow talons.

Below ground, in the dim fluorescent corridor, Kassem broke into a run. Soldiers rolled heavy metal tanks of DF on wood slabs with wheels noisily into elevators. With seven mixing trucks outside, he feared something catastrophic.

He found Sami on the phone in his office and felt a stab of guilt that so often with Lilia, he had greatly ignored his best friend. Sami immediately hung up and turned to Kassem. "They've ordered missiles this time. Here."

"How many?"

"Maybe a hundred."

"What kind?"

Kassem almost hoped they were long-range, but arching them towards the Zionists might mean the obliteration of Syria with his estimate of their having between 80 and 300 nuclear warheads, some deliverable by submarine.

"Very short range," Sami said, shaking. "140mms mostly. The M-14s. A few larger ones. Some mobile missile launchers have taken up positions inside the compound and higher on Qasioun."

"Across the country?"

"No. Only in Damascus."

For literally a year, Bashar had taken baby steps with his gas as if testing how far he might push Obama without a backlash. Each time nobody knocked him to the ground, he stood taller and strode farther.

"Ghouta or Dariyya?" Kassem breathed in despair.

Sami looked away and squeezed his eyes. "Ghouta."

Inside the capital, the FSA stronghold in the eastern suburbs was like a woman's slap across Bashar's face. The fighting there had ebbed and flowed like a tide. The army ducked in and sprayed bullets street by street, and the tenacious rebels fired from windows and bunkers and drove them back. Kassem could not fathom the coming catastrophe. The UN chemical weapons inspection team was in the city *right now,* led by that bearlike Swede, Ake Sellstrom. Bashar was about to thumb his nose at the world, especially the preacher Obama. Nobody would invade. The blasting winds of Iraq and Afghanistan had exhausted the meek West.

Kassem did not reveal to Sami that he had an idea of how he and Lilia would help Ghouta. Likely a legacy of his father's humanity, he had never hated the Sunnis. His desire to help them now did not rise from the shock that he had been born one of them, was one of them. He had always breathed this way and hated the cruelty of the horse-riding polo boys, especially toward lower-caste girls. He saw that his father did what he could from inside his own line. He felt a newfound pride and purpose that to help, he would cross the line his father had stood safely behind.

An hour later, picnic basket in hand, but not laden this time with his mother's largesse, Kassem approached the dozen stone arches and Roman columns at the entrance to the Souq al-Hamidiyah, Damascus' largest shopping area and a tourist attraction until these foreign visitors, like the Romans, were no more.

The patient Romans, believing they'd be around forever —and not that far off as their empire survived 2,000 years— began the Temple of Jupiter, to the God of sky and thunder, during the reign of Augustus (27 BC to 14 AD.) It was intended to outdo the Jewish temple in Jerusalem, where that God resided at ground level in the Holy of Holies. The sheer enormity, which included the 1,500-columned *Decumanus Maximus,* the east-west road in the New Testament and now named the Street Called Straight, required a couple of hundred more years until Constantius II hauled up the last pillar. In 634, the Muslims galloped in. Early in the next century, Umayyad Caliph al-Walid I razed the Temple of Jupiter, though he preserved the outer walls for use in a new complex. Over nine years, thousands of men from across the Islamic and Byzantine worlds labored on the mammoth rectangular enclosure and mosque. Four thousand square meters (43,000 sq ft) of gold mosaics depicting plants, flowers, and buildings filled the courtyard, the world's largest area of gold mosaics. Not unlike the mere men before them, the new empire believed large-scale grandeur signaled its power.

Kassem reached the old Roman gateway. Wares and dresses hung in shops behind the surviving row of arches. People and unlocked bicycles sat on the black stone ground and against the columns. One of them hurried towards him.

As Afra strode quickly to Kassem, she threw her arms around his neck.

"I'm sorry," she whispered, assuming he had asked urgently to meet because of last night's row.

She gripped him and kissed only his cheek as he was chaste in public. She was embarrassed by her tantrum. After she had offered to shop, he'd gone himself and forgotten both the bread and the za'atar. Sleeping around a bit with guys she kind of liked pummeled her with insecurity when she cared greatly for someone. If she could disrobe casually, might he feel the same way about her? Kassem was obviously a different breed. Still, maybe she was only the teacher of his unrestrained experience and would be left behind at graduation. She held him tighter and silently demanded of herself that she stop. She felt his love in his every gesture.

"No," he said, letting her drop. "That's forgotten. I need you to contact that woman undercover FSA officer at the university. *Now.*"

Afra had met her at the outdoor cafe just inside the black metal gates surrounding Damascus University. Afra had observed that most of the women wore white head coverings that wound around their hair and necks but exposed their faces; many with loose hair donned jeans. As a moderate stance, various women dressed in pants yet covered their hair. All chatted easily with each other. It made her feel excited about how women lived together easily here.

As he handed her the heavy basket and she listened, she knew Shai would recoil at the risk Kassem was proposing. But she, too, could not remain idle and later watch the slaughter on television.

Two hours later, heavy basket in hand, Afra walked alone through the southern orchards beyond Mahaad Aali Sinaai, Damascus' premier technical college. The high walls were pock-marked from shells dueling with rebel forces encroaching from the south. With all her heart, she wanted to see this people freed from the *mukhabarat* yoke around their neck.

Afra watched through the apricot trees in the dry heat as sparsely spaced cars sped on the wide highway away from the city. Focused on the task before her, she suddenly felt lifted over her insecurity, for now anyway, and with fields beneath her feet, she headed towards the small farm between the trees. The apricot harvest that had begun two months earlier was near an end. The late-arriving fruit still on the trees kept company with closed pink buds.

At the small farm, a young man she knew was Ali, cap worn backward, short dark beard, in a t-shirt, stood at the spout of a small vat suspended on metal stilts. From a distance, the sweet scent struck her. Compressed apricots in a thick paste dropped from the valve into a metal tub, the brightest orange she had ever seen.

He closed the spigot.

"*Qamar al-din*," she said excitedly.

Ali smiled, said nothing, and motioned for her to follow him. They moved along an ancient stone irrigation canal their ancestors had hewn from the Barada River tributary. *Qamar al-din*, the apricot nectar exported and drank everywhere in the Arab world during the holy month of Ramadan, originated in Ghouta, which grew the sweetest apricots on the planet. The paste would be dried on wooden boards, cut into sheets, and packed for shipping. Ali led her to an area where the last of the picked fruit was stacked in plastic crates, ready to be washed in a giant metal tub on the ground. This late in the season, the bottom crates were empty.

"You can get into Ghouta, where the people live?" she asked.

The military surrounded Ghouta's fields to sever them from starving. "I have a way through the trees. I bring apricots but rarely. It's dangerous. The roads..." He laughed at the impossibility of circumventing the soldiers. "Even most of the paths."

Ali's eyes darted around the area, searching for his disapproving father, but all was silent, save for the leaves quietly moving. "I was told it was an emergency," he said, assured his father was not near.

"You have to leave immediately." Afra opened the picnic basket, removed some cloth and picnic utensils, and pointed to the tall stack of atropine syringes.

Ari recognized the syringes. The rebellion worried about sarin with every breadth.

"You're certain?"

"Sometimes they back down," she said without hope. "This time, it looks not. From the number of missiles, it's going to be big. Awful."

"When?"

"Tonight. The latest tomorrow. But likely tonight. There is a plastic decontamination tent at the bottom. They must find their own poles. Instructions too for dousing off the arrivals. Very important information on how not to pass the contamination from victims to workers. If you touch clothing or even skin that has sarin on it, it's very dangerous. They must find gloves."

Ari swore under his breath. "There's no place to evacuate to. No place for them to hide. Maybe the roofs?" Sarin dropped to the ground.

"You cannot," Afra said. "The source has to be protected. They can prepare ambulances to take people to medical clinics. Ready areas inside to wash the victims. Read the instructions. There are ten copies." A heaviness dropped through her like a physical weight. It was so little, so late. She managed, "It all will help."

Ali was terrified for Ghouta, for himself. Two months ago on Facebook, Aleppo medical workers staged a chemical attack practice drill. He had not believed that Bashar would explode the gas on civilian streets.

"Maybe it's just a government drill?" Ali said.

"No." Her voice choked. "Not this time." Orders reached Kassem to join the two sarin elements.

"I usually wait until dark."

"I'm sorry. I didn't know sooner. You cannot wait. Get back quickly. Before dark. But I cannot be sure it will not start in the daylight. But we think the cover of night."

"*Stand at the edge of your dream and fight,*" Ari said, quoting the Arabic verse appropriated by this revolution from the Palestinian poet Mahmoud Darwish.

Afra felt her worlds collide like head-on cars, the fighting at home, years of ears on the pilots about to slaughter here. Tears rose in her eyes as she pictured what was coming.

Though she was not a believer in either God, she said, "*Allah maeak dayiman.*" *May Allah be with you always.*

Ari grabbed the heavy basket, started to run, then turned back and shouted, "*Sukran. Allah maeak dayiman.*"

She was terrified for Ali that if the missiles struck soon, she had killed him. She feared the sarin reaching Hezbollah and their missile stockpile in South Lebanon. She worried about Kassem's emotional vulnerability to mass murder and to her. Strangely, she thought, she wasn't worried for herself. If she were hung here, her life would have circled to where it began. She hurried back through the fields, thinking for Kassem's sake she had to reach safety in case sarin hit here.

CHAPTER 10

GHOUTA

AUGUST 21, 2013

I t was not yet dawn when the sounds of nearby ignition, then the dull whoosh of ascent followed by the closer shrill return to earth reverberated through East Damascus. With stone rendered into rubble and days into dust for the second year, people in the Ghouta agricultural belt leaped from bed and found whatever places in their homes might offer safety from the familiar rockets. In the heat and doldrums of late summer, people tried to avoid television and printed news, to relax, to hug hope, to pretend. Electrical power was long gone. They had candles and flashlights, and the Syrian Free Army had plans to storm the Nasib Crossing and rush in supplies from Jordan.

In the darkness at the Sheraton Hotel, across from the Ministry of Education and the National Museum, the United Nations team leader, Ake Sellstrom, wrestled with frustration and sleeplessness like a bear with one foot in the claws of a trap. Secretary-General Ban Ki-moon had tasked him with investigating the smallish number of mysterious deaths in recent months across the breadth of Syria. Bashar al-Assad had agreed to the chemical weapons use probe after people inexplicably expired in March in Khan al-Assal, an Aleppo suburb. Witnesses reported an unseen but horribly sweet odor and twenty-six dead, ten civilians, and, peculiarly, sixteen government soldiers.

Angry at the delays, the gray-haired Swede looked out his tenth-floor window at the inner courtyard. Floodlights reached across the stone facades. He could make out the huge pool surrounded by deep blue cloth-covered lounges, and white umbrellas shut for the night, like the Arctic Starflower whose petals collapsed until warmed by the sun. He dropped his tall frame to the floor and did push-ups. Sellstrom's team had yet to be granted access to any sites to scoop up soil samples. He had hoped they would only be here a few weeks. Into his third month, he had nothing to show for their stay in this obscenely opulent hotel while people across the country starved.

Suddenly he heard a noise like a loud backfire or fireworks. He went to the window but saw nothing. His view was south. Sellstrom walked quickly to the bathroom whose corner window opened to the north and Mount Qasioun. He saw the fire from the tails visible in the blackness as the missiles arced south and east a short distance and then dropped. He stood mesmerized and terrified because there were no explosions less than five kilometers away as the tail glow descended below his line of sight. That really scared him. He ran to the phone to rouse his team. He was going out there *now*, permission be damned.

The siege against this Sunni rebel stronghold had scattered the population like rats bolting from a flame-licked building. Now a ring of regime tanks and troops blocked all departure. People boiled weeds to eat. Children roamed the streets like wolf cubs searching for a teat. Even the garbage they poked through offered no sustenance as those on two feet had already licked there. The Covert Intelligence Command Center in nearby Jordan, staffed by the CIA, the General Intelligence Presidency of the Kingdom of Saudi Arabia,

Jordan's General Intelligence Directorate, with an occasional furtive visit from the increasingly restless Israeli Deputy Director of Operations, Shai Shaham, saw nothing of note on their screens that dawn. Rocket fire often lifted with a flash of light from the hills north of Damascus and arced a short distance eastward, or southward. This barrage was more extensive than most, like rage trying to assuage frustration at the recalcitrant. Such rage succeeded no better than in marriages.

Everybody on the ground, those who survived, reported the same surprise at the near silence. After the dull landings, this time, no explosions rocked the buildings. One elderly man, who had survived Hafez and remembered Hama, came out from under his bed wondering if all the rockets could have misfired. Had young rebels sabotaged them all before launch, he asked himself gleefully. Then tears involuntarily dripped down his cheeks. That was too good to be true. Allah had turned his face from Syria. The soft booming continued and continued. A muffled hour passed for those farther away and not yet dead. The old man had heard confusing loud thumps. Then one landed near his home, which shook gently.

After that hour, the climbing sun gradually brightened the horizon. As if exhausted, the black plumes refused to rise in the sky and dropped and blanketed the ground. The old man crumpled dead on the spot and did not hear the approaching regime conventional bombers. Designed for World War I trench warfare, chemical gas was heavier than air and sank to where people were breathing.

A younger man, 24, not a rebel, not a believer in Bashar, but an artist who captured the struggle on canvas, staggered outside gasping. His breathing inside had been like acid screeching down his throat. He inhaled hard over and over noisily, but his throat was blocked, and nothing entered. His head pounded. The street spun. He was strong, lifted heavy weights, and pulled himself up repeatedly on the door frame. It felt like daggers struck his eyes. He wanted to vomit. Choking, he noticed the smoke hovering at the ground in the distance though the air was clear on his street. Suddenly a rasping breath drove through. He put both hands on the sides of his head and sucked life in. Instinctively he ran towards a hill to get above the dark death. As he forced one heavy leg in front of the other, bodies lay still in the street, eyes bulging. Blood tracked from a young girl's eyes and nose. He stumbled at the end of the block and heard voices inside a lower floor of a tall building. Crying, wailing. Mortar shells shrieked towards him and exploded on all sides, destroying buildings as dust and pieces of homes soared.

He staggered inside and skidded on blood. A woman in traditional dress threw buckets of water at her screaming children. Men pounded the chests of people lying in the blood. An old man with a long gray beard like a ghost stabbed the young intruder's shoulder through his shirt with a syringe. The old man shouted, "We have to get to higher floors." He did not know how he knew; he just did. The artist felt lopsided like a stroke had contorted his face. Fury coursed through him like a new friend as he ran and stumbled up the stone stair hall. For the first time, he craved an AK-47.

As they emerged on the roof, they saw makeshift ambulances, cars, and flatbed trucks with lights and sirens racing to take people to the hospital and nearby clinics. To his surprise, he saw two buses similarly outfitted.

Nearer, those sounds were drowned out by the crunching of tank tracks tearing up the streets as they came for those who had emerged. Free Syrian Army fighters, some in gas masks, appeared, and the tanks charged after them like parents after mischievous children. Lured to explosive devices, the lumbering giants rose into the air in flames and then crashed back loudly, their flight inordinately brief. This smoke rose.

Regime troops arrived clad entirely in chemical gear, looking like giant black insects, their eyes behind gas masks. As the sarin dissipated, men of every age in bulletproof vests spilled from the buildings firing AK-47s and M4 assault rifles. Regime troops greeted them with mortars. The ragtag group hurled grenades. The heavily clad Bashar troops could not maneuver in the narrow streets and were cut down on block after block. Russian-manufactured tank shells loudly decimated buildings. Then the tanks themselves were hit by American anti-tank devices and set ablaze in the street, the smell of burning everywhere. A regime soldier on fire climbed from a turret, fell down the side of the tank, and continued to burn beside his blackening tank. Ghouta was on the clandestine rebel weapons supply route from Jordan that circumvented the crossing.

Two hours later, a free fighter grabbed a dead soldier's radio and heard Bashar's 4th Army commander's call to retreat.

* * *

That afternoon in Jerusalem, Shai watched the video feed somehow already broadcast from Ghouta. His mouth was dry as he absorbed the bodies in rows, mostly children, infants, and babies, many in pajamas or underwear. Without visible injuries, they looked like the Angel of Death had winged over them, hand outstretched as they slept. White foamed from some mouths and noses, but most were unblemished and serene. The feed shifted to men carrying adult bodies, one by the arms and another by the feet; they lowered them in rows. Two women in dark Arab dress from head to toe marked the names in masking tape on their foreheads. Orient News, the Dubai channel, broadcast this clip. It then turned to men, like the children laid in rows, these on prayer rugs on the stone floor.

Elsewhere two children sat together propped against a wall. In diapers, the girl was softly dead. About the same age, three or four, tape secured an oxygen line to the boy's mouth and three EKG electrode patches to his chest. A man and woman sat on the floor, each pressing oxygen masks to a different infant. The screen jumped inexpertly to a man in a checkered shirt, his wife's head darkened by a black scarf; they sat beside three small bodies shrouded in white sheets on an extended length of plastic sheeting. The man's hand obscured his face as he cried. In a green floral dress, a young girl of maybe ten lay dead as a man held her head up to the telephone video. Blood clogged one nostril, her lips white; both eyes slid into her head. A small boy sat against the wall, a tuft of brown hair peeking through head bandages. Pock-marked and red, his face was ruined. Blood congealed below one eye, both pupils screaming. Another girl, maybe seven, held a portable oxygen mask to a younger mouth, likely a sister, and cradled her to her chest with one arm.

Everywhere rescue workers poured water on the faces of those newly hurried in. Some shook in spasms, some screamed, and some moaned. Some soon stopped breathing. Slippers had been eased from all the dead of all ages in preparation for washing their feet before mass burial. Everywhere Shai saw the dead in straight rows. Preliminary estimates, an announcer intoned, were a thousand killed, and numbers were expected to climb.

The feed switched to a spent chemical bomb in the dirt, a massive 330mm surface-to-surface rocket Shai recognized with such rage that he thought his head might literally split. Like a torpedo propeller, the fins at the top stabilized the descent, stem to stern 2200 meters. After the fins came the motor housed in a long round metal encasing, followed by the amber warhead. On impact, a soft explosive charge detonated and the thin metal casing disintegrated. Then sixty liters of sarin fled the two containers. Shai bet some old M-14 Soviet 140mm rockets mounted on trucks with a maximum range of 9.8 kilometers, a little over six American miles, had been mobilized for the near target, where precision was optional.

Outside on the pavement a bevy of volunteers dipped cups in buckets and washed the injured. This was all wobbly bystander footage forwarded to friendly news agencies.

The videographer must have run inside then, the ceiling images bouncing. They steadied into people lying crowded and haphazardly on the floor. Tall green tanks fed oxygen through translucent tubes to masks, some bodies below them convulsing. A camera moved into contracted pupils. Everybody was wet; the floor puddled from washing off the sarin. Outside again, dead animals filled the screen—dogs with blood running from their mouths, pigeons after abrupt unguided landings. Beside a small cinderblock building with a large square hole in the wall, three dozen sheep lay tangled in the dirt, some mouths desperately open. Sounds of sirens rose during the presenter's pauses.

Shai darkened the small TV screen in his office. He wanted to talk to his son, who would see some of this in his electronic universe and should, but later. Shai hurried through the shocked hall, people speaking in a symphony of ranges from whispered flutes to the rise of violins to angry percussion. When he heard his name called, even by Goodman, Shai did not respond or was slow.

Outside, in air that he was fortunate to breathe, he walked without a destination or clear thoughts. Tears tracked down his face when he stopped at an intersection to slow his breath.

An hour later, his legs aching, Shai collapsed at an outdoor cafe in the Old City behind the Church of the Holy Sepulcher. The proprietor arrived and hardly heard him, Shai thought as he ordered an espresso, which must have been right because soon he noticed a small, drained porcelain cup before him. Packs on their backs, Palestinian school boys played in the stone lane. Bells from the black cupola sang on the hour and began their deep chant. To the left stood a postcard stand. To his right, in front of the coffee bar, a large table with mounds of oranges and pomegranates. The Palestinian shopkeepers immediately recognized Israelis and spoke Hebrew. Colorful shawls and small carpets hung behind Shai. Leather purses and backpacks of a startling breadth of quality—you had to know which to pluck down, Shai thought, fingering the rose in a vase before him—climbed the wall below the shawls.

Shai watched a small boy hiding behind a table next to a customer as the bells continued pounding. His skin was perfect olive brown, dark hair barbered short, and he stared at his friends down the limestone blocks of the lane with more curiosity than concern. The boy lifted a single finger vertically to his lip to alert a friend not to betray him. A good distance away, four boys looked to see if he had ducked into a shop there.

Down the lane, two men sat in plastic chairs against a stone wall beside a closed grate with carved stone lions hunched on both sides. Shai was more at home in the Old City than anywhere in the rush of modern Jerusalem. He took the red rose from the tiny vase on the table and willed himself not to pluck the petals. The proprietor startled Shai as he set down a double espresso and a small plate with four almond cookies from the glass case between the pomegranates and the coffee bar.

"With my compliments," he said with a small smile. "I was worried you'd eat the rose."

"Thank you," Shai said. "You have time to sit?"

Inside was empty, and the proprietor dropped into the pliable rattan.

"Have a cookie," Shai said as he lifted one. "I'm certain they're excellent."

The proprietor demurred with a smile.

"You watch the gassing in Damascus?" Shai asked.

The Arab let out a long sigh like the moan of the wind. "The Russian, that Lavrov, is saying that the American charges of a chemical attack are well, ill-informed. Other Russian leaders are saying the people gassed themselves to bring the UN and America to help them. Lavrov says, why use chemical weapons when Assad is already winning the war? Maybe this is horrible enough for the world to act. They have kicked away Obama's *red line* like it was chalk." The proprietor shrugged.

"Then again, hardly anyone comes to our aid. I expect it will be no different for the people of Ghouta."

Shai inhaled two cookies in the sudden quiet as the boys had moved on and the bells rested.

"There's always a chance," Shai said, "for them and us."

The proprietor placed both hands on the small wooden table and pushed himself up. "I have hope," he said. "Everything changes over time. On occasion, for the better."

Shai's phone screamed in his pocket. As the proprietor disappeared inside, Shai fumbled it out and saw it was McEnnerney. He had to push the green button three times as his finger was damp before it connected.

"You got what you wanted," McE said.

"Expected," Shai corrected him.

"Not among your most brilliant prognostications, if I may."

"Agree. Boys with toys like to play with them."

"Russians are doing their usual tap dance for the cameras," McE said.

"I think we can ignore it," Shai said. "For exactly that reason."

"I'm going to the White House later this week. Big pow wow. All the chiefs and a few of us Indians."

"Maybe one line crossed and one door opened," Shai said hopefully.

"Nah. Never works that way. Always have to have a few doors slammed in your face first."

Despite everything, a small laugh escaped Shai. There was an opening now to rebalance the scales of justice in favor of the Free Syrian Army and the civilian population.

The competing despair at the dead and the opportunity the gassing afforded, as well as his sidestepping Goodman about his actual plan, exhausted Shai. He had expected to feel better now that he and McE were about to turn up the heat on their long-simmering pot.

"Let me know if the chiefs call for the peace pipe or

tomahawk."

"What I live for," McE said.

Shai heard the line go dead in his ear.

* * *

President Barack Obama strode into the National Security Council room in the White House, where Chief of Staff Dennis McDonough, chairman of the Joint Chiefs of Staff Marty Dempsey, Vice-President Joe Biden, Director of National Intelligence James Clapper, Secretary of State John Kerry, Deputy National Security Advisor Ben Rhodes, various greater and lesser generals, and the CIA's Paul McEnnerney filled every seat around the conference room table littered with papers, laptops, binders, and water bottles already drained and toppled from the battle.

"New suit?" President Obama asked McE, shrouded in double-breasted white linen.

"Wife had it at the back of the closet, rotates the stock like in a paint store. She wants everything used. Little tight around the waist, if I'm confessing."

"Come shoot some hoops. I'll work it off you. Call up to the residence anytime."

"Love to. Good thing I'm not competitive."

Obama released his big smile, not long captive even in the worst of times. He slid elegantly into a cushioned chair, his demeanor somber before he landed.

"So Bashar did this while the UN chemical inspection team was two miles away cooling their heels in the Sheraton swimming pool?" Obama said matter-of-factly.

The avuncular, bald Clapper said, "After a delay, they're on scene in Ghouta. They are collecting samples. All signs point to the Assad regime having launched a sarin attack. The case is not a slam dunk."

Obama spoke immediately, "Jim, no one asked you if it

was a slam dunk."

McEnnerney saw the stress in the deep webs at Obama's eyes. Rhodes, too seemed agitated, unfolding a paperclip with a vengeance. He was half-Jewish by birth and understandably highly sensitive about killing gas. Everybody was elevated on eggshells because of Iraq. George Tenet, Bush's CIA honcho, had promised Saddam's stockpile of nuclear weapons was a "slam dunk." McE hadn't bothered to read his book to see if it contained a mea culpa, with the "but" these chiefs always appended.

Obama turned to him, "McE?"

"We have a high confidence assessment. It's sarin. A good deal more than a thousand dead. The regime is saying the rebels bombed themselves. I supposed they hauled the missiles to the rooftops and pitched them over."

Dempsey had been arguing that if they charged into Syria's quicksand, they'd sink and disappear. Now his face reddened with the convert's conviction. "We can't remain on the sidelines any longer. We need to take decisive action. Even if we cannot predict the outcome with any certainty."

"I'm concerned about the UN inspectors," Obama interjected. "Can something be done to get them out of Damascus before we launch?"

Kerry spoke softly. "They're going to say they want to finish. They'll need maybe three days."

"We cannot wait any longer than that," a miscellaneous general said. "Enough pussyfooting. We need to hit them hard, a lesson they'll feel. Otherwise, we're complicit in mass murder."

Clapper said, "They may already be moving civilians into the potential targets to deter us. They like to crowd prisoners into the military airports, make them sleep on the runways."

"They could, even will," McE informed. "But haven't yet."

Obama looked at him, absorbed this contentedly as if he was at the law school podium and McEnnerney his star student.

McDonough said, "Legally, we're on thin ice. Congress is demanding approval. The real question is, what happens the morning after? What'll this petulant boy, Bashar, do? Drop all hell from the skies?" He turned to the boss. "Are we willing to send in troops to seize the stockpiles? What do we know about how they're guarded?"

"*Assad or we burn the country,* seems to be their theme song," McE said quietly. "Top of the charts. More than a few of them mean it. We're not sure about Bashar. Maybe he has a villa waiting in Sochi? My take, he does—for the nickel it's worth."

Clapper leaned forward, looking agitated. "I don't want an assessment for public release. Let's get everything we know to Rhodes. Facts. What the inspectors have. Options. He can write it up. We'll review for accuracy and sign off on it."

Rhodes spoke, his voice like sandpaper. "I want to see the videos, everything that's out there on the internet. Photos. You're asking me to justify our going to war."

McE saw Rhodes would be knocked about in the scalding Congressional waters if it all went up in flames. McE thought about how much he loved operating hidden in his leafy apple orchards with an encrypted sat phone.

Obama said, "I want that UN team out of there by tomorrow."

McEnnerney leaned back in his chair, a little shocked. He realized Obama would order a strike as soon as the UN team was safely out of Syrian airspace, Congress be damned. This was precisely what he and Shai had hoped for. It seemed that if not for the mortal danger to the UN inspectors from missiles, ours and theirs, Obama would have pushed the 6th Fleet button on the spot.

"Get me Ban," Obama said to McDonough. *Now.*" Ban Ki-moon, UN Secretary General. As McDonough grabbed a phone, Obama drummed his fingers on the polished conference table.

When Ki-moon came on the line, Obama put the call on speaker as he often did for the assembled.

Obama pressed that they needed the UN team flown to

safety now, yesterday, immediately.

"I cannot," Ki-moon said with the equanimity of a Buddhist monk. "Mister President, you must understand. They need to finish their work. Many sides make many claims. It is crucial that we fully determine what has occurred."

"I cannot overstate the importance of their not remaining in Syria for a lengthy period," Obama said.

"Forgive me. One minute, please," Ki-moon said.

McE could hear a muffled conversation in Ki-moon's office. Sounded like French.

"I'm afraid they will need three days. Regrettably, they could not secure the authority to visit the site for five days. It is complicated, as always. That is not what I would wish. They could not go in while the government was shelling."

"What's Bashar agreed to?"

"A cease-fire for five hours today. Then the same for the following three days. The government is guaranteeing the team's safety only through no man's land. They cannot go to the other side. Sellestrom wants to finish."

"Ban, I need them to leave by tomorrow night."

"It is impossible. I am deeply sorry, Mister President. Three days. They must have three days. I now have a meeting. But please call for updates about their progress as you wish."

"Where are the Brits?" Obama asked after Ki-Moon disconnected.

"They're voting Thursday," Rhodes said. "August 29. Three days from now, so that syncs with the UN team's timeline. Exactly seven days ahead of the President's meeting with Putin at the G20 in Saint Petersburg. So everyone is looking at the ducks through the same sights. Cameron says he can deliver a vote for military action against Syria. His party obviously holds the majority. We're moving fast."

Joe Biden spoke. "I've talked to Cameron. He wants to launch immediately after the vote. Night of the 29th, morning of the 30th."

Obama rose. "So I need you boys to figure out where we

hit. Don't be shy about a target assessment. Quietly make that ready."

After a moment of collective silence, a chorus of "Yes, Sir" sounded through the room.

Obama turned to McE. "I have some time now. Let's shoot a few. Someone will have some shoes you can squeeze into."

"Sure, Mister President. Can't say I have anything more important to do."

Shortly after he moved in, Obama had yellow lines painted and baskets added at both ends to the outdoor chain-link and pine-surrounded tennis court. The existing indoor court only had room for a single basket. The white tennis markings remained, and the low net could still be rolled out from the adjacent pavilion.

Obama had sent the Secret Service packing. As the two of them came out on the green surface, the only sound was the whistle of a sparrow above the President rhythmically bouncing the ball as they stood at one end.

"See McE," Obama said, nodding towards the heavy blue padding that covered the pole from below the net to the ground. "They said I agreed to this. I can charge to the basket through LeBron James, anybody I want."

"Good decision, sir. I presume not the wounded warriors?"

The President released his smile. "I do hold the line at wheelchairs." Obama banked a ball off the backboard that dropped softly through the netting. After it hit the ground, he let it roll. "Your opinion McE. Not the Agency's. Nobody's listening. Only my wide ears."

"You remember what the Israelis did to the Egyptians in sixty-seven?"

"Historically speaking, yes."

"Effectively ended the war before the sun came up. You could take out all the helicopter gunships, all the fixed-wings, massacre the runways, the hangers, the whole shebang—no need to dirty any boots on the ground. We know where they make most of the barrel bombs. Without them, without the ability to drop them, it would give the Free Syrian Army a chance to wallop him." McE walked over and picked up the ball where it rested against the tarp-covered fence. He arced a shot which hit the rim with a thud. "You'd give the Syrian people a chance at life."

"If we do that, will Bashar use the sarin on civilians in many places? I take it he has plenty of the old Soviet mobile missile launchers. We can't possibly get all those trucks."

"Well, that's the question, now, isn't it?" McEnnerney retrieved the ball and went in for a lay-up as Obama kindly watched. "Mister President, nothing's near certain. But I think not. He knows if he did that, your next volley would be at his head. I'm sure you'll find time to have a stroll alone with Putin at the G20. You raise the stick that the missiles were the warm-up to crossing your *red line,* and you're readying to send troops in. Then the carrot that the cruise missiles are a one-and-done. After a lot of insincere outrage, Putin'll muzzle Bashar. Ultimately, he wants to march into Syria, expand Russian naval and air bases there, and doesn't want American soldiers smiling on any roadblocks." McEnnerney bounced the ball to the president, who held it in his large hands. "Some indication Bashar has a set of bags already packed," McE continued. "Comes from MI6. I can't confirm. The psych profiles all say he's paranoid, vacillates, and is weak. Beauty queen wife, but still shags other women to buck himself up. As the Brits have it."

"Which could mean if I humiliate him from the air, he then tries something very nasty to feel big and better."

"Well, yes, there's that, isn't there?"

Obama fired the ball and missed everything. As it skidded with a clink against the chain link, he loped after it. He bounced it back in loud, hard slams against the soft tennis court.

"So it's a coin toss whether he runs to the Black Sea or opens the gates of hell," the president said, slamming the ball higher against the ground.

"Or does nothing, which is my take, as well as some friends of mine. Other than maybe speed up a bit more of the regular murdering. I don't think he will risk anything that might get you to send in troops."

"The Free Syrian Army ready?"

"Who's ever ready? You open a window for them, and they climb through it. Ninety percent of the civilian deaths in the country, more are blood dripping from Bashar's hands. You silence the scream of the barrel bombs, and it's a brave new world for them. The FSA's a hundred fifty thousand very determined hombre. Without fear of fire from the sky, they can put a lot of pressure on Assad on the ground."

McE watched Obama bounce the ball pensively for a long time and saw the tug of war in his eyes. From the psychology of his youth, he was a community organizer, a peacenik. Didn't want to send yet more boys in Humvees where modern IEDs flung them around like ragdolls. For what? To play Taps and watch them stagger back, ignored as the drug companies held out colorful M&Ms. McE got that. But from the American, from Obama's own—unique among recent presidents—moral center, and the R2P, The Responsibility to Protect, the international norm adopted by the UN in 2005 that the international community would never again fail to halt mass murder and crimes against humanity—this president had to at the least decimate the runways, adjacent aircraft, and the barrel bomb capability.

Obama bounced the ball to McE. "Shall we sweat a bit now?"

"You're not already?"

Obama opened a wide grin. "I feel a good deal better when I'm sweating on the outside too."

CHAPTER 11

AL-SHAALAN MARKET

FREE GIRL

U mbrellas with blue, yellow, green, and orange panels shaded the shoppers from the powerful sun on the outdoor lane of the al-Shaalan Market. With plastic bags in both hands, Fuad threaded through the women shoppers, most in headscarves and wearing pants or dresses that descended midway between their knees and shoes. Fatima was slipping with startling rapidity, both her memory and ability to walk distances. Fuad did all the shopping now. It was his duty, and he enjoyed the physical effort which carried him for a time from his thoughts. Yesterday they had gone to a movie at the modern Cinema City with its vast glass facades and broad cushioned seats. An hour later, she had forgotten they had. That same evening, she had sung along to songs on television for over an hour she had not heard in thirty years, which made her very happy. Kassem explained that they accessed different parts of the brain. They had ensconced her mother in a home where she could be cared for when she was a little older than Fatima's seventy-one years. With a leaden heart, he had begun inquiries at that fine residential facility.

Everything accelerated like a multi-car wreck, with one

crash slamming into the next. Fatima, Ghouta, and especially Kassem hurtling at high speed on a highway with no seat belt. Fuad did not believe he could survive the loss of his son.

Grapes, figs, oranges, and apples climbed outside shelves. For Fatima's favorite pistachios, he would stop at the nut seller's *souq* on Assad ah-Din Street, where men sat at square tables in the wide lane and drank coffee. He stopped and marveled at a crowded, colorful boutique, all glass and white lettering only in English above the glass door: FREE GIRL. The Chinese company descended on the Middle East like locusts. Who in Beijing devised that genius name to entice young women, already eager to join the high fashion of their peers around the planet? Ladies' clothes, purses, shoes, scarves, and colorful t-shirts with both D & G for Dolce Gabbana and Victoria's Secret PINK ANGEL were visible inside, copyright complaints filed and forgotten. Mannequins in the floor-to-ceiling glass window sported orange shorts, turquoise mid-length pants, and a potpourri of orange, gold, and turquoise blouses. Scarves circled the plastic necks, not the tumbling three different colored wigs. Inside, he knew from a foray of curiosity, that young women queued for the yellow and orange sweatpants. The only wave to the ongoing war was the pink number on the outside glass: 50%. Fuad thought that if the Americans tried to embargo Syria, as they had Iran, they'd slip and break their faces here too. America had abandoned the future to cultural bickering while the Chinese jet skied and waved in their wake, often holding hands with the Russians.

He sighed audibly. Damascus lived with the uprising the way those in London tolerated the traffic, and he supposed in Los Angeles the smog, without excessive notice. Cement barriers and roadblocks rose permanently outside all government offices, the way unpleasant change always encroached. Still, rebel fighters nibbled at the city's periphery from the east, south, and west like mice at cheese.

After Ghouta, the military elite feared an American invasion or, at the softest, the thunderous rain of cruise missiles, which Fuad secretly hoped for. In his paranoia, Bashar was terrified they'd strike the presidential palace. The elastic Mitqal believed that at the first radar blips of American missiles, Bashar would bolt for exile in Russia in the already waiting helicopter. The Council with Fuad and the likes of Mitqal at the tip of the spear would thrust out his young perfidious entourage. Still, Fuad was accustomed to disappointment, and it was safer always to expect it to come with the inevitability of the sunrise. He got on with his shopping.

Beyond where a woman in head-to-toe black climbed into the back of an old, yellow Mercedes taxi, Fuad approached plastic crates on the ground brimming with tomatoes. He reached his stubby fingers in and felt for several that would ripen soon and later. He brought a handful to his face and inhaled the freshness. This activity calmed the unaccustomed terror newly flooding through him. He had not told Kassem that he found common cause on occasion with the Israelis, though the boy suspected much had gone unspoken. Fuad was also uneasy that his son knew Afra only as Lilia from Daraa and was scared about how he might react to the abiding deception. It had always played in the back of Fuad's mind that if Fuad were caught, Kassem would not survive at Institute 3000, or at all.

"How much?" Fuad asked inside as the proprietor weighed the tomatoes on his scale.

Salim knew Fuad both by station and his recent regular appearances in his wife's stead.

"For you, general," Abel said. "Special price."

Fuad would not bargain, which some shopkeepers took as an insult to tradition. Everybody in the country was less fortunate than he. "Salim, full price, please. If not, I will have to leave a very large bill there." He motioned to the bin of cucumbers on the floor below the scales. "Some young jackal may get it."

"*Anta labiq* (you have a way with words,)" Abel spoke the

traditional compliment.

Fuad responded in kind, from a cornucopia of far-reacting tradition, "*Atfaluka yabduna bishhatin wa quwwatin qayyidatayn* (may your children be successful.")

Next door, beside alternating bins of shiny black and green olives, Fuad repeated the same process for the finest figs. That a new Syria should be days away intruded into his thoughts again, and this time he could not elude his hope.

As he walked quickly, Fuad carried bags heavy with food, the narrow plastic pulling at his fingers. He passed bananas hanging from string and bags of oranges trapped in netting swaying beside them in the strong warm breeze heavy with manure from the fields.

Though the danger focused Fuad on the moment and the possible sparkling future, his thoughts had headed elsewhere. The mannequins behind the glass in FREE GIRL had for many steps carried him back to the exhilaration so long ago on Carnaby Street in London when everything changed. The Syrian Army then had resembled a train toppled off its tracks. During the French mandate, Paris had ferried troops to Damascus as Syrian soldiers had difficulty hitting the side of a house with a rifle. Ferocious frequent coups from the 1940s through the 1960s had left the country like one of those plastic clowns weighted at the bottom that hit the ground at a single punch. Each grand new government shook the military trees of the one before and tossed everything that fell behind bars. Soldiers regularly ignored orders from rival ethnic, religious, or political persuasions. As a young recruit reaching for the stars, Fuad was uncertain how to climb the ladder to them or, of more immediate concern, how to keep his head attached to his shoulders.

In 1967, he had met Shai, entirely not by chance, he surmised very quickly, while both on a course with other freshly minted Syrian junior officers at the Department of War Studies at King's College. He later wondered if the British had cooked up his group's invite to go fishing in the Syrian pond for anybody they might hook. Shai hadn't seemed much of a soldier, freewheeling and portly even then. In what he surmised was Palestinian Arabic dialect, Shai suggested that they have a stroll on Carnaby Street, the fashion apex of a now bygone world, whose psychedelic prints made Free Girl tame. They met outside the Lady Jane on Carnaby Street.

"The very first fashion boutique on the whole street," Shai had informed him, with a penchant for history even then. "Opened last year. A dairy stood on this very spot. Imagine, Yussuf, if I may be so informal. Shows you how the world's turning, and the Middle East has hardly gotten aboard the Ferris wheel."

In the window, three women casually stripped down to their panties and bras. Fuad laughed at himself, literally out loud as he walked through the Syrian *souq*. He had been excessively excited by the tall blond with a Beatles mop of hair in her undies, preparing to step into the next wild attire. Then she removed her bra. He was shocked and embarrassed and even more aroused. Short, he seemed to overcompensate with desire for tall women. A woman entered the window with a paint bucket, expertly brushed a blue bra on the nakedness, and then dried it with a battery-powered hair dryer. If that was not enough, the model dropped a plastic see-through dress over herself. To this day, Fuad loved the ease of the 60s abroad.

His memory was near photographic. They walked through the crowded Carnaby lane, three stories of red brick apartments, and above the shops, a jungle of signs jutted out: His 'N' Hers, Lord John, Chubbies Sandwich Bar, John Stephan Wig Centre. They passed a woman in a British flag dress. He was drawn to the low Triumph Spitfire parked at the corner and everywhere bare legs that descended forever below mini dresses. A Bentley idled with a sign in the front grill: Free Lifts to Carnaby Street. STOP ME, and I'll take you to "TAKE 6." The Bentley rested from its small labors under TAKE 6 in purple letters, of course, the men's fashion retailer, loads of wool and cashmere coats in the windows and inside the door.

"This will all disappear soon," Shai said, chatting in Arabic of no note in London even then. "Who knows what's next? My point, actually. On your patch, particularly difficult to tell. Certainly must be hard to navigate waves in a perpetual storm. Everyone around you capsizing. I might be able to help you keep your ship steady as she goes. A long pull ahead of the pack. Do some good too, which I believe matters to you."

"Israeli?"

"Of course. We go outside, breathe, and Arabic comes in. Hear it everywhere if one's listening."

"I will not betray my people."

"Of course not. I have something else in mind entirely. You're going to protect your people, well, as much as possible. Politicians on our side are better than your lot but not by much. This Golda Meir quote, *Peace will come when the Arabs love their children more than they hate us.* Condescending, ugly. Worst part, my take anyway, is she believes it."

Fuad watched a platinum blond in a neck-to-floor striped mink outside the red exterior of Carnaby Girl, peering in the window. It then became clear to Fuad, like a rainbow appearing through dark clouds. "You're suggesting we work together to circumvent the politicians when necessary. To moderate excess. If it's not too grandiose—to save lives on both sides."

"People of the secret heart. That is the picture I'm attempting to paint. Less talent though than that glorious blue brush in the window."

"I'm not important," Fuad said directly. "I'm afraid I'm not worth your time."

"Speaking about change. I can do something about that if you will allow me."

"I thought you might be heading there." Fuad stopped walking. "Maybe I was hoping. Stronger sails for the ship?"

"More like the captain of a destroyer. Have someone for you to recruit. Budding intelligence officer on this actual program. Young but with promise. And he has some golden nuggets, well, a whole mine, to be more precise. Disaffected.

We've run up some reasons—rage and rebellion at a bullying, disapproving father, strait-laced high military officer. Anyone pokes around, as close to the truth as Van Gogh was unappreciated in his time. Me and mine, as it is, in fact."

"And the gold?"

"A career maker. Not entirely a coincidence that we're talking precisely today."

It was June 4, 1967. "Anything in your life a coincidence?"

"Not if I can help it. So, shall we?" Shai began walking again and lowered his voice as Fuad caught his step. "Tomorrow morning, a bit before dawn, two hundred jets are off on a short journey. Before the sun's up, they'll blow up the Egyptian air force on the ground. The Egyptians, as you know, are pawing at our border like a racehorse at the gate. We prefer you not alert them. Infinitely better for what I have in mind for Syria. Still, our consensus is that you won't be believed anyway. My apologies, but given your station in life. We'd like you to get on the phone and suggest the Syrians stay out of the fray. Once we control the skies, we can take the Golan in under a week. Though better for everyone if Damascus sits on its hands and lets the Egyptians bear the thankless burden of attempting to run us into the sea. You can save a lot of lives on both sides. End up a hero as a bonus. And Syria will keep the Golan."

"What if I convince the Egyptians you're on the way?"

"Then you're a one-trick pony, and so am I. A lot of people make one great call, and the world expects it to continue. It doesn't, you sink. Like many of my disaffected brethren, I'll end up repairing garage doors in Los Angeles. As it is, let me say I don't have full permission to share what I'm telling you, so I may end up in LA anyway. Which I suppose is not all bad, beaches without humidity and all."

"You're not offering me a girl, too, to seal the arrangement?"

"Last thought on my mind. Mostly because you'd be

insulted."

For the first time that afternoon, Fuad smiled.

In Damascus, as Fuad headed home to Fatima, tired from carrying the fruits and vegetables, he recalled how he had agreed immediately. He glimpsed a future and a way to achieve more for his country—and admittedly for himself—than he had even imagined. He looked at the ground as he walked. He had never anticipated that he would risk his son's life.

His intelligence persuaded Air Force and Military Intelligence to rein their Arabian stallion from the conflict for the first four days of the Six-Day War. The memory reminded Fuad that worlds shifted on single decisions he might influence. Then, despite doubts, the generals and President Nureddin al-Atassi were inexorably drawn to the Siren's Song of Cairo's dispatches; Egyptian troops poured into a burning Tel-Aviv, bombed by their heroic jet pilots. In a world where people did not believe their fantasies, those planes had been flipped into flames on the Egyptian runways as the Prophet Shai had foretold. Rather than suffer a loss of face on the sidelines, Syrian artillery abruptly shelled northern Israeli settlements and a dozen Air Force MiG 21s and MiG 15s bombed and strafed kibbutzim in the Galilee. Within 48 hours, Israeli Centurion tanks dug in atop the formerly Syrian Golan Heights, with smoothbore guns pointed towards the desert.

* * *

On the evening of August 29, 2013, Shai, Tami, and 10-year-old Asher sat in front of the living room CNN news broadcast. Shai was impatiently optimistic about the British Parliament vote in progress for joining hands with their American cousins in blowing up some of the nastiest parts of Syria, of which there were innumerable choices.

"So, what's the deal?" Asher asked, kicking the floor from where he sank near it on the old bean bag he and his friends had jumped on when younger from his bed.

"The British are voting to join America in retaliating for the poison gassing in Syria you saw on TV," Shai said.

"Of course, they have to hit them. I saw what happened, especially to *kids*."

Tami's desire to shield such cruelty from their young son had long been overridden. Initially, she had hoped for an innocent childhood but quickly saw in this house, and maybe in this world, that was impossible. When she saw her boy tugging to untie moral Gordian knots, she had gradually, though hardly wholeheartedly, acquiesced.

"There's some opposition," Shai breathed, more worried than he wanted to acknowledge.

Angela Merkel had howled at the moon that they wait for the UN team's full report and then submit it to the Security Council for a vote to gavel action. Her hesitation had tugged at Obama's resolve, McE told him. McEnnerney had not been in the room, but Merkel's warning had spread, low and dirty like the sarin itself. She wanted the comprehensive report, time to build European consensus, after Iraq, proof the Gods would look at and cheer—this time, you have it right. She had told Obama: *What I say to you as a friend is, you do not want to be left out on a limb where there are only vague allegations.*

Vague allegations. In a rare retreat into rage, Shai thought of McEnnerney's apples. This was precisely how politicians took bites of a good thing down to the core until exactly nothing worthwhile remained.

"Some leaders want proof it was poison gas," Shai said as evenly as he could manage, as he wanted Asher to think unencumbered by his father's weight. "They can test for it in clothes and soil, but it takes time."

"That's *so* stupid," Asher said loudly. "What do they think, someone cast a sleeping spell over those kids? They were dead, Dad. Obviously."

"It is stupid. But sadly, there's no shortage of stupidity everywhere."

"Why would anyone continue to let Assad do this?" Asher asked.

Tami joined in. "They shouldn't. They won't." Though after the world failed to bomb the railways to Auschwitz, when they had known, citing crucial strategic targets elsewhere, she was less than sure. And still more than furious.

"Cameron, the leader of Britain, has pledged to honor the vote," Shai explained.

"That sounds good," Asher said. "It will be a landslide, for sure."

BREAKING NEWS flashed. Wolf Blitzer's familiar face filled the screen. Shai knew him well. Blitzer had pecked at his typewriter as the Washington correspondent for *The Jerusalem Post* before his reporting caught fire during the Gulf War in Kuwait. He came to Israel often, spoke marvelous Hebrew, and remained down-to-earth despite stardom. Blitzer's deep voice, though only modestly elevated, came at Shai like a howitzer:

In a stunning defeat for Prime Minister David Cameron, the British Parliament has rejected the motion to join an international response to a chemical weapons strike that the United States has blamed on the Syrian president, Bashar al-Assad. By a mere 13 votes, 285 to 272, Cameron's Conservative Party members voted with Labour to oppose their Prime Minister. During the raucous debate, members of his party cited considerable concerns about the evidence. British resentment, they said, remained strong over the previous false assurances that Saddam Hussein possessed nuclear weapons. One MP said that current British intelligence reports could only cite that it was highly likely that Syrian government forces had perpetrated the attack. Mr. Cameron's pledge to honor the vote is a blow to President Obama, who is seeking an international...

❊ ❊ ❊

Shattered, Shai pressed the remote and blackened the screen.

"What happened?" Asher shouted. "I don't understand."

"I don't either," Shai said. "I think the easiest way to explain it is that the West is tired of wars in the Middle East."

"So they just let him kill *whomever he wants*?" Asher screamed. "When I'm tired, I still have to do my homework. Everybody makes mistakes. Does Obama have to listen to them?"

"Come sit on my lap," Shai said.

Asher ran to his father on the couch, folded onto his legs, and threw his arms around Shai's neck. Bereft, Shai hugged him, needing it probably more than his son did. Shai was shaken, had allowed for this possibility but did not believe he would be punched by it.

"Obama doesn't have to. But it's a big blow to him."

"Why he's the President *of the United States*."

"They say they're worried about the war spreading. The Russians coming in, terrorists getting the chemical weapons."

"That's all bullshit. You should do the right thing. Always. Then things get better."

"It is bullshit," Shai said, finding some solace in his son. There was no mood in Britain to march blindly behind an American president as Tony Blair had with George Bush, despite how fabulous Bush looked on a carrier deck in a bombardier's jacket and the unlikelihood Obama would embarrassingly don one.

"What happens now?" Asher asked.

Shai was reeling. "How about ice cream?"

"Don't try and bribe me!" Asher said. "What happens next?"

"Obama cares deeply about the right thing. It'll be hard for him, but he can strike alone without the Europeans behind him. We'll have to wait and see if he will."

Asher buried his head in Shai's chest. "Okay. But I don't like waiting, and I want a lot of ice cream. More than usual.

Chocolate and strawberry."

Tami approached and kissed the top of her son's red hair that was darkening to auburn. It had come out of her thin and bright. She hated that his childhood was racing by so fast and wanted to hold onto it.

She said, "Coming right up. Both."

"Good."

Shai watched Tami bound into the kitchen, which gave him hope. On interminable flights, to fall asleep. he imagined her breath in the purring engines. Neighbors told him that when he was gone, they often heard her late at night baking. She brought it all to the youth center in Shuafat, where the high concrete separation barrier hemmed 70,000 Palestinians in that East Jerusalem neighborhood so violent Israeli firefighters dared not enter. With parents both child graduates of Bergen-Belsen and Auschwitz, respectively, she was more nervous sitting on the sidelines, not unlike her husband. Kids followed her there in Shuafat like the Pied Piper. If anybody moved to harm her, the Palestinian girls would tear their eyes out. She taught them how to bake poppy seed cake and Sacher-Tortes. Guilt that he was so often away from her and Asher plagued him. He wondered if someday soon he might stop sloshing upstream in the cold like a fat salmon constantly pounded by the current and remain in the hearth of home. He knew he would continue upstream as long as he could swim.

Shai lumbered towards the window, looked out, but saw nothing. He was inside his mind mourning what the arrogant Iraq War had cost the world in subsequent fumbling.

"I have to go to Monaco," he said.

Tami returned with two mammoth scoops in each of three bowls on a tray. She looked at him and nodded, not disappointed. For his next absence, she had been thinking about initiating the Shuafat girls in the challenging yeast-risen chocolate Babka. She felt they were ready.

✳ ✳ ✳

Five kilometers along the serpentine road from the Casino de Monte Carlo, views from the four bedrooms all looked out from second and third-floor balconies. Occupants gazed over the swimming pool and Jacuzzi, which readily welcomed ten with or without bathing attire, over the grass where the open umbrella-shaded four cushioned lounges lined with precision, and beyond the stone wall and steel gates to the blue Mediterranean, and to the left the green mountains shading Monaco. Smooth marble surrounded three sides of the pool, and the fourth comprised wood planks to secure wet feet. Alisher Karimov guarded against accidents other than those of his own design.

The villa, white marble everywhere, even the tall round bathroom sinks towering from the floor, comfortably slept eight or the aforementioned ten or more, if a third slipped between any couple. Other than the occasions his wife and daughter bustled down from Moscow to march imperiously into the shops while he leaned forward on both elbows researching baccarat odds with the intensity he brought to all his endeavors, typically only two were in residence. Karimov once entertained any of the pearls on a string of young Russian women his consigliere ushered from commercial flights. Despite their refreshing disdain for conversation, he did not trust the local talent, whom anyone might suborn. They preferred the sound of crisp Euros counted out. Against all expectations, however, and Karimov was a man who bent people to his expectations, he found himself against all intention a man blissfully in love.

Shai and McEnnerney lounged on the bench at the cliff across the two narrow lanes from the villa, backs to the short, rocky slope to the sea. It was Sunday, September 1, 2013. Vladimir Putin would declare the G20 summit open in Saint Petersburg in four days. The chances of grounding the barrel bombs had dimmed like clouds discouraging the light from a night moon. Though clouds sometimes did move on, even at night, Shai reminded himself. At nine years old, in Europe by Eurail with he and Tami, Asher had written in his journal:

> Sun. July 11 Nice, Monaco, VF Sur-mer, Nice, Paris
> Took the train to Monaco, the most boring country in the world. On the way to Monaco, we saw kids get off at Villefrance-sur-mer. We got off at VFSM and swam in our underwear on the way back. The beach was little pebbles, not sand. Swimming in the ocean was so much fun unless it got in your mouth. Ptooy!!

Shai knew the journal from memory and often recited passages to himself when in need, like now, of cheering up. He agreed about Monaco. He stared out at the placid sea, a bit stunned even in his general lack of expectations. McEnnerney slipped a consoling arm around Shai's shoulder.

"There's still time and a chance," McE said. "Satellites show no movement to crowd the runways with civilians. Maybe they can't spare the time from torturing them."

Shai said nothing, was reading the news on his phone. Republican members of Congress wrote Obama and, of course, released the letter:

> *Engaging our military in Syria when no direct threat to the United States exists and without prior Congressional authorization would violate the separation of powers that is clearly delineated in the Constitution.*

Speaker John Boehner added a personal letter to the President:

> *Even as the United States grapples with the alarming scale of the human suffering, we are immediately confronted with contemplating the potential scenarios our response might trigger or accelerate. These considerations include the Assad regime potentially losing command and control of the stock of chemical weapons or terrorist organizations—especially those tied to al-Qaeda—gaining greater control of and*

maintaining territory.

Shai handed the phone to McEnnerney, who read rapidly. Boehner was a smooth and arrogant player, McE thought, flaunted his perfectly coiffed head at Capitol no smoking requirements with a Camel cigarette between his fingers. Not to mention dead wrong. Americans on both sides of the aisle were running from a burning world and quickly had forgotten how they'd had to run literally from the World Trade Towers. The idea that anybody was safer anywhere with Bashar in the presidential palace was cock and bull. These barrel bombs were the same homemade concoction Timothy McVeigh packed in that Ryder truck in 1995 to flatten floors in the Federal Building in Oklahoma City, along with everybody on them. Merkel wanted to sidestep another Iraq War. Okay, Syrian refugees were already trudging toward her open borders like Mongolian hordes. She probably feared a strike would blast shock waves that propelled more flight to her swollen refugee camps.

White House lawyers, too, were trying to steal the mallets from the attack drumbeat. They cited Boehner's missive that no claim of self-defense could be cherry-picked out of even such a rotten harvest. They had been graced with a UN resolution to bomb Libya, where none existed here or would be forthcoming. In yet another lounging around the table, the National Security Council tepidly voiced support for strikes *if* the President could secure Congressional or UN authorization. If Obama were going to act for the mere morality of it, he would have to stand tall and very alone. McE felt he had it in him.

"It about time?" Shai asked, looking out at the sea and taking a deep breath. When he turned back, his energy was elevated, and he was ready for battle. If he couldn't get the barrel bombs, the sarin had, against its natural trajectory, floated up his list.

McE consulted his substantial watch with many dials

that made Shai a bit dizzy. "Sure."

As they reached the gate, it slid apart on noisy chains. Shai tried but could not spot the video camera. Across the drive, past an orange Lamborghini with a black grill like a laughing hyena, the oak fortress door groaned open. A tall redhead in a long blue sundress with a slit at the thigh, which at the very least showed off her tan, bade them enter with a quick, silent turn. Her hair whirled, and her dress followed.

Up a flight of marble steps and outside, three place settings surrounded one end of the substantial table. In the breeze heartier here, two bottles of champagne in a silver bucket anchored the white tablecloth. Junipers with long skinny trunks and leafy heads like sprouting adolescents were silhouetted against the sea and mountains.

Alisher Karimov burst out of the villa to the patio. Tall with short wire brush black hair, flat features, and quick blue eyes, his ancestors hailed from somewhere along the trek between Turkey and Mongolia, the exact location unclear given the trade routes and various pillaging of his native Uzbekistan.

"*Vas makhstu yid?*" he said to Shai in Yiddish.

"Can't complain too much," Shai answered in Yiddish. "Unless I have the time." He nodded to McE and transitioned to English, which Karimov handled like someone slicing steak with a machete. By way of introduction, he nodded to McE. "Paul McEnnerney, a fine American who can speak for them. If he's not quoted."

Karimov let out a roll of laughter. "So good. Alisher tell no persons. Well, maybe tell Putin some things. Maybe tell Yana too. You meet Yana, no?" Karmiov playfully slapped his head. "Sure, you Yana meet. You here. No climb wall. Not Shai guy, too fat. No climb nothing."

During World War II, Stalin packed up whole Soviet industries from vulnerable western regions and lifted machinery and their operators onto trains bound for the Central Asian republics. As a boy, Karimov found himself in his Old Samarkand playing with the kids of Jewish tailors forced into the long trek from Kyiv with their Singer Sewing Machines. For many years Karimov's second language, Yiddish, outstripped his third, Russian. Thirty-three million people in Uzbekistan, Afghanistan, and other corners of Central Asia chatted in Uzbek.

Karimov turned to McE and fought with English, "Uzbek Turkish language. Me, Alisher. Ali mean strong. Sher it mean lion. So strong like lion. Except when drink too much. Then I pussy cat. Sit. Sleep. So to no give you what want, must drink much."

Karimov hoisted one of the bottles and showed the label to McE. "Henry Giraud MV. Good. Not best. Best for when I want from you." As they settled around the table, Kiramov poured each crystal goblet to the brim, splashing here and there. He sat, lifted his glass, and toasted in Russian. "*Za ada ro vye.* Have much health." He clinked his glass with McEnnerney. "You know how I meet this Shai guy?"

McE decided to let him retell it. "He think, I speak Yiddish, I Yid friend. He fat fool. I like Yiddish, not so much Hebrew." Karimov laughed. "I joke. I love Zhids. Just no, if they ask so much." Karimov drained the narrow crystal in one very long pull. "So story of meeting. I am in Switzerland. Ski with wife. On big vacation, no mistress in different hotel. Treat wife respect. So this Shai guy. He ski right by me on slope. Except not ski. He sliding downhill, arms." Karimov set his glass down and swung his arms wildly. "No act. He can't ski shit. I must carry him uphill. You think maybe he smaller then? *No!* Since then, I love him. Mostly. He terrible lover. Always want more. And talk. Oy, not stop." He turned to Shai and shifted to Yiddish with the ease of a race driver moving up a gear. "How long did you wait for me to show up on that slope?"

"Two hours," Shai said.

"Great. I hope your toes froze off is the reason you walk so poorly."

"It was worth every moment of the pain to arrive at this

moment."

Karimov bellowed and returned to English. "This better than Yana. Almost. She beautiful, no? Men stupid. What difference beauty not beauty? Sometimes not beauty more smart. But not always. Ok, drink with almost friends now. Good rest for the lion. I more drink." He poured, challenged the unyielding rim, and champagne spilled down the glass in rivers. "Need drunk to hear this Shai shit."

Putin's boy Friday, Karimov bulldozed cavernous Soviet movie theaters, and a good deal circling them, into giant entertainment complexes. He was busy given the surfeit of old movie houses in Moscow and other Russian cities. His centers housed artificial ice rinks, beauty salons, and shops for proper presentation while skating, bookstores, and bowling alleys. Inside children's centers, youngsters could be abandoned for a good deal of the day in the Russian tradition but without the old Komsomol youth group instruction on informing on one's parents. Impresario of the nearing 2014 Winter Olympics in Sochi, where Karimov had another albeit more modest residence, he was a deft and fast skier. Shai had great difficulty ramming him. However, he was known not for his downhill prowess but for swooping low as a helicopter pilot.

McE lifted his glass and downed half. "Tastes like the good stuff."

"This okay. Worse shit I give for Yana's dog." He raised his thin goblet in a new toast. "За любовь. This means, 'To love!'" He looked at McE. "You know why I love this Shai guy? Right away, he tell. Okay, not right away. After vodka, he say, 'I Yid spy.' I like this so much. This tell me he will lie. In Moscow, everybody tell me best friend, then try fuck me. And not like Yana. From behind."

Shai sipped the champagne, could not discern the spirit's excellence but thought he might recognize the difference from Yana's dog's vintage, given the opportunity. Shai returned to Yiddish, "My friend McE has brought you a gift."

Karimov stayed the course in English. "Gift. I see no

suitcase dollars. Diamonds, maybe? Yana love diamonds but say enough. Maybe special some such thing, diamond guys in Tel-Aviv?" He took a steady finger well accustomed to inebriation and circled the Orthodox head curls beside his ear. "Maybe antique glass you dig up? But that too I buy on internet. Yana like eBay so much. Wife too. Moscow, we get everything. Much more freedom than West. You want see doctor, you see free in a week. Real bad, so that day. Ambulance, free. Health care, of course free too. In new Russia, bad form inform on neighbor. High scores, university sometimes free. You see movie with Tom Hanks work FedEx in Moscow. I love movies. I tell Vlad. We not destroy *all* old beautiful theaters." He lifted his goblet and the yellow liquid vanished again. "Shai, you intelligent man. I ask you. Who believe the great Tom Hanks work FedEx? You see this movie?"

"I liked it."

"Never mind. It's the movies. I cry like baby that he and wife cannot love more. But so go love sometimes. It end. Not like my good friend, Shai the spy, who will at my doorstep forever. For sure."

Shai nodded to McE, who removed a single sheet of paper, unfolded it, and set it on the table in front of him, not Karimov.

"As you know, Alisher," Shai continued. "There is no full suitcase I can bring that is larger than the one already under your bed."

"It in wall, if we precise. Behind Monet. You emergency, need cash, no problem. Take. No interest even for the Shai guy. Favors, of course, you will owe. Alarms no problem for your tech kids, for sure."

Shai smiled. "The Americans worked this list up for you and Putin."

"And you people?"

"We added a few names we'd run across. While looking at other matters." Shai swept the sheet over to himself. "McE tells me some journalists have noses to the ground about the world's oligarchs. Abdullah in Jordan. The odd Czech, Pakistani and Kenyan. Private jets that nobody owns but still manage to fly. Van Goghs known and the other kind. Skipping taxes here and there. Bank accounts for some reason always on islands. And mansions, well, they're the flavor of the month."

Karimov slipped into an easier Yiddish. "Quite a few Russians on the list, then?"

"Top of the class. Swept all the honors and then some." Shai consulted the dossier. "A woman here, a close acquaintance of Putin. Not implying she's his Yana. Russians, like other people, have actual friends."

"Who else besides me is there?"

Russia's income inequality rivaled Ancient Rome, Shai thought. "Stepdaughter of the chairman of the state defense corporation Rostec has a place to put up her feet on the Spanish coast. Twenty-two billion rubles outside the motherland, and what a yacht. Says valued at 10 billion rubles. That could be a mistake."

"No," Karimov said, and slapped his glass down without delicacy.

"The head of the state-owned oil pipeline company. Transneft, is it? His whole family, let's call it, are busy abroad."

Shai pushed the sheet over to Karimov, who chose instead to refill his goblet carefully without dousing the tablecloth or yet these fires.

"Journalists are onto this," Shai said softly. "Coordinating in a lot of countries far better than the allies did in Iraq. McE and his friends are throwing up roadblocks wherever they can in the interests of our mutual friendship. But eventually, they'll publish. Could be a long time off, even years if everybody made their work a bit harder."

A smile lit Karimov's face again. "So this is head's up. Do what we want. Cover the trail. Bury the bodies. Type up the *dezinformatsiya*. Trash the messengers."

"We have bigger fish to fry."

Karimov was all Yiddish now, for clarity and maybe to freeze out McEnnerney. The list disappeared into his pocket.

"You want food now? It's no problem. I have cold shrimp in the fridge. Big ones, of course."

"Let's do a little more work first before I earn my supper. Syria, if I may," Shai said. "Specifically their sarin."

Karimov steepled his hands together and sat as quietly as an empty cathedral.

McE, hearing *sarin*, which Shai had spoken in English, stepped to the altar to sermonize, and like most southern preachers, he began by playing loose with the facts and then found no reason to halt there. "Obama's going in. We don't know yet where or how big. Assad is sticking his finger in Obama's eye about the *red line*, not what we Americans like to see. More important, Obama's a moralist. He's not going to allow Ghouta to blow in the wind unanswered. He does nothing, it gives Bashar the go-ahead to gas everyone he can't easily shoot."

Shai transformed the words into Yiddish though he saw Karimov understood.

"This is big matter, Shai guy. It is no secret that Vlad intends to enlarge our warm water port at Latakia and much more in Syria. Shoot at these ISIS terrorists who hate Assad, and maybe when miss, hit many Free Syrian Army. Putin will not sit on hands if America invades." He returned to English. "About this I make so big promise!"

"Yes, all that's on our radar in bright blips, no question. Alisher, this is embarrassing for Putin. Mass murder by his vassal with *poison gas*. Just like the Fascists you hate as much as we do, with their Zyclon B. We have an idea. Putin can come out the hero while forcing Obama to be the one to sit on his hands."

"Alisher, he listen. But maybe only listen, no promise more." Karimov pounded the table with one hand; plates leaped. "For this, need food."

He pushed back from the table and once inside the house yelled, "*Yana! Yanala!*" Then Karimov turned back as if he remembered something he actually had not. "How much missiles Hezbollah looking at you from Lebanon?"

"If I'm rounding, hundred thousand. Our cave count is imprecise."

"Not good for you, Assad's cowboy sarin on those."

"It is something we'd like to avoid."

Karimov abruptly launched a wide grin. *"Saving Private Ryan.* This Tom Hanks Alisher believe with all his heart."

Soon the two Russians emerged bearing silver platters of fat shrimp, quartered lemons, and dumplings, contents unfamiliar and unidentifiable to Shai. Barefoot with new glistening blue nails and gripping two platters, Yana had abandoned revealing one leg for a blue bikini. Muscles rippled at her calves, and Shai suspected she ran barefoot on the beach. A small gold cross on a thin chain dropped halfway into her top.

"This *manty,*" Karimov said, delivering that platter directly onto Shai's plate with the clink of silver on china. "My mother made me—meat, fat, onions. I teach Yana how to steam. My wife say steam bother her nose. I no argue. Eat with Yana."

"Please give Yana our apologies for invading her balcony like Cossacks," Shai said. "Tell her that we will soon be gone and the pool and everything else hers again."

Karimov parroted Shai in Russian, and her face tightened as she responded. Karimov turned to Shai. "Yana informs me tell you first, house too big for two peoples. You invite stay. She personally change bedding in two bedrooms to make nice for you. Second, as girl, she experience with Cossacks along Dnieper River. She prefer not tell. She certain you no Cossacks but request not such matters again in joking way."

"Tell her thank you for everything," Shai said quickly. "We would be honored to stay another time, but today we are in a bit of a hurry. And about the other, my deepest apologies."

Karimov translated.

"Spaceba," she said with a smile that lit the copper flecks in her green eyes. She turned. Her hair spun in a perfect arc,

and she was gone.

"She happy," Karimov said. "No want me leave wife, asks nothing, appreciate all things. More jewelry, she say *nyet*, only more laughing please. She crazy loves for me to take her in helicopter. Fly high and fast and low and fast."

"You need her," Shai observed.

"Yes, so. Sometimes I don't wish make more money when she not near. She says if I leave wife, she disappear. She believe in Saints, will not kill marriage." He laughed. "I lucky she not believe in them more deep."

Shai peered towards thick palms at the edge of the property shielding a cluster of satellite dishes. Food was swept onto plates. The cork from the second bottle sounded like the pop from a Beretta.

McE spoke, "In the years after the Berlin Wall went down, we successfully worked with Russians to secure the former Soviet nuclear facilities. And chemical containers, which in some cases had uncooperatively been leaking."

As Shai translated, Karimov held a shrimp in midair as he listened.

McE continued, "We are suggesting that Putin come up with the idea and propose it to Obama privately at the G20 next week. Maybe during a walk around the sumptuous grounds. Obama won't know it's coming. I assure you. Mostly because the only two people who do, are eating *manty* just now. Fabulous, by the way. Please deliver my compliments to Yana."

"Idea," Karimov said in English. "Please stop shit and tell me. Precise."

"We are currently developing the technology to render sarin harmless aboard a ship we are modifying. Not specifically for Syria, but it will be perfect for this. It's at Norfolk. We're very close to getting the technology to work," McE greatly exaggerated but believed they would get there. "We want Putin to whisper to Obama that he will support him in having Bashar transfer all of his sarin by land to these American ships. In exchange for the removal of Syria's chemical weapons, Obama will stand down. No troops, no cruise missiles. Only applause all around."

Karimov whistled, set the shrimp down untouched, and lifted his goblet. "This really big shit." He turned to Shai. "Up glass, both you."

To distract himself from his misery, Shai thought about how General Colin Powell learned Yiddish toiling as a teenager in a New York baby equipment store. He wondered if he and Karimov had ever whispered in the *mamaloshen* as cover at a summit.

"*L'chaim*," Karimov said. "Putin love fuck Obama, not cause he Black. He love fuck all American pussy presidents."

Clinked glasses quickly were all drained. The champagne pounded inside Shai's head at his right temple.

"We Russians emotional. Throw glasses on stone floor. No now. Yana make me on knees and clean."

"What do you think Putin will say?" McE asked.

"Putin, I think love. America troops come to Syria big..." Karimov couldn't find the word and pointed his free hand to his head.

McE tried, "Headache."

"Yes. Big cruise attack is big headache for Vlad. He already decide send superior tanks, T90A. So send what more?" Karimov picked up the sheet gift and adjusted to Yiddish. "This is helpful. Putin will appreciate your thinking of him, even when strictly not necessary to persuade him to agree. He can tell Obama, 'For you, Barack, all the sarin can disappear into the sea. We will walk hand in hand like at Potsdam; again, we save the planet.'" Karimov clapped his hands. "Everybody will love the heroes Barack and Vladimir. Same time, we save the Syrian people, almost."

"How about Bashar?" Shai inquired. "Your guess from anything Vlad might have breathed. Will he put up a fight? Pitch a tantrum?"

"Bashar biggest pussy president of all. He kill nobody without MiGs and Kalasnikovs. Maybe make few barrel bombs with local talent. Putin snap fingers, Bashar bows. In private naturally. *Horosho*, now we eat everything. Alisher, bring best champagne."

"On one condition," Shai said.

"You're not done. *Oy*. More?"

"Only this. Please tell Yana that she must join us or begin to swim, as she wishes. I don't want to inconvenience her further."

Karimov bolted to his feet and turned to McE. "Love this guy. He think people. Good man. Maybe bad spy. He worry too much."

Karimov slid the glass door open again, and given the distance his voice needed to trek, he bellowed, "Yanala."

Shai smiled, but beneath it, his despair was boundless. If Shai had to choose between taking out the barrel bomb capability and the sarin, he wanted all the runways and gunships decimated. Fuad believed a new Syria would relinquish the sarin Bashar had turned on his own people. But Shai did not think Obama would swim over the European wave pushing him back to shore.

On a grander scale, Shai worried about showing Putin, already eyeing Crimea and Ukraine, that *red lines* could be crossed without much consequence.

CHAPTER 12

G20 SAINT PETERSBURG

SEPTEMBER 5-6, 2013

In St. Petersburg, Shai trudged heavily through the 18th Century Smolensky Cemetery. The host Russian Federation had issued the lofty and tedious G20 agenda of "developing a set of measures aimed at boosting sustainable, balanced, inclusive growth and global job creation." Actually, on everyone's minds, and in some hearts, pulsed the Syrian conundrum and the interminable rows of bodies broadcast almost everywhere fifteen days ago from Ghouta—attribution still unreasonably debated. In the run-up to the summit, the gladiators Russia and China had stretched a thumbs down to Obama's motion for the UN Security Council to send in the Imperial Roman Army or, in its stead, a hail of lances. Six days ago, the House of Commons had said no can do to Prime Minister Cameron, their vision clouded by the sand in their eyes from driving behind the Americans into the last desert storm. Yesterday Obama arrived at Strelna Palace and buttonholed leaders as disparate as Cristina Fernandez de Kirchner of Argentina, Shinzo Abe of Japan, and Saudi King Abdullah for justice meted out the old-fashioned way. The window was closing on Obama and shutting the cold in.

Multiple bridges over narrow waterways connected this small Vasilyevsky Island to St. Petersburg. Gone were both the name, Leningrad, and the yellow beer tankers off Nevsky Prospekt, like lions squatting in the savannah. Mammoth ugly apartment blocks surrounded the rectangular burial grounds as they could not be as easily removed. In the densely forested cemetery, withered leaves littered the narrow walkway where Shai trekked in search of Alisher Karimov. Shai inhaled the dampness. Through the thinning branches, he saw the Smolensky Church at the edge of the dead, neoclassical bell tower and dome, flawless azure, supported by white Greek columns. One of three churches in the cemetery, and Shai thought, tradition died hard everywhere.

Shai headed off a slimmer path, even more deserted than the empty walkway. Up ahead, Karimov sat on the base of a ruined stone monument, like many along the way in Russia having lost a head.

"I love this place," Karimov said. "We honor dead. Pushkin's nanny here. Xenia of St. Petersburg, patron saint of city. I cannot bring Yana. Too much crosses. Maybe she never leave. Want to touch every one."

"How is our Yana, if may I ask?"

"Busy, busy. Stalin call Jews rootless cosmopolitans, true love to Mother Russia. He can then kill them. Then have pure Soviet culture, stand above Western degeneration, so he say. New Russia now big cosmopolitan. Yana learn saxophone. Her niece refuse practice. Girl want quit, greatly upset Yana's sister who loves Kenny G. Yana sign up in class with niece, practice with her. I say, six months if girl stay, I buy her saxophone. All day long I must listen Kenny G. vinyl records. Not sophisticated but very smooth. When listen, Yana likes make love even more, which before I think not possible. So I big fan of this second rate sound."

"She is very Russian. Big heart."

"Big soul, my Yana. We walk, and I share news. First, I share this place Alisher love. Czars build Imperial Academy of

Arts on this island edge of Neva River. Big building, beautiful views to inspire. Best students, they send Europe to be more best. Stupid Communists think they can make whole country island. Stop send people Vienna to learn best piano. If island so beautiful why afraid let people out? You like history, Shai guy?"

"It's how my people still exist."

"*Horosho*. So Alisher continue such talk. Come 1937, Communists want destroy cemetery, make yet another Park of Recreation and Rest. Seem Communists make people very tired, so need much rest. They say, for sanitation. More true, not like crosses everywhere. People hide entire tombs, to rescue. Hitler make big noise, interrupt plans for rest park, as leaders very busy. Communism kaput, children of those peoples, bring tombs back. Alas, you see, some a little break from travel. Vlad have open mind. Fix Smolensky Cemetery Resurrection Church. Much damage. More from river flood than Communists, to tell truth."

Shai decided to focus on current exigencies. Shai had been desperate to halt Putin's march across the globe, and with Bashar gone, send Putin scurrying from Syria.

Shai's voice betrayed none of this tempest and came out as his usual breeze. "How is your boy, Vlad? You find some time to talk?"

"Of course. We talk many things. Hunting. Movie theaters. And Shai guy. Though Alisher not mention this name or even country. McE, that name comes out Alisher's mouth instead. Putin want assurances nobody fucking him."

"Perfect all around."

"So Putin need know. He ask Alisher. Obama know this idea about the sarin? Or Putin tell his idea?"

"We thought it best to keep Obama in the dark. For authenticity. Keep his righteous anger full steam ahead. So Putin might eventually, as they stroll, offer this magnanimous gesture to his pal, Barack. Make Barack happy. Make Congress happy. Make world happy."

"Make Putin very happy."

"Yes," Shai said. "Counting on that, as well."

"Okie dokie. We go Strelna now. Alisher need talk Vlad. Have badge for Shai guy. With bad English accent, Alisher make you from Turkey. Small delegation. Please to avoid Erdogan. You meet maybe somewhere? Try kill or something?"

"I haven't had the pleasure."

"Haha. Erdogan have big knife. Think Syria big pie. He hungry. We drive. Not far on ocean. Gulf of Finland not Amalfi Coast but something still. We could go helicopter but inhale sea so healthy."

* * *

The Constantine Palace at Strelna reminded Shai of Versailles. With good reason, as in 1714 Peter the Great enticed the Versailles designer to turn the smallish Swedish outpost into summer quarters befitting a czar. With its doppelganger geometric gardens, Peter's Russian palace held the advantage of ocean views from all its floors, which Moscow was always eager to flaunt over Paris. Despite ascending to invincible emperor in 1721, four years later, Peter I succumbed at the advanced age of 53, far outlasting his inbred half-brothers. In 1797, the palace was bestowed upon the Constantine branch of the Romanovs, who continued to enjoy the ocean views until they were sent running for their lives by the Revolution mob. The palace soon went the way of Czarist grandeur under the people's protectors. It had seen better days. Youngsters first from a youth labor commune and then a school raced through its high hallways. On their clamor to Leningrad, the Nazis parked at the palace and summoned *Decima Flottiglia Mas*, a newly minted Fascist Italian flotilla replete with commando frogmen, to keep their own craft company at the shore. Eventually, the Germans fled but not before packing up everything but the bare walls. All of this Alisher meticulously imparted to Shai as they raced along the coast towards Strelna in a yellow Porsche Boxster, top absent.

"The walls remained but broken more than little," Karimov further explained. "Year 2000, come our heroic Vlad. The West, I impart on you Shai guy, not appreciate Vlad vision. Example, he fix big time. Fountains, rivers, walk roads, bridges all come back. Again like Versailles. Honor Russian history, bring from Riga famous bronze statue with Peter the Great on big horse. Put outside entry door. Now state conference center and presidential house. Share together, no problem. Big, of course obvious. 2003, three hundred years exactly existing St. Petersburg. Fifty big heads of state come palace. All put in little houses by sea. Each have name for historic Russia city. Old stable, Putin make hotel for people they bring. Beautiful, no? Everyone like hear sea from bed."

"Even I would sleep like a baby."

"So sorry, Shai guy. Only for very important people."

Later, as Shai walked alone along the shore and came upon the "little houses by sea," he laughed so hard that he lost his balance and nearly toppled face forward, albeit into sand. The spasms of laughter brought unexpected release, and the pulsing in his forehead headed out like the choppy tide to his left. Twenty considerable two-story stone edifices with slanted roofs, a considerable distance between each, marched back in two rows from the water. Spruces surrounded each structure, and heavy branches shaded the narrow, paved roads to front doors. The yellow palace, four floors in a U, a trek back across the gardens, went on forever like most palaces, given the lack of neighbors.

Instinctively Shai turned and saw Karimov's irrepressible smile heading towards him at full gait.

"Shai guy." Karimov came to a full stop, unwinded from the exertion at a fast clip along the numerous artificial waterways and many fountains. "Glad you no inside. By sea, no hot air. Prime Minister Manmohan Singh. No wonder India so mess. Give long, not big speech. World economy trouble. Eurozone uncertain. Unemployment large everywhere. India want strong World Trade O. In Russia, fourteen-year-old give same speech, girls too. Girls smarter than boys, mostly, so they can give younger. I had wait take Vlad outside. You see tonight, Vlad and Barack will walk, after big food. No other peoples, just your Alisher make translation. Not so good English, but Vlad think enough good."

"Putin speaks excellent German, and his English is good enough to reprimand his translators. He often speaks English on the sidelines of a summit."

"Yes, it *horosho*. But Vlad want Alisher by side. Like Robin to Batman though Alisher for sure no little Robin. You like movies? I ask this, no? Who favorite Batman? Alisher love Michael Keaton. Less muscles, more genius. Yana loves *Beetlejuice*, hate *Batman*. Yana no like violence. Certain things Alisher not tell his Yana."

"Alisher, I want to send Yana a present. *Jerusalem Icon of the Mother of God.* The Palestinians do them up in the Old City —the best ones with mother-of-pearl frames for the Russian tourists. Who somehow all pay in extremely crisp hundred-dollar bills."

"Yes." A big smile raced up Karimov's face. "Russia big success country now. This will be very wonderful of Shai guy. I think Yana cry."

"I'll have someone leave it with the guard at Monaco."

"No, no, send Yana's home. Russia friend everybody now. Israel new friend. Buy Israel drones. Your Heron best endurance for fly over Ukraine. We hide nothing. Well, some things hide. You need address?"

"Actually, no."

"Of course. You Shai spy. You want hear what Vlad say? No need answer. Of course. Karimov playing. World is big beautiful park. Karimov like play. Shai want to swim with Alisher in the ocean?" Alisher looked at the waves hitting in small crashes and reaching up the sand. Helsinki was too far to be glimpsed across the bay. "Cold. But big excitement."

"Sure," Shai said. "Worst it can do is kill me."

"Alisher is Robin, watch. If need, save you. If Shai guy swim like ski, then Alisher stay big close."

"I appreciate as much help as I can get."

"Good. Sign strong man. I continue about Vlad, yes?"

"Little would make me happier."

"*Horosho.* So, Vlad tell Barack tonight. Barack my friend, American missiles attack Syria no good. Only kill more peoples. Sometimes fire cruise from aircraft carriers, kill children. Vlad not disappointed, no angry. It happen. Understand Americans try hard murder only military. But mistakes everyone make. Even Vlad. So Vlad, he tell his mistakes. Example, sometimes not see kaput oil market in time. Vlad not pay attention, move slow like polar bear. American soldiers in Syria big mess. Vlad must send more ships Latakia. Tanks, big guns, best MiGs, best Russians fly MiGs. Then *really* big mess."

"Obama's been trying to corner him about Syria's chemical weapons every time they're together."

"Yes. So, is truth. Vlad tell Barack guy, like with oil price busy other things. But always things change. This Ghouta not new Russia. Like Fascists. Sarin bad for everybody."

Only now that Obama had justification to launch, Shai thought. "Putin willing to twist Bashar's arm?"

"Of course. Vlad grab whoever arm Vlad want. Keep America out, maybe even Bashar agree without Vlad pulling arm off. No matter, with or without arms, Bashar must say yes. No say *nyet* to Vlad. Lose more than arm, for sure."

"There's a ship in Norfolk, the *Cape Arthur*." Shai unpacked the herculean efforts to refit her.

"She magic ship? You have Merlin for this Arthur?" He waved an arm approximating a sorcerer's wand. "Make sarin to salt water?"

"Tying the last loose ends," Shai joined McE's exaggeration. "The machine works. More a question of not killing everybody if say the uncooperative seas spring a leak. After throwing the required soft punches, Sergei Lavrov and

John Kerry work better together than the American Congress. Given that they actually want to get things done. They might meet somewhere historic and neutral, say Geneva. Beautiful views of the mountains behind the lake."

"Yes, yes. Alisher and Vlad say same just now." Karimov swung his head towards where he'd walked with Putin. Karimov then feigned anger, his voice loud. "You listen us, Shai spy guy? You put listening machine in Alisher's underwear?" Karimov could no longer suppress his smile. "Of course not. Underwear is sacred thing. Only in most extreme case FSB put Novichok kill powder in underwear. Sergei Skirpal betray motherland to British spies. Not like Alisher and Shai guy, saving all motherlands. So, must wait for small summit of two big leaders. Now swim, yes?"

"We have time to get through. Not my strong suit. Bit impatient if we're sharing all. Sure, into the breach, let's swim."

"Stay this place, wait me. Alisher bring towels from horse hotel. Only four stars but good. Towels best cotton, come by Turkey. We make sacred." Alisher slapped Shai's back. "Swim in underwear."

As the icy water lapped against Shai's ankles, his toes froze. A soft late summer sun, low 60's Fahrenheit, felt warm in comparison. Beside him, Alisher was his height, though muscled and bronzed unlike Shai's pale girth.

"Big warmer on top water," Alisher advised with great seriousness. "So no deep. Few times *only* some Estonians swim Tallinn to Helsinki." Karimov waved his arm south towards the again independent Estonian capital. "Swim whole day. Very macho. Understand, please, Great Patriotic War Soviets invade, free Estonia, so take whole country. Put tens thousands Estonians on long train time to camps. Half maybe no come back, as in die Siberia. Always they remember. Strong in mind these Estonia guys, which make strong body. Nobody in Russia too forget nothing. Now free, these crazy guys swim for fun. Must be very careful. Many mighty boats watch Finland Gulf, so no bad guys enter Neva River and heartland St. Petersburg.

All Russia more safe than US. Come take Robin's hand."

Alisher grasped Shai's hand, and Shai's heart nearly accelerated through his chest. They ran, feet splashing. A frigid wave slapped Shai's chest. He escaped Alisher's grip and dove ahead, mindful to land atop the water, which he hit like a whale. Every part of him frozen, Shai swam somewhat straight ahead, rotating strokes with all his might. In Jerusalem, when he woke in the early morning hours, on occasion to slow his already racing thoughts, the Russian woman manager of the public pool on Emek Refaim Street whisked him to the Olympic lanes a half hour before the 5:30 a.m. unlocking for the serious swimmers who had demands on their time ahead. She always bolted the glass door behind him. In the worst of times, when he had hardly moved for protracted periods and compensated for it with voluminous eating, he had to begin by walking the water chest high, back and forth horizontally, hence the need for the early hour as he occupied all the lanes.

As the cold knocked the headache from him like a heavyweight's punch, which Shai had counted on, what surprised him was the low salt content of the waves that struck and hurried past him. Russia knew no moderation. The wide Neva River, he realized, gathering at Lake Ladoga churned through St Petersburg and spilled into the Gulf of Finland, diluting the sea landlocked by Russia on this end. In another dozen strokes, the cold seized Shai like a hand clasping his heart. He stopped, threw his weight in a backflip, and headed to shore with everything in him afraid that if he stopped for a second, say to breathe, he'd sink. He raced past Karimov, leaving him a good distance behind.

Bent on the shore, heaving noisily and painfully for breath, shivering with Alisher hovering over him like a cuckold, the Russian said with seriousness, "Maybe you ski too, and everything about you big lie?"

"I swim because I can't walk far. Wouldn't mind those hundred percent cotton Turkish towels, if I might trouble you." His teeth chattered.

"Now, I think you like even bad Russian towel." Karimov's laugh bounded out to sea, and he ran up the sand to retrieve them.

* * *

At the InterContinental Hotel in Geneva, the grand American delegation assured by breeding—if not their elite educations —that they would hardly ever be mistaken, were certain that Bashar's fortunes would soon deflate like a balloon left over from a party. But efforts to speed his departure were reserved for another date, as the chemical caves occupied center stage for now.

Across from John Kerry at the isolated corner poolside table, shaded by a vast umbrella, a bespectacled Sergei Lavrov wore a dark suit, shirt, and tie, all of blending blues. At 63, Lavrov was yards shorter and seven years younger than the peripatetic US Secretary of State, John Kerry. A week after the G20 pontificating, the scents of cold and snow were not yet in the September air. At the small table, the two American state department women, the Russian foreign minister's male aide, and his female chemical weapons specialist all sported dark business attire despite the welcoming, warm weather.

Foreign minister since 2004, Lavrov was arguably the more visible of the two after a previous decade as permanent Russian representative to the UN, with Russian appointments uninterrupted by authentic presidential elections as the US endured. Small submachine guns were visible behind the Russian security agent's jackets, a not-so-discreet distance away. The young American secret service men stood casually but steel-eyed, whether that glare aided alertness or not. They relied on compact SIG-Sauer P229 pistols at their hips which interfered less with running than the earlier and heavier P226s.

Before his early posts at the Moscow State Institute

of International Relations, Lavrov mastered Sinhalese and Dhivehi, the languages of Sri Lanka and the Maldives. He often apologized that his French was decidedly inferior to his English.

Young John, a military brat, his father a lawyer and Foreign Service officer, finally found solid footing at boarding school in Massachusetts where friends at award ceremonies spoke of him as a graceful athlete and irrepressible debater. Expectedly, John Kerry strode into Yale, where his long legs gained him acclaim on the soccer, hockey, and lacrosse teams on their way to grander fields.

"I'm afraid that you are asking far too much," Lavrov said to Kerry, who, unlike Putin, utilized his excellent English in formal negotiations. "These so-called rebels are in fact, terrorists. You saw what they did to the military intelligence building during the morning commute. They placed those car bombs not to slow intelligence operations. But to *kill* children on their way to school."

Pinned in this third day of arm wrestling with Russian Foreign Minister Lavrov, Kerry's frustration scaled new heights. Obama had told him if there was no quick deal on the sarin, Congress be damned. For starters, he was ready to arc cruise missiles from the Nimitz-class carriers, The USS John C. Stennis and USS Abraham Lincoln, prowling off the Syrian coast.

Kerry blurted out, "So shoot them. I don't care how you take them out. But *not with chemical weapons.*"

Lavrov displayed no surprise on his poker face, which by now arrived without summoning. Kerry's exasperation concerned him as it likely indicated that he and Obama, if thwarted, would pile on a potentially far-reaching offensive.

"But you see, John," Lavrov said with the air of a school marm enlightening an intelligent but headstrong pupil. "In the way Israel officially has no nuclear bombs, Assad has no chemical weapons. Both deny..."

"Both are lying."

"Of course. Nobody believes otherwise. But to ask Bashar even to admit he has sarin while Israel claims the Dimona nuclear reactor is a solar energy research center. The only part that plays is Dimona's in the desert. That alone is a major concession."

"Why don't we skip the nonsense? You know theirs is a necessary deterrent against total annihilation. And they're not nuking their own people."

"Moscow is sympathetic to their precarious position. So we are making no counterproposal that Jerusalem dismantle that arsenal. But Bashar feels the same about his, I'm afraid. In light of the Israeli refusal to allow inspection, you must understand his reluctance to part with *his* deterrent."

Kerry's deep voice shook with anger. "Do I have to give you the citation where chemical weapons are banned by international law? Signed here in this very city by the League of Nations. For damn good reason, given the indiscriminate gassing in World War I."

"My friend, we too make that important distinction. Because of that treaty, Moscow and Washington are greatly in agreement. We respect international law. I am here, am I not? Mutual escalation in Syria serves no constructive purpose."

Kerry's glasses slipped down his aquiline nose, the temple ends disappeared in his thick, precise silver hair. At seventy, Kerry found himself increasingly emotional and equally determined. Upon arrival, Kerry had split his team: half to vault the legal hurdles, the other to tackle the nuts-and-bolts logistics of securing, transporting, and destroying everything to do with Syria's chemical weapons.

A delay swallowed precious time as Lavrov had fielded no troops for the battlefield, arriving instead with a few advisers. Outplayed, Lavrov quickly blew the trumpet for reinforcements, who took a day and more to wander into the InterContinental. Fearing a stall in the first quarter rather than the more easily overcome fourth, Kerry martialed his legal eagles to tap out a near-final draft of a written agreement for the Organization of the Prohibition of Chemical Weapons. If Putin herded him to join the Chemical Weapons Convention, the agreement would handcuff Bashar al-Assad to its terms. Kerry demanded that everything be signed here in three days, expecting the other side to dither and try and run out the clock, banking on the world's myopic attention span to eventually unravel the pact through delay. Kerry would not backpedal on his three-day finish line. Lavrov wanted to play Russian roulette. Obama just might fan the trigger.

"Obama's not kidding, Sergei. The Republicans will just have to swallow whatever he serves them. We'll move, and it's going to be much bigger than you think. We're ready this very minute. I'm telling you this because we'd prefer an agreement." "As do we, John. Our Russian Ambassador spent two hours with Bashar last night. We impressed upon him the gravity of his situation and even our own displeasure at this terrible gassing of Ghouta. We now have a breakthrough. However, to agree to relinquish all his chemical weapons, the Syrian president has several modest requests."

Kerry did not yet release a sigh of relief. Sometimes this was political posturing, others a wrench tossed in a purring engine. "Such as?"

"First, the obvious. No air strikes. No troops. No increased weapon support delivered to these terrorists. Let's not quibble about what we call them. Personally, to move this along, I am happy with *the opposition*."

"We can agree only to the first two. You know that."

"Yes. In fact, such was explained at considerable length to Bashar. He has promised to look the other way. Though he has asked us for a modest upgrade in his capabilities which we have taken under advisement."

"In other words, you said yes. In exchange for an expanded presence of your own along his beautiful ocean."

Lavrov said nothing and instead poured more water from a plastic bottle into his glass.

A family headed towards the pool, father, mother, maybe

both German, Kerry thought, from the entitled stride even to swim, two girls with plastic tubes around their waists. A pair of guards, a Russian and an American with a blonde crew cut, wordlessly searched their bags without explanation. As the mother protested in what Kerry heard as Swiss German, the Russian opened his jacket where the machine gun hung from around his neck. Silent now, the scowl on her face deepening, she allowed the pawing through their things, the removal and replacement of the cell phone batteries. Then she defiantly marched her daughters into the still water. Her husband lifted their bags to a row of empty lounges under umbrellas. Kerry gazed across the pool and thought about the photos of the dead in Ghouta in his room. Assad banked on hardly anyone other than their families remembering for long, which enraged Kerry. The gall of this attack while the UN inspection team was two miles away informed Kerry that if let off, Bashar would send the sarin sailing again. Kerry was tired and a little sad, which he didn't want the seemingly stone Lavrov to see.

Tables immaculately set with water and wine goblets filled two lengths around the pool; shaded by beige umbrellas, the fabric matched the backs and seats of their wood chairs. All rooms on the far side of the hotel tower looked out at the nearby Jet d'Eau geyser ascending from Lake Geneva.

Kerry realized Putin seemed to want this accomplished double-time, lest Obama grow atypically impatient and belligerent. Kerry's voice came out matter-of-fact. "Anything else?"

"No UN resolutions. No authorization of international force, no condemnations of any questionable behavior."

"Okay, but for now only. He behaves himself in the future, that's one thing. If not, we're back with a full-court press."

Lavrov smiled. "Obama loves his basketball."

"This is it. Today, here, right now. We have a document for you and your people, and we'll accept modest suggestions. But starting tomorrow, Bashar al-Assad has seven days to identify everything. We want it all and no last-minute Arab haggling. We're not buying a backgammon set in the *souq*. Syria is to reveal the locations of every storage facility. Every production facility. Inventory of every ounce of sarin and mustard gas. Exact totals and locations of all component chemicals in case he has in mind to mix up more as soon as we turn around. We're going to melt down or cut up the storage tanks on the spot."

Lavrov smiled. He did not think that he and the Americans had ever come to an agreement this rapidly. Russia had deeper designs in Syria and desired no American roadblocks. The Americans seemed weak-willed these days to him and Putin.

"We are happy to come to this understanding," Lavrov said, "that will protect Syrian civilians."

"Whatever he tries to squirrel away for a rainy day, we'll know."

"Eyes and ears everywhere I take it?"

"Tell Bashar we're clairvoyant."

A waiter approached, hoisting a round tray with water bottles, condensation dripping down the plastic. With an abrupt sweep of his long arm, Kerry shooed him away. Kerry was running flat out and had no time to be distracted by another water break. The waiter, in all white, backpedaled and then turned and fled.

"Sergei, we want the missiles, the warheads, everything stacked to the ceiling to deliver this garbage. Tell Assad they need to burrow underground like rabbits looking for forgotten warrens. I'm utterly confident that Moscow will see to it that he'll have enough missiles to kill copiously in his ordinary inhumane way. We don't need a public renouncement. Giving it *all* up will suffice."

"You will be able to destroy the anticipated quantities in nine months, as you suggested previously?"

"For logistic prowess," the Navy man Kerry suggested, "think D-Day. There is no compromise on our inspection teams, and we dismantle his equipment. Our people are free to head anywhere and overturn any rocks their heart's desire. No impediments or the deal's off then and there. Bashar convoys the chemicals to Latakia on the Mediterranean."

"All acceptable."

"Anything else you want to propose to be polite," Kerry said warmly, with his genuine friendliness towards Lavrov. "That I can decline and sweep off the table?"

"Let me instead tell you what we must have in the written agreement." Lavrov leaned in, his head still below where Kerry's was bent towards him. "That you will have this finished and be completely out of Syria in nine months. Preferably to the hour. No excuses for any of your troops to remain on the ground."

"Absolutely. With the danger of any of this falling into dangerous hands, we consider lightning speed imperative. Couldn't agree more."

"This ship, the *Cape Arthur*."

Kerry wanted this deal, knew he'd never reach the presidency now, and didn't care at this twilight stage about that. For the greater good, he wanted to stop mass chemical murder.

"Sergei, I don't recall anyone mentioning that name."

Lavrov shrugged. "Lucky guess."

Kerry waited. He'd leaned around the slalom hairpin turns, and now it was an effortless downhill to the flat runout.

"Our *Cape Arthur*, if I may." Sergei tapped the wood table with the other four silent participants pushed back so they all fit. "That you have reconfigured to render the sarin's ability to kill no longer historical fact. You have finished it? We have indications you are still working onboard."

"We are."

"This technology. Of course, we may be wrong, but we believe that it does not yet exist. The potential difficulties and dangers do not elude us. You have mastered it? You will be able to do it aboard ship as you promised, without poisoning an entire ocean? Or killing all your valiant crew?"

Kerry did not miss a beat. "I won't tell you there weren't setbacks. It's full speed ahead." He sipped from his now cold cup of tea, the squeezed lemon on the saucer. "The technology works, and the Pentagon green-lights the mission," Kerry lied to buy time.

* * *

In Norfolk, Virginia, Shai and McE walked along the red brick pedestrian quay beside the silent Elizabeth River. Across the way, gulls wheeled noisily in front of a stationary gray battleship whose shadow darkened the water. A row of sea cranes towered behind it. Farther up this six-mile tidal estuary, an aircraft carrier sat motionless like a tourist boat waiting for patrons to snap away to create the memories that otherwise would slip away.

"Tell me the bad news first, then the worse news," Shai suggested.

"The bad news is, we're knocking on doors to see who might take the sarin if we can't break it down at sea."

"Oh, good. I'm glad that's not the real problem."

"We're searching for anyone who might grant us a temporary storage site until we can get our high-tech gizmos aboard the *Cape Arthur* to stop belching mayday."

Shai looked out at a civilian tugboat noisily clunking by, leaving two lines of bubbles in its wake.

"Of course, everybody wants to help for the good of mankind," McE said. "Our great hope was Jordan, being next door and all, but you didn't much care for that."

"Abdullah's done a lot. Has a million Syrian refugees jamming his falafel stands. Of course, the nearby advantage of just across the border means just across the border from the kind of people in Syria and Iraq eager to show up with water jugs to haul off as much as they can carry."

"We did see your point rather readily. We discovered

a couple of the EU countries, more specifically France and Belgium, actually have hazardous waste incinerators."

"Designed to render mute what?" Shai asked without enthusiasm.

"And therein lies the problem. In France, battery acid and stuff akin to very old and rancid red wine."

"The slightly worse bad news, if I may inquire?"

"Belgium. It looked promising in a historic way. They built a plant, highly unexpected, in that it's still operating specifically to render chemical weapons as calm as a baby's bath water."

"My ears perked up at historic. As in charmingly obsolete?"

"Alas, mostly the case. For our needs, a no-go. As people plow fresh fields and wander around the forests, they seemed still to trip over World War I artillery shells. Vintage coups for eBay. Except..."

"Not quite hollow steel, then?"

"They made things to last then. My fucking new dishwasher is all plastic, and the guy said, 'Give it five years tops.' So yes, fabulous steel and inside, mustard gas galore."

Shai suggested, "The French, of course, in our new multicultural era said, *nyet*. I'm sure the Belgian's denial was heartfelt."

"Correct on all counts. Brussels pleaded regulatory hurdles so high elite equestrians couldn't clear them. Local jurisdictions, city mayors, federal mandates, and long waiting periods for public input. They ache to aid, but it would take years."

"Any progress here in the good old USA? Since you happen to have the shiniest incinerators for the express purpose of beating chemical weapons into submission on the planet?"

"Brick wall, I'm afraid, high and thick and growing higher by the minute. With the current state of the two warring parties, we can't get them to agree on where to meet for lunch. Mutually do the 'gee, love to, wish we could welcome it to the land of the free, but my constituents would create quite a ruckus.' The Brits tell us their island is too small and that they've retreated from all the ones where they might have done a *hey look that way* on the heathens." McEnneney sighed. "So we wing to Albania."

"America's greatest friend among the former reluctant Soviet bloc partners. They're all Europeans now. Especially, I gather, in Moscow on international dating apps." He had read something to that effect in *Vogue*.

"Has a better ring than Slavs," McE agreed.

"So, what does all your American aid buy you from the new colorfully painted buildings of Tirana? I hear Aperol Spritzes are all the rage, having navigated the Adriatic from Italy far easier than the Syrian refugees have the Aegean. Albanians clamoring to get into NATO? That's a card you can play?"

"The ace up our sleeve," McE conceded. "Looks like they're at the table and eager to go all in. We actually already built them a post-Berlin Wall party chemical weapons disposal unit. They had lots of this and that around. They didn't want to blow up any of their spritzer parties."

Dark clouds edged over the sun, throwing a shadow over the quay. Shai tried not to see it as a portent, though he did. "Love to see what cards you dealt on the felt, face-up."

"Since they already saw what we can do, we pitched them a new bigger and brighter permanent site for one of their many isolated ocean coves. Build 'em something to take the sarin that can also clean up everything they can produce that might foul up those exquisite waters. Let their once- and no-longer-Communist neighbors ship, truck, and train in whatever they can't successfully douse with water. The Albanians charge them to turn mealy loaves into baguettes. We throw up this new facility for them, no IOUs."

"Other than taking everything Bashar has managed to concoct."

"With government spending elasticity, we pay them for

that too. Anything, so we don't have to dirty our pretty hands. Now we arrive at our last resort. What if the Albanians, too, fold and throw in their cards? I sadly report that, as of now, Pentagon and intelligence alike have sped into a brick wall, crashed, and declared all this impossible in nine months, nine years, and likely nine lifetimes. Like with most unsolvable problems, we punted it to the people who get most of the world's work done."

"Women."

"I told you?"

"Not yet."

Shai thought about Afra in Damascus, and a shiver of dread and guilt shuddered through him like stepping into the sun coatless on a bright New York winter day that looked welcoming. She reported Mitqal had asked Kassem to sniff out the mole, which could mean he suspected or was even on to Fuad's son. Now that Bashar seemed likely to balance atop his tottering country, Mitqal was doubly dangerous.

McE withdrew a cigar tin from his linen long-sleeved shirt with hood, a last-minute grab in the Casablanca airport at double the cost. He slid it out, crushed the tin, and deposited it back in this outside pocket to avoid a signature trail.

"Can't smoke this aboard the *Cape Arthur*, even docked. More than getting the machines to purr, the obvious concern is for those aboard ship." With a lighter, the cigar tip flared, and McE took a hurried deep drag.

Shai chimed in, "The only place to hide is over the railing."

"A ship severely cramps options. As to the aforementioned seas, a spill will create unprecedented havoc. We're nowhere near sure where it leads. So to our gal team. Young by chance. Or likely not. Not sure who rang the bell to shove all the men overboard. We have a string quartet. Army major toiling as a microbiologist. Air Force Lieutenant Colonel who in her spare time climbs into F-35s and has a thing or two to say to Lockheed Martin on the design. Given all those expensive recruiting trips to New Haven, we had to have a CIA Yalie. A biologist. The youngest, an international relations scholar, Jewish as it happens. Looks about twelve years old, an overachiever, maybe battling those childlike looks? Then maybe just trying to fit in as the proverbial outsider?"

"How much do they know about chemical weapons?" It struck Shai to inquire, suddenly feeling hopeful at their distance from decorum.

"Diddly squat. Perfect, it is. We have to turn the sarin into bilge right there on the ship. They're running simulations, equations, and tragedy likelihoods on computers I can't even turn on. All those parents whining about their poor babies having electronic childhoods and not enough dodgeball have turned out to be full of shit. They're all over the docks like hungry seagulls. Our ladies of the night don't bother sleeping. They pull in Navy experts, dockyard old hands, some men even. Rather a lot of them as it happens. These are smart women. When in the French countryside, they ask which way to the vineyard. None of that macho wasting centuries trying to find it themselves. You know what a 'ro ro' is?"

"Not even remotely."

"Roll on, roll off. Big mother cargo ships. You have to roll on something like the Empire State Building. Too heavy to lift. Navy crew says, 'which way you want it to point?'"

Shai grinned. "We going to have a gaze at the *Cape Arthur* anytime soon?"

McE threw his cigar on the bricks and ground it out, suddenly wishing he'd saved the tin to rehouse and smoke later. Alongside his inherited wealth and casual spending, he was as eager to save a buck as those who needed to. McE walked the remnants to a trash receptacle at the water. "Turns out we have loads of these 'ro-ro's' all over the globe bobbing at the docks. So next time we start a needless war, we'll have them at hand. Let's go see the gentleman the ladies have fallen in love with."

Soon McE drove through an open gate in a chain-link

fence and parked at a quiet quay. A huge gray ghost ship rose before them, empty and silent, four decks running atop each other from stem to stern.

"You'll like the provenance, cosmopolitan like you. Found her mothballed in New Hampshire, Portsmouth," McE said as they exited opposite sides of his top-down Mercedes convertible. What hair Shai had was windblown, and, to his surprise, the speed had quieted his head. "Came into the light of the world in the Imabari Shipyards in Japan in the year of our Lord 1977. Spent half its aging life in Saudi Arabia, carting oil drilling paraphernalia here and there. Navy grabbed it in the run-up to the first Gulf War, being already in the neighborhood and all."

"Quite a luxury. All our wars are fought in our backyard."

McE led Shai to the side of the monster. Preserved in the most recent freshening of the gray was the outline of a short Arab sword with a curved blade that broadened toward the point. "Why's it get fatter at the end?" McE asked.

"Lightweight, designed for desert warfare. Arc of the blade in harmony with the sweep of the rider's arm as he slashes his enemy. Presuming he's galloping."
"You know anything about ships?"

"Bit less than scimitars," Shai conceded. "Get a little seasick, if I'm forced to tell the truth."

"Meet the *Cape Arthur*." McE swept an arm like introducing a bride. "For the sarin killing machines, we're tinkering with prototypes twenty-feet high. Each. The floor below the top deck is as big and open as anything on the water. Twenty-five feet high. As you can see, it goes on as long as she does. If that wasn't enough, variable-pitch propellers and stabilizers like my old dishwasher, built with the excellence and pride of bygone days."

"And these implements of propulsion?"

"Keep the gentleman on his feet even when drunk with sarin. Our women of the docks are greatly pleased that the *Cape Arthur* remains on the calm side out at sea."

"Six hundred feet long, maybe?"

"More than maybe, six hundred forty-eight. Will she set sail and not sink with all Bashar's barrels and gleaming tanks of poison and the ones we need to pour the neutralized byproducts in? Our ladies' mountain of printouts say *da*."

Shai absorbed the enormity of it. Everything aboard one behemoth. It was an achievement of scale and wonder only the Americans could manage.

"The cost to outfit her?" Shai asked to tread water; he didn't much care.

"We spend more on toothpaste for the troops at the government contractor special inflated price. It's cheap compared to rebuilding Albania, which I'd still prefer due to the risks aboard. Hundred million. Includes sprucing up the scimitar."

Shai's irrepressible smile lifted off and as quickly landed. "How many needed to flip the on-switch and swab the deck of non-chemical spills?"

"In its previous life, to haul drilling rigs from one port in the sand to another, say twenty. The ladies suggest we'll need a hundred and fifty but whisper that due to the extraordinary hazards at sea, they could lop off some number, to be determined later. While we're hermetically sealing that one extraordinarily large deck, we'll have to build something between hammocks and condos somewhere. Additional food facilities, showers, and latrines. We'll make them nice, given a lot of these engineer types, as it happens, have never been to sea."

"The alchemy machines?" Shai asked. "I noticed you skipped over how fabulously they work."

"Not there yet, my man. We're close. Cautiously optimistic. At the finish line. Minus a couple of breakthroughs."

"The sarin will never leave Syria unless there's a way to render it drinkable."

"It is irrefutable that *we* can't take it ashore. That America has set sail. The new breed of politician, these *patriots* shout spills and kills. They shake in their boots about what Fox News might say about endangering our precious population. Let's find a watering hole in the great American outdoors. I'll explain the best that a mind unable to penetrate calculus in high school can manage about where the alchemy problems lie."

Shai said nothing and headed alone back towards the Mercedes. He noted that McE said *problems* in plural.

"The timeline's a bit outside the way engineers think," McE said as he slipped in and slammed his car door shut. "They said, 'this is something that's never been done aboard ship. We can figure this out. Give us two years.' So I told them, 'how about two weeks?'"

Shai held onto the window frame as McE screeched a hard left to spin them around. "The compromise?"

"We're negotiating somewhere in between. Say two months. Even with amazing stabilizers and propellers, this big guy bobs in the water. Sometimes left, sometimes right. The ladies inform me, sometimes forward, and then sometimes it has a mind to briefly head where it just was. The forklift operators, understandably, are used to hauling around the worst poisons man has conceived on unmoving dry land."

"With her weight, there's potentially lethal pressure on every pipe, welded seal, joint, hose, and gizmo they invent that has no name yet," Shai said quietly.

"That's just the most obvious difficulty on the list, but nowhere near the top. The ship's elevators work hunky-dory with empty tanks, but our ladies promise that with filled ones, they will grind, stall or crash, depending on their mood."

"If we skip over that, a chemical fire kills everyone on board," Shai suggested. "Even a small leak can get into the ship's ventilation system."

"That would be the top of the charts," McE said, entering and accelerating through a yellow light near the end of its brief life. He looked hard at Shai, who would have preferred

McE notice, at his speed, the car in front of him approaching rapidly.

McE continued, "We'll open the curtains to NATO for Tirana. Turn it into a Hollywood premiere on the Adriatic. Nobody can resist Tinseltown. That's how we get them to say yes."

Shai felt a surge of hope. Albania hugged the Adriatic Sea north of the Greek coast. It was a fabulous option—Latakia to their port Saranda, across from the island of Corfu, three days flat.

* * *

Eleven days later, Shai shuffled into Levi Goodman's inner sanctum. Rows of books haphazardly crammed the bookcases on dueling sides of the office: English, Hebrew, and French novels on one wall and of equal girth non-fiction. Goodman didn't trust ideologues who had no time for novels, who shunned exploration of competing human desire in favor of firing bullets loaded with facts. Anyone could pull facts from a file cabinet and ease the drawer closed on those they preferred to remain in the dark. Historical facts, in particular, were an army martialed to delegitimize, to bayonet the other side rather than ride together up a mountain to a view both cherished.

"I just got off the phone with McEnnerney," Shai said, collapsing his tired legs into the small chair opposite Goodman's desk. "Obama's alone looking out the window, as much as that hurts him."

"Basically, this we know."

"Kerry used the phrase *we're hungover* with Brooks Newmark, a British Conservative MP who argued with him for destroying every barrel bomb." Shai had kept up hope, like blowing on an ember, that like Winston Churchill when overwhelmingly pressured by Parliament to do a deal with

Hitler, Obama would stand alone against the storm and fight. "Newmark was in DC trying to push the Americans into action on their own. Nothing new from Kerry other than eloquent imagery, which we've come to count on from him when all else fails. 9/11 created a voracious appetite for war. Americans got drunk on it. They're left with that hangover. Now that we are at a moment for a justifiable intervention to stop a massacre in Syria, people are worn out. It isn't viable for any politician to support even cruise strikes. So the world's great leaders retreated."

"Being stuck with the lesser good of getting the sarin out of Syria is not a small thing," Goodman said consolingly. "It may actually be the greater good—no certainty over there. What do the mobs chant: *Assad or We Burn the Country?* Given present realities, how about we play the cards we're clutching in our hands? The *Cape Arthur*?"

"Slammed into an underwater mine. Not yet sunk but leaking badly."

"Friend or foe. If there's a difference?"

"Navy paper pushing experts."

Goodman threw his feet on his desk, which only made his lower back hurt. "We shun such restraints here, preferring to remain alive."

"Came down to Norfolk from Washington in full regalia, narrow ties, those plastic pen holders for their shirt pockets. Produced an inspection report, pages upon pages. Sent out far and wide like wedding invitations of a couple with no means otherwise to acquire china and silver. Pentagon upper floors, along with a lot of other lesser hallways where the worry about career advancement runs deeper. If it had a headline, it would read: DISASTER, DON'T!"

"A sample of the highlights, if you have them at your fingertips, Shai."

"The way cover your ass runs. Machines designed to work on reliable dry ground. Unforeseen weather likely. Too dangerous even in a calm. Rescue of crew in the event of a spill or leak, precarious, maybe impossible. Sailing into the complete vast unknown. Considerable concern about engineers who might have trouble standing on deck to begin with. SOS. Abandon ship. Look for alternative."

"Dare I mention these concerns were all front and center from the get-go?"

"I think there was a lapse in not considering the paper pushers would spread them like the plague."

"Suggestions for workarounds in all this flowing print?"

"None," Shai breathed, exhausted. "They murdered it. Now that they've been summoned to put their signatures on it and reject these recommendations, the higher-ups are worried about a disaster on their watch."

"And their records."

"Yes, mostly that, I'm afraid."

Goodman swung his short legs down and groaned from the back pain.

"Our lady quartet have anything ready for a rainy day?"

"Lacking experience in the rarified corridors of power, our ladies of the ocean were knocked to the sea floor. They swam right back up. These are women used to getting things done in a man's world. They want to re-draw blueprints for greater security, large and small. Fly in the world's welding experts. Those with sea legs preferably, used to ship stresses. Reweld seals so King Kong couldn't yank them off. Every pipe possible, swap with flexible hoses. Weld the big stuff right to the floor and walls. Do a trial run, a few days at sea."

"In other words, the Americans have no backup plan. Without one, the sarin stays in Syria."

Shai stood. "What are we doing if we have to count on Albania as our last best chance?"

As he reached for the doorknob, Shai watched his outstretched hand tremble in the tension but didn't care. It was benign and didn't slow him. He turned.

"If you draw a *red line* and you don't stick by it, you're giving Bashar a green light. He can continue using chemical weapons with impunity. It will say to the Russians that America's word is meaningless. It shows Putin that the West has no resolve. You need a stick as well as a carrot. Otherwise, if people realize all you're doing is talking, they'll talk you to death. And attack. It could lead to Putin launching adventures in Crimea, Ukraine, against all the breakaway republics. It's not the Democrats or the Republicans. They're all the same. It's the end of an empire."

Then he was gone.

CHAPTER 13

SOUQ AL-BUZURIYAH

DAMASCUS

In the outdoor Souq Al-Buzuriyah, Kassem stared at a giant poster of President Bashar al-Assad in blue slacks, a white shirt unfettered at the neck, and an unbuttoned tan blazer. Ropes strung above shoppers secured the president, here the height of four Kassems, to a stone wall above several bicycles resting equally casually on kickstands. On the other side, the supports dipped across the crowded lane to iron rings above the row of shops. One woman, feet secured in orange plastic sandals, western jeans with fashionable knee patches, her ripe form snug in her orange blouse, arms bare to the sun and clutching a child's hand, stood intent on a message on her phone. Nobody glanced up, as larger-than-life aspirations of leaders were commonplace in the Arab world; anyway, they all knew that the vote was rigged. The Arabic caption infuriated Kassem: Hope in Science and Knowledge.

This mocked his years of late-night scientific reading. The Assads murdered with his science. At Bashar's right elbow, the lie heralding his upcoming presidential campaign read: HOPE. Kassem quickened his pace until he found he was running and pushing people aside. As a woman he brushed past almost fell, he caught himself and her with the same outstretched arm and embarrassed, squeezed his eyes and slowed.

He wanted to show Lilia the Khan As'ad Pasha. He hated that the world greatly likened his Syria to a barbaric animal. The khan warehouses had risen like gargantuan beasts in the early Ottoman Empire. Vast lines of a thousand camels trudged west from the Tigris and the Euphrates bearing spices, rhubarb, and silks. Upon arrival, their drivers struck their beasts between their ears, and they dropped to their knees inside the paved colonnades to be unloaded. The Janissaries, the elite soldiers of the Turkish Empire, in high red boots, billowing red capes, tall white caps, and matching green leather shoulder and arm armor, patrolled and protected the wares. The camels departed bearing pounded brass, ironworks, and garments woven from the formless bales of Chinese and Indian thread.

The grandest of all Syria's khans, one of the proudest anywhere, 2,500 square meters (27,000 square feet) had long decayed since the governor of Damascus, As'ad Pasha al-Azm, raised it in the mid-18th century. In the 1990s, the renovation garnered the Aga Khan Award for Architecture. Kassem looked down, his face hot. He was ashamed about the sarin storage breakthrough he had devised.

Inside the showpiece of alternating horizontal lines of black and white masonry was empty. The main cupola reached as high as any in Rome. Iron-grated windows that beckoned the sun surrounded the cupola; a half-dozen smaller domes circled lower. The supporting pillars, the same white and black basalt rose from the floor and widened into arches below each smaller cupola. Halfway up, striped walls, inside each dome, more arches flared and led everywhere like a black and white Escher drawing. In each towering cupola, round black iron circles decorated the white plaster above the grated windows. Kassem walked on the original small black uneven stones.

There were no tourists. Alone, staring up, only Lilia.

As she heard his familiar heavy steps, she turned. "This is, *wow*." She said the last word in English.

"You were never here?"

"No," she half-whispered. In time, she would tell him she was a Jewish girl from the ghetto, believed he would not care, but Shai had been explicit. No matter how much she trusted him or anyone, that was not to be breathed.

Nervous, he grabbed and kissed her. She kissed back, lingering, trembling, and he saw she must be frightened too under her marble veneer. He wondered whether it was fear of arrest or about them. Last night she had slept without her night garments and this morning told him, "It was terrible. But I want to try again, just not tonight."

"Let's walk outside," she said, taking his hand, enjoying how hers disappeared in it.

They walked under the vaulted ceiling towards the open-air end of the *souq*. People shopped, their feet clicking on the gray flagstones. Equal numbers of men and women walked in the street, but only the women carried plastic bags.

"They intend to truck the sarin across land to the Mediterranean," she told him quietly, still holding his hand. "The Americans have a ship. They want to try and neutralize the sarin at sea. It doesn't quite work yet. They have a field deployable hydrolysis process..."

"I understand what they're intending," he snapped.

Rather than pull her hand away, she kept them laced together. This was not him. She felt a slight dampness on his fingers which scared her.

"They *cannot* put the VX through that process."

"What VX?" She had not been briefed on VX. "Or put another way, what is VX?"

"Venomous agent X," he said in English, then returned to Arabic. Outside now, in the blinding sunlight, they were away from people. "British discovered it. Deadliest nerve agent on this deadly planet. A hundred times more powerful than sarin, to be accurate. One drop killed North Korea's Kim Jongnam. Longer lasting. Invisible. You touch it, you're dead. The problem for the Americans is its very low volatility."

"What am I not seeing? I would think low volatility is good." She smiled. "Like with a woman."

Kassem did not respond to the humor. "In chemistry, volatility explains how quickly a substance becomes vapor. VX does not vaporize. It remains oily and sticks, which is why it remains deadly to the touch for protracted periods. It persists. But that is not the fundamental problem."

Afra waited and looked at the bare-bulb electric lights inside the shops. She suddenly felt naked and unprotected in Damascus.

"It would not even take bad weather aboard such a large ship," he said. "If one tries to alter that calm state, it likes to fight back by bursting into flames. It cannot be neutralized that way."

"How much of it do you have?"

"A small amount compared to the sarin. Still many thousands of liters. Shall I explain how it can be deployed?"

Her nod was so slight Kassem was not sure he saw it. He trudged forward. "It is very much like the sarin in deployment. SCUD C rockets can carry it 500 kilometers. The SCUD B's, 300 kilometers. The 302- and 320-millimeter artillery shells can carry either sarin or VX a shorter distance. Fifty kilometers. The rebels in Idlib are just over 300 kilometers north from Damascus. In the other direction, Jerusalem is 218 kilometers, again to be precise."

"How might the VX be neutralized?"

"The Americans helped the Russians neutralize their large quantities after the Cold War. If they are to be believed, the Americans are in the process of neutralizing their massive stockpiles of sarin and VX, which they keep secret from their people everywhere across their country. The British. VX was first developed in 1952 at their Porton Down chemical agent facility. We used the exact British chemical composition for our VX. They could take it apart. At Porton Down, I mean."

"Where's the VX?"

"Not in one place."

She felt her accelerated heartbeats repeating like car tires on a grooved highway. "How many?"

"I don't know."

"Could you get me a list?"

"I don't know. Maybe. I believe some is in a secret site in the desert. In the northeast near Iraq. Midway between At-Tibni and where the Islamic State is threatening Raqqa. It has both the DF to mix the sarin and accomplished VX. It is not even on the maps in my boss's office. I don't know whether we will report it to the inspectors. We call it "the strip." Single desert runway. Hanger. Storage in a cave inside a small hill. Everything else in every direction, sand. You would not locate it if you did not know where to look. I do not know the exact location myself."

"Do the Islamists know it's there?"

"Unlikely. Almost certainly not."

"But they might learn it," she breathed, just above a whisper.

"So I am thinking. There was no ISIS, no idea that Raqqa could fall when we hid it there."

"If ISIS overruns the entire area, someone might sell it or its location," she pressed.

"I can try and get a list of all VX locations. It will be dangerous. I would have to enlist my boss, Sami. He is my closest friend."

She was terrified for him, for herself, for everybody everywhere she could imagine. "Would he do it?"

"Even asking could mean a death sentence. They would take you too. My father."

She wanted to send up the evacuation flare, clear out by helicopter, by sea, back through the Nasib Crossing, and cart them all with her, Kassem, his parents, the entire Syrian people.

They passed a cart with every kind of dried fruit and nuts

in tall barrels.

"I want some," she said, stopping.

"Which?"

"Doesn't matter. Just something to chew on. You choose."

He saw the anxiety in her eyes, the nervousness in the quick movements of her hands as she pointed. From each barrel, a yellow sign protruded with the starting price.

She reached towards large walnuts. "These."

He motioned to the proprietor, who was standing back where onions in netting hung from the walls. Next door, a narrow entrance between black and white striped stone led to a coffee house. "Let's sit inside," he said. "Afterwards, there is something else I have to tell you."

"No. Now. What?" she said too loudly.

He waited until the owner finished scooping an assortment of nuts and fruits into individual small brown bags. Kassem paid, and the proprietor bowed slightly and backed away.

"We also have chlorine gas. Vast quantities. It is commonly found in household products like bleach. Used to make pesticides, rubber, solvents. It is *not* deemed illegal by the International Chemical Weapons agreements, and was last used as a weapon in World War I against the trenches. It's heavier than air and sinks down to truly terrorize. You can't hide in your bunkers or your homes. The only thing they can do is flee the country."

Afra almost choked on a whole walnut, and the symbolism annoyed her. She coughed hard and spat into her hand. She put it in her purse. "He wouldn't give up all his nerve agents and then start bombing people with chlorine? That's insane. It makes no sense. This is supposed to be a great diplomatic coup for the Russians. Stop the poison gassing. The Russians would never stand for it. Would they?"

"I am only telling you that we have a great deal of chlorine gas. The question first, I believe, is do I ask Sami for the locations of the VX? Risk us all?

"I don't know," she said. "I can't think. Help. Coffee."

He laughed, enjoyed her antics. As months passed, he was not surprised that he impossibly loved her more.

Inside, as they sat alone at the small table, men across from them sucked on tobacco gurgling from water pipes.

"I have to prioritize," she announced. "Cookies. Get me cookies."

He smiled. "I presume the kind doesn't matter."

"Compared to all this. Obviously."

He rose slowly, and she watched him look for the waiter, tall and contained; she was shaken and delighted and terrified that she so loved him. She wasn't at all certain Russia would cap the chlorine. She knew the culture from their pilots over Syria; they bombed helpless suburbs and then dove and soared in aerial acrobatics. The Russian Jews in the underground bunker had tutored her. Each year in Putin's Russia, on May 9, to celebrate Victory Day over the Nazis in what they called The Great Patriotic War, 12,000 troops strutted, then tanks and missile launchers rolled through Red Square. Jets burst overhead, chased by lumbering attack helicopters. Post-Soviet Russia scribbled over memory. The new elite eviscerated the Party for the 27 million Russian corpses. In this rewrite, Putin-style military men rode shirtless on horseback and crushed the Fascists. Nobody had buried more soldiers or killed more Nazis than the Soviets; the boast that they rescued Europe was not misplaced. They believed that they soared still, on a continuing messianic mission against absolute evil. Or, as her former lover had ranted as he roughly stripped her: they exploited that old sacrifice to legitimize intervention.

That night, above him on his narrow cot, Afra was loud and suddenly heavy as if the weight of her burden had entered her bones. He worried the neighbors might hear her and later not say something; they never would but look away embarrassed as he passed. He wished he didn't care, but they were not yet married.

Only as they sat on the roof together, only a blanket

covering them, her leg over his, did he realize her fear had entered him, or maybe more accurately, drawn his to the surface as one might suck out the poison from a snakebite. Though he was not cold with her small warm length against him, as they sat, he shivered.

"The city's beautiful," she said.

He looked out. Lights shone everywhere in the low houses and on the pencil-thin minarets. A quarter moon lit the eastern mountains. He saw a shooting star. He was about to explain that it was a tiny meteor plunging at a vast 60 to 130 kilometers into the atmosphere. As it burned, the air glowed along the trajectory. He caught himself and decided not to dim the magic and less comfortably said nothing. The city seemed eerily quiet, but he supposed it was he who was.

"There's lots about me I haven't told you," she said.

He was silent and rubbed the bottom of her foot with his. "You think I'll be disappointed?"

"I don't know. I hope not. I think not."

"Can you tell me?"

"No. Not yet."

He stayed silent. Whatever she was hiding, whom she was working for, where she had been before she erupted into his life, he knew it would not matter. He was aware though that he could be naive and see the world as he needed it to look.

He said, "I'm going to talk to Sami tomorrow. I have to."

She leaned her head softly against his shoulder like a spent storm, the earlier ferocity gone. "Yes," she said. "I know."

"You hungry?"

She laughed. "All the time now. Onion and potato omelet?"

She rose, and the blanket dropped over him. He looked at her nakedness, still a little surprised that she was silky and hairless everywhere, unlike the two Syrian women he'd lain beside. He both loved and was equally frightened by her abandon.

Kassem said, "I know where to take Sami, what I need to

show him. And how he'll react. It will convince him."

Kassem and Sami hiked slowly up the last rise on Mount Qasioun and both breathing heavily, stepped in tandem onto the flat crest at 1,151 meters. A hot wind blew the air fresh, the quiet almost a sound of its own. Kassem had slept long, surprisingly deeply, and woke with renewed optimism. Lilia had slept even more encumbered by clothes than usual, including socks.

To the east, he gazed at their nearby destination, Adam's Cave. Syrian lore had it that the first man, Adam, had dwelled there for some time. Kassem loved these fanciful fables where inconsequential man clung to a history that elevated their importance. He felt it was the frail human condition. Syrians were simple, childlike, with hearts as open and warm as the desert. People ascended to the cave to pray for rain.

Sami pointed just below them to the student and activist *Ala agsadona* site where Sunni, Christian, and Bashar Alawites camped on twenty-four-hour vigil. They splayed their bodies as human shields to protect the dozen antenna of Syrian TV, radio, and communication broadcasts atop Qasioun. Tents flapped, and the deep tones of a stringed oud suddenly lifted towards them. Foam mattresses lay outside many tents. They celebrated Syria's ten-thousand-year history and its civilization, felt their country was being threatened from beyond and within—though opinions varied on who internally was victim and perpetrator. The encampment name translated as "over our dead bodies." Unidentified mortars had defaced the mountainside last spring but managed little else.

"They started with two hundred and now, with a website, are two thousand," Sami said, excited. "If I could, I'd sit there with them."

"You just want to meet women," Kassem joked.

Sami reddened. "It is easier to talk to them while they're preparing food around the campfire than it was trying to sit next to them at the university."

Kassem studied the steep rocky eastern slopes devoid of development. Since the civil war, a new Qasioun Republican Guards Military Base had fenced in much of his father's beloved purpled-bordered *Iris damascena*. From here, he looked down at the glass-fronted restaurants lower on the peak. Deeper down on the city floor, houses and small domes crowded against the Great Umayyad Mosque from all sides. Three minarets ascended from the surrounding walls, two at the corners and one from the center of the opposite length. The Old City was so dense that the Great Mosque could not be seen in toto anywhere other than from Qasioun. He shuddered at the thought of all this turned to rubble.

"I understand their pride as human shields," Kassem said. "It does not matter either that the group at *Ala agsadona* who want to protect us from foreign invaders is led by a charismatic Hezbollah woman from Hermel in Lebanon. Those who come are true of heart. What matters is that in the world of Institute 3000, they are pretending. Trying to escape helplessness. Everywhere they turn, there are rebel mortars or the president's barrel bombs. Bashar crossed Obama's *red line*. If America strikes, it will not be at radio antennae."

A song rose from the encampment in English, a single woman's high voice having rewritten a classic American protest spiritual:

Go tell it on the mountain, from the Peaks of Qasioun and everywhere,
Go shout it out from Adam's Cave, where Syria's blessed resistance was born!

Kassem abruptly found the utter ignorance appalling. *Blessed resistance* to American bombers with stringed instruments, while children slid into mass Ghouta graves. It was difficult for him to accept how long he had pretended too that sarin would never be dropped inside the country.

"If we give up the sarin," Sami said anxiously, "they

will not strike. It is the understanding. We are making the preparations."

"Does it include the VX?"

"There has been no mention of VX. It is not my position to raise..."

"Let's walk to the *Maqam al-Arba'in*," Kassem suggested but did not unveil why.

Sami followed his friend across the white rock towards the small two-story mosque. It nestled just below the peak, its small dome lit green at night. A long dirt staircase with peeling light-blue wood railings, wood X supports all along the railing wound up the mountain's flank from the city far below. On both sides of the walkway only a few determined brown shrubs grew between the white boulders. The stairs ended at the *Maqam al-Arba'in* shrine, built over the cave where it was said Cain murdered Abel, the son of Adam. Inside the cave, a grotesque image of a mouth screamed in the rock where the mountain cried out at the killing. In the two lower *mihrab* prayer niches, below the upper forty, Abraham and Al-Khidr, it was also said, prayed during their flight through Damascus. Each night from the cave, the spirits of Damascus' forty saints slipped through a narrow shaft in the mountain wall, dropped across the city to protect, and ascended again before dawn. The people below often referred to Qasioun as the Mountain of the 40 Prophets.

As they descended from the rear of the shrine, circled, and then neared the front entrance, Sami stopped in shock. "*No,*" he cried out loud. "NO!" Sami was not religious, but this was history, lore, memory.

Kassem had been here recently with Fuad on the way to walk through the irises. The glass windows were gone, shards lonely in the frames, the wood front door ajar, swinging and squeaking. The wind brought the scent of the burnt carpets. Only the sky above the mountain was untouched, cloudless, and serenely blue.

Kassem shrugged. "Where the country is now,

unfortunately, there are too many possibilities of who dared do this."

"I can't go inside," Sami moaned. "The walls. From the fire..." The inside stone was whitewashed, the marble steps more a smooth slide from the years of pilgrimages to the prayer niches. The low walls down to the caves had glistened white too.

Kassem was shaken that someone on some side of the war had done this. He and his father had not entered. ISIS swore to burn the Islamic world clean and erect a pristine Caliphate from the ashes but had no adherents in Damascus, though he supposed some might have slipped into the city. Just as likely lonely, drunk Republican Guards wandered from the nearby base. Maybe it was the handiwork of loyalists: *Assad or We Burn the Country.* But it was hard for Kassem to believe anyone would ransack the *Maqam al-Arba'in.* Though he knew of such things growing up, cloistered with his experiments under his father's umbrella, he remained naively optimistic.

"Sami, Syria's cracking apart. If this holy place can be destroyed, if we blanket Ghouta with sarin, what cannot happen? *What?* How far can it go?" He looked out at the creaking door. "I could not have imagined this. So, I conclude with that logical certainty that I cannot imagine how it can end. Right now, the American cruise missiles are on pause. We have a deal. I do not know what happens if they discover that we have hidden the VX. If later we use the VX. Obama aches to attack, even now. What if we give him the opening? What if some VX falls to ISIS?"

Sami fell to his knees. "It's unraveling so fast. I'm alone. You have Lilia. I went to *Ala agsadona.* You are right. They are children. 'We are prepared to take the cruise missiles with our bare chests.'" He laughed crazily. "Worse, unlike the American hippies, most of the girls went home at night."

"It *is* coming apart fast. Hard to be alone. Maybe Lilia has a friend at the university. I will ask. I am very sorry that I have not sooner. I have not been a good friend." Kassem meant every word, was ashamed in his happiness that he had not thought more about his friend's.

Sami stood, gazed up at the dome of the decimated shrine, abruptly hugged his tall friend, and whispered in his ear though nobody could hear them here. "If we share about the VX with anyone, we are all at risk. Our lives."

"Maybe if we love the country, our lives don't matter. If we can stop it from burning."

Sami backed away from the embrace and looked at his feet. "Kassem, I'm afraid."

"My father always taught me, 'You should feel the emotion that is right for the moment.'" He reminded himself that Lilia's suddenly donning socks in bed was appropriate. "You have Syria's history in your hands. How could you not be afraid?"

Sami was frozen, unable to move. "Kassem, aren't you afraid?"

"Now that I have Lilia, more than ever. But if I don't fight for Syria, what will remain will be a country where I cannot live. I do not wish to leave here. I have nowhere to go. My heart is on the Mountain of the Forty Prophets."

"Their spirits could not protect Ghouta nor even their own home from being burned," Sami said with an eerie, ghostlike laugh.

"So we must."

Sami was silent for a long time. If he ran from this, he would indeed be nothing. Finally, he swung an arm around Kassem's high waist. "Okay. So to save the country. Two awkward, brainy, one formerly and one currently lonely scientist."

"Yes, not in whose trust anyone planned to hand anyone's fate."

"Okay. Then tell Lilia to wait to look for a woman. I cannot stand so much anxiety at once. It would make me brag to her about my great feats in rescuing the country. I will get the locations and other information you need. Tell me nothing more."

Kassem swept an arm around Sami's shoulder.

Sami gazed at the white rock slab sides of the enduring mountain and said, "Let's save Syria first. Then we will save poor Sami."

❊ ❊ ❊

Two weeks later, upstairs in Waterstone's Bookstore in Oxford Circus, Alisher Karimov burst towards the blackboard menu at Union Coffee like a charging lioness, her cub Shai trailing. The high ceiling was open, with metal beams, intense single floodlights, rectangular ventilation shafts— nouveau decor. Books crowded sections headed HISTORY, COOKERY, TRAVEL, YOUNG ADULT. Bare bulbs slung low on strands like Christmas decorations but all bright white. Picture books rose in stacks from small wood tables. Colorful Harry Potter hardcovers peered out from an entire wall. There was so much space, Alisher thought. Turning around, he felt he was in Russia.

Across from the traditional list of Negroni, Old Fashioned, Espresso Martini, Long Island Iced Tea ran the list of literary alcohol inducements: L'Etranger, Voltaire Sour, Catcher in the Rye, Master and Margarita, Hemingway Daiquiri, Dorian's Grey Goose. Below that, another chalkboard askew on a pillar offered French and Italian wines.

Karimov turned to Shai and roared with laughter in this paper jungle. "Bars in bookstores, cappuccino. *Master and Margarita* drink so funny. You know Bulgakov, Shai guy? This publish only after he so dead, in Paris, even, first. Maybe best book twentieth century anyone write. Longing Russian man for be forgiven. This everyman, no? Even Shai guy, I think. Maybe especially Shai guy?" And without waiting for a response. "Alisher add *alcohol* to entertainment center bookstores."

Alisher had released a quiver into the bullseye, and

Shai yanked the arrows out before the blood was even more noticeable.

"Read it three times," he said quietly. "At least."

Karimov roared again, followed, and then loped towards the metal counter to his right as if after a zebra, though he settled in front of a Kilimanjaro of pastries. Behind the espresso machine, bottles of spirits stood at the ready. Above them, wine protruded from a wood niche, beer bottles lined atop it. Brown bags of coffee beans commandingly rose up the wall to the left, nearer the busy whoosh of the milk frothing and the coffee dripping into glass.

"Use space so good. No waste," Karimov said. "Little country, so understand." He clapped Shai on the back. "Alisher follow Shai guy. See so crazy things. Yana happy also. Alisher shop for wife while Yana go St. Paul. Wife happy too. Beautiful world, yes? If we no look Syria, where not so beautiful."

"Yana," the barista called, the name Karimov had supplied. He approached and lifted the tray from the counter with the four espressos and almond biscotti, each protected in plastic for the journey from Italy.

A short distance away, McE held the fort on one of the few small square wood tables; most were long communal affairs. By necessity, McEnnerney had commandeered a fourth chair from one. Down the way in front of picture books ascending face-out optimistically promising Posh Rice, Posh Toast, Posh Eggs, and Happy Soups in a country of barely edible fare, beyond the chess players, Shai watched Sir Nigel Davies of MI6 move swiftly, thrusting forward a walking stick he apparently did not much need. His full silver mane was longish to offset the recede; a soft, inexpensive Marks and Sparks lambswool jumper, light gray with darker diamonds down the center, matched his patterned gray ascot. Shai had met him once before with McEnnerney in Washington. Uniquely Sir Nigel had risen the slippery ranks on the ladder of congeniality. He always sought common cause through the door, and when met with obdurance or ignorance—which usually came as a team—

he considered his brutality warranted.

"Sorry, no drink name your country," Alisher said to Shai as all converged where McE stood to welcome the mini UN.

Shai smiled.

As chairs squeaked on the gray floor, drinks and biscotti marched across the table, and McE made the introductions.

"Pleasure to have you on our patch," Sir Nigel said to Karimov. "I'm sure not your first occasion."

"Of course, no," Alisher said. "But first with big friends at little table. Big honor." From his waist, he bowed.

"President Putin is well?" Sir Nigel inquired.

"Of course. He run against no real peoples. So, no stress. Russia most efficient. This lovely, Waterstones. I think efficient too. Alisher learn. Like play chess when buy books. Russians so love chess. Many ideas arrive."

Sir Davies lifted his espresso and turned to McE. "I gather from the report you flashed over that you just discovered you have a bit of VX on your hands. Cheeky. Let that one slip. Wanted to keep it for a rainy day, did they?"

"We have our eye on a bit of it up near Raqqa that thus far seems to have escaped anyone's notice." McE kept at the head of the presentation. "Like to get it out before anyone does. Maybe five thousand gallons of the sarin elements ready to stir up. Great deal less of the VX, small quantity, but helicopters gassed up in an adjacent hanger."

"Doesn't take much of the VX to make an impression." Sir Nigel smiled at Shai. "Rather like you Israeli chaps. Seem to draw a lot of attention despite how few of you there actually are."

"We landed in a noisy corner of the globe," Shai said. "We took immediately to the environs."

Sir Nigel's lips came together almost in a smile. He remembered this about Shai and liked the fortitude to not take offense. Sir Nigel returned his cup to the table. "I asked around a bit. You say you can't take the VX aboard your supership. Our chaps at Porton Down, by the by, concur. Enthusiastically.

Not a word I use much about them, I might add. The VX put through your otherwise brilliant technology will blow everyone aboard a good deal of the journey to the sun. The sarin you might manage that way aboard the pitching seas. Might."

Shai had explained to Karimov that Porton Down, the fenced facility in the south, housed the Ministry of Defense's Defense Science and Technology Laboratory. It had plowed ground in 1915. Soon buildings rose to test mustard gas, chlorine, and phosgene to defend British forces against Germany's eagerness with them. Over 7,000 acres, above and below ground, they practiced seeding Britain's own clouds with sarin and its associates. Later they were tasked with determining precisely what killed the various Brits and Russians the FSB jabbed while strolling in Hyde Park. To which Karimov had replied, "This subject, Shai guy, we spoke one time, so too much. I thank you."

McE cradled his small cup in both hands. "We don't have all our t's crossed and i's dotted aboard the *Cape Arthur*."

"Ah," Sir Nigel released a knowing sigh. "Technology or the bureaucracy?"

"Latter worried about the former. Still inside the boxing ring, dancing around. I'm afraid the bureaucrats are sticking in their corner and punching from there." McE took a small pull of the espresso, which was Italian and surprisingly good. "If it all goes to hell in a handbasket, might Porton Down take the sarin too? Not much of a journey from Southampton?"

"Right as British rain. I thought you might put that to me. So we ran that one up the chain of command. *Ever so sorry* came back and *if you please, don't ask again.* Too many jihadis on the prowl, eager to swing a sword if our neck's out there for a century. Too much of the bloody sarin. Take forever and longer to transfer."

Karimov leaned both elbows on the table. "You, I mean Great Britain. You invent this VX thing at your Porton Down. So you know it like your baby boy. Alisher correct this, yes?"

"I'm afraid, sir, you have pulled down our knickers. This Nazi who started us all on this ignominious nerve gas escapade, the IG Farben chap, what's his name? Can't recall. I'm afraid all those names sound identical to my aging colonial ears."

"Gerhard Schrader," Shai said evenly.

"Wasn't there a Schroder chap too, a bit more recently?"

"Yes, Gerhard Schroder, chancellor of Germany in the early oughts," Shai obliged. "We still have a lot of dealings with the Germans. Big war reparation discounts on nuclear submarines still on today. As the guilt continues. He stood down so Merkel could stand up."

"Yes, see." Sir Nigel loosened his ascot. "Schrader, Schroder. Though I suppose they feel the same about our lot. Sir Nigel Davies. Must sound to them like a vanilla lolly. So yes, Alisher, if I may, come the 1950s, we're as crazed about you Russkies as the Americans were about the Iraqis before the tits up in Baghdad. So we take Herr Schrader's fertilizer eugenics, tweak here and there, and bring to the world from between our British loins venomous X, I'm quite ashamed to say. With all lesser-known V nerve agent cousins to come and join the unholy family." He turned to McEnnerney. "If I'm not mistaken, your Blue Grass Chemical Agent Destruction Plant is near Richmond, Kentucky. Crushing 155mm projectiles, M55 rockets. Not to mention what was in them. I have that about right? In the ballpark, at all?"

"We have chemical weapons stored south of Richmond and Lexington," McE countered tiredly, without an edge, keeping this friendly given that Davies was right. "We try not to put such places in the cities. Even if they're filled with trusting southern folk who don't pay much attention."

"Wouldn't be awfully taxing for you to make magic with the VX there. Given that they're disposing of your very many tons of VX. It seems like something you Americans might do for the cause, American exceptionalism and all. So we muse here in our spare time."

"Yup. If only we were so enlightened. We have a nasty chemical stockpile at the nearby Blue Grass Army Depot. Though it's a mere pittance of the 4,400 tons of VX we whipped up in the 60s and had stockpiled across our glorious heartland. Which of course was nothing compared to our 34,000 tons of sarin. Nobody pays attention to this, so before flying over, I decided to have a look-see on the off chance it came up."

"Thoughtful of you," Sir Nigel said with a smile, genuine enough, saluting him with his small cup. "Even appreciated."

Once running, McE continued around the track. "Brewed in one place then distributed to nine army chemical weapons depots from sea to shining sea. Almost. One on Johnston Island, 800 miles off Hawaii. I suppose in case we decided to go after Beijing and Shanghai this round. Then we head to Umatilla, Oregon; Tooele, Utah; Pueblo, Colorado; Newport, Indiana, VX only there as it happens, specialty stop, no sarin welcomed. So, on to Aberdeen, Maryland; Pine Bluff, Arkansas; and Anniston, Alabama. We wanted to make sure people in all different parts of the country had equal opportunity to die horrible accidental deaths. A good deal of it done, finished neutralizing about ninety percent as I eyeballed it. Hydrolysis, incineration, supercritical water oxidation at Newport for the VX. Been a while since the 1997 Chemical Weapons Convention that prohibited the use and stockpiling, which we're getting Bashar to ink his John Hancock to. Had to build most of these take-apart jobs from scratch. Blue Grass's got a good way to finish up. Unfortunately, in our present state, we can't get our powers-that-be to green-light the *Cape Arthur,* not to mention actually bringing a glass of Syria's VX onto our hallowed shores. Lest there be an accident, theft, or some unanticipated mischief."

Sir Nigel smiled. "So you want us to do what you won't?"

"Unfortunately, it's the American way. Pass the Buck, Chuck," McE said. "You can shoot the messenger. I'll happily take a bullet for the cause if it gets something tidied up."

Shai remained silent; he could not rise from where he

was sunk in sullen despair. The West was whispering that you can kill hundreds of thousands of civilians with big blunt instruments, just not with chemical weapons. Beside him, Alisher studied the lettering on the biscotti plastic, then ripped it open. Assembled and having made the slow journey from Tuscan Lucca, it was scentless and tasteless as he bit into it. He decided that he would need his own biscotti factories.

"Sorry about our MPs," Sir Nigel said to McE. "Twelve votes. Traitors running to Labour just because Blair and Bush gave them the fast shuffle. We have our heads up our arses. Follow the Americans into the dark, and run the other way when there's daylight and a clear view. Could have given those brave Syrian lads a chance against those barrel bombs. What a cock-up."

Alisher set his biscotti down and turned to Davies. "Sir Davies..."

"Call me Nigel, lad. If we're going to clean up the world's poison, let's have none of this British stiff-upper-lip nonsense."

"Okay, new friend, Nigel. So Vlad tell me, tell them. He much sorry. VX, he cannot take himself. Our destruction not so first class. Other reasons too. However, many things he do. Big things. So he promote favor. Nigel and bigger people. Sorry, no insult to my friend, Shai guy. Everyone have bigger people. Maybe even Vlad. So, if Porton Down murder this VX, do such favor. Sometime Nigel come to Alisher, this favor return. Alisher go to Vlad. Vlad open arms. Also, Alisher open arms. Not as big when open as Vlad. But not nothing." Karimov stretched his large arms wide to hammer in his point.

Two young women at the next small table eyed Karimov and giggled the way young women did when eager to jot down their phone numbers.

"Greatly appreciated on both counts," Sir Nigel said. "Will bear it in mind." He then pulled his coffee nearer and lifted his attention directly across the table to Shai. "Want to make sure we're not putting the cart ahead of the camel here. There was no VX on the original Syrian sworn declarations."

"I think they temporarily misplaced their hearts," Shai said.

"Which they've now suddenly found."

"So it seems."

"You have a source? Electronic? Human? Some new hybrid of both? You fellas are bang up with technology. This Q Cyber Security group of yours in Herzliya. Doing the nasty on cell phones. A declared Chinese wall between them and the Mossad? Tissue paper, maybe. Anything you can't do, if you put your minds to it? In the name of survival, of course."

"How about I don't lie to you?" Shai suggested. "I much prefer not to though some say I have a talent for it."

Sir Nigel let loose a grin. "We're all just meeting for a friendly cuppa. You confident it's comprehensive, what McE's given us?"

"If not, it's close."

One of the girls stood shyly, her friend physically nudging her. She tottered near on high narrow heels, her boots rising most of the way towards her very short skirt. Her wispy blond hair jumped as she wobbled.

She giggled, thrust the scrap of pink-lined paper with her phone number out, and set it before Shai. "I'm Amy. You remind me of my dad. He's super." Before he could say anything, she darted away, and holding hands with her friend for balance, they ran off.

Alisher roared with laughter, and proper British eyes from other tables arrived disapprovingly.

"If I'm not interrupting," Sir Davies said with a playful smile. He drained his coffee and slowly turned to McE. "Let me run this up the food chain and see who's willing to bite. Maybe some cold hearts will be warmed by the reminder that we delivered this plague to the planet. We have a military aircraft testing site, RAF Boscombe Down. At Amesbury, Wiltshire. Been there since the first cows ever went to pasture. Private, just two hardly noticed runways. In your parlance, as the crow flies five miles from Porton Down, who obviously are up to the task."

Sir Nigel pushed the biscotti away and patted his stomach to indicate the need to keep it flat, which it was. "Alisher, you think your Vlad might spare a couple of large cargo planes for flights from Mezzeh Air Force base in Damascus to Boscombe Down? They'd be helpfully inconspicuous at Mezzeh if any of the baddies are about. No need to waste ink on flight plans. Especially with everybody so busy and all in today's fast-paced world."

"This not even question. Vlad proud help. This certain fact."

"Okay boys," Sir Nigel said and stood. "I'll see what kind of enthusiasm I can muster. But everything on the hush-hush, obviously. We've paid rather a sizeable price for our colonial adventures in terms of the people we're forced to let inside our very insecure shores. Don't want any attempts at a grab of the VX."

After Sir Nigel bid his goodbyes, Alisher picked up the pink-lined paper. "You no call, I think. Pity. Maybe world go bang tomorrow. Never know."

Shai smiled. "Always heartening to hear someone speak well about a parent." He took the scented pink scrap and tore it in short lengths.

"This Sir Nigel," Alisher asked. "Why he *Sir*. He save country from the Fascists? Or maybe the Americans?"

"He's a virtuoso violinist," McEnnerney explained. "Violin, very good." As he saw on Karimov's fact that he did not understand. "Goes into poor neighborhoods far and near. Sets up music classes. Orchestras. Buys everyone instruments. Even has them wrapped."

"I so love this," Alisher said. "Maybe I do too in Russia. Not in entertainment centers. There pay, of course. But poor places, I want. Alisher's duty help make such music."

Shai turned to McE. "Any decision on the *Cape Arthur?*"

"Just checked my phone. Doesn't look good."

CHAPTER 14

INSTITUTE 3000

DAMASCUS

A bead of sweat dripped down General Muhammad Mitqal's forehead and sped down the side of his face into his meticulously trimmed gray beard. It was stifling again as he strode down the underground corridor of Institute 3000. Stark overhead fluorescents created a shadow of himself in front of him; for a brief moment, he thought of himself as double an ordinary man. He could not understand how they could revolutionize the readiness of sarin, yet the air conditioning regularly groaned at anemic levels.

Mitqal nodded at a soldier who pulled open the blast door, which squealed on unoiled hinges. Inspecting what he had achieved here calmed him. He glared as the two electric lights flickered in the room.

"You can't make those *work*?" Mitqal thundered at the guard.

"I'm sorry, General. As soon as you are safely out, I will replace them again. I think it's the wiring."

Rows of bulging steel tanks rested on wood stilt supports, each with 2,000 liters of DF. He nodded towards the blast door on the far side of the room, and the soldier scurried to pull it open. This door too cried out. The corridor was dark. Rooms without doors stood off both sides of the hallway deep underground. He entered the first to his left, and annoyed with the poor light, removed his cell phone and quickly found the torch, felt it crucial to master new technology. He moved the small beam meticulously from wood barrel to wood barrel of isopropyl alcohol in search of leakage. Not trusting his eyesight, since he shunned the need for glasses, he ran his fingers along the barrel bottoms as these were safe to touch. All felt dry. Farther down in the annoying corridor half-light, a door led to the mixing room. He did not want to risk heading there, even in the unlikelihood of a spill. Mitqal himself had procured the gleaming German stainless-steel vats where the sarin was alive. He'd gotten the glass reactor vessels necessary for mixing, reaction, distillation, and chemical filtration from a company in Victorville, California that manufactured them for pharmaceutical companies. Not a single one arrived even cracked. Nobody knew how to pile up money, Mitqal thought, like the Americans.

He was not particularly pleased that Bashar had revealed the secret of the sarin in Ghouta, like pulling the veil from a bride before the wedding, though they had dropped it four months earlier from a single helicopter in Saraqib. Like a maddening football match, first, the rebels charged down the field for a goal, then were thrown westward only to regroup and mount another fearless coordinated effort towards the town of 30,000. Apoplectic at the inability to take the vital junction between the M5 that burst north to Aleppo and the M4 west to Idlib, they experimented with the sarin clearing the way to the opposition citadel. One woman succumbed from the sarin before arriving at a hospital in Turkey. Several others, shaking with nausea, and vomiting, staggered across that northern border and stretched out their arms to offer blood samples. Gratefully, with the delay, all were inconclusive.

Mitqal had adjusted easily to the horse trade of the sarin for no disruption of their other terrors from the skies. Like

Bashar, he couldn't believe their luck that the Americans had agreed so quickly to take only a prize Arabian stallion and sail home. He had been prepared to join the Council of Elders in a new Syria, even secretly hoped for that eventuality, and would keep that communication channel open to bring them into Bashar's tent.

Content with his ministrations of his realm, Mitqal walked into Sami's office and gently eased the knob back until the latch clicked. He reserved rage as a secondary resort or for those far down his hierarchy. Maybe because of self-consciousness at his wandering eye, he wanted to be liked.

"How is the mood here, now that we are giving them the sarin?" the general asked as he softly sat opposite the chaos of Sami's desktop.

Sami felt trapped. Thin and nervous, he smoked foreign Newport cigarettes, a status symbol in Damascus that had tripled in price since the uprising. With the new EU sanctions, many smugglers wandered from weapons to tobacco, which is far more lucrative per kilo. The Islamic State controlled a third of Syria across the north and outlawed a litany of vices, including cursing and all tobacco. In East Syria, a severed head in the dirt in al-Mayadin had a cigarette placed between the lips. Though Islam permitted smoking, ultraconservatives banned it as slow suicide so *haram*, forbidden. The head had formerly sat atop an Islamic State official. To Sami's terror, danger was spilling from every direction, near and far.

Recently the Islamic Front had wrested the Bab al-Hawa border crossing into Turkey from the Free Syrian Army. Those extremist Salafist and Islamic believers had set aside disputes, mostly, to join hands in a 15,000-fingered fist to hammer Bashar al-Assad. Atop pickup trucks on the Syrian side of the crossing, they poked their rifle muzzles through all imports. Mountain rebels with little food but with tribesmen among the smugglers bragged online about smoking four packs a day instead of eating. The Salafists sought to spread the understanding that Islam had peaked in its first centuries after

Muhammad and his followers migrated from Mecca to Medina in 622. Since then, Muslims had tumbled down an endless mountain, humiliated by Crusaders, Zionists, and apostates. The only true identity was not national but membership in the *umma,* the community. Arm in arm, global Muslims would return honor, security, and comfort and reverse the slide of history. They were the Lions of Islam they shouted as they beckoned the downtrodden. In the gulf between ideology and breathing, Sami felt, Salafist Jihad fighters laid out corpses of Muslim villagers, townspeople, and few Westerners. Maybe Salafists destroyed the *Maqam al-Arba'in?* The scent of the burned carpets remained in his nostrils. Since he and Kassem climbed there, Sami felt that the world was coming apart. In revealing the VX locations to Kassem, he was knee-deep in quicksand and sinking.

Sami's stomach clenched, and recently he had been bolting to the bathroom. The only correct answer to Mitqal was adoration of Bashar, but cheering too rapturously might arouse the suspicion that one was concealing truer thoughts.

"People here are saying little," Sami stalled, though that was true. "There is confusion and fear about what will happen now. That with it gone, they will have no place. Or worse, be taken away to create a new history that the sarin was never here."

"All of you are to be congratulated," Mitqal said. "You have accomplished everything that was asked of you. No need to worry."

"I will try," Sami said, his hand shaking as he lit a now despised Newport. Or maybe he hated himself for smoking them.

Mitqal leaned forward and tapped Sami's desk with a forefinger. "Nobody will be imprisoned. Or even removed from here. You are the great minds in science and logistics. Maybe the best in the country. A new mission will be found for you. Tell them. I promise it personally." Mitqal did not want any of them flowing into the fleeing flood and then rising from the waters into propaganda positions that attacked Bashar from abroad.

"It will help that I can say it comes from you," Sami said, just above a whisper.

"The regime will emerge even stronger. We are at the center here, remaining in power, with our Russian allies, of remaking the world."

A sadness tumbled through Sami. He tried to imagine the future but could not because he did not know where he fit now. He regretted that he had Lilia wait to find him someone to hold. He would have Kassem ask her now if she knew someone who would accept his uncertain station.

"I will let people know," Sami said meekly. "It will greatly calm them."

"Now, I'm afraid we may have another problem."

Sami sat unmoving and said nothing, his terror with him now at every moment.

"The Americans seem suddenly to know quite a bit about our VX program."

Sami's mouth was dry, his hand trembling as he held his cigarette. He saw Mitqal's gaze light on his hand and then as quickly depart. Sami smashed the Newport out and lowered his hands beneath his desk.

"Spies, you think?" Sami tried. "Maybe the American satellites can penetrate our communications. The Israelis can reach into cell phones. All security can be overcome."

"It is almost certainly what happened," Mitqal said with the calm of a still high-circling steppe hawk. "Foreign spies have always tried to burrow here."

"I *don't know* what further precautions we can take," Sami said loudly. "It's not my fault."

"Of course not, my boy. We are past the days where we punish those who have served honorably but have been defeated by some superior outside enemy. We are still a small country without American resources. I am certain that when the Americans were shown the extent of what you have accomplished here, sarin and VX, they were both impressed and surprised. It's a masterpiece."

"Maybe someone afraid of losing his job or waking up in Saydnaya Prison sold the information? My office door has only a simple lock. Down here, I never thought to..." Sami looked down. "Everyone is afraid, general. Ghouta made us more so. I can't explain exactly." His head came up slowly. "Maybe because it's so close and not what we imagined we were readying here."

"You did not think we would send the sarin into Damascus, did you?"

"Did you plan it all along, general?"

"Sami, more things surprise me than not," Mitqal answered truthfully. "It is how one bends that determines a man's strength. Tree branches bow in a storm. Otherwise, they'd snap. If he had lived, Bassel might have built a bridge to the opposition. With his strength and charisma, ease them to a middle ground and move there himself. Bashar has not bent in a hurricane and is one of the lucky few not uprooted. He rained sarin on Ghouta and is now stronger for it. I imagined none of this. I am a soldier. I respond to changes in what is." Mitqal's steppe eagle floated lower toward the prey. "It is how you can enjoy a long and comfortable life too, Sami."

Sami was so nervous, his hands shook under his desk. He was a coward, not meant for any of this, and ached to run.

Mitqal sensed Sami was attempting to hide like a desert rabbit looking to blend into the gray rock. Mitqal soared down, talons out, as he had in so many interrogations when younger and making his mark. Though he rarely engaged in any now, he saw he missed them. "Maybe you are asking what you owe your country when it's so changed that you no longer see yourself in it?"

He couldn't hold it all in any longer. "Atropine was missing," Sami blurted out. "A lot of it."

"When did this come to your attention?"

"I went to the storage room immediately after Ghouta.

Don't ask me why. I don't *know*. I think I was worried the Americans would drop bunker busters after we had mixed the sarin." He then murmured sotto voce. "I'm sorry that I was afraid."

Mitqal offered a small paternal smile. "Anyone who isn't afraid working here is a liar. Fear is part of bending. Those who pretend they aren't eventually break. Who has access to the atropine?"

"Many people. There's a keypad with a code. I would not discipline anybody for sharing it."

"What are you hiding, Sami?"

"Maybe someone wanted more for their department. That's what I thought, why I said nothing—Obama's *red line*. We charged across it like a bull. In the end, the bull is always lying on the ground."

"Bashar has been president for thirteen years. He is forty-eight. He will be leading the Syrian people when your grandchildren are born. About that, I can assure you. Sami, what are you not telling me?"

Sami fumbled with the pack of cigarettes on his desk, again furious at himself for the insecurity of buying this American tobacco. He had stupidly imagined the women at the Qasioun campsite would be impressed. "There is *nothing* general," he thundered. "I promise you."

Mitqal had made a career of listening to the scales of fear and believed the notes on Sami's were too high. If he pushed too hard now, the boy might find reserves of strength. He would take him on an outing later, sure to melt his resolve like lard in the burning sun.

Mitqal said, "Get Kassem."

Sami nodded a little too vigorously, he thought, and picked up the phone. He would say nothing about the VX data he had handed Kassem, he promised himself, even if they tortured him. He might not be able to hold out to save himself, but for his friend, he could. He had told Kassem about seeing him near the atropine storage room. He would not tell Mitqal either about Kassem and the picnic basket. He had bent in revealing the atropine so he would not break.

When Kassem walked in, Mitqal rose elegantly to his feet in a fluid motion, the metals on his uniform softly clinking. A smile livened his face as he saw his friend's son. Mitqal stretched out his arms, hugged the tall boy, and they kissed on both cheeks. Mitqal affectionately ran his hand through Kassem's curly black hair, then patted him on the back.

"I don't see you enough," Mitqal said. "You must come to my home with your father for coffee. Please tell him that I insist. Soon, or I will be insulted."

"Of course," Kassem said. "I'll call him tonight."

Maybe because Sami had piqued his concern, Mitqal realized something he had noticed before, but that had not penetrated but dropped away like rain from the Burberry trench coat in his office closet. The tall Kassem looked neither like his short father nor his tiny, round mother. Though Mitqal reminded himself that the next generation is always grander. Certainly, Kassem had never huddled under his bed covers hungry. Still...

"Leave us," Mitqal told Sami.

When Sami had shut the door hard, Mitqal invited Kassem to Sami's chair. "The Americans somehow learned much about the VX. What have you heard? The preparations and movements of the sarin across the country last year reached the American's ears very quickly. Sami tells me that atropine disappeared just before the operation against the Ghouta terrorists. Might someone have smuggled it to them?"

Kassem was not sure how he felt so calm. He suddenly wondered if it was because, if caught, he had finally fulfilled the purpose he had longed for.

"We have enough in each department," Kassem said. His father had instructed him, if questioned, to disarm with inconclusive truth. "Everyone here is loyal. Maybe someone has childhood friends there? Would someone choose to save women, children, elders?" Kassem shrugged. "I cannot promise you I would not myself. It was atropine, not missiles."

"You have been looking for a possible leak, as your father instructed? I am becoming more certain that one exists. Though you are quiet, you observe. I know this about you. What is your instinct?"

"Someone would have to be very careful. I will not find someone with a hand in a drawer. I am watching states of mind. But everything is changing so greatly and fast. It is normal to feel nervous."

"What about Sami? I believe he is worried about his future when the sarin is gone."

Kassem laughed. "Never. He's a master logistician. He can move and hide material like nobody. There is always a place for the Samis of the world."

"Can he be blackmailed?"

"No." Kassem smiled. "Only for smoking foreign cigarettes. No hashish. Doesn't even touch shisha."

Maybe to sidestep his worry, Kassem's mind went to last week when he watched television with his father. In a rare, televised speech Bashar had said: *The homeland was for those who fight in its defense and not for those who smoke shisha while its people are being killed.* Kassem filled with outrage at his charge that the homeland was only for those Syrians lined up behind him. Immediately loyalists waved flags in a campaign to revoke the citizenship of Muhammad al-Halqi, the Prime Minister's son, after he appeared inhaling a shisha hookah, wearing shorts, a t-shirt, in sunglasses, and, in defiance, *enjoying* himself. Kassem watched his father halve himself like a walnut. Suddenly exposing his soft inside, Fuad seemed to unburden himself to him. Behind the curtains on the public stage, he explained, he battled this single-minded absolutism wherever it reared. He told Kassem that a large wise Council of men and women from every class and corner of Syria who felt identically waited offstage. Kassem had excitedly wondered if there was a seat at such a feast for him.

"I *want* the traitor," Mitqal said quietly, increasingly

worried about the consequences of one he could not snare revealed betraying the country under his nose.

"I believe they have penetrated our systems electronically. But if not." Kassem rose to exit. "General, I will find him."

"Hacking our systems would not explain the disappearance of the atropine."

"They may not be related. Anyone might have wanted those syringes."

"I want to see you and your father at my home. Immediately." Then he added quieter. "For coffee."

Kassem strode down the hall. Once away from Mitqal, fear struck him like the icy waterfall from the nearby Zabadani spring. He had thought his father untouchable. He realized he had been naive.

Shai waited outside the Holy Trinity Cathedral in Jerusalem's Russian Compound for Alisher Karimov to emerge with the latest bad news, of which there never seemed a shortage. Eight magnificent steeples, tall narrow windows encircling each, rose high above the white stone facades. A few steps from the Church of the Holy Sepulcher and out the New Gate from the Old City, in 1860 Russia shoved an army of spades into 68 prime dunams, the Ottoman land measure still used in Israel today, or more conventionally, 17 acres. A decade later, passersby admired a surrounding limestone wall that protected a men's and women's hotel, a hospital, the Russian consulate, and the cathedral's painted icons and elaborate gold work. In turn, the Russians, Ottomans, and Brits flew out of Jerusalem's revolving door. The Jews, who needed more friends than most, returned the cathedral to the Russian Orthodox Church and leased the Consulate to whoever was in charge in Moscow. The door kept turning. The Israelis got off inside the police station and prison that Whitehall had thrown up inside the compound to welcome members of the Jewish underground sniping at their heels like rabid dogs. Now, traditionally dressed West Bank Palestinian women waited daily with hard plastic shopping bags filled with food for their incarcerated husbands and sons, though apparently more to occupy themselves than from necessity.

Shai watched Alisher hurry toward where he waited in the small parking area. Karimov had refused Shai's offer to personally escort him around airport formalities, declaring, "Underling most fine for suboptimal task."

"Yana is okay inside?" Shai asked superfluously, as Karimov had assured him she would be.

Karimov laughed. "This nave. She to memorize every painting. Happy I go and no bother sacred time."

"How was the flight from Tirana?"

"Flight fine. Stop only Istanbul. Bad news, Alisher tell in person. Good news, okay telephone. So come Jerusalem."

"Let's walk. I appreciate your coming, though it wasn't necessary."

"What is necessary? Love necessary. Only little food like in Siberia camps. Everything else for friendship. I do much business, this Tirana. Many old movie places. Need entertainment centers for young with multiplex. This new President, I like so much. Anyway, I explain. Albanian people like cows, long under Communist how you say in English? Like cows pull wagon?"

"Yoke."

"Yes. As exactly. Yoke. I like this superior word. Under Communist *yoke*. Now, in after time, people demand much talk in goings of government," Karimov heavily told Shai. "Students the most. Away from other young peoples across planet for long forty years. They hate so much. Worse problem, no strong leader. After Wall down, all go to pieces, so fast."

"Tirana, capital of the Ponzi scheme," Shai said. "I have some vague understanding of what happened. Post-Communist government can't handle the challenges of capitalism, so it ushers everybody into get-rich-quick schemes. People cash out their homes, their cattle, go all in. Always ends only one way."

"Incredibly shit show, of course." They reached Jaffa Road, the city's long main street that ran east-west from the Old City to the Jerusalem-Tel-Aviv Highway. A light rail train whooshed by. Low old stone buildings, shops below, and iron rails of the apartment balconies above, flanked the pedestrian mall. "This beautiful, Shai guy. Tell truth, we come a little. Yana want see Jerusalem. Maybe Alisher, a little also."

"We're happy to have you both."

"So Alisher, back to telling. After such horrible things, peoples outside say loudly, 'No have place to go home to.' Run in streets. Yell. This become big tradition."

"Protests, I gather," Shai said. "Not homelessness."

"Of course. Having home is sacred thing. This new guy they elect President. He Minister of Culture, Youth, and Sports. Before time, he big basketball player, Dinamo Tirana. Team captain even. Some guy. Artist too. Organize students meet when teach Arts Academy. Bother Communists, so much."

"A man of the people." Shai scratched his forehead, which sometimes moved the blood around to less active areas of his brain.

"You *understand*," Alisher said excitedly. "He exactly that guy."

"Bashar leak it to the Tirana press, that Albania was soon to be the new home of his creation? Though with some optimism for our team, temporarily."

"Vlad think *nyet*. Think maybe from Tirana government somewheres. So, hundreds young peoples come big square. In gas masks even. Make big signs. Also outside U.S. Embassy. This too big tradition everywhere, I must tell. Two days later, now thousands. Chanting, make with fists in air. Small country, so seem big number."

"You spoke to him privately?"

"For sure. That why go. This goings in street, Shai of course, already know. So I tell this president, Albania do great thing. Go in history. Save Syrian peoples. Destroy bad poison. Then destroy from many places in new factory by sea. Make big money. Make big friends. Tell him even I build big entertainment complex for free, one only. Kids leave street, turn to love him. He cry, Shai guy. I not lie you. Big fat tears. He want but tell me, so much must do. Economy like Berlin Wall, falling down. Police so corrupt. Judges still used Communist tell them how decide law. Government weak like baby. Opposition side in street yelling with kids. Want throw him in sea. He want help. He cannot. Everybody sorry. I tell Yana. She cry too."

Shai had arranged for a Russian-speaking guide to do the spiel through the various religious quarters of the Old City, the Via Delarosa, the Temple Mount, and on the far side across the small Kidron Valley up to the Mount of Olives. They would rendezvous for dinner with Tami.

When Alisher and Yana were off to see the sights, from his car Shai dialed McE. For some reason, Shai hadn't expected the Albanian option to materialize, so he wasn't much disappointed. Shai briefed him.

McE said, "The ladies and the paper pushers are still arm wrestling. The women are demanding a trial run. They want to wait for a storm just to make a point."

Despite himself, Shai laughed. If anybody could get the *Cape Arthur* out to sea, it was this gutsy female quartet. None of the gizmos better spring a leak.

✳ ✳ ✳

Thirty kilometers north of Damascus, General Muhammad Mitqal drove Sami towards the secret Saydnaya Military Prison. Ten thousand of the unlucky newly slept under the sands outside its walls. Mitqal paid little attention to numbers, and the deaths accelerated so rapidly that these figures were best erased from memory. From the high mountains, Our Lady of Saydnaya Monastery gazed down upon the prison in the inhospitable valley below. Given Syria's envied position as a crossroads between East and West, the convent resembled a stone fortress more than a Greek Orthodox Church run by an order of nuns.

Seat of the ancient Patriarchate of Antioch, the nuns sang in celebration of the Most Holy Theotokos, Eastern Christianity's claim on the "God-bearer," the mother of Jesus. According to legend, in 545 A.D. Byzantine Emperor Justinian I, while marching troops across Syria, either bent on Jerusalem or dismantling Persian armies; the lore was vague. Still, in all variations, Justinian chased a gazelle to the spring of Saydnaya. Before his arrow could penetrate its flesh, the animal morphed into an icon of Theotokos, inevitably circled by bright light. The voice emanating from the brilliance, not unexpectedly, requested a church be raised on the spot.

In Rome, difficulties with the architectural sketches for the edifice atop Mount Qalamoun, a challenging 1,400 meters, required Theotokos to reappear to Justinian in a dream where she ironed out the difficulties of construction atop a towering cliff. Modern probes found no 6th Century sediments in the stone structures. Across the outdoor stone plateau floor from the domed church, the renowned *Shaghoura*, the illustrious icon of the Virgin, was secluded behind silver doors in the pilgrimage shrine. The pigments were more reliably dated to the 8th century. Icons blackened from candle smoke climbed both sides of the small, dark vaulted *Shaghoura* niche. Gold lamps plunged on chains from the ceiling; candles flickered in them, and atop a central table flanked on both sides by gold drapes tied with sashes. In a yet smaller crevice, gold and silver necklaces, bracelets, and crosses hung from the silver grill before the *Shaghoura*—gifts across the millennia from the poor in adoration of the incorporeal, who could not lift them. In the library crowded with dusty tomes, documents from 1708 cited forty nuns, a superior, and fifteen monks, so in the many corridors and secluded niches were prospects for the assignations the nuns abhorred.

The convent maintained an orphanage for girls, long swollen from its original thirty-seven. In 1948 the Mother Superior, seizing the obvious opportunity, founded a school for nuns and ushered the orphan girls to its desks. The nuns harvested much of their own food and stored it in cellars below their individual cells. Below the cellars, four wells supplied more than sufficient water from the spring, a plethora of gazelles, if not Justinian, had certainly discovered. Second only to Jerusalem as a regional pilgrimage destination, nuns from every edge of the Middle East and from across oceans flocked to Saydnaya to beseech the "God-bearer" and receive her blessing. They were either unaware of the horrific prison in the valley below or too ecstatic to consider concerns. In better times, Greek Orthodox families from Damascus and abroad summered here to pray and evade the heat.

As for the prison, unseen in the valley from outside its high walls, the mainstay was a vast Y-shaped structure named for the red facade. South of the three-story Red Building, past a small clump of trees and hardly much of a hobble even for those whose legs had been considerably compromised, executions were accomplished in a small square white building. In the main room, nooses lined all four walls. Fifteen to fifty were invited out each afternoon; they shuffled eagerly at the assurance of transfer to a civilian prison.

Inside off to the right was a courtroom, desks, a podium for the accused, a long table with ledgers, and inkpads for fingerprints to be pressed into those pages; blood stained the white walls. From Soviet pedagogy, inmates faced the chimera of due process at this Military Field Court, rapid-fire like a Kalashnikov. Deep in the night, meat trucks descended the boarding ramp and rumbled into the desert to the newly dug holes.

Beyond Saydnaya in the daylight, before Mitqal's care passed through the gate in the outside walls, Sami had seen only moonscape.

"We have no prejudice," Mitqal told Sami as he

drove up the arrival ramp alongside the left Y of the Red Building. "Doctors, lawyers, students, bloggers, laborers, professors, rebels, people helping rebels, businessmen, those who unwisely chose to join a demonstration—we house them together. No one is lower than his brother. Bashar has reformed society."

Mitqal parked at the top edge of the incline. Sami slowly got out. The howl of wild dogs outside the walls broke the stillness of the dry heat. Sami was so frightened that he feared he would scream.

"We greet newcomers with a welcome party," Mitqal said matter-of-factly as if opening his front door to these guests. "Knock them to the ground. Greet them there with electric cables with copper wire hooks, the regular electrical apparatus, pipes, and our innovation here, the 'tank belt.' Shall I explain?"

Sami was trapped and wanted to burst down the ramp, run free. But to where? He was inside the prison walls. With less than no choice, he whispered, "Yes."

"Isn't it obvious? A belt made from tank tracks. If not immediately available, old tires will suffice temporarily. The sound in the air and when it strikes is memorable. What it produces, more so."

"Why am I *here*?" Sami half-shouted, his walls of defense already cracking. "You know how hard I work."

"Standard inspection. I did not want to be alone. Sometimes, if I'm not feeling myself, I become saddened that we still need such places. Wanted the company. Everything's fine, Sami. I trust you like I trust the sun will set today. Nothing to worry about at all."

Sami believed not a morsel of it.

Inside, the stench of sweat, excrement, and bleach bombarded Sami. Guards in both military and police uniforms lounged against the walls. As they saw Mitqal stride down the left wing of the Y-corridor with its individual cells, lit cigarettes disappeared under their boots. After twists of legs, postures abruptly straightened. Mitqal and Sami had already passed the group rooms in the wider main walkway before the two diverging paths. Sami had looked through the peepholes into the communal cells, incredulous that dirty white-cloth blindfolds wrapped around everyone's eyes. Moans escaped the small cells. However, the unnerving sounds emerged from the wall vents—a high wail, the thuds of "tank tracks," crying, pleading, electrodes sizzling flesh, a never-ending scream after an eternity finally trailing off.

"One person tortured is like everyone feeling the blows," Mitqal said off-handedly, either to manipulate or because torture had become humdrum, not entirely certain himself. "Because they hear it, they feel it is happening to them. It was not planned. But the air conditioning here chooses to work wonderfully. Sometimes the universe dispenses horror the way it wants."

"If Bashar loses the war, the world will not forgive this," Sami said.

"At the very worst, a new regime will empty the prisons. Who will remember what was never seen? Beyond that, the best of us will be needed to ensure the transition. You could be among them. But for now, let us continue our inspection. Amazing innovations happen here," Mitqal said, this time with actual excitement. "Scientists come together in the group cells and invent new medicines. Engineers, imams, and teachers give lectures to the other prisoners. Scholars impart great wisdom. Even blindfolded. Those who are eventually released will go on to lead richer lives."

Sami was so blind with fear that, for a moment, he believed it could be true. Then inside himself, he collapsed.

Small hatches were set at the bottom of each metal entrance, like dog doors. "To eat, we place the plate on the hall floor. They stick their heads out." Mitqal pointed to a guard and then moved a stubby finger to a low door. "Open that one."

The guard bent, and the metal squealed as he lifted it. Clasps caught and held. Soon a bloody bald head poked out.

Mitqal shrugged. "There's no light in the cells, so he

thinks it's dinner." He turned to the guard. "Help him back in. But gently, please. His suffering is sufficient."

The guard looked at the general, puzzled.

"Never mind." Mitqal bent, placed hands softly on the man's shoulders, and eased him back. "My brother, please. I am sorry to disturb you. The food is not yet ready."

The man emitted no sounds and, on all fours, backpedaled into the cell. Sami's breath caught in his chest, and he felt a squeezing tightness; he must be suffering a heart attack. The small portal eased shut with a metallic whisper.

Mitqal came closer to Sami. "Terror teaches. It reaches far. Most of the older generation has not joined the demonstrations because they remember Hama."

Sami fell back against the corridor wall and said nothing, worried he might be unable to stay silent.

"You are young with so much ahead of you. I will explain how the world works," Mitqal said, like a school director to a child. "While vowing to destroy us, ISIS is our shield, our protector. Videos of beheading westerners excite the world. The outrage makes them feel like they are doing something, and then onto dinner. What a voice that Jihadi John has in English. Another British Lawrence of Arabia invading our desert and believing he knows our ways. The American drones search the skies for this Jihadi as if nobody who speaks only Arabic knows how to slice a throat. Not a single photo of the inside of Saydnaya exists in the West. Their human rights groups demand inspection. We tell them there is no Saydnaya. We are as quiet here as our desert. We only execute Syrians. We are boring. Nobody sends drones after the boring."

Born on the air conditioning, screams bounced through the corridor like leaves in the wind. To Sami, they were incorporeal, ghostlike.

"What do you want?" Tears dripped down Sami's face.

"Hard to hear oneself think in here. Don't you agree? It will be better outside, away from all this. Calming. Shall we walk?"

Eager to escape being misplaced in one of these cells and forgotten, Sami spoke, and his voice came out a small and throaty, "Please, yes."

Beyond the perimeter walls, night had darkened the desert. Stars winked in the inky black. In jeans and a t-shirt, Sami shivered in the sudden cold. In the quiet, he heard and then saw the silhouettes of mountain gazelles releasing small rocks as they scampered up a hill.

Mitqal deeply inhaled the crisp air. "Sami, do you believe everything happens for a reason?"

"I don't know. Yes. A life is not granted for no reason."

Mitqal released a loud laugh that bounded through the desert, scaring the gazelles who ran full-out higher, some noisily slipping, but only momentarily before they regained their footing, unlike Sami. Mitqal began to walk on a dirt road in the dark, and Sami hurried to catch up.

"We lost three wars against the Zionists. I am a realist. The Golan, like my heartbroken father, is gone forever." Mitqal found, so long cloistered in his office, he was enjoying the crossed swords of interrogation. "Sami, God does not hear these pitiable cries. I'm afraid that when needed, God is napping. I don't want to be forced to leave you inside Saydnaya. Truly, you have been a great help to me. It would hurt me to return to Damascus alone. My bones would ache to think of you here. Who is the traitor in Institute 3000?"

"No one. Everyone is loyal to the president. To the man. We have allowed in only the best of the best."

"Nobody was outraged about gassing Ghouta? Not a grunt. Not a murmur. No gas masks slammed against the wall? Only jubilation at how perfectly their creation killed?"

"No. *Nobody*. General, nobody would say if they were horrified. They know what would happen..."

"Maybe your memory fails you. I can arrange for you to spend some time in a crowded cell. Just to focus your thoughts. See what comes to you there."

"Please, general. I am thinking."

Mitqal remained silent for a long time. "I understand why God always appears to all religions in the desert. It can be very lonely for those who aren't one with the silence. Though you would not have that problem in a communal cell."

"I think Kassem took the atropine," Sami stammered, hating himself. Maybe they could all escape if he gave him *something*, an understandable morsel. Passing atropine to women and the elderly was something the general could understand and forgive. "Saw him near the storage room before the attack. It doesn't mean anything. He could have taken it for a hundred reasons. If he did. I didn't see anything. Just him by the door."

"Sami, was he carrying anything?"

Sami was shaking in the cold. "No. Nothing. Nothing."

"Then why are you so nervous? This is Kassem. Son of one of the most respected officers in the *mukhabarat*. I trust Kassem more than I trust my own hands. His hands were empty, yes? He was maybe clapping them to some song he was listening to through little headphones in his ears?"

Sami crumped to the ground. "A picnic basket. He was meeting a girl, I think, must have. He's happier than I've seen him in a long time. He had a picnic lunch."

"Kassem has been unhappy. Is that what you're saying?"

"No!"

Suddenly three vans burst onto the dirt road they had been following. Mitqal jumped out of the way. Sami turned to the vehicles and remained still, like a gazelle frozen in the oncoming headlights.

Mitqal abruptly ran, grabbed Sami's arm, and dragged him through the dirt to safety. The vans, accustomed to traveling this road in the darkness, sped past without slowing.

Back inside the main building, a strong arm—despite his age—around Sami's shoulder, Mitqal propelled him towards Group Cell 2 in the main corridor. Sami was near spilling everything, he thought with satisfaction, like a pitcher of water knocked off a table.

Eyes squeezed, Sami listened to the abrupt quiet, heard only water dripping somewhere and their footfalls. Mitqal nodded at a guard to open the door.

"Sami, you will be woken at five-thirty. You will know the hour as you can hear the Dead Sea Sparrows at first light this time of year. The rock partridges have beautiful necks, but they are farther in the hills. Unfortunately, you will only be able to hear the guards shooting at them. However, they are very tasty. I am told that if you lack diversion, some here count the tiles in the floor. Or count the broken ones. Man's ingenuity to pass the time is boundless. You had all the locations of the VX."

"I'm not the only one," Sami cried out. "Others do. And anyone down there could enter my office. Or they hacked my computer from another country."

"Yes, of course. All of that is true. Please enter."

The talk inside stopped at the swing of the door. Sami shuffled into the cell. In the dark, he saw only a mass of men and some boys, indistinguishable blindfolded bodies asleep, standing together, heads reaching for the walls. Most rested on the man in front of them. He never did anything entirely right; he feared torture more than death.

Sami felt a sharp pull at the back of the t-shirt, turned, and Mitqal hauled him back into the corridor. With a flip of Mitqal's head, the guard pushed the door closed.

"If I can count on you to say nothing to Kassem, I can take you home. Then none of this has happened. Like the prisoners, you have not been here. And we have not talked."

In shock, Mitqal's fist still at the back of his head pulling on the cloth, Sami managed a jerky nod.

"Good. You are like a son to me, Sami. So let us forget this cell. You stay silent, and this is over. If you bend, you won't be snapped."

Kassem certainly delivered the atropine to Ghouta, a sentimental and not highly effective error, but it signaled the boy could go further. Mitqal felt certain he would not do so without his father's knowledge. If Fuad's boots trekked in this treason, he would consider Sami's disappearance a flashing warning light.

* * *

With Kassem beside him, Fuad drove along Fayez Mansour Street, sunlight glaring on the windscreen as he glanced at the three lanes in both directions, cleaved by a grass parkway with lofty palm trees like generals above the battlefield. The Mezzeh municipality of 150,000 in this southwest swath of Damascus reminded Fuad of the European Mediterranean: three and four-story white houses, balconies, terra-cotta roofs. Foreign Embassies clustered here among the prosperous. They were due at General Mitqal's house near the Mezzeh Military Airport. Fuad felt a reckoning coming, but he had many friends, and Mitqal could not close a cell door on him or Kassem without incontrovertible proof.

The French had thrown the airfield up during their attempt to tame the heathens after the West, knives sharpened after victory in World War I, carved up the Ottoman Empire; as the Japanese would later, the Turks greatly regretted teaming up with German overreach. The airport had done double duty as the civilian airfield until Damascus International unveiled its runways in the mid-1970s beyond the southern suburbs. Shorn of its duties as the Syrian gateway to the world, Republican Guards and the Air Force Intelligence Directorate found ample room to stretch their legs at Mezzeh Airport. The abandoned terminals offered space for a new prison, a short drive after scooping up city recalcitrants. Old airplane tires abounded and were rolled in for their traditional role.

Since the uprising, rather than risk the open highway to Damascus International, the Assads flew only from Mezzeh Military, given the field's proximity to the presidential palace, which commanded the entire flattened top of steep Mount Mezzeh. With its spectacular views of every edge of Damascus, empty rooms of Italian Carrara marble, tinted windows, leafy perimeter trees, security wall, and interval of watchtowers, the presidential hilltop was either a gilded cage or the cat's meow. Maybe depending on which Assad peered from the windows; their two sons and a daughter ranged from ten to fourteen.

A previous Mezzeh Prison had squatted atop a lesser hilltop below the presidential mount, filled with his father's doubters after Hafez bear-hugged the country in 1970. In 2000, shortly after Hafez died, Bashar emptied those cells of his father's peers, and with early creativity, the prison, after a good deal of labor and new stone, sparkled from those heights as a science center.

Fuad believed Bashar and Asma had longed to reform and revitalize Syria after decades of Hama rule. Meek, unproven, and unsure of himself, Bashar had been unable to rise toe to toe with the military elite who considered Hafez a visionary who calmed the country. Bashar's vast hurt as the afterthought son drove him to prove his toughness, even after his father was in the earth and still not listening. Bashar grandstanded, and Fuad was unclear whether these stunts were designed to buck up the people or himself.

Weeks before, a hundred and sixty helmeted cyclists in shorts and white t-shirts, insisting that "Syria Pulses with Life" as the event was called, commenced at the Mezzeh Communications Center. Soon they pedaled past another life-size poster of Bashar, this one growing from the sidewalk before a tall, elegant rose-colored apartment building fronted with palms. With a seemingly limitless wardrobe, this time Bashar donned military camouflage and a matching cap. Small MiGs rose into the blue yonder behind him, and painted missiles blasted from just above the pavement, the gold script: "Syria Glorious in Victory." Given the ubiquity of these varied likenesses, nobody bothered to look. After twelve kilometers, riders pushed down kickstands at the Mariamite Greek Orthodox Cathedral, which rose first in the 2nd Century and had endured the pain of multiple successful facelifts. The bikers crowded in through the Bab Sharqi, the Roman Gate of the Sun, the eastern portal to the Old City, and the Street Called Straight, where Paul the Apostle lodged in search of Saul of Tarsus. It was called the Gate of the Sun because morning rays first brightened that stone entrance ahead of the other six perimeter arches.

Syria leaped ahead at the same time it was blown backward. Women pedaled, long hair flowing freely with their overall momentum. The crush of cyclers, including teenage boys, smiled in front of the white stucco church, providing a photo-op for the restless international media walled away from the regime's regular operations. In November 2012, Free Syrian Army mortars struck a 10-story Mezzeh residential building here for no readily discernable reason other maybe than it was in the presidential palace arena, and the opposition controlled most of the Dariyya suburb farther to the southwest. Then too the launchers may merely have been desperate. They had good reason with what was to happen in Dariyya.

In silence, Fuad and Kassem walked along a towering mosaic wall that earned the Guinness Book of Records award for the longest mural of all recycled material, 720 meters, a mile-and-a-half. Maybe three times Kassem's height, it was a tour de force, with pieces of every rainbow color, tiles, dinner plates, car parts, bicycle wheels, ceramics, mirrors, soda cans. It signaled beauty and hope. Amid the war, housewives had ransacked cupboards to contribute.

"It's saying," Kassem said excitedly. "Creating beauty from debris means we can rebuild our broken country. It's something I want to be part of."

"It's wonderful and optimistic," Fuad said quietly as they headed up several steps with pastel blue railings to a door in the decorated mosaic wall, newly planted at the sidewalk's inner edge. Each stair face boasted a colorful mosaic. Small blue, orange, and yellow tiles, old keys, and spark plugs festooned the door in the wall to Mitqal's building beyond. "Even true. Most everything is eventually rebuilt."

"But you're not impressed, Dad?"

"It's graffiti. It is rooted in the schoolboy's courage on their school walls in Daraa. It's the most extreme statement someone can make here without ending up inside a tire. But it won't save a single life. Stop a single barrel bomb."

"It matters how people feel."

Not really, he declined to say and while at it, said nothing. After a clandestine lifetime, he had reluctantly come to see that in the grander scheme, rarely did operations matter. From a drone, the Americans had splattered Anwar al-Awlaki, the Yemini-American imam, across Yemen; traffic to his sermons surged, and his pronouncements carried greater authority today. Intelligence continued their work out of a kind of inertia. He'd been at it a long time, felt worn down like a car tire too long on the road.

"I got atropine and a decontamination tent into Ghouta before the attack," Kassem said quietly, fearing his father's disapproval.

"Sentimental."

"It saved lives."

"Without doubt. But how many? At what risk?" Fuad's voice did not divulge his displeasure. He understood the carousel of emotions circling inside his son, that he felt he had to *do* something. Anyone can build a mosaic wall to feel they are not betraying by sitting idle. He felt waiting was a higher art, which he realized he had failed to impart to his son. Fuad spoke quietly, "Is this why we're here? Does Mitqal know?"

"Sami knew atropine was missing. Mitqal walked him through Saydnaya, threatened him. He was told not to tell me. Though he is terrified, we walked on the mountain, and he did. He saw me near the atropine storage facility. So he gave Mitqal that. Felt it could be explained."

"Only that? He said nothing more?"

"He swears."

"You believe him? Everything is on the line for him. Mitqal could leave him at Saydnaya."

"He was ashamed, felt he was weak. I told him he was terrific. He was."

They were speaking softly. Through the mosaic, they had stopped outside the residential building with its high pillars, shelter for cars to enter from the rear and rest.

"How much influence does your friendship have with Mitqal?" Kassem asked, unburdening the high tide of fear inside him to his father.

"I am not certain. I have known him for a long time. He prefers not to slam doors shut. If he believes I can be of use to him, even later, I may have some room to maneuver with him."

"He suspect you?" Kassem asked. "Of anything."

"Everybody watches everyone. More than that, I don't know. Even Manaf Tlass defected." Brigadier General Tlass was the first Republican Guard commander to walk away from the violence. In July 2012, with two dozen disgusted officers, Tlass disappeared and surfaced in Paris with his family. Former Deputy Prime Minister of Syria, Abdullah Dardari, with degrees from the University of Southern California and the London School of Economics, materialized in Kabul. After being accused of ambiguous ties with both the Syrian government and the rebels, he now stood atop the United Nations Development Program in *Afghanistan*. Syria was boiling, its great talent evaporating, leaving a residue of thugs.

Margaret had recently sent a postcard explaining she was now in remission from the breast cancer she had not mentioned. Stunned, he had sat unmoving for a long time, holding the photo of the yellow and orange buildings in the Saint-Jean Quartier in Vieux Lyon. Crazily it felt like holding her. Terrified to lose her, he had wondered if their memories would still sustain him if she passed. He wanted to flee and rest forever but would not leave Kassem in Damascus without his protection.

"Mitqal attempted to negotiate with the revolutionaries

early on," Kassem said, by nature hopeful. "In many cities."

"Then, yes. We are a long way from those early days. Sides have hardened. With America turning her back, the great chance for the FSA is over. Mitqal will think the same and act accordingly."

Kassem threw an arm around his father's lower shoulder. "If I haven't caused you enough trouble, father. Lilia, I've never met anyone like her."

Though excitement and dread for his son mixed together inside him, Fuad laughed like the lethal sarin components combined.

"In what way?"

"She's terribly vulnerable but afraid of nothing."

"High recommendation. Does she love you the way you love her?"

"Yes," he said immediately, then hesitated. "I believe so. There are things about her I don't know. But I think you do."

"You will have to ask her, Kassem. I cannot tell you if now is the right time. You will have to decide but also accept her wishes and her timetable."

His arm still around Fuad, Kassem hugged his father tighter.

Upstairs on Mitqal's balcony, they sat around a small chiseled brass tray table with intricate Moorish designs. The removable tray rested on six narrow folding legs, mosaics in oak. Handle-less frothy cups of Turkish coffee rested in brass holders, the muddy grounds sunk to the bottoms. The hot breeze, in its familiarity, comforted Fuad.

After the requisite pleasantries, Mitqal lifted the hot cup with thumb and forefinger. He turned to Kassem. "What have you learned?"

Again, Kassem felt surprisingly calm. "I have spoken to Sami. He is my closest friend. I ask you to honor that bond between us. He shared that he told you about the missing atropine. A decontamination tent was also taken. I know because I removed both."

"You gave it to widows and orphans, I presume. You have your father's heart with none of his common sense. Smaller men would consider this a betrayal." Mitqal brushed this confession away with a swipe of his hand. "I want to know how the Americans knew we were sending the sarin to bases across the country last year."

"I cannot find anything further. Satellite surveillance? Paying off truck drivers? Any one of hundreds of people on our bases? Inflation topped 120% recently due to present circumstances. Makes it far easier to pay off maybe a lot of people to take photos with their phones."

A pair of jets slowed noisily low overhead, descending to Mezzeh Military, a MiG-25 and MiG-23 delivered decades ago, secondhand and dented then, Mitqal thought angrily, and never a match for the Israeli F-15 and F16 pilots. In the last month alone, they lost two Su-24s and an L-39 to Turkish-backed rebel missiles. Syria under Bashar was a hapless third-world power. They never dared rise to challenge the Israelis who flashed over their air space as if it was Tel Aviv. Ten days ago, the Zionists decimated multiple installations and trucks laden with missiles in Al Bukamal near the border crossing with Iraq, the chief Iranian supply route into Syria and across the country to Hezbollah in Lebanon. The same night black clouds billowed over arms depots in Deir al-Zour, an Iranian militia and Iranian Republican Guard center on the M20 Highway in the Syrian northeast. They knew everything, he thought, enraged.

"I want answers, Kassem," Mitqal said barely above a whisper. "And I don't want them next week. Or I'll bring Sami over to the airport facilities and introduce him to the main hall. Why drive to Saydnaya?"

Kassem did not know what Mitqal meant and looked at his father.

Fuad was shaken and not surprised that ripping apart flesh affected him in a way it had not when he began his career. Age had peeled away blind ambition and left a soft caring for loved ones.

"Seven hundred people, no room to lie down. Open wounds, moaning, children, rebels, elderly. No ventilation. In the heat, the expected odors. Supervised by criminals from Adra Prison with electric wands. They avail themselves of the teenagers in front of the full audience. Then everyone is screaming. Word spreads, and it keeps people at home." Fuad was dropping his mask that he could participate in the regime in the hope of producing better days.

Kassem did not shudder. He was not playing with colored mosaics on a wall which he now saw as infantile. Whatever allegiance remained for the regime was now ripped from him, like gauze and tape from a wound still bleeding. He came from and was one with those inside that horrible hall.

"The Americans are the most arrogant people on the planet. Worse than the French." Mitqal drained his cup too quickly and tasted the muddy residue that stuck to his mustache. He wiped it hard on his sleeve. "Obama's *red line* speech filled the rebels with hope. It is a lesson, son, not to promise emotionally. After Ghouta, they believed with all their hearts that the American missiles were coming. For sure America would enter. If not toss Bashar down his mountain, at least create their celebrated "no-fly" zone. To ground the barrel bombs. Their honor demanded it."

Kassem now understood. "The rebels saw no help was coming. That they were completely alone."

"Exactly," his father said. "We are seeing a tsunami of recruits joining the Islamic State and al-Nusra. The Jihadis love Obama's *red line* retreat. It is a smile from Allah for recruitment."

Mitqal took up the thread in his deeper voice and pulled hard at the unraveling American garment. "They're telling everyone who will listen, and who wouldn't? The Americans lied. They don't care about you. You are brown, not like them."

"It's true," Kassem said, his broken and patched heart bleeding anew.

Fuad stood, moved to the railing, and looked out at the traffic moving casually in both directions on Fayez Mansour Highway. No matter the tragedy, whoever succumbed, pauper or patron, the world sped ahead without slowing, other than to momentary dim lights. Activists had spilled across the globe to tell their tales of imprisonment. Released by Mitqal's underlings, the gaunt Mazen al-Hamada clambered onto a boat bound for Greece and ultimately docked with asylum citizenship in the Netherlands. Over and over again, al-Hamada recounted Air Force Intelligence receptions. Spoke to audiences, recorded video testimony of wrists broken by chains holding him as he dangled from the ceiling, of leaping guards who snapped his ribs, of electric current charged through a pole up his rear. Tears always escaped from the dark eyes that seemed to recede into his skull. Before his arrest, he had documented the cases of detainees and fed them to the news media. He drove and snuck food and infant formula to the starving in the rebel volcano of Dariyya, where 3000 FSA soldiers held the municipality. The population of 130,000 was shrinking rapidly. Last month, two massacres over four days, two hundred and beyond executed, mostly dragged to basements of vacant buildings, never to climb the steps out. Another fifty rose atop each other near a mosque; people packed and ran. Eight kilometers from the city center, they would empty Dariyya and relocate everything that could still move to the far north.

Fuad dropped both elbows on the railing and supported his head with both hands. Nobody knew Mazen al-Hamada's name. He turned and headed back to the table where Mitqal and Kassem chatted, trying to cling to the shrinking hope that had livened his steps in his darkest hours. The Council of Elders was blossoming into a committee representing all of Syria and would spread its roots and branches for a time when it might flower like the white beauty of the apricot bloom. As he waited for that time, Fuad first needed to consider the danger Mitqal posed to Kassem, the woman he loved, and, lastly, himself.

The Americans had left Bashar safe to prowl his palace. Mitqal's future lay there now. Hafez's Air Force Intelligence chief and all since, including Mitqal as second-in-command, toiled from offices inside the palace, across the hall from the president.

Fuad needed the young woman to contact Shai for him. He had moved his crumbling wife to the elder care hospital with profound sadness. He would invite the couple to dinner tonight, cook himself, and find a moment alone with her on the balcony. The window was closing on them. Fuad loved Syria and knew Kassem did even more, and Fuad was devastated. He had believed that after Bashar ignored Obama's *red line* and slaughtered an entire suburb of the capital, the West would launch cruise missiles to aid a people who desperately needed that small amount of help to tip the balance in the fighting. Now instead of Kassem finding a seat at the Council, Fuad knew that he could not protect him.

CHAPTER 15

ATLIT BY THE SEA

Two days later near their home, Shai and Tami walked on the raised concrete railway ties of imitation wood in Train Track Park in the cool of almost-evening. The metal rails had been pulled up all the way to the old Khan Terminal. Grass, landscaping, and granite in two directions designed for bicycles flanked the narrow seven-kilometer design. In 2005, Israel had erected the modern Malha Rail Station. In its best use, the empty tracks from there to Khan were jammed with illegally parked cars, and in its sadder days, with beer bottles and other adolescent detritus. Much like the Mezzeh mosaic wall, neighbors bustled together and demanded healing fresh air rather than succumbing to yet another clogged artery to the heart of the city. Old bus shelters found new purpose as open-air libraries, minus formalities, volumes exchanged for another and returned at the borrower's alacrity or lack thereof. The path briefly widened at intersections into small squares with benches, playground swings, seesaws, and water fountains, showcasing old railroad gear.

It was about the only place Tami could prod Shai to exercise his legs, as Asher's patience for Shai's swerving as he attempted to bike beside him had long ended. She slipped an arm between his, more to steady herself than him.

"Your worrying has turned my hair even grayer," she said matter-of-factly.

He touched her hand. "I like when we do things together."

With her free fist, she punched his shoulder. Her security clearance was not much below his, and when he wanted to talk to her, which was mostly always, he did without concern if he could.

"They took the *Cape Arthur* out," he said without enthusiasm. "The quartet wasn't allowed to search for a storm, but they managed to run into one anyway."

"How'd the ship do?"

"No laundry detergent leaked. Not a drop."

"That what they had in there?"

"No," he said with no joy. "But what they had stayed put."

"So the sarin extraction is a go?"

"The Americans abandoned the Syrians. Putin will trumpet his great act of diplomacy. I expect it will get done on the easier side of how most things do. The Brits will take the VX. There's a Russian delegation landing in Damascus now to oversee their flying it to England." He stopped walking and said quietly. "A few years back, 2008 was the turning point for the world as we know it."

"The Russian invasion of the Republic of Georgia." She saw it all now, what tormented him, how he had failed to turn the globe back as he'd hoped.

Shai nodded. "When nobody stopped Putin in Georgia, he saw he could do whatever he wanted. The West had a great chance to draw a hard line in Syria. A new regime would have stopped Putin's new airfield from going in on the Syrian coast. Now he'll build that base and invade Syria from there and the port he already has at Tartus. While claiming otherwise, he'll help Bashar take out the Free Syrian Army. Since nobody's stopping him from this complete success, it's a short hop back to all the breakaway republics he feels were unjustly stripped from Russia."

"So you've felt all along this was the time and place to stop him?"

Shai walked without responding, looked down at the faux tracks, and finally said, "The Jaffa-Jerusalem railway opened in 1892. French actually built it. Took three years for an entrepreneur from Jerusalem to get the Ottomans to take his 5,000 Turkish lire and scribble out a permit."

Since he wasn't going to answer her, she tried different geography. "You going to go see Prince Bandar now? You think he'll fund the training in Jordan and the Stingers?"

In addition to his money-making media enterprises, the Saudi prince and Prince Khalid Al-Faisal had created The Arab Thought Foundation to strengthen the unifying Arab identity.

"My sense is he wants to. The Jordanians would be perfect to train the Free Syrian Army. I've suggested they take groups in six-week stints to turn them into a more disciplined force. The FSA's not far from taking the Nasib Crossing, which would make all this easier."

"You going to get to the "but?" I can wait if it means you'll walk farther."

They neared a street overpass, everything unusually quiet. Ever security conscious, huge streetlamps rose at close intervals on the walkway. Palms and other trees climbed the short hill between terraced limestone walls to their right. Shai was panting slightly, and Tami stopped and circled her arms around him, so his breath could slow.

"Bandar is all in on the training costs, which he'll see are covered. The *but* is," Shai said and gazed away. "ISIS is on the march. Al-Nusra share their lack of restraint. Concern haunts all quarters. Either get their hands on Stingers, maybe they point them not at the presidential palace but at civilian airliners. It's another mistake, another abandonment of them. We can secure the Stingers."

She hugged him. "That why you're delaying meeting Bandar?"

"No. Goodman can sneak me into Saudi any time. It

seems we have our own jetway in Riyadh, brothers in arms against the Shia. Though I'm not so convinced the enemy of my enemy is my friend."

She smiled. "Anything you're not worried about?

"Sure. Asher." He kissed her on the forehead. "Let's head back. I can't be away any longer."

She eased from the safety of his broad arms.

"People I care about are in some danger. I'm in danger of being too late."

"Can you help?"

A Palestinian breezed by pushing an old Jew in a wheelchair on the bike path. Both were laughing, and Shai felt more hopeful, if not for Syria, for this land.

As they walked, she saw he wasn't answering, which meant he heard her, but his thoughts were elsewhere, and he chose not to answer.

"How's the head?" she asked helplessly.

He was charging forward now, barreling towards their apartment and his car, and only his hulk was in Jerusalem.

His phone rang. He wrenched it from his deep pocket, saw it was Levi Goodman's secure line, and, his hands shaking for reasons he had no incentive to analyze, the phone dropped on the railroad tie.

Face-up, it wasn't cracked or apparently broken as Goodman's insistence persisted. Shai reached down and swiped the phone up.

"You better get to Atlit," Goodman said with angry urgency. "Interagency balking. Best handled in person. There's a helicopter heading to the Knesset pad." The rest Shai just knew before he heard it. Except for the last bit.

"The military is hitting Mezzeh Airport tonight. It shouldn't complicate your job. Other than risk it completely. Worse than the usual— long-range Iranian rockets en route to Lebanon. I can't get it delayed. Not a day, not an hour. Surgical precision promised on their children's lives. Warn anybody you value to head for the hills."

Shai looked back towards Tami, horror and cranial pain pressed into his face, an accustomed silence on hers. He said nothing, turned, and began to run. After a dozen steps, the throbbing in his head was mercifully overrun by the pain that shot up his legs.

As Tami watched her husband struggle to hurry, to her surprise, believing she could not possibly love him any deeper, she did.

Half an hour later, after he placed an urgent call, as the light four-passenger observation Bell 206 lifted gently into the afternoon, Shai gazed down at the park across from the Israeli Parliament. Fifteen thousand white, pink and red roses lined paths shaded by slim Jerusalem pines in a small way, a sign they were a nation that had arrived. As they pushed higher, he saw Joan Miro's bronze sculpture, *Tete,* a black brain with lines of pain slashed across it, and laughed that his problem was not so unique.

A bit over an hour ahead, on a natural bay south of Haifa, Atlit was home both to the remaining walls of the fortress Chateau Pelerin, raised by the Knights Templar during the Fifth Crusade, and of Shayetet 13. Among the least publicized of Israel's elite units, of late Shayetet 13 busied themselves in the Red Sea, relieving Iranian freighters of misery bound for Africa. Once carried ashore in Port Sudan, trucks moved the missiles through a chaotic Egypt into Gaza where they heightened Hamas's stockpiles in the basements of residential buildings.

As the helicopter cleared Jerusalem, the pilot thrust the throttle forward, and they lurched northwest. Shai peered down at the new superhighway plunging down the mountains to Tel Aviv. High concrete walls snaked on both sides of the four lanes where they veered through the West Bank to shorten the hour-long trip. As they hemmed in the Palestinians, the Jews similarly circumvented memory of the European ghettos.

The familiar rotor sounds in his ears, instantly they were

over the green fields of the heartland, the ball of the sun about to touch the endless sea ahead. The chopper bolted past the Palestinian metropolis of Tulkarm, 50,000 off to the right just inside the West Bank, with another 10,000, if anyone cared to count, interminably in the adjacent refugee camp.

Shai required one of the Sa'ar-5 class corvette missile boats, the largest frigates in their small Navy. He could easily make do with either of the two specialized Sa'ar 4.5s of the eight in that older group. He wouldn't need the advanced missile capability or, with luck—generally in short supply in his experience—any firepower at all. Though he'd ask if they could round up a submarine or two because it never hurt to be prepared.

* * *

That night, a few minutes after 3 a.m., four explosions, one virtually on top of the other, rocked Mezzeh and Muhammad Mitqal awake. More precisely probably half-awake, as he'd anxiously been shifting between dozing and eyes open terror throughout the night. He did not think he'd been asleep but was not sure. He feared the blame could come at his neck like a guillotine if he didn't unmask the traitor. As his building stopped shaking, he jumped out of bed, twisted his ankle on an errant shoe, swore out loud, and hobbled to the window.

Low yellow flames and orange-black smoke in huge plumes ascended from Mezzeh Airport.

His wife sat up in bed. "The presidential palace?" she screamed, frightened. "The *children*."

He turned to the presidential hilltop, whose high perimeter lights were like open eyes in the black night. It had not been struck.

"No," he said impatiently. "The airport, here."

In the sudden quiet, his bedside phone sounded. He limped over and raised the receiver.

"Israeli missiles," the voice of his third-in-command spoke quietly so as not to enrage the general. "Trajectory from the Golan Heights."

"What was hit?"

"Three Iranian planes, long-range missiles not yet unloaded. A fuel storage tank, likely by error."

"Any of the visiting Russian planes hit?"

"No."

Mitqal dropped onto the edge of the bed and could see the flames dancing higher in the sky into the smoke itself. They probably knew not to hit the Russian planes? *How?* This failure to intercept the missiles at an airport so near him while Russians were here could be pointed at the medals on his chest.

Mitqal breathed into the receiver just above a whisper. "Give an official report to the Syrian Arab News Agency. An electrical fire at the fuel depot. Apparently, bad wiring. No planes were damaged in the fire. We deny any reports of Israeli missiles."

"General, should I issue the denial before the accusation of Israel is made?"

"Yes. *Now.* The trajectory, some teenage rebel in his pajamas with a laptop already has it figured out."

Mitqal returned the receiver with a loud vengeance and cracked a plastic corner, making him feel even more helpless. If they acknowledged any of these Israeli bombings of Iranian assets, Bashar would have to retaliate or lose face. Firing inside Israel would bring a hellfire response. The result had become declaring Syria accident-prone.

Though such targets typically were spotted by satellite or drone surveillance—on this occasion, the latter—Mitqal felt impotent and frightened that someone under the spread of his falcon wings might be chattering like a small bird unseen in the rocks.

Could it be Kassem? Mitqal wondered as he struggled to the window, his ankle impeding him. He could imagine nobody else Sami would protect with his life. The smoke was disappearing into the darkness like an artist repairing his background; small yellow flames jumped near the ground from what must be the runway. And if Kassem, then Fuad too? It had been tugging at him too that Kassem resembled neither of his parents. He tried to remember if Fatima had been pregnant, but he had known Fuad only distantly then.

"Are you coming back to bed?" his wife asked from completely under the covers, hiding from the noise inside and out.

"In a moment." He would first take Sami to the Mezzeh Airport torture rooms and wring him dry. He no longer cared if it tipped off Fuad. If Kassem was in on this with Sami, Fuad could do nothing. Exhaustion tugged at him, so maybe he could sleep? He fell heavily into bed, thrust his head onto the pillow, but his mind was jumping. On the other hand, he felt grateful that Fuad introduced him to the Council. Had the Americans turned their military might on the airports, Bashar would have fled.

With the Council's passion not to trek in the Assads' notion of transition, alongside Fuad, Mitqal would have survived until retirement. He wouldn't have minded a gentler Syria. He was worn out from this prolonged internal bleeding and the certainty of years of it ahead now. He no longer had a younger man's illusion of the future as limitless.

He flipped onto his back, and as his trembling wife tried to hug him, he pushed her away. These doubts plagued him when he couldn't sleep. What was the matter with him? He needed to locate and hang the traitors. With that done, he would be safe. He prayed he find sleep soon. He always felt stronger in the daylight.

✳ ✳ ✳

Kassem parked at Institute 3000, surprised at the quiet outdoors. He gazed towards the peak. The campsite peace protestors under the red and white zig-zag communications antennae had disappeared. He wondered if they'd moved to a new party or had concluded the threat was over. Since the almost exquisite fear when he'd handed Lilia the VX locations, the following day and since he had been in a kind of subdued daze. When Mitqal questioned Sami, he felt like someone had thrown a hood over him too from behind. He could not see or breathe.

Lilia had turned even quieter except when atop him. Last night, her small hands grabbed his shoulders so tight her nails hurt him in a way that frightened rather than excited. She'd released loudly with sounds and a quivering body, and he was so worried for them both that he did not care who heard through the walls. She was undoubtedly Syrian but often asked questions about things that were common knowledge. She could be someone who went to America as a child or from the Jewish ghetto near the Bab Sharqi, now bereft of Jews. Which meant she could be an American or Israeli spy, and Fuad knew which. None of that mattered after the motionless children in rows in Ghouta and the way the regime used people like kindling to warm themselves at the palace heights of power. He knew a chance existed, more than a chance, that she was pretending, and he was *her* kindling. She might disappear without leaving footprints and unplug his life at any moment. He was fine before he had met her and could be again, he tried to convince himself.

Sami exited from the catacombs inside a large group of Russians in military regalia: dark green with red accessorizing on epaulets and military caps and younger FSB security in unflattering dark suits despite the heat. Next to Sami, General Mitqal spoke through a local translator to two Russian officials high-ranking enough to wear designer khakis and elegant short-sleeve shirts.

The size of this Slavic mass, maybe two dozen, spoke to the VX. The Russians were eager to immediately move the first shipment from Institute 3000 to Porton Down for the diplomatic coup. The American bean counters had a cornucopia of sarin components and the stainless-steel containers to tabulate here and across Syria. The quantity of liquid components would require months of Syrian convoys to the American ship. The runway at Mezzeh Military Airport was just long enough to accommodate the Russian Antonov An-225, the largest cargo behemoth on the planet. Three Ivchenko D-18-T turbofan engines on each wing and seven pairs of landing tires on each side of the fuselage assured the VX the smoothest possible touchdown. The Russians wanted the VX ready for the Antonov to glide down here in two weeks.

As the Russians separated towards several arriving black Mercedes stretch vehicles, Mitqal parted from two tall men with kisses on both cheeks. The uniformed one seemed sweaty and impatient, while the other in khakis had flat, almost Central Asian, features and an impish grin.

Engines roared, and dirt rose from departing tires. When Mitqal finally stood alone with Sami, he abruptly clutched Sami's upper arm. Kassem watched his friend shake as if touched by a torturer's electric prod.

Kassem approached and gratefully heard his voice come out calm. "How'd the meeting go?"

"Fine," Mitqal said abruptly. He tugged Sami towards his burgundy Peugeot.

"Where are you headed?" Kassem asked.

"He's going to help me," Mitqal said. "Inspect the damage at Mezzeh Airport."

Two levels below ground, Kassem sat still at his desk. Though the air conditioning was suddenly blasting, dampness gathered at the back of his neck and under his arms. Lilia was in class and had neither picked up nor answered his texts. The clock on his computer promised the sun had set. Sami had not returned. He dialed his friend's number, which again rang singly and flipped to voicemail. He did not leave a message, as the phone would indicate he had called once before. Mezzeh Military Airport had erected a new Branch of Investigation building alongside the existing prison dormitories. As the uprising spread, the Air Force Directorate closed the runway near the first bridge to the Fayez Monsour Highway and quickly threw up a new compound with rows of small cells and torture facilities. Kassem closed his mind to the image of Sami in one.

As Kassem stared at the phone on his desk, willing it to ring, it startled him and did. The gray LED screen read his father's cell. Kassem grabbed the lifeline irrationally joyous.

"I've had a long day," Fuad said. "Seems to have become my every day. I'd like to stretch my legs. A short hike?"

"I have some work," Kassem lied. He ached for Sami to burst through the door, wanted to wait for him. Though he knew that Sami might be inside a tire, electrodes anywhere, and retching out everything they had done.

"Please indulge me, Kassem," Fuad said tiredly. "My calves had been in spasm again. I need to move them." His father's casual insistence was like someone grasping his shirt collars.

"Okay. When?"

"Now. I'm in the car to you."

Kassem imagined Mitqal striding through his door with armed escorts. He had not returned either. Still, Mitqal surveyed his domain from the mountain palace near the airport prison, where Kassem knew Sami was suffering. He grabbed the hiking boots from his tall narrow closet, didn't slow to put them on, and raced to the elevator with them.

Outside, the early night was still. Stars winked above the mountains, the city below lit, sprawling and calm, the war elsewhere. Jumbled, Kassem waited for his father with almost desperation. He loved this city. Instead of Bashar being the man of the people he could have been, he lived with ghosts in his father's palace behind masonry walls with vast marble hallways and hidden courtyards. One room alone, Mitqal had whispered recently, contained 100,000 marble tiles and set the treasury back 10 million dollars. Kassem had thought, *while those in Ghouta searched for weeds to eat.*

Afraid he might not survive the night, to his surprise Kassem thought not about Lilia, whom he had known such a short time. His feelings dropped down to the city below. If imprisoned, he might never walk those alleyways again and inhale the scents of time, past and present.

Fuad slowly drove up and stopped. Kassem jerked open the passenger door.

"Mitqal took Sami to Mezzeh Airport this morning. He hasn't returned. Doesn't answer his phone."

"Get in, Kassem."

When Kassem slammed the door shut, Fuad drove towards the front gate. The military guards ran to throw the tall chain link open.

"Mitqal asked me to come to the palace to speak to him," Fuad said evenly. "I told him I'm on my way."

"How long ago?"

"Thirty minutes."

"He mention Sami?"

"He didn't have to. He's too close. We need to leave Syria. Now."

Fuad swung his car at high speed down the dirt roadway towards the city.

"Where?"

"The border crossings are too dangerous for us. You'll see soon." His arms trembled on the wheel. "I have to focus on the road."

Kassem buckled his seatbelt with a snap as the car raced. He could not ask about Lilia, was afraid of all answers. At the crossroads low on the mountain, Fuad turned right towards Al-Muhajirin and Assad's palace.

"We're going to Mitqal?"

"No."

Traffic was light to non-existent. Kassem saw they were approaching Tishreen Park, Damascus' largest, from the west side. Shaped like a giant green diamond, it narrowed at its point on the opposite end at Umayyad Square and the sword monument. The park was even more magnificent illuminated at night. Kassem realized he was emotional about everything now. To steady himself, he stared out as his father drove silently.

Lights blazed from the palms and pines along cement paths that wound through meticulous grass and flower landscaping. Annually, the international flower fair filled the air with fragrance. Daily, people tried to close their eyes to tragedy and fear, to stroll and play here. Young, traditionally dressed women with scarf-hidden hair gathered in groups to meet army men on leave. Soldiers in the comfort of civilian clothes danced together until emboldened to approach potential wives. Young boys sold cotton candy in individual plastic, tied together like a cluster of balloons. On the outdoor stage to celebrate Eid al-Fitr, the festival at the close of Ramadan, before Lilia, alone he watched children perform 'The Adventures of Smurfs.' He had thought even then that at this historic crossroads, Syria *could* be a bridge between East and West. He'd been like those men in the park, searching for courage, and was afraid he would be back there again. He was battling the despair of *leaving Syria,* maybe, likely, never to return.

His father parked just down from the tall Shami Hospital, green lettering in Arabic and English, each language on opposite sides of the flawless stone: DR. SHAMI HOSPITAL MEDICAL CARE CENTER. Kassem looked away, terrified for Sami. His guilt was like a hammer striking an anvil in his head, and he shuddered. And then he saw her on the sidewalk, walking purposely towards him with her signature short, rapid steps.

"Let's go," Fuad said, rising from the stupor behind the wheel Kassem had been afraid to penetrate.

As father and son reached the sidewalk and Afra ran towards them, Fuad's phone rang. Kassem glanced over, saw it was Miqdal, and to his surprise, his father answered.

"Hello, Muhammad."

"Yussuf, I hope you are having a pleasant evening. You with Kassem?"

"I am."

"Please confer my condolences. His friend, Sami, has unexpectedly died. It was not what I wanted, but so much is out of my hands these days. The torturers are guilty of excesses. But then you know this. Still, he had the opportunity to tell me much."

Fuad, who had witnessed and inflicted death himself, breathed hard but felt steady. "Is this why you're calling, so we will know about Sami?" he asked evenly.

"I want you and Kassem to come to the palace. We must talk. We will find a solution. You have served the country for a lifetime. I confess I would like to avoid the public embarrassment of my subordinate's behavior becoming widely known. We can find other work for your son. Teaching at the university, for example. You can retire. Even advise the Council of Elders."

"Let me speak to Kassem, and I will call you back."

"Instantly, Yussuf. You understand?"

"Five minutes, my old friend. On my honor."

He disconnected and turned to Afra. "Where are you parked?"

"Across the street." She reached and took Kassem's hand.

A sigh of hope fell from Kassem like a leaf slowly descending as he still feared it could be lifted away in even a small gust.

Fuad turned to his son. "Give me your phone."

Kassem handed it over.

Fuad looked at Afra. "Yours is dismantled?"

"The one everybody knows, yes."

With their two phones, he strode quickly to a nearby trash container at the park's edge. He left the SIM cards in place. Nothing on them would reveal anything more to Mitqal. Fuad dropped the phones in.

He took Kassem's other hand, and the three crossed the

wide empty street together.

Afra broke away and ran towards the car, a black Honda, one of the most common vehicles on the roads, Fuad had secreted in a garage. She had left it unlocked and stopped in the street outside the rear passenger door. "Kassem should drive. He's the best behind the wheel."

Kassem asked nothing and climbed in. His mother was lost to the world, and Kassem knew she would not be bothered in that residential facility. He suddenly fully felt that they were fleeing Syria forever. His heart shattered like a ceramic pot dropped in the street. Fuad dropped hard into the passenger seat beside his son.

From the rear, Afra handed him the keys. "Go," she said. "Into Mezzeh."

Hide in the regime stronghold, he thought, trusting her implicitly.

"Turn at the Al Mouwasat Hospital onto 7th April Street," she ordered in a firm voice that seemed to him devoid of fear. As he did, he wondered who she really was.

Kassem realized that this would take them into the desert and the highway to Beirut. A long 60 kilometers to the border on highway empty at this hour, and Kassem did not believe Mitqal had waited even the five minutes to start the full-out hunt. He could not fathom how they could avoid those chasing them on it, even in this car.

"Steady yourself for what I need to tell you," Fuad said to his son.

Kassem gripped the wheel tighter and pressed harder on the petal as the car raced in the dark.

"First, reduce your speed," Fuad said.

Kassem felt foolish and immediately saw a million reasons why and pulled his foot from the accelerator.

"Sami is dead, son. We will mourn this later."

Kassem slowed and carefully took the turn at Al Mouwasat, the older squatter government hospital; lights dropped on the cluster of palms and shorter trees at the entrance. He continued past the Edge Restaurant, across from a five-story stone apartment building, people dining at outdoor wood tables in chairs with matching wood backs and seats, the legs white metal. He longed for that normal.

A twin-turbine, old Soviet Mi-8 helicopter, green with windows all around, burst towards them from the direction of Mezzeh Military Airport. Kassem knew they flew both as a gunship and for reconnaissance, the most utilized helicopter on the planet. He saw his father watch the chopper beating the air low toward them. Of course, Mitqal would send helicopters. Nervous, Kassem swerved and quickly brought his attention to the road, though he feared the helicopter had seen them. He reminded himself that hopefully, they did not know about this Honda. But in the sparse traffic, they would stop every vehicle. He realized they would not reach the border.

The helicopter veered toward the nearby presidential palace, lit brightly like a carnival spreading over the high hilltop. It was disconcerting to be driving into the mouth of the serpent. Just before Hospital 601, his father pointed to a dirt road.

"Turn here, slowly. Careful."

Kassem was piqued at his father for again instructing him how to drive but knew that he was on an emotional cliff and feared the compulsion to jump. Sami was gone. He was numb, like the pain hidden by dental anesthesia before it wore off. Kassem expertly made the right. Soon they were in a dense industrial area in the middle of nowhere, low stone buildings, dead at this hour. Kassem had no idea where he was. It seemed like a manufacturing zone. Though maybe only one manufacturer as he looked again:

Safelator Elevator, in flowing white Arabic script on a blue background.

Sino-Japan Joint Venture
Hengda Fuji Elevator Co. Ltd.

"Park in the street across from the entrance and down just a little," Afra said.

Then she was on an iPhone Kassem had never seen, speaking English rapidly as he swerved to the curb, slammed on the brakes, and the Honda rocked to a stop.

"This way, quickly," she said and hurried out of the car.

They backtracked around the way they had come, towards the back of the building. Kassem saw large wood crates with Japanese lettering. Chinese capital, he realized.

As Kassem turned the corner to the back, in the barren countryside between the factory and the palace, squatting like an oversized bug, sat the Mi-8 helicopter he believed he had seen pass overhead.

Afra ran. On the far side of the chopper, a tall man bounded down the ramp, which did not reach the dirt. He leaped the last step and came towards them as father and son hurried.

He was wearing khakis and a light bomber jacket. Kassem stopped short. He had seen him that morning with the Russian delegation.

"So, please, fast," he said in heavy English.

Kassem dashed now after his father and Afra and followed behind them up the short ramp. Fuad grabbed onto both rails to hoist himself up the last small distance inside.

All in, the Russian pulled hard on a chain, and the steps clattered up. A small woman sat in the co-pilot seat without headphones, a redhead clutching a small gold cross at her neck with both hands. She wore a Russian flight parka, puffed green with a fur hood considerably too big for her.

"Thus so. I am Alisher," he said, sliding easily into the pilot's seat. "We go little trip. Please to seatbelts. Better in case stupid Syrians shoot at us. Bad too, we bring no missiles."

The rotors turned slowly, quickly accelerated, and sucked dirt up around the windows like a sandstorm. The Mi-8 lumbered into the skies, and Alisher turned back and tilted his head towards the co-pilot.

"This my Yana. Well known she love helicopter sights at night. So borrow helicopter. Very usual. No worries. Base commander happy give for Alisher. Maybe we go Beirut, jewel at sea, Alisher say him. Gamble in casino." Karimov laughed. "Make joke. No time sideways trip. Must return helicopter before so late. Maybe Alisher tell land empty beach, make Yana love. We see how goes all such things."

Now level with the palace, Karimov raised his hand to his head and saluted. "Must honor president, even if he kill everybody. Still president, maybe for life like Vlad? So good idea, honor. Of course, until choose murder him. One moment, so sorry."

Karimov studied his navigation screen, punched buttons, and brought the helicopter far higher. "Now straight. To Lebanon, so ten minutes. See Beirut in sky only. I make flight plan with commander. No Syria army make bothers. Almost no army, Lebanon. Nothing country but beautiful. More no worries."

In the rear, she touched Kassem's hand. "My name is Afra."

He gave a slight nod, non-committedly feeling so much he could not focus on anything. "Where are we going?"

"I don't know," she said. "But to friends."

Through high in the nose, she saw the flash of three F-15Is, tandem seats, heavy weapons load, her boys. She saw Alisher watch them calmly. It suddenly struck her that when they first met in the Golan, Shai had been probing, even then, for methods to defend them in the event of such an escape.

Kassem leaned back in the seat, and with the motion, the full force of Sami's death pressed on him.

Soon Yana grabbed Alisher's wrist excitedly, one hand still on her cross. The Mi-8's entire nose left, right and center, was transparent for reconnaissance. She pointed at the view as they passed over the anti-Lebanon Mountains bright with snow in the half-moon. Karimov sent the helicopter in a steep dive. Pines filled plummeting valleys, and a river roared though there was no sound over the rotors.

Kassem knew Syrian pilots saw no barrier at the border

and would chase them and fire if ordered. He was torn between fear and the desire to die. He thought of his mother and ached that he had not said goodbye.

"It's like Switzerland," Yana said in Russian. "Prettier. Less touched by man."

"For sure, sadly fewer entertainment centers."

She hit his forearm hard, then leaned over and kissed him briefly, not wanting to distract him.

Karimov said loudly over the blades' beating, "Pretty woman with phone. You can talk this Shai guy?"

"Yes," she said softly, not wanting to overload Kassem.

"You tell this things to Shai guy. Alisher make list of favors he owe. Need much paper to write. Still thinking. Not call yet. Alisher tell when."

Afra nodded. "Thank you," she said. "For all this."

Karimov laughed. "Thank later, when more sure no dead."

Karimov examined his navigation again and plunged them in a steep dive. Yana released her cross and pushed her face forward in the helicopter nose.

"Yana love low. So, good too if danger watch us. We make like tourist."

He switched to Russian for her and pointed to a Greek Orthodox city in the hills, spread between the long mountain ranges that delivered the Bekaa Valley. He pointed to the navigation for her to the word. "It's called Zahlé."

"Oh my God." She leaned farther, pressed her face against the glass, and quickly crossed herself.

In the moonlight, Fuad gazed out the side window and saw the white marble tower with outside winding steps inside overhangs, easily 50 meters high. From it rose the bronze statue of the Virgin Mary, as ubiquitous in the Christian Levant as Bashar's image in Syria.

"Yana," Fuad said in English, "It's called Our Lady of Zahlé. There is a church at the bottom for two hundred. In the dark, everywhere there are grape vines for making wine. Many around people's own homes. You can make them out."

Alisher translated into Russian for her. She briefly turned to Fuad and said, "*Spaciba.*"

He brought the Mi-8 high again. Once over the second mountain range, Fuad said to his son. "Midway to Beirut now."

Kassem knew he would never see Syria again, or not until it was a different country and the regime had been washed out to sea. He felt numb, like some clay object his father's words stuck into. He said nothing. He had never been outside of Syria, and this was more of his father's life that Kassem did not know.

Afra looked high in the nose and saw one of the F-15Is ahead; the other two would have their back. She was suddenly happy to be headed home.

At the base of the green mountains, Kassem managed to look out the side windows as the Mi-8 greatly reduced speed and dropped low over the sea wall. To his surprise, grand hotels many stories higher than Damascus buildings fronted a wide corniche with lights on high poles and palm trees set in the cement, he supposed in dirt squares, which was crowded with people. Like slate as far as Kassem could see up ahead, the dark sea churned ferociously here in white foam against a wall that protected the plaza. A double-lane highway clogged with cars ran between the hotels and residential towers.

"Much built again after war," Alisher said. "Maybe hope you."

Kassem closed his eyes.

"Woman, please," Alisher said with urgency Afra had not heard before. "Make known, we Beirut south. Need coordinates *now.*"

Afra sent an encrypted text, and numbers flashed back on her screen as soon as she hit SEND. She rose, balanced herself, accustomed to rising in fighter jets, and walked to the pilot. She held her phone to Karimov so he could enter the coordinates. As he did, he eased the Mi-8 five degrees south.

"Four minutes," he told Afra. "Sit *now*, fast."

She turned and watched tears silently crawl down

Kassem's face and willed herself not to feel yet.

Karimov veered south along the beaches, then dropped precipitously to avoid detection throwing up a maelstrom. He abruptly banked and burst out to sea, so low spray splashed the windscreen and brushed away the sand.

CHAPTER 16

THE GEULA

On the enclosed near-empty bridge of the Sa'ar 4.5, Geula, Shai sat in a seat gratefully bolted to the deck. The captain stood and peered at the clear night. Geula literally meant Redemption, which Shai found a bit too much, even for the moment. Shai wasn't much for these symbolic names, like those dreamed up for their military incursions into Gaza, the most recent, Operation Protective Edge. What edge? he wondered, thinking they had the clear advantage over the refugee camps in Gaza.

Considerably nauseous, he made his way across the bridge, holding onto whatever he could, other bolted chairs, the wall.

"I'll get someone to accompany you," the captain said.

"No need. I'm used to staggering around on my own."

Shai heaved a door open and ventured into the deep darkness outside, all lights on the ship switched off. A brush of wind struck him. He hardly felt the cold, warmed by their two babysitters, Dolphin 2 class submarines, the INS Dolphin and the other whose name he forgot, armed with torpedoes and Popeye Turbo cruise missiles that could be launched when submerged. When he had casually mentioned at Atlit that an IDF female Air Force officer would be aboard, rival resistance melted like butter in the sun.

Though the gray sea was calm, he gripped the railing with both hands and took some breaths through his nose as Tami instructed to settle the jumpiness in his stomach. He headed towards the stairs. After the second, he stopped and looked up at the raised empty helipad and the hanger where a helicopter sat in an open bay like a hen on her missiles in the unlikely eventuality she needed to be woken. Shai clutched the railing with both hands, pulled himself forward, and wind in his face, the frigate bobbing, made his way slowly towards the waiting area below the helipad.

As he did, he gazed eastward but neither saw nor heard a helicopter approaching. Whenever anything went this easily, before it was done, he began to worry gravely.

* * *

Alisher barreled so close above the water that the rotors threw up concentric waves in the sea. He peered through the windscreen and swore quietly, "Where fucking lights." Smack on the coordinates, he worried he could ram into the ship.

Beside him, Yana clapped in fear and excitement.

"Tell ship, light up like big party," he shouted toward Afra.

As she began to type, directly in front of Alisher, as if someone had pulled a switch in a ballroom before yelling to the birthday boy, "Surprise," the Israeli corvette blinked brightly, alive in the blackness.

"Stop. See," he shouted, but Afra, gazing ahead, had already ceased pecking.

Alisher drew back hard on the throttle and rose as he blasted past and just missed the *Geula*. He saw Shai guy on some steps nearly falling over and smiled. Karimov slowed further and came to an abrupt near-halt in the skies as the engines sang. He circled back.

"You need to talk to them?" Afra asked.

"Why? One ship. One Alisher. We make sandwich."

The frigate was anchored. Karimov saw a submarine periscope in a swath of moonlight on the water. His chest tightened.

"Woman person. Israel have submarines?"

"Yes. Five."

Alisher breathed easier. "*Horosho.* Everything so good. No need grandmother come watch big dance for boys make trouble."

Alisher slowly eased the Mi-8 towards the stationary helipad. When the twin skis hit down solid without a bounce, he slowed but did not cut the engines.

Alisher jumped up and lowered the ramp in one tug on the chain. As it came down, he saw Shai struggling up the steps to the pad, hauling himself up the rail with both hands, thin hair flying in the rotor's breath. Alisher bounded down the Mi-8 stairs, jumped the last one, and stretched an arm towards Shai, who grasped his hand. Karimov yanked him up the last foothold onto the ribbed pad.

"It went well?" Shai yelled above the slow noise of the rotors.

"We here so can only say yes."

Behind him, Shai saw Fuad start down the ramp first, and joy leaped through him.

"Shai guy, you listen." Alisher half shouted and poked his forefinger in Shai's chest. "We must make movie of so big adventure. For success in entertainment centers, make like comic movies. Not stupid but excite, like Michael Keaton *Batman.* Young people's love. In movie, *mukhabarat* follow us in cars. We get helicopter, shoot, hit glass. Near Lebanon, send gunships to shoot us to small pieces. Syrian pilots. Russians no shoot at Mi-8. Alisher escape with mighty maneuvers. Here on ocean big storm. Hard to land. Seas angry. Shai guy scared. Alisher worry, try several times set down. Cannot. Maybe peoples have jump in sea. Commandoes prepare go in big waves. Then Alisher do miracle landing."

"Of course," Shai said, laughing. "Everyone goes to those movies."

"So. Next. We must Tom Hanks play Alisher. In *The Terminal,* he do accent *horosho.* They make up country. Forget crazy name. Like Kazakhstan, but some no exist place. He can do little accent change, so easy. Again no stupid like great Tom Hanks work FedEx. Our Tom Hanks hero, escape pirates Somalia, fly Mi-8, so like Alisher Karimov. This everybody believe."

Shai threw both arms around Karimov and hugged him. "We'll find someone who knows Steven Spielberg. Maybe even start with a novel."

"Yes. Very *horosho.* Bookstores already in entertainment centers, coming *Master and Margarita* drink. This book everybody buy. Maybe name it Shai's peoples. Now Alisher make quick before some stupid peoples think helicopter missing. First Shai greet Yana."

"Of course. This sacred thing."

Karimov laughed.

Shai smiled at the entourage now on the helipad. He ran the short distance to Fuad. As they hugged and kissed on both cheeks, Shai saw the consternation on Kassem's face and decided it best not to approach him. While embracing his old friend, Shai looked towards Afra and mouthed a single word, *todah, thank you.* She gave a tight nod.

"Give me a moment," he said to them loudly over the noise.

Shai placed his hands lightly on both ramp rails and, with steady legs, ran up to thank Yana.

❊ ❊ ❊

Nearly a month later in Old Jaffa's Peak Park, Shai and Afra sat on the low wall in the stone square waiting for Lilia Wassaf. A small bag with a few things for her rested at his feet. Afra wore her silver star with the turquoise points still tarnished.

Shai brought his gaze to Jaffa's tallest building at the edge of the square, St. Peter's Church, built the last time from the bottom up in 1654. Its stone clock tower above brick facades had alerted ecstatic pilgrims at sea—the Holy Land is near. Late in the 13th Century, Louis the IX of France found the citadel leveled and raised a cathedral over the ruins. So when beseeching a generally indifferent God, one might have the solace of these views. The century before Holy Roman Emperor Frederick 1, variously king of Germany and Italy had thought of a citadel fitting for the promontory. About everybody had trod their patch of sand and still did, Shai thought, and that demanded of them a moral obligation as its custodian. Pretty much the way Shai felt about everybody's responsibility.

An old woman in a colorful headscarf opened the main entrance and scurried in late with an agility that belied her years. The mass in Polish briefly washed towards them, one of a bevy of languages rotated inside.

"The Acts of the Apostles say Saint Peter raised Tabitha from the dead in Jaffa," Shai continued, as a warm wind off the water rustled the palm fronds around them.

"We might need some help raising Kassem from the dead," she said, a sadness slow and quiet in her voice.

"How's he taking being here?"

"Not the problem. I don't think he much cares that I'm Israeli. Suspected it. Your nature types have been showing father and son trails and caves around Jerusalem. It's the only time he perks up. A bit."

"Sami?" Fuad had made calls and confirmed the death.

"Entirely. He can't forgive himself. Sweats in his sleep. Wakes several times a night. Paces. Sometimes outside. Sometimes cries. I fear Sami's death opened a door to a room he kept closed. Everybody hid a lot. Fuad, me. With little to do, it's all crashing down on him. He hadn't anticipated having to leave Damascus."

Shai turned to the brown palm trunks with green heads, the blue sea behind them. He understood as Kassem felt about his land the way Shai did this place. Nearer in the square, the modern sculpture, The Gate of Faith, brilliant white Galilee stone led to nowhere corporeal. A stone cross of four meters rested on two four-meter pillars. On the twin uprights, bodies entwined like a Picasso—Biblical, so none of the sex Shai would have found more interesting—instead, the patriarchs, recipients of The Promise. The gate of entry to the Promised Land. Shai felt fortunate enough to have once sat at the feet of the preeminent Zionist scholar, Arthur Hertzberg, at his home in Englewood, New Jersey. The short scholar in his stentorian certainty called this the *twice-promised land*. The Palestinians, he argued, were belated but equal recipients, their history no less inscribed despite the absence of a book.

"How are you?" Shai asked, turning and trying to penetrate her small dark eyes.

"A little jumbled," she said, "since you're my confessor."

"You're just more open now after your journey."

She gave a small laugh. "Entirely true. I won't tell anybody else, but I like it."

"I gather Fuad shortly will take him to Lyon. Get him away from the Middle East."

"You know about Margaret?" She laughed. "Of course you do."

"Never lucky enough to meet her. Hope to. I'm a great fan of anyone who can care for someone, separated that long. If it's not overly prying, will you go?"

"I think so. At least initially. I truly love him. Not sure what I would do there."

"I can find something for you with the team. It would require abrupt disappearances. No explanations. Not the mortar of a good marriage, should you go that way."

She put a small hand on his. "I'll think about it. But I suspect that it wouldn't work for him. He's still that traditional guy."

"Babies?"

She chuckled. "Nice try. Been expecting that pitch. Your reputation precedes you. *No.*"

"It's really too bad that love is not enough," Shai said. "We can introduce him to some scientists in Paris. There is something to the international Jewish conspiracy. The opposition to Assad has some presence there, though the center's in Istanbul. He might find a home in either place."

"I think he'll be okay in time. He has his father at his side. Though I think he and I are broken. Shai, I can't go back to the military. I'd suffocate."

"Same offer to travel the world from here," he said. "We have plenty of time for more comprehensive training. It would be a privilege to have you."

Shai watched Lilia Wassaf heading towards them, her short steps quick, and he saw tension in them.

Afra jumped to her feet, ran to her, and the twins hugged tight, the warmth of skin beneath their t-shirts building tears in Afra's eyes. Afra decided, despite her newfound penchant for openness, not to cry.

The tears, however, on Lilia's cheeks knew no such bounds. "I told you I'd see you again." Then immediately, "I can't go back, can I?"

"Not even under a new identity. It would be too dangerous. For your family too. Right now, you're just one of the many who disappeared." Afra laced an arm in Lilia's and walked her back to where Shai had now stood. "We have another idea we're hoping you'll like."

"Tired of the Holy Land yet?" Shai asked as Lilia reached him.

"Very."

"Come sit next to me," Shai patted the warm stone.

A handful of people, none younger than Shai, emerged from the church, chattering in Polish. The two young women descended beside him like bookends.

"Feel free to hate this," Shai said to Lilia, "And tell me

what *you'd* like. I'll do whatever I can to make it happen."

"Try me," Lilia said. A yellow rubber band captured her hair in a high ponytail, Israeli style, her face free of makeup. She was thinner, and he saw new lines at her eyes. Shai thought uneasily of Kassem and how much damage he inflicted on the road he traveled.

"One of the largest Syrian refugee camps is outside Munich. They're housed temporarily in a big army base. Of course, the authorities are completely short-handed."

Lilia was puzzled. "I don't understand."

Afra put a hand on hers. "We can get you papers through friends there. Legal. The younger generation has a lot of guilt and cuts corners for us. An apartment in Munich and work helping the refugees transition."

"I speak no German."

"So here's how we remedy that," Shai said. "I have a tutor that can start with you anytime you're ready."

Afra took up the approach. "He has an apartment in Munich about ready for you. Just needs your go-ahead to get the last bit together. A tutor there. A monthly stipend for some years. You can leave here anytime. Soon, if you want."

Shai reached into the bag on the ground, withdrew a crisp German passport, and placed it on her lap. "I'm sorry, but we had to give you a new name. Once there, you can start work right away or take some time to settle in and advance the language."

Lilia didn't react and then started to cry. "My family..."

Shai reached to the bottom of the bag, extracted a cell phone, and handed it to her.

"This one's German. It's yours. We took the liberty of taking your family's numbers from your old phone and programmed them in."

She grabbed the phone. "I have to wait until I'm there?"

"Actually, some of our boys played a bit with the phone. It will show the call coming from Germany. We'll adjust it back before you leave. But you need to tell them you're there. And please, no last-minute photos of our incomparable beaches."

Afra added, "Before I leave today, I'll take a couple of photos of you inside your apartment against a blank wall. You can send those. When they ask, you tell them you had a chance to escape, but you had to go immediately. You lost your phone. Went to Turkey, then by boat to Greece. It capsized. You almost drowned. Hit your head. Have been in a hospital in a coma."

Lilia laughed. "That's a Turkish soap opera. Where's my prince?"

"That you have to manage on your own," Shai broke in. "Sure, it's ridiculous. But when they hear your voice, they'll be so happy they won't care if you told them you've been on the moon."

Tears spilled down her cheeks, and Shai wasn't surprised when he found they ran down his too. Lilia opened the passport and looked at her new name. "Okay." She tried unsuccessfully to wipe the tears away but more replaced him. "I want to go. Thank you."

"Am I the only one not crying?" Afra said loudly.

Shai stood. "Just wait. You're going to be with her when they hear her voice."

Shai stood. "Thank you. It's an honor to know you both."

Quickly, he ambled across the square towards the snaking concrete path through the palms, the scent of the sea behind him, his steps heavy. Like so often, his operation had met with gains, death, lost opportunities, and hopefully some success. But this time, he had achieved so much less than he'd hoped. More than in a very long time, the future frightened him.

His phone rang. He dug in his deep pocket. A smile brightened his face as he saw it was Karimov.

"How's my favorite Russian?"

"Of course, wonderful. Listen, please. I think so hard this. In movie, who play Shai guy? First believe Anthony Hopkins. But problem. Very handsome but old. Then think wonderful Paul Giamatti. Still, little young. But then think good Shai young. Audience like, buy tickets more. So maybe forget Giamatti. Get Tom Cruise. What Shai guy think?"

"I'd be honored at any of them."

Shai stopped walking and was surprised, had not considered what he said next. "Alisher, this cruelty against civilians in Syria. The world didn't stop it. Vlad sees this. It's a taste of what could happen elsewhere to civilians where he has designs. There may come a time when the world stands up. Or your own people may. If you are ever in trouble or need a quick exit, you find me. I will move heaven and earth for you."

The line was quiet for a very long time. Finally, Karimov said just above a whisper, "Thank you, Shai."

AUTHOR'S AFTERWORD

In February 2014, five months after the G20 Summit in St. Petersburg, Russia invaded Crimea. In February 2022, Vladimir Putin's troops stormed into Ukraine.

The Russian military intervention in the Syrian Civil War began in September 2015 after the regime requested military aid against the rebels. In August 2015, the Syrian government entered into a treaty with Russia where Russia controlled and operated the Khmeimim Air Base, newly constructed by the Russians, adjacent to the Russian naval facility of Tartus near Latakia on the Syrian coast. Beginning in 2015, the Russians greatly expanded their port facilities.

Simultaneously, Russian bombers lifted off from Khmeimim and attacked military groups opposed to the Assad regime. These included the Syrian Free Army, the Syrian National Coalition, the Islamic State of Iraq, and the al-Nusra Front. Russian special operations forces deployed across Syria. In 2017, Russia announced that Khmeimim Air Base had become a permanent Russian military installation. Ostensibly there to bomb ISIS positions, they released regularly on Free Syrian Army targets. At the end of 2017, Russia announced its troops would remain in Syria permanently.

The all-out military assault on Daraa commenced on

April 25, 2011. On May 5, the last protestors dared dart into the streets. So many disappeared that the civilian death toll was estimated, with little confidence, at 250. The children of Daraa had ignited the Syrian Spring uprising.

The graffiti in Daraa, Bethlehem, and on the Mezzeh Mosaic Wall, the 1982 Hama massacre, the Military Intelligence Directorate bombing, the sarin attacks on Ghouta and elsewhere, Institute 3000, Saydnaya Prison, Mezzeh Military Airport Prison, the destruction of Adam's Cave, the Nasib Crossing, the British House of Commons vote against intervention, the G20 gathering in St. Petersburg, the Kerry-Lavrov tete-a-tete in Geneva, and the demonstrations in Tirana are all factual. Often a historical novel is easier to write as actual events exceed imagination.

On January 7, 2014, slightly less than four months after the Kerry-Lavrov agreement, Syria delivered its first shipment of sarin to the Syrian port at Latakia. The chemical weapons were loaded on a Danish ship that sailed into international waters. China and Russia provided escort to the US ship, the MV Cape Ray, for neutralization using hydrolysis.

On January 16, 2014, Italian Transport Minister, Maurizio Lupi, announced that Gioia Tauro, a port in southern Italy, would be used to transfer Syrian chemical weapons to the Cape Ray.

On June 17, 2014, the last 8% of Syria's chemical stockpile was transferred from Latakia to the Danish ship Ark Futura.

On July 2, 2014, over 600 metric tonnes (158,000 gallons) of the precursor chemicals for sarin gas were loaded onto the Cape Ray in Gioia Tauro. In six weeks, the first 581 metric tons were neutralized aboard the ship.

Syria's VX stockpile was neutralized at Porton Down in Great Britain.

At room temperature, chlorine is yellow-green and twice as heavy as air. Chlorine reacts promptly with water in the mucous membranes and airways to form hydrochloric and hypochlorous acids, leading to acute inflammation of the conjunctiva, nasal mucosa, pharynx, larynx, trachea, and bronchi. Those exposed may suffer acute lung injury and acute respiratory distress syndrome. Severe exposure leads to death.

On April 10-11, 2014, while sarin was en route to Latakia, the Syrian regime dropped chlorine gas on the rebel town of Kafr Zita north of Hama. 107 were affected, five seriously.

On April 11 and 16, 2014, unidentified chemical gas was released in the suburb of Harasta, in Ghouta in eastern Damascus. From the effects, it appeared to be sarin.

April 12, 2014, chlorine again descended on Kafr Zita, hospitalizing five.

On April 12, 13, and 18, 2014, chlorine gas was launched at rebels in Al-Tamanah in Idlib province. 137 were affected.

Chlorine attacks continued on April 18. In Kafr Zita, 100 people were affected, and 35 were hospitalized. On April 21, 2014, two chlorine barrel bombs struck a residential area. 133 were affected, four seriously.

On April 22, 2014, chemical barrel bombs hit Dariyya, the western suburb of Damascus, killing four and wounding 30.

Al-Tamanah was hit again with chlorine on April 29, May 21, 22, 25 and 29

Kfar Zita on May 19, 21 and 22

Al-Lataminah in the Hama district on May 29

July saw chlorine attacks in Kfar Zita and Aleppo

August in Kfar Zita

February and March 2015 witnessed chlorine attacks in Dariyya, Aleppo, Idlib, and Daraa, the seat of the uprising in the south. That year the number of chlorine gas attacks climbed into the hundreds. Most often, the regime targeted opposition-held suburbs to cause panic and force fleeing. Residents did, and those loyal to the regime commandeered their homes.

The Dariyya municipality of Damascus west of the Mezzeh Military Airport held 130,000 before the uprising. By August 2016, the population had shrunk to 7,000. Unable to break the siege and starving, the 700 remaining rebels surrendered and were allowed safe passage to the opposition stronghold of Idlib. After the forced resettlement to the north of the remaining population, the city was empty.

On March 24 and 30, 2017, sarin was used against rebels in al-Lataminah in the Hama district.

On April 4, 2017, a government air strike dropped sarin on rebel-held Khan Shaykhun in the northwest. It injured between 300 and 400 and killed 80. In response, President Trump initiated a strike against the government airbase at Shayrat, located near Homs, from where the bombers departed. In a UN emergency meeting, Russia vetoed a motion for international retaliation against the regime for violating the Chemical Weapons Convention treaty Syria had finally signed in 2015.

On April 7, 2018, Syrian forces dropped two chlorine canisters on residential areas in the city of Douma, ten kilometers northeast of Damascus. One did not release its payload. The other, with a high concentration of chlorine, struck an unstable roof of an apartment building and within minutes killed between 40 and 50 and injured up to 100. On April 14, France, the United Kingdom, and the United States launched missiles at four government targets associated with this attack. The strikes claimed to destroy Syria's remaining chemical weapons capabilities.

On June 2018, a Syrian Mi-8 military helicopter operating out of Dumayr Airbase, forty kilometers northeast of Damascus, dropped a chlorine bomb on the rooftop balcony of a residential building in Douma. 34 deaths were known to have been tallied.

On July 6, 2018, a helicopter dropped a chlorine payload that struck a multi-story apartment building in Douma, killing 49 and injuring more than 600.

Chlorine gas attacks continued.

On April 1, 2015, the Syrian liberation forces overran the Nasib Border Crossing from the Daraa region into Jordan, closing the chief conduit for bilateral trade valued at two billion dollars annually. At that time, in the north, the Bab al-Hawa and Azaz crossings into Turkey were also in rebel hands.

On July 10, 2018, the regime recaptured the Nasib Crossing.

In September 2021, Jordan reopened traffic through the Nasib Crossing in a move to boost the two countries' struggling economies.

Civil War toll between 2011 and 2022:
- 500,000 civilians killed
- 8-9 million displaced internally
- 4 million displaced externally
- Bashar al-Assad responsible for approximately 96% of civilian deaths
- ISIS responsible for 2%
- Russia 2%

The remaining came at the hands of the Free Syrian Army and Kurdish forces.

On April 15, 2021, the Syrian Network for Human Rights in Paris (SYNR) estimated that in the first nine years of the civil war, the regime had dropped 82,000 barrel bombs.

On August 30, 2021, the SYNR in Paris published its 10th annual report on Enforced Disappearance in Syria. The known number since the March 2011 uprising was 102,287, including 2,405 children and 5,801 women, the vast majority detained by the Syrian regime. The report indicated that the first years of the mass uprising saw the highest percentage of enforced disappearances because the demonstrations were taking place in areas under the control of the Syrian regime.

The torture victim, Mazen al-Hamada, returned to Syria —maybe wracked by the West's failure to help, maybe bones increasingly brittle from the world's coldness, maybe longing for the hearth of home, maybe so haunted from those fifteen months of torture, many in Mezzeh Military Airport Prison—

perhaps he could no longer bear to stroll along Amsterdam's canals with their colorful houses reflected in the water. Apparently fantasizing he could mediate between the regime and the West, in 2020, Mazen al-Hamada reversed his exodus. After three visits to the Syrian Embassy in Berlin to negotiate terms, he flew back to Damascus. Upon arrival, he disappeared. Nobody has seen or heard from him since.

While a college student at UC Berkeley, I traveled to Lebanon where I met a Syrian student at the American University of Beirut. He suggested I take a shared taxi from Beirut to Damascus, as visas were readily granted at the border. I spent a day in Damascus, was followed by the *mukhabarat,* and fled back to Beirut. In 1977, Dutton, Hodder and Stoughton in Great Britain and a number of countries worldwide published my first novel, *The Damascus Cover.* Forty years later, in his final film, Sir John Hurt and Jonathan Rhys Meyers appeared in the movie adaptation of my novel. The member of British Parliament, Brooks Newmark, whose conversation with Secretary of State Kerry is referred to above, had read *The Damascus Cover.* While walking together in Los Angeles after the film was released, he said, "It's time for you to return to Damascus." He meant with a new novel.

On the way home to Los Angeles from my first trip to the Middle East so many years ago, I traveled to the Soviet Union to meet dissident leaders and bring some of their writings on microfilm to London, which I managed unimpeded. The British group tour conducted by Intourist, the Russian tour operator, took me to Moscow, Leningrad, Kyiv, and then to Tashkent and Samarkand in Soviet Central Asia. On my own in the Old City of Samarkand, I happened across a group of tailors, all working on sewing machines. When I indicated I was American, they pointed at their American-made machines and chorused, "Zinger, zinger." It is mere conjecture that I met someone resembling Alisher Karimov then.

Made in the USA
Monee, IL
13 March 2023

29814703R00173